THE RULE OF CLAW

as

another

era

dawns,

SURVIVAL IS ALL.

THE RULE OF CLAW

JOHN BRINDLEY

CAROLRHODA BOOKS · MINNEAPOLIS · NEW YORK

First American edition published in 2009 by Carolrhoda Books
Published by arrangement with Orion Children's Books, a division of Orion Publishing
Group Ltd., London, England

Carolrhoda Books
A division of Lerner Publishing Group, Inc.
241 First Avenue North
Minneapolis, MN 55401 U.S.A.

Website address: www.lernerbooks.com

Library of Congress Cataloging-in-Publication Data

Brindley, John, 1954–
    The rule of claw / by John Brindley.
        p.   cm.
    Summary: Ash and her friends live in a future where they are the only human
    teenagers left, but when Ash is kidnapped and becomes a pawn in a power struggle
    among the formidable Raptors who captured her, she begins to reconsider her own
    humanity.
        ISBN: 978–1–58013–608–2 (trade hardcover : alk. paper)
        [1. Science fiction. 2. Good and evil—Fiction. 3. Kidnapping—Fiction.] I. Title.
PZ7.B76874Ru 2009
[Fic]—dc22   2008018907

Manufactured in the United States of America
1 2 3 4 5 6 – SB – 14 13 12 11 10 09

For Francesca

THE
ORIGIN
OF
SPECIES

PART ONE

one

Birds were gathering in ever-greater numbers to scream at him. He couldn't hear them any longer; the roaring inside his ears was too loud. His head was spinning as if he was about to pass out again.

"Dead down," he murmured, as if speaking to someone. There was no one. He had lost his two best friends. "That's sick, that is. Dirty down and sick."

Derri's bare feet were bleeding. He was very dark, but the blood was being taken from his face, away from the skin. He had hardly any energy left. The forest floor was littered with broken twigs and branches, thorns and the sharp husks of broken nuts. More and more forest debris rained down onto Derri's head and shoulders from the outraged birds in the canopy. His feet were badly cut, but that alone was not what was taking his blood. Something else was with Derri, something he couldn't see or even feel, beyond an impression of being ridden, of extra weight and tightness in his back.

All he had on was a pair of old torn shorts. He was probably about sixteen years old, roughly the same age as all the surfers in the seaside camp he loved and so wanted to get back to. His legs and feet were working as if by themselves, without effort on his part, but without strength. The stranger's legs on the forest floor down there buckled and gave way, and Derri went over again.

He had to lie face down, breathing in the dank fungi stench of the ground. At least it was cool for a while. But the birds above gathered in number and fierceness the longer he stayed in one place, and the reptiles hissed at him, and the insects clicked too close.

"You're wrong," he said. His words were lost in the ground. He had to keep going. If not—there was no "if not"! If he stayed here any longer, he'd never make it back to the ASP surf camp and the other seaside dwellers.

He started to recite the five Camp Commandments, as he had when he was much smaller, learning them by rote. *"Honor Your Father and Your Mother,"* he said. The familiar words reminded him of home, his friends, who felt like his only family, and the sound and smell and the cool feel of the sea.

"You Shall Do No Murder," he said, heaving himself up. His back felt so tight, so heavy. His head almost took off from his shoulders as he stood. He went so dizzy he staggered sideways. The insects clicked in his ears. The birds above cackled with amusement. He tried to look up. He wanted to shout at these creatures that he wasn't afraid.

"You Shall Not Steal," he muttered. *"You Shall Not—Shall Not Covet Your Neighbor's House!"* he tried to shout. "I'm not—not scared. Not 'fraid!"

But he was afraid, more than anything, of ending up here in the forest like the other two, his best friends covered with insects, coming to bits, becoming so quickly food for animals and vicious plants.

Derri recited the fifth commandment, scratched onto the signs much later: *"Surf's Always Up—Honor the Best Rider Like Your Father and Your Mother."*

"Surf's always up," Derri repeated. All he wanted was to see the sea again, just once. There was nothing in the whole world like the sea. It was his home. He had to get back there, to the shore, to the camp. Out of the forest.

"Whatever," he said. "Whatever it takes. Whatever."

TWO

They would have found him, sooner or later, but the clatter of the birds and the hiss of snakes and lizards told them right away and showed almost exactly where he was.

"It's them!" Ash said.

They had been looking out for Derri and the other two for three whole days, as far as anyone could see beyond the periphery wires of the ASP camp. The forest canopy came in close and had to be hacked back every other day. The camp was a collection of bare wooden huts enclosed not only by wire, but dense forest and sand dunes on three sides, with the sea lapping at the fourth.

"They're back!" Ash called. She started running for the wire, where the birds were most active and agitated.

Laura tried hard to keep up with Ash but was left far behind as always. Jon heard her and came running out, dragging Rich with him.

There was a sign fixed to the wire where the birds gathered. It was rusting, with a hole in one corner. On the outward side it read, "Admittance Strictly Prohibited" in bold red letters on a white enameled background. Below the sign, Derri lay sprawling face down in the undergrowth.

Ash halted at the sight of the thing clinging to Derri's back. She reached out and tugged at the taut wire. "Derri!" she called out.

"What's that?" Jon shouted out, coming up beside Ash. "That's sick, that. Dead down!"

"It's Derri," Ash said.

Rich came up beside Jon and looked as if he was about to throw up. "Sick," he said. "Oh, no! What is it?"

"It's Derri," Ash said again.

Then Laura was with them. "Get the thing," she said. "Cut the wire."

"Don't!" shouted Jon. "Don't let it in!"

"It's Derri," Rich said through pale lips. "He's breathing."

"Don't," Jon growled. "You don't wanna. Not so sick things. Don't let 'em in."

"Cut the wire," said Laura. "Ash, cut the wire."

Jon would have stopped her if he could, standing to one side there with that disgusted and aggressive look on his face, with Rich by his side, simply disgusted.

"Don't be 'fraid," said Ash. She had the thing with the crimpers and wire cutters.

"Not 'fraid!" Jon cried upward, trying to appear bigger than he was. "Who's 'fraid?"

Ash snipped the wires and the ASP sign fell to the sandy soil. "With me," she said to Jon and Rich; but they did not move as Ash the champion rider of the surf stepped through the gap. Laura alone followed. Together they stood over Derri, listening to his labored breath but watching the appalling slow squirm of the huge black-brown creature clinging like a growth to the center of his back.

"It's eating him," Laura said, quietly.

"With me," Ash turned and said to Jon and Rich, but still they never moved. "With me!" she called out to the rest of the camp, knowing what effect this would have on Jon. "Here! With me! Anyone! Over here! It's Derri!"

Jon puffed up and stepped through the wire suddenly, still dragging Rich with him, before anybody else could get there. "Get him up," he was saying, heroically, as the others started to arrive. He and Rich and Ash dragged Derri from the ground. Laura watched; with her thin, spindly wrists and arms, she'd have only got in the way.

"You," Jon said, to some of the others gathered about the gap in the wire, "get the legs—not you girls!" he tried to order.

Ash looked at the boys. They stayed where they were.

"Easy!" Jon said to the girls as they hauled Derri up almost higher than Jon could reach. "Right. Go."

Derri's head fell back as they carried him through the broken periphery fencing. His eyes were open. In a daze he looked out under fluttering lids at the open sky. "The sea," he said. His lips were bloody and cracked. "The sea."

"What happened to the other two?" Ash said, touching his hot forehead. "Derri, where're the others?"

"Eaten," he said. "The forest. Eaten. The forest! The forest!" He passed out again.

THREE

Jon and Rich went out of the hut as soon as they had dumped Derri face-down on his bed. "Not having that near me," Jon was saying as he stamped out of the door. Alex and Nicholas, twins, the camp's only close relations, shared this hut with Derri. Like most of the other camp dwellers, they were waiting outside.

"Wrong," Rich was mumbling, creeping out behind his best friend. But before he left, he turned at the door and gave Ash a glance of pure apology.

"Crets," Laura said. "Craps!"

Ash was inspecting the massive sluglike creature stuck between Derri's shoulder blades. There was a knock on the door of the hut. Nobody knocked on doors. It just wasn't done. All they ever did was shout "with you" before coming in.

"With you?" Jess's voice peeped through the doorway before she did.

"With us," said Ash.

Jess crept in and stood away with her hand covering her mouth. "Will," she mumbled. She turned away. "Will! With me! Will!"

When Will came loping in to be with her, as he almost always was, Jon and Rich traipsed back in behind him and stood skulking in the far shadows. Will inserted his huge presence between Jess and the dark dangerous blob on Derri's back. "That don't go," he said. "Sick, that is."

"Someone gotta do something," Laura said. "Someone," she looked up at Ash. They exchanged glances.

"Shouldn't have let him back in," Jon was saying loudly, as if to Rich, but really to everyone. "Shouldn't have done it."

"Could be anything," Rich ventured. "Could get any of us."

Laura looked at Ash again. Ash shuffled. Nobody said anything.

Jess held onto Will as he looked down onto Derri's back from his great height. Jess looked up at him. Rich would have held on to Jon if he could have got away with it. Nobody would have minded. Only Jon. Jon minded everything.

"What shall we do?" Laura asked Ash.

Ash watched Jon glance at Will. Neither of them was going to volunteer. Jon wouldn't, if Will wasn't going to. They both looked willing to leave this one to the Camp Champion. Ash looked more closely at the giant sluglike leech. From the tapered shape of it, the thicker end seemed to be the head. Every now and then the leech moved slightly, as if breathing in. It wasn't breathing in—it was inflating, filling with blood. Derri's blood.

"Don't touch it," Laura whispered into Ash's ear. "Please don't. Don't know what it'll do."

"Got to," Ash said, approaching the thing with her fingers. At that moment, whether it sensed it was about to be touched or by coincidence, the massive greedy lump gave a jelly-shudder, a wobbly revolting jerk. Ash's hand came away as Jess gave a little squeal.

"Don't," Laura whispered. She was tiny, thin, with massive, frightened eyes.

Ash glanced at Laura, at her best friend's large eyes, then at Jess's perfect face peeping from Will's shoulder, and finally at Jon and Rich floating in the gloom in the far corner of the hut. "Got to," Ash said again, preparing her hand for contact with the bloodbag of a leech. "Has to come off," she said, watching with horror as her own fingers approached the thing's bloated body.

She was revolted to feel how packed tight and warm it was. It was huge, covering way over half of Derri's back now.

Ash had to run her hand over it. It looked slimy but wasn't. It was mottled but shiny, like a snakeskin, softer than that though, more rubbery. She placed her other hand over it. Ash tried to push her fingers between the leech and Derri's skin. She felt the thing hunker down, sucking harder to stay in place, like a sea shellfish against a rock. The harder Ash pushed against it, the harder it held on.

"Hates us," she said, as she could feel the greedy malevolence in its perverse strength, its determination to hang on until the job it was doing was finally done. Even then, she felt with a shudder of nausea, the thing would probably never let go. Even then there would be more and more juices for it to suck.

"Hates us," Laura repeated.

"Hate it!" said Jess from Will's shoulder.

"With you there," said Will.

Jon and Rich stayed where they were, watching from the shadows as Ash's fingers pushed hard between the body of the creature and Derri's back. Every move she made, the jelly solidified against her hand.

"Vile jelly," she grimaced, tugging at the leech. "Out. Out!" Ash pulled as hard as she could. The leech hunkered harder. "The tail," she said. "Get the tail."

"Where's it?" said Will.

"No," said Jess, holding harder on to him.

"The end, down there," Ash said through gritted teeth. The thing was tightening ever harder over her fingers, cutting off Ash's blood supply. No wonder this thing was killing Derri. "Will," she said. "Help."

"Will," Jess said, in warning.

But Will eased Jess away and came to Ash's side. As he did, Ash noticed Jon approaching, trying harder to gather enough courage to beat Will to it, but the look on Jon's face told Ash he was going to let Will have this one without a fight, for a change.

"Lift it from there," Ash said, nodding toward the thinner tail of the thing. She herself was stuck, both her hands fixed in place by the fingers. "Pull it," she said. "When I say. Ready?"

Rich appeared, stepping up sheepishly by Jon's side.

"Ready," said Will.

Rich looked away.

Ash took a deep breath. "Pull!" she shrieked, dragging upward as Will ripped up the tail. The leech-thing came away with a slurping plop and a tear and a splash of blood that arched through the air. The creature thumped against something before dropping heavily to the floor, where it shook with a sickening sucking sound that turned everyone's stomach.

They all stood and looked down in horror, then at the huge red sucker-mark it had left on Derri's back. Then they all looked at Rich. The leech had flown through the air and splattered against his chest as the arc of Derri's blood flew and striped him from shoulder to hip.

Rich looked down at himself, at the blood, before looking at everyone looking at him. His eyes went up to the ceiling then disappeared into his head as he went over, fainting clean away and falling to the floor, quivering like the blood-creature he was lying next to.

FOUR

Ash and Laura were sitting outside in the shade waiting for their turn. A night and most of the day had passed since Will had volunteered to take the leech and throw it as far as he could over the wire and into the forest.

"Kill it," said Jon.

The thing was still alive. Its gruesome mouth pouted and sucked at the air.

"You kill it," said Will.

"Don't mind," Jon said, puffing up. "Me an' Rich. With me, Rich?"

"With you," said Rich, looking quite sick enough to faint again.

"*You Shall Do No Murder,*" Ash quoted from the sign fixed in every hut. She had always interpreted that as killing nothing, eating nothing but the fruit and nuts from their trees. "*You Shall Do No Murder.*"

"Not murder," Jon said. "Not with that thing."

But in the end, Will took it and threw it away over the wire. Since then, between them all, the teen surfers were keeping a continuous vigil by Derri's bedside.

The sun was high and hot. Every day it was the same, except when the storms came. Laura sat tucked into the dense leaves of a bush, while Ash squatted farther out in the dappled shade, intensely wiping down her surfboard. "Shouldn't have," she was saying, for the hundredth time. "Should have stopped it. Shouldn't have let 'em go. No, Laura. My fault."

Laura was shaking her head. "Why?"

"You know why. *Honor the Best Rider Like Your Father and Your Mother?* You know what the sign says. You wrote it."

"Didn't," Laura said, for the thousandth time. Most of the dwellers believed she scratched the fifth commandment on to establish her best friend as leader of the camp. Laura always denied it. The commandment stood anyway. Surfing was everything now.

"Doesn't matter," Laura said. "They were going anyway. You can't stop 'em."

Ash had been angry with herself ever since she'd allowed the girl and the two boys to set out. "It's not right," she said. "They shouldn't go."

"No stopping it," said Laura. "It happened before," she said. They were thinking of the unplanned expedition outward, the other frightened boy who broke out looking for his mother and perished screaming in the woods within earshot of the camp, and the girl who tried in vain to rescue him. "It'll happen again. One day."

Ash shook her head. "No. It won't. They don't come back. Only Derri, ever," she was saying, as Will and Jess came out of Derri's hut blinking in the blazing sunlight. "With him," Ash said, getting up. "How's it?"

"Any good?" Laura asked, hopefully.

"Not good," Jess shook her head.

"Down. Dead down," said Will, walking away. He didn't want to speak about it. None of the dwellers did. So nobody spoke. Sometimes they would grunt or growl, snarl or sneer. It was a common form of communication between them all, this kind of growl-grunt that depended on body language and facial expressions, or signing, like Tori and some of her friends did, to get the message across. It was very effective because the dwellers were very good at it. Will hissed as he walked away, expressing the disgust and anger Ash and Laura could see in the solid set of his shoulders.

"Poor Derri," Jess whispered, before turning and following Will.

Ash and Laura glanced at each other. They stepped out of the shadow of the bushes together into the full sunlight. The heat not only bore down on them from the sun above, it came up at them, reflected from the pale yellow of the sand outside the hut Derri had shared with Alex and Nicholas. They, inseparable twins, had slept beside a fire on the beach last night, rather than return to where the delirious sick lay mumbling in the bed by the dark stained floorboards.

Inside that red-flecked hut it was at least cooler. Derri, however, was burning up. "Me to go," said Laura, marching out to collect fresh water from the giant daffodrill flowers.

Ash tried to get Derri to drink. She wetted his lips with warm water. His breath smelled sour, like acid. The suck-mark on his back where the leech had clung had turned into a kind of scab, raw and raised and angry. At one end of the mark, where the head of the thing had been fixed, a black wound pouted, something like the damage a bullet might have made coming out. Beneath the skin, going away from the puncture, it was possible to follow a huge dark alien vein squirming down Derri's body, disappearing into his insides.

"Derri," Ash said softly. "Come on, Derri. Please. Please. Make it." She heard Laura coming back into the hut. Cooler, fresher water appeared in a plastic pail beside the bed. Ash dipped a cloth and wetted Derri's lips again.

"Poor Derri," Laura said.

Ash wiped his face. As she did, it seemed as if she were wiping his eyes open. The cloth passed across his brow, and Ash and Laura stepped back in alarm as Derri's wild eyes fixed upon them. He was still chest down on the bed, with his chin on the pillow, looking up through red-rimmed eyes from under his dripping brow.

They both stepped back, then instantly regretted it. "Derri," Ash said first, stepping forward again. "Derri."

He looked as if he was trying to speak but his tongue was stuck. Ash helped him release it with the wet cloth. He coughed and retched, falling forward onto his sopping pillow.

Ash and Laura turned his head to one side. His eyes were closed again. The air rattled hard out of his chest.

"Awake?" Ash whispered close to his ear. "Derri?" His eyes fluttered, opening and closing, before settling on a heavy, halfway position.

"Awake?" Ash asked. "Hear me?"

"With you," he said. It didn't sound at all like Derri speaking. His voice was too low and too rough, coming from somewhere seemingly much farther inside him than his throat and mouth. The whole hut smelled of the deep down air that carried Derri's voice.

"Drink," Ash said, holding some cool water to his lips.

He gagged. He couldn't swallow. "No good," came his hoarse whisper. "No good no more—listen! Listen!"

"What is it?" Ash said.

"Is it—" he breathed. "Is it the sea?"

"It's the sea," Ash whispered close to his face; closer, she knew, than any other camp dweller would ever now get. "It's the sea, Derri. It is the sea."

He let out a massive sigh. "That's all then," he said, with a smile flitting for a moment across his face. "That's it." The smile instantly gave way to a grimace of pain.

"It?" whispered Ash. "What's out there? Why so bad?"

Laura came in closer. "Is he—"

"The sea," Derri breathed.

"Derri?" Ash asked. "Derri, what happened?"

Derri coughed, and Laura drew away.

"Everything," he sighed. "It all eats. Everything murders."

"It eats?"

"We're eaten away out there," Derri coughed. His eyes came open with a start. Laura stepped farther away. "They—everything murders! The forest—plants, animals. They eat us, chew us—to bits! That's all! That's why we're here—we don't have—anywhere else!"

He lay his head back down, sideways on the pillow. He was looking at Ash, looking hard at her. "Nowhere," he sighed.

Ash touched his face. Derri's sigh went on and on. Then it stopped. His eyes never responded. Ever. Gently she closed his eyelids. They never came open again.

FIVE

Jess was helping Ash and Laura prepare Derri for the ceremony. They were wrapping him in his bedsheet with his few tattered belongings: just an old and rusty knife, his shorts, a couple of tops, some beads and bangles. And his surfboard. Everybody had a surfboard, although some, like Will, too tall, and Laura, too frail, never went out on it. But still they took pride in their boards, bringing them to the beach for all the celebrations. Many green-bee stings were suffered trying to get wax for the boards. Ash still looked blotchy from the stings she'd taken to prepare her own as well as Derri's board for today.

"I shouldn't have let them go," she said again. Ash couldn't stop saying it. "There isn't anything. There's nothing out there. Harm, is all. Nothing else."

"Is," Laura said, without conviction. "Must be. Look." And she pointed out the stuff, the artifacts that had been collected from the beach over their eight or so years there. The camp was littered and decorated in plastic pots and pieces of wood and broken bones and lost teeth, all held together by bits of old rope and string. The dwellers drank from plastic bottles and cups found floating in the sea. Other animals, kinds they had never seen, were sometimes washed up on the shore, mutilated by sharks and giant seagles, but showing odd fur and feathers and strange, distorted faces. Or sometimes, an old rubber boot or a piece of lifejacket with all the life gone out of it, long ago.

"Must be," Jess said, equally as unconvinced now. "All sorts out there."

"Yes," Ash said. "Not for us though. No more. You heard him, Laura, you heard Derri. This is all—this is it. Nothing else, not for us, not for years. Once, maybe. When we were little. Before all the sickness."

They fell silent. Derri's surfboard had been placed on his bed. Now Derri's wrapped body was bound on the board, the three girls gathered around him as if waiting for something else to be said.

"When we were little," Ash said, "maybe. When I was seven—I don't know. Must have been different then, when they put us here, when the magazines were."

"The magazines are," Laura said, as she kept a great pile of them by her bed.

"They *were*," Ash said. "That's what was. That's what's in the magazines. This is what *is*," she said, as they all three looked down upon Derri's stained shroud. "The magazine stuff—people like those—they were, but now not. They're gone."

"But might still be," Laura said. "Somewhere."

"Somewhere they might be," Jess halfheartedly tried to agree with Laura.

Ash shook her head. "Something's changed. The world. It's different now. I can feel it."

"But you don't know," Laura said.

Ash didn't say anything more. She didn't know, it was true, but whenever she looked at the images in the old magazines, the people, the places, she felt it. The sun was too hot for most of the clothes those people wore, except for the swimwear, which was too small.

But the girls' silence was broken by a sound, some kind of commotion nearby. The camp had been almost as quiet as Derri for the past two days, but for the everlasting lapping of the sea.

"I'll go," said Ash quickly, to get out of that hut for a little while. A couple of huts along, she saw, the dust was rising as Alex and Nicholas shoved another pile of papers out of the gaping doorway of the "Library." "With you!" Ash called.

What was left of the old broken and rotten books was strewn across the sand outside the hut. Alex appeared in the doorway with Nicholas inside over his shoulder.

"With you," he said.

"All this?" Ash said, kicking at a few of the worm-eaten pages.

"Can't go back there," Alex said, indicating the hut they had shared with Derri. "Not now."

"This is library stuff," Ash said, with some concern. It seemed somehow important that, years ago, the library hut had been full of shelves stacked from top to bottom with books. The tables had been piled high with magazines and comics, set up with care when the camp was new, but then left to decay under the bleaching sun like everything else.

Now, as Nicholas appeared with his brother in the doorway, they all looked at the broken covers and single, senseless pages, wetted and dried and worn out, purposeless and mostly illegible. The camp "Library" was nothing but litter fading underfoot.

"I used to look at these," Ash said, bending to pick up a few pages. One crumbled and fell in half as she held it. "Pictures, in some. Animals. Cows. Mice. Things like you've never seen."

Alex and Nicholas blinked simultaneously from eyes in very similar faces. Their shared expression cared nothing for animals they had never seen.

"They weren't real anyway," Ash said, dropping the rest of the pages. "Once. Not now. Like the magazines. Doesn't matter now," she said, remembering that night during a season of great storms, when the roof had been blown from the library hut. Laura and Ash had rushed to save what they could. They took what they liked best. The pile of magazines still sat by Laura's bed. The shelves were blown down and the books soaked, then subjected to the full force of the sun, then soaked again, blurring the millions and millions of useless old words into obscurity. "Doesn't matter now," she said again.

"Can't go back in there anyway," Nicholas said, also indicating the other hut. "We'll put a roof on here."

"We'll be here," Alex said.

They were looking at her, their united face awaiting her reply, as champion surfer, as ASP number one. Ash might still have stopped them. She thought of the end of the fourth Camp Commandment— *Keep to Your Own Hut!*

But the library pages were useless, and the hut they were moving into belonged to no one, just like their old hut, now that Derri was ready to go.

"With you," she said, stepping on crumbling paper, treading the remnants of dead books further into dust in the sand.

"It's nearly time," Ash said, turning, leaving them to it. Their floor sweepings billowed out of the doorway like smoke.

"With you," called Alex, or Nick, as it was even more difficult to tell the difference between their voices.

Back in the other hut, Jess had left Laura with Derri's shrouded body to go and search for Will. Laura looked so pale and delicate, as if she could have hovered over Derri's body like a protective spirit. "With you," Ash said.

Laura glanced at her with those huge eyes. She didn't say anything but went back to gazing down on the shroud.

Ash joined her. "Like Baz," she said, sadly.

Laura glanced again. Her eyes, always so expressive, told what she was thinking: that this was not like Baz, because boy Baz had gone first, of everyone. He was the first, and still the worst, because Baz had looked how he looked. When he had died, all that time ago, when boy Baz went, his face had gone all . . .

SIX

The first time any of the dwellers paddled farther than the rubber reef where their lagoon lapped at the real ocean's edge was when Ash took Baz out there on two surfboards. She was petrified then. They all were. And still were, very often, but had grown much better at hiding it.

They were still little when the last of the adults had gone away and had never come back. It didn't happen like that, not quite so suddenly. Kids were being brought here from all over the place, different nationalities, different languages. Most spoke English though, so they all did eventually, those who spoke at all.

There were adults around for a while in the beginning, but not always the same ones. They made this place. They erected the wire, they built the rubber reef to form the lagoon. They hung the signs all along the fence to keep others out—*Admittance Strictly Prohibited*—ASP! They brought reels and reels of wire and a tool to mend the fence. They brought books and bedding. They brought magnifying glasses, powerful ones to concentrate the rays of the sun and make fire. They fixed up the Camp Commandments on every hut, locating the boys to their huts, the girls to theirs. Why? Why do all that and then leave, sadly, with sickened faces, one by one?

Always there was some small child crying for its mom or dad, being consoled by someone else's mom—until that mom went away without explanation, Ash wondered, but with that pale and putrid look on her departing face, and another little kid was left crying.

Ash still remembered some of the dads trying to fix up the Camp Commandments signs in every hut, each bearing the four camp rules, before the fifth was scratched onto the end:

Honor Your Father and Your Mother

You Shall Do No Murder

You Shall Not Steal

You Shall Not Covet Your Neighbor's House—Keep to Your Own Hut!

But how weak they were, these men, almost unable to stand unassisted, taking turns to try to knock a little nail into the wooden frames of the huts. All the adults were like this, very thin and slow, with painful breath and red-rimmed eyes. They had hardly enough strength to finally walk away, but still they disappeared, one by one.

In the end, the camp was full of nothing but crying kids looking out through the wire for someone to come. They never came. Never.

"Where are they?" Ash remembered them saying, with crying all around her. Her own mother had died a long time ago, and her father was a stranger with a kind but crinkled face who said how sorry he was, but he would have to go.

"There's a special thing," Ash remembered him saying to her, "inside you. It keeps you safe when people are getting sick."

"Why?" she said. "Why are they?"

His face, in Ash's memory, was worn and wrinkled with worry.

"It's just the world," he said. "We've changed it. Now it'll change us. I have to go. There are others like you. I have to find them. You have to look after this place for me, keep it special. Can you do that, for me?"

Ash could never remember what she answered. She was too confused; there was so much she didn't understand.

"You will," he told her. "One day you'll understand."

But day after day, there was nothing but grief and desperate want. Others came with fathers or mothers; but they were always left alone. Then, one night, Ash woke to find her father standing over her, looking down at her, with his face pale and thin and worn and weary in the ghostly candlelight. "I've done all I can," he said, so very softly. "It's over." He lay down on the bed with her, and Ash fell back to sleep in his arms.

In the morning, he was gone: they all were, the last of the adults, for good.

"Where have they gone?" the children cried in the oppressive heat of the morning, waking to find themselves entirely alone.

Ash cried quietly. "It's over," was the last thing her father had said to her. By this, she knew that it was final; that this was all there was and all there ever would be, from here on. The crying intensified. One frightened boy got through a small hole in the wire and ran away into the forest. For hour after stifling hour, he cried from somewhere out there. As darkness began to fall again, his cries turned to screams of terror. One of the little girls couldn't stand it any longer and went out to look for him. They both screamed.

Then, abruptly, they stopped. The night was once more full of bird cries, great animal growls, but no sound of children, other than the stifled sobs of the ones left behind hiding in their beds. The forest pressed in ever harder at them and the sea beyond the reef churned in frantic turmoil, but it would be a very long time before anybody dared go outside the wire again.

Ash had been seven when she'd arrived at the camp. She was eight when the last adults evaporated. Her father had asked her to look after this place for him, but she was terrified, like all the others, hiding her head under the pillow until the screams died in the forest, fading out like the adults themselves.

In the morning, the weather turned. It grew hotter and hotter. The canopy of the forest stood still but seemed to waver under the heat. It had always been hot, but now the lagoon smelled of bad fish and a terrible silence came down, relieved by nothing but cries and moans, until the insects came up. The buzz and click-clamor was everywhere, but concentrated in the ears, on the ankles, and behind the knees in great boiling bites. Any piece of fruit falling from the bushes burst and was attacked immediately, black with ants or brown with termites and massive millipedes.

The water in the lagoon felt sticky and stank of disease. Something dreadful was coming this way, something even more than the horrors they had already endured. The ASP camp kids, all around the same age, cried even louder for their missing moms and dads.

Something had to change. Someone had to do something, or they'd all perish, dying of nothing more than dread and self-pity.

Ash remembered her father telling her of the special thing she had in her that kept her safe. She tried to get a feel for what kind of thing that could be. There wasn't anything to feel, nothing but anger growing as she realized that it must have been a lie. She wasn't safe. She wasn't special. She'd arrived at the camp before everyone else; that was all. She'd been shown for a longer time how to live without anyone's help: that wasn't special—it was cruel!

It was Ash who first broke the giant dandeliar plants open in anger, and then bathed in the milk of their stems to moisten her skin from the sun and the viscous salt water of the slow sea. She was the first to discover how the smell of dried dandeliar milk repelled insects. It was she who organized the repair of the hole in the fence and the almost daily cutting back of the vandal forest in favor of the fruit and nut trees in their compound and made everyone start going into the far bushes to do their business and never in the sea. She swept her hut using the coarse dune grasses and started to console her crying *hutmate*, helping the tiny Laura to drink some water from the daffodrills and eat something for the first time in days. It was Ash who massaged Laura's painful back every day.

If not for Ash, Laura and many others might have perished. When boy Baz fell ill, Ash and Laura tried to nurse him back to health. The camp-dwellers had been told, but had not yet learned for themselves, which berries not to pick, where the freshest water lay cool in the deep wells of the daffodrill trumpets. Sickness was everywhere for a while. But not like it was with the snake-charmer Baz.

In his fever he turned venomous. His gums began to leak an evil orange-yellow fluid that seeped down his teeth as if he had a mouthful of poisonous fangs.

Boy Baz, always catching and keeping the snakes from the dunes, was left unable to blink or shut his eyes at night or wet his eyes by closing them. Besides that, he had no tears. He lay on his back in his bed staring and staring as if in stark horror at the ceiling. His skin changed color, darker in some places, paler in others. Ash and Laura watched in horror over the space of a couple of weeks as Baz's skin broke into pieces and hardened into what looked like scales, running in dark and light bands down the length of his body. Laura cried out the day Baz died when she went to give him some sips of water. A sleek black tongue, separated and forked at the end, shiny and firm, came slipping out toward her, as if tasting the air around her body.

And when Ash moved closer, trying just to protect her friend but with all the appearance of an assault, boy Baz attacked first, hissing and opening his mouth too wide, striking at the bare flesh of Ash's arm, dropping from his bed in a splash of dirty orange venom, writhing in all his scales on the floor and snapping his poisonous jaws as the very last of his hair fell away and he was gone.

He was so toxic, in the end, that Ash and Laura didn't dare touch him. In any case, he had no eyelids to close. They wrapped him in his sheet with his black eyes bare and his forked tongue hanging out. They told no one what had happened, only that he had died and that there was only one way of getting rid of his diseased body.

The surfboards had been toys, floats for little kids, until then. When Ash had paddled Baz out to try to get the current to carry him away, the age of the surfboard started. The breakers only pushed Baz back toward the beach. Terrified as she was, Ash had to wait for a lull, for a low-wave period, to push Baz out past the reef of old rubber tires. Once out, the boards were taken farther and farther. Ash had to fight to keep her board in one place on the sea, watching Baz until the giant seagles came out of the sky to have at him and an orange and black tiger shark appeared, all head and mouth and—and Ash had to look away.

Massive white sea eagles always swooped over the ASP camp, scattering dwellers, looking as if, without actually doing it, they were about to attack. Now, out on the open ocean, they were fiercer, more fired up, diving for Ash as she struggled back toward the crash of the reef. Several times as she waved the birds away her hand made momentary contact with a clutching claw. They screamed in her ears.

She had to get back in. She looked behind for a big wave to carry her across the reef to safety. The wave she caught was even bigger than she had anticipated. Ash found herself flying, away from the white sailing seagles, toward her home in the sun.

It was exhilarating! Ash discovered that she had time to think, to look around. Although she had the time, she didn't think about standing up on the board: it just seemed to happen.

Ash stood. She was surfing on a wild wave with a water tube forming just behind her. As she glanced back she saw and heard and felt the power in the motion of the water. Ash felt a part of it.

Before she fell off, Ash had already fallen for the sheer adrenalin excitement of riding the ocean. She did fall off the wave, and it was hard; but she retrieved the board and paddled in to a riotous reception.

The girls had gathered on the shoreline, waving the plasticated leaves of the beach palms, banging the bottoms of buckets, whooping and screaming for their champion as the boys looked on, smiling sickly, each wondering why he hadn't taken the initiative, leading the ASP dwellers out onto the waves, to give the camp its real character in discovering this, their reason to live.

Jon had watched the celebrations that day, standing on the sand with the girls all around him laughing at the boys, laughing, particularly, at him.

Ash had noticed the expression on the boys' faces, but on Jon's, particularly, she noted for the first time ever the damaged pride in the face of an enemy.

seven

Ash walked to the door. "With us!" she called. "It's time. He's ready."

So was the rest of the ASP camp. The flags were out on the poles, the plastic drums prepared. Everyone was dressed up in feathers and all the finery made out of the plastic and rubber flotsam. Alex and Nicholas came coated in gray dust. They moved like specters through the colorful crowd as it gathered, entering their old hut to collect their ex-hutmate on his freshly beeswaxed surfboard.

The twins picked up Derri on the board from the bed and carried him out. As they appeared in the sunlight the old cry went up. "With you!"

"With you!" they saluted, the crowd of ASP camp dwellers, decorated with plastic bottle-tops and the jawbones of unknown fishes.

Will went from Jess to help lift the surfboard high above their heads to transport it to the beach. Jess stayed with Tori, her hutmate, who made signs but never, ever spoke.

Jon tried to join in with the lifting of the board, but he was so short he couldn't actually reach it. Rich had to take over as Jon stomped angrily nearby, blaming Will for being too tall.

Laura helped Ash carry her surfboard to the beach, following on behind the wildly colorful procession. At the water's edge, the funeral surfboard bearers lowered Derri to the sand. The mild sea in the lagoon lapped sadly at the side of Derri's board. Other surfboards were dug into the beach, standing upright, scattered like waxed tombstones.

Ash placed her board some respectful distance from Derri's. Everyone gathered around the shrouded body on the sand. Tori bent and touched Derri, as if to say it. The others said it for her, with her: "With you."

"Derri, with you."

Some cried. Not very many. Ash noticed Rich wipe away a tear, but six or so years ago, when Baz had gone, for days, until Ash had seen to it, the camp had cried for the dead body decomposing in its midst.

Now the camp was quiet, but for the sound of the sea. Ash stood, first among the ASP dwellers, speaking to them all through the breaking water's silence.

"The sea!" she said.

Nobody else said a thing, but Jon turned and tugged his board from the sand as if uninterested in listening to anything anybody had to say.

"The sea, Derri. It's what he wanted. He came back. He came back for the sea. It's what we are. This! The surf. There's nothing else for us, Derri said. The sea!"

She looked around. All eyes were on her, except for Jon's as he wiped down his board with an old wax cloth.

"The world's not there," she said, looking deliberately from face to face, "not like it was, in the magazines. That's gone. Derri said. We're eaten up out there. This is what happens," she said, looking down upon the shroud. "Can't afford to lose any more. Too precious," she said. "Too precious. Derri, with you—Total!"

"With you—Total!" they chanted, all but Tori, who made a sign, and Jon, who made no sign.

"It is time," Ash announced, just before they all took turns to give Derri a tiny push outward, with Ash sitting on her board ready to take him out way beyond the reef.

"Why you, though?" said Jon, refusing his turn to touch Derri's board. He had already stepped forward, before any of the others could, ready for the beach wake, the surfing competition they always held in celebration of a life or lives now lost.

"Because it's Ash," Laura spoke up, her delicate nostrils flared, her cheeks reddening further than the sun's influence. "The fifth commandment says—"

"Who writ it?" Jon demanded, not for the first time.

Rich cringed on the sand in his long shorts.

"I didn't! It wasn't—" Laura started to say.

"Don't!" Ash stopped her. It wasn't worth it. Neither Jon, nor any of the other ASP surfers had even beaten Ash out there on the open ocean. "You know why," she simply said. "The fifth commandment stands."

"She's the surfer," Jess said, with Will like a long shadow behind her.

"We all are," Jon said, without looking at Laura or Will, neither of whom ever went in or on the water. "We're surfers, all!"

"No," Will said, bearing down on him. "No we're not."

Jon turned away and addressed himself to the two dusty twins. "You write it?" he said to one. "Or you?" to the other. "Anyone could've writ it," he said. "Except me."

"Surfing's it," said Alex.

"An' surf's always up," Jon mocked, holding up his board.

"Yes!" Ash said. "Yes, it is. So, who is it?" she said, looking from face to face in front of her. "Who is it? Is it me? Or what?"

Alex and Nicholas exchanged glances. "With you," they said, simultaneously. "With you, Ash."

"Not with you, *Ash*," Jon said, mockingly. "I don't see why—"

"Take him out, Ash," Will said, stepping into the shallow water, stooping to push Derri's board from the shoreline. "You take him," he said, looking at her, but threatening Jon as much as speaking to Ash.

So Ash took Derri away, and those who could crossed the great barrier of the reef, following on behind to watch as Ash let Derri go to the seagles and the sharks and to wait for the funeral to finish and for the fiesta competition to begin. She left the beach the ASP Camp Champion, number one surfer, pleased with the way the twins and Jess and Will and just about everybody but Rich had supported her against Jon's antagonism, little realizing that, when she got back, all that would have changed.

EIGHT

Ash came kicking and spitting out of the sea, flinging her board. "Did you see?" she was asking Laura and Jess. "Did you see it?"

"Now we're for it," Laura said.

Jess's impossibly pretty face appeared strained and nervous. She was looking about for Will. He stood apart from everything that was going on. Jess ducked out of the way and joined Will as he towered on the other side of the bonfire that was built on the beach.

Will was watching closely as Jon was being carried on the shoulders of Rich and some of the other cheering, sweating boys. A few of the girls beat out a mis-rhythm on halfhearted palm leaf drums.

Jon was looking down on them all like a king. Even the twins were beneath him now. He didn't seem to notice Will by the bonfire. "Okay," he shouted. "Okay! Okay! Put me down! Put me down!"

Ash had to stand there with only Laura by her side as Jon made his way over to her with that look on his face.

"Yeah," he said. "Never mind." He held out his hand. "Had to happen."

Ash inspected his hand. She had never been beaten out on the surf before, but she had to accept it, reluctantly. "Lucky for you," she said, as they shook.

"Lucky?" he said, with a slanted face. "Lucky? No luck. Outsurfed you, is all. You went down, I stayed up. You lost. You lost, is all!"

"Yeah, but the seagle, right in my face."

"You lost! Is all! No seagle! Bad loser!"

"No. Almost in my face. There was one! It came after me. I let Derri go. It came after me. A seagle! You must have—"

"Seagle?" he shouted. "No seagle! Bad loser! I won. I won! Fair and square."

"I'm not saying you didn't. You won. All right? You won."

"Fair and square!"

"Yeah. With the help of that seagle."

"Who saw a seagle?" he cried to the crowd gathered closely around, glaring from face to face. "Who saw it? You?" he demanded. "You?" The faces blinked at him. "No? Rich? You? See anything?"

Jon was stomping on the sand, as he did so often, as if inviting someone to come and fight with him. Rich, as always, tried to diffuse the situation, confirming that there was nothing out there but the new champ and the old one and the wave.

"Anyone?" Jon clenched, with his teeth gritted, challenging the whole beach, the whole ASP camp to defy him.

Beside her, Ash could feel Laura quivering with indignation. "I'm not saying," she started to say, just to prevent Laura from trying to stick up for her.

But Will came in, saying, "Yeah, I saw it. Big seagle. Right there, on the wave. You saw it Jess, yeah?"

Jess nodded, blinking at Ash.

"So did I," Alex said.

"And me," said Nicholas.

The others started to join in then: "With you." "With you."

Jon was glaring at Will. He could feel his victory slipping away.

"We all saw it," Will said, ignoring him. "It was there. Couldn't miss it."

A moment passed. The drums had halted, the flags faltering in the still of the late afternoon.

Will had got too many to agree with him, too many for Jon to attack. He glared at Rich. "What did you say?" he demanded. "What did you say you couldn't see?"

Poor Rich shifted nervously. "A seagle," he said, looking about. "I couldn't. But I was—you know, too busy. Building the fire."

"The fire!" yelped Jon. "Yes, the fire! The championship! Some seagle? Who cares? She was scared," he said, cocking a thumb toward Ash, "not me. Am I scared? Some seagle? Am I?" he went at Will.

Will just shrugged.

"Who's 'fraid?" Jon bawled at the blank faces. "Rich knows, don't you, Rich!"

Poor Rich nodded, not really knowing anything.

"Rich knows. He built the fire, Rich has."

"We all have," said Jess, standing on the other side with Will.

"Yeah," Jon said. "Why? Eh? Why?"

"Something's out there," said Rich.

"Right! Rich's right! Something's out there. We know it. Derri said it. No good saying nothing out there, nothing out there. Something—all those things. They're waiting for us. They'll get us.

They will! So what do we do? We do something about it, don't we! A seagle down after us? What am I, scared? Am I 'fraid?"

He wasn't, not at that moment. Usually, yes: they all were. In darkness, they cowered under thin sheets, still falling asleep with tears on their eyelashes. When the perimeter wire broke, they couldn't rest until it was mended, with all the "Admittance Strictly Prohibited" ASP signs back in place. The signs were of no use, but it was the name of the camp and it made them feel somehow safer.

"Am I scared?" Jon blared at Will. "Are you?"

Will drew himself up to his full height, way over everyone else. He was aloof up there, with only Jess by his side.

"Will's not 'fraid!" Jon declared for him. "Seagles? Crooks? Screech-owls? Look at this!" he said, dragging out one of the pointed sticks the flags were fixed to. "Let 'em come! Let 'em come!" He pulled out another flagpole and tossed it to his sidekick. Poor Rich was supposed to catch it. He fumbled and the stick plopped onto the sand. Jon pulled another, tossing it to Will, who deftly caught it without so much as a blink. "With me?" Jon shrieked, holding his spear in the air.

Nobody moved. Some looked at Ash to see if she was going to stand for this. But there was nothing she could do.

So they looked to Will. He was too long and gangly to be any good at surfing, but he was big and not worried, confident and self-contained. His opinion had always counted for so much.

"With me?" Jon asked him again.

Will was with no one ordinarily, except Jess. Ash was sure he'd refuse Jon. Then there'd have to be a fight. She had always known the fights would start again, when the boys got more power—or as soon as Jon assumed seniority over Will. Ash always had the power to prevent it from coming to blows in the past, with Rich's help, but now she, and he, were powerless.

But a roar went up as Will's arm rose like Jon's, both bearing a spear. All around, at the sound of the huge cheer, birds soared from the forest canopy and from the surface of the sea. As sudden as the fright and flight of the birds, ASP camp dwellers were running for more spears, roaring at the sky, their drums rolling out the excitement like a quickening, hysterical pulse.

nine

Laura and Ash stood on the sand as the new tribe rallied around, growing in fury and sound. A crying, crowing mass of painted faces bristling with weapons and fear turned into aggression. Ash felt Laura step closer to her as, to the rhythm of the madly excited drumbeats, a little sand lizard was impaled on the end of one of the new spears. The savagery of the act made them gasp as the little creature struggled with the wooden stake that had gone into its back and come out of its belly. Its tiny mouth opened and closed. Ash and Laura were astonished at how funny and exciting it was. It was scary, but the more the lizard thrashed in agony, the more the ASP dwellers celebrated their brand new savagery. Hysteria swept over them all, until what they were doing seemed natural and fair.

When Jon took the dead lizard from the end of the stick, everyone cheered. Ash stayed with Laura at the back, as the thrashing crowd armed themselves until they were bristling with sticks, running around the huts, and streaming out back onto the beach. Birds shrieked from the forest but were shouted down.

"This is it!" Jon crowed. "This is it!" as they ran to the far end of the beach where the dunes were, screaming along the sands, streaming over the little hills, through the dune valleys. Creatures that weren't usually afraid quickly scuttled away. Spears were thrust at them.

As they ran whooping between the hills, a giant seagle tried to take off, leaving its lizard-kill belly-up on the sand between coarse grasses. The seagle, especially one of that size, was fast, clattering out of the sky with such falling force not much could escape its attack. But it was cumbersome on takeoff, too huge to get away from the ground without a long run at it. As the braying mob rounded one of the biggest dunes, the seagle panicked and ran for the air but toward them, as if propelling itself forward for an attack.

Jon and Will were at their head, hurtling forward face-first. Jon screamed like a real warrior, "Look it, Ash!" as if this might have been the same one that attacked her earlier. "With me! With me!"

But most of the others had stalled at the sheer size of the creature, the massive hooked raptor-knuckles of its talons. Jon ran on to meet the exposed breast of the bird, running into it with the pointed end of a flagpole. It swooped to one side and crashed a wing into the grasses of the dune with a screeching sound none of them had ever heard.

They were going to kill this huge creature, regardless of its life, its hungers and thirsts, its own anguish and pain. All that was beneath them in their frenzy.

Ash still stood just outside as they tried to surround the flapping bird. One of its wings hung down to the ground, but its beak and brute talon lashed out, forcing them back.

They stalled. Ash grabbed Laura and held onto her. Up close, the seagle had them in its sight, bringing them down with its accusatory eye. Jon grabbed Laura's spear from her. She was never going to use it. Will tried a lunge at the bird but was pushed back by a dangerously serrated beak that took the end off his stick in a bite.

"Don't let it!" Jon shouted above the caw-cries of the seagle. "We're stronger! It's what we are! This! We can beat this. Then we can beat anything! Come on! Come on!" He was screaming at everyone.

Ash felt Laura shaking, trembling. She looked into her face to give her some assurance but saw only excitement and anticipation there.

"This," Jon crowed, "is nothing. These things think they can beat us! Can they? Why're we so scared? Is this it? Is it? I tell you, nothing can beat us! All the things we're 'fraid of! What are they to us? They're no different from this!" he screamed, turning and running in one smooth moment into the bite radius of the maddened bird.

Everybody thought he was going to be killed. But he drove Laura's spear deep into the proud breast of the seagle, far into its hidden heart.

A gasp went up. No sooner had it, than Will was in and lunging into the dying flesh of their prey. Another after another of them ran into it until the bird was still and bristling with brightly decorated flagpole spears, as if their first real kill had been dressed up and adorned.

Jon had to put an end to it. He stopped them. They stood in a crowd around the huge dead body. Jon looked around. "Ash," he said, picking up a fallen stick from the sand. He pushed Laura aside using the wooden shaft of the spear.

The crowd stepped away from the kill, leaving Ash standing on her own with a clear path leading to the dead bird.

"Ash," Jon said again. He held out the spear.

Everyone else was empty handed now. Everyone but Ash and Laura had done the deed, but nobody would bother counting little weak Laura in something like this, so there was only Ash. Being offered the sharpened stick.

She looked around at the faces like tiger sharks snapping all around her, before taking the spear, before glancing to Laura for approval, before taking a deep breath and lunging forward, last to penetrate the broad breast of the dead seagle.

Ash expected a huge cheer. Instead, silence fell, like regret. Heads were bowed. Nothing else stirred. It could have been that there were no other birds and no adults left now. Everything had changed. *You Shall Do No Murder*, the command signs said. No ASP dweller made a sound. Not a single frightened sand lizard broke cover. A saddening breeze blew through hair, through feathers, flicking the fallen flags before dying.

Jon gazed around the ring of blackened brown faces as if seeing everyone for the first time. He was small, but he drew a mighty breath.

He exhaled luxuriously. He looked at Ash before looking away at the so dead seagle once again. Then he went to it, drawing his heart-piercing spear from its deep breast. The shaft at the tip end was bright red. Jon held the spear high in the sunshine.

He opened his mouth, exposing his clean white teeth. "Party Time!" he screamed out.

A cheer went up at last, echoing from the blanket of trees that covered the far green hill.

Ten

As the sun went down into the sea at the open end of the valley, even the evening scream of bird and unseen beast could not drown the sound of the drums. A savage heartbeat pulsed out across the open canopy and up the far hillside and back again.

The dead seagle had been plucked of all its feathers and thrown onto the heap of the bonfire. "It's time!" Jon announced, when it was properly dark. He was wearing a new headdress of feathers. "The fire! It's time!"

They took glowing hand torches from smaller fires to the stubble of broken branches and dead leaves at the main bonfire's base. The flames blazed upward, throwing sparks into the sky. The beach was too far from the forest to cause any damage, but nobody would have cared, not at that moment.

Around and around they danced, screaming in the firelight. As they gyrated, screeching, throwing their arms up, hands to the empty sky, every pair of deep-breathing nostrils started to catch something, a new, enticing aroma. The bird had begun to put out a smell where it sat in the heat, until at last Laura went over and told Jon what it was and what cooking meant. She and Ash had seen it in their magazines, dead meat heated up before being eaten.

"Eaten?" Jon said. He went as close to the edge of the fire as he could stand. He turned, silhouetted with the light at his back. "I remember, when I was really little. Meat!"

"Yeah," said Laura.

"No!" Ash shouted. "No. Murdering it's one thing. We don't eat that."

"Why not?" said Laura. "They do it in the city. You've seen it. Recipes, it's called."

"That's them, not us. We don't!"

"Who said we don't?" said Jon. "Who said? Adults? Is that what they told us? What else they tell us? Remember? I can! I remember. Their promises. They were going to look after us. Where are they now? No, we killed it. Why not eat it? Who's going to stop us?"

"It's wrong," Ash said.

"Nothing's the same now," Laura said.

"But that smell!" Jess was saying to Will. "I love it! I love it!"

"Yeah," Will said. "With you there."

"With you too," said Alex, said Nicholas, said many others. "With you," signed Tori.

"Nothing's the same," Ash had to agree. "We can't go back. Ever. But—not that! That's too far. Not that!"

"Why not?" said Jon again.

"It's going too far," Ash tried to say. "That's where the harm is. Remember Baz? Laura, tell them. Baz! Tell them."

Laura shook her head, licking her lips.

"That smell!" said Jess, coming closer with Will.

"Go for it," said Will.

"No!" Ash shouted, as they gathered around the fire. "We can't! Not that!"

But even pretty Jess, along with tiny and gentle Laura, helped to turn the bird so that its charred skin was exposed. Oils were dripping out of the carcass through the spear holes. Jon bent down and gouged out some of the heated flesh with his fingers.

"Laura!" Ash yelled. "Don't let him!"

"Try and stop me," Jon said. He divided the big pieces he was holding and offered some to Will and Jess and Rich.

They did it. They put it in their mouths. Ash couldn't watch them start to chew it up. If they went through with this, she was thinking, it would change them. There would be no end to the savagery. Every day they would be taken further and further from innocence and into sickness and destruction.

"Not this!" Ash was still trying to say. Now she realized that she had always been trying to achieve something with the camp, to keep it clean, to prevent the dwellers from contamination. "Don't! Don't!"

But Jon, acting as the new leader, had masticated meat and swallowed it. The shine of melted animal fat reflected the firelight glow from his chin. "Yes!" he said. He shouted. "Yes! We eat this! It's what we do!"

"No!" Ash shouted back, her lonely voice failing against the roar of the savage cheer that went up. "We don't know what'll happen," she said to herself under the cheer as they tore the hot broken bird to bits. Ash began to feel quite sick. She couldn't breathe. Not one other person was against it. Even Laura grinned, in the thick of it, surrounded by flesh-grabbing hands. The sound of their greasy, greedy cries was coming at her from the darkness closing all around as Ash turned and ran. They started chanting: "Eat! Eat! Eat! Eat!"

Running with leaden legs through the darkness, Ash dashed into her hut, smashing closed the door behind her, falling back against it, breathing. She crossed to the open glassless window to look out along the beach to the glow of the fire. Opaque silhouettes shuddered in the parody of a dance, feathered, furious. Everyone was over there. Only she was in here, on her own. "They don't know what they're doing," she whispered to herself, because she was on her own.

Then, then—what was it, a sound? Something told Ash she wasn't on her own. Everyone else was on the beach dancing, but somebody, *something*, was there with her. She thought she heard a shift in the pattern of the silence of the hut, a faint, unfamiliar odor, a sense of another presence.

She froze. The thing clicked behind her. One of the dry floorboards creaked. Ash's breath came into her suddenly, stayed there. She was about to turn around.

Then everything went black.

eleven

Ash struggled. She tried to scream, but she was in some kind of bag, thick and dense. There was hardly any air. She cried out, although she knew the meat-eaters on the beach would never be able to hear her.

Big hard hands clasped the bag. Kicking out, Ash could still feel the motion as she was being carried away. She fought as hard as she could. The rough bag rasped against her face. All kinds of grit and dust came into her mouth. There was no point in opening her eyes. The dried-out air hurt her lungs. Ash could feel it against her teeth. So many bone-hard hands had hold of her as they carried her from the hut.

"Laura!" she cried out.

The dreadful dusty air shut her up. Ash thought she was going to faint. The only thing to do was to concentrate on breathing, breathing, while crying out for help in her head, hoping Laura would somehow be able to feel her terror. Please, please, please, she was crying. The tears on her cheeks were dried to nothing in an instant.

"Let me go!" she cried. Some spoilt air was coming in through the sack, so some sound was probably getting out. "Don't! I tried to stop it! If it's that, I tried! We didn't mean it! We didn't!"

But *they* had meant it. "It wasn't me!" she cried, betraying the others, the meat-eaters out of sheer panic and dread. "I tried! Don't do this! Let me go! Just let me go!"

She was so alone. Every moment that passed Ash felt herself removed farther and farther from the camp and everyone she cared about. She was so afraid she could taste it. All her muscles went tight and stayed like that. She froze. Solid with fear, Ash felt the motion carrying her away, swaying with purpose. What their purpose was, how could she know?

If only she could have got a look at them, if she could have seen their faces! It made it worse, not knowing who or what her abductors were and why they wanted to take her like this. Her heart was thudding against her ribs, worse than when she came off her board today. That was a thump, a struggle to the surface, but she could drown in this sack. "Help!" she screamed, struggling to the surface again. "Help!" as if still underwater, as if she'd never made it back to the top.

But the grip of the pincers down her arms and legs held tighter, harder. It felt as if these hands, if that was what they were, were not made of flesh and bone, but something more metallic, sharper, and crueler.

TⱲELVE

Laura staggered back to the hut with her ears ringing and a very unusual and unpleasant taste in her mouth. Collapsing with a sigh on her bed, she found she was thirsty, but couldn't find the energy to get up and go outside for a drink. The drums were still pounding out there, with a few slow silhouettes stumbling around the embers of the low fire.

"Ash," Laura said, speaking into the darkness in which she imagined her hutmate fast asleep in the bed next to hers. "Ash," she said again. "You 'wake? With me, Ash?"

But Ash hadn't been with her for some while. Laura supposed her friend had been asleep here all this time, which might have been hours but felt like minutes. Laura still felt dizzy from all the dancing, the spinning in circles. She wondered, from where had she got the energy to carry on through most of the night? It wasn't like her, but she could get used to that level of energy, the strength and vitality that must have come from eating the seagle meat.

As soon as she thought that, Laura's thirst stepped up several notches, until her head was thumping so badly it felt as if the drums were still as loud, or louder, right inside her ears. Her mouth was entirely moistureless now. She thought about calling Ash again, waking her and asking her to go and fetch some fresh cool water, but Laura's throat was so parched she couldn't speak.

She dragged herself from her bed. Her shoulders ached like crazy. It was the old problem coming back again, or getting worse now. A great weight was sitting on top of her, dragging her down. Laura stumbled as her feet touched the wooden floor of the hut. The floorboards felt especially rough and splintery. She had to practically stagger to the door. All the strength had gone from her legs.

A huge daffodrill collected the dew of the evening close by the hut. Laura stumbled and tipped the whole contents from one of the bright yellow trumpets into her mouth. Her face and hair were dripping as she went back inside, tripping at the door and stumbling forward onto Ash in her bed.

Only Ash wasn't in her bed. Laura fell onto an empty sheet and an undented pillow. "With me?" she said, looking about.

No answer.

Laura smiled. Earlier, she had thought Ash had been angry for losing out to Jon and upset by everything that followed. Now, Laura supposed, Ash was like everyone else, out celebrating in one way or another, no longer constrained to the old ways, the Adult ways, but free to dance till they dropped and sleep anywhere, or with anyone, they chose.

Still smiling to herself, Laura fell onto Ash's bed, lacking the stamina to make it back the few more heavy steps to her own bed. She collapsed onto her front to keep the pressure from her shoulders, dropping into a deep sleep as the camp grew silent—a sleep and a silence that was to last until late into the next hot morning.

THIRTEEN

Her legs were going again. Ash tried to think about Laura, her pale thin arms and legs, the blue of her veins so close to the surface of her skin. Laura was so very often ill, Ash doubted that she would have made it this far without her. They looked at their old faded magazine pages together, gazing at the pictures of a lighted city peopled with beautiful men and women who smelled good and washed with shower gel under water from faucets and slept in big cool beds. They both remembered their lives before they were brought to the camp, living in a world of cars and normal houses and cooked food and beautiful clothes—the old world that Laura still tried to keep alive through their magazines, while Ash remembered but never repeated her father's last words to her: "It's over."

The old world was gone forever. Ash only knew the camp now, and she wanted to go home. However tough and hard and dry it was, the ASP camp was Ash's home. She wanted her family back.

The forest was all around. The sea had disappeared. In every direction, the night-birds bickered and cried. Every now and then, Ash would hear a closer click, a strange sound like a rough purr. In quieter moments, she could hear her kidnappers breathing. There were two at least, if not far more. They were big, by the feel of them against her, the long lope of their stride through the trees. Ash thought she may be able to hear them speaking, but all she got were clicks and purrs, or ratchet sounds like the metal machine they used back at the camp to mend the wire fences. There was massive strength in the grip of the huge hands that held her. Not once did Ash feel that she was about to be dropped.

On and on they went. Ash's memory was of a long journey to the camp. Others had similar tales, but of much longer distances. So just how big was the world? Massive, by the feel of it pressing in at her: she began to think it would never stop.

They did stop, but only after a long, long time. They halted and Ash felt herself lifted higher before she was dumped onto a flat surface. It felt like the floor of some kind of hut. Several clicks and ratchets clattered before something else changed. The floor under her shuddered, and Ash felt a smoother motion taking her away. Although carried by arms and hands no longer, she was still being transported, driven forward on something solid, something moveable.

Now that she was not being carried, she was able to hold the fabric of the sack away from her face, Ash tried to explore the confines of her sack, and through it to the limits of the flat platform. The sack was tied under her feet. She rolled one way. Some kind of metal bars stopped her. She rolled the other way. The same thing.

Every so often a huge jolt bumped her up and down. Apart from that, the feeling of being taken farther, and farther, and farther away. She tried not to think. There was nothing she could do. It had been a long, long day, and it was very late. She dropped suddenly into a dead sleep, more like falling into unconsciousness. Her brain just turned off.

Then instantly back on!

Everything was different. There was no movement, no motion. The outside sounds had changed from night to day. Ash could hear it was still early, but the sun was up. The heat was beginning to build inside the sack. This could be even worse. If she were left in the sun inside this thing, what a death! What an end! She was as afraid of this as she had ever been of the dark threat of the forest. Ash squirmed, kicking to see if the sack was still tied at her feet. It was.

Ash had to stop herself again, to try to keep calm, breathe deeply and think; or to try not to think, because thinking only led her back to fear. Breathe, she lay telling herself, just breathe.

Then she felt it. First of all she thought it was just her nerves. But then it happened again. There was a little tug at the sack at her ankle. She halted, holding her breath. It tugged again, as if trying to drag the sack but unable to. It felt so different to the angry grab of the hard hands from earlier that Ash shifted, moving toward it.

The effect, the little, gentle pick moved farther down, below the soles of Ash's bare feet where the tie of the sack gathered. Something was pulling at the strings.

All she could do was lie still while whatever it was picked and weakly pulled. It didn't seem to have any strength. She waited. It stopped. Ash thought it had given up.

Then it went again and the gather relaxed as the sack untied and was lifted. Ash found herself blinking in the sudden light, staring down the length of her body and legs, past her feet where the pinkest, whitest, pointiest little face poked in at her.

For maybe a full minute, they looked at each other. Several times it blinked its pinkest of pink bulging eyes.

"Where—" Ash started to say.

The face pointed away from her in panic. It came back. "Yuk!" it said, and vanished.

FOURTEEN

The sack fell onto Ash's feet. She lay there for a second or two wondering what to do before the light came back and that little pink pointy face made a sound at her like Shsh! Then it fell dark again.

This time Ash scrambled out into the sunlight, squinting through the bars of the cage she was in at a tiny boy. At least she thought he was a boy. He had sloping shoulders, thin arms, and fine, four-fingered hands, almost no neck and a pointed pink head. He shuffled from foot to foot. Ash was in the cage, he was outside. They examined one another.

"Yuk," he said again.

"Yuk? What's it mean?"

He seemed to stagger back. "Did you—speak?"

"'Course! Did you?"

He stood aghast, with his pink eyes bulging. "Well, you'd better speak quieter then," he whispered, stretching a hand through the bars. His fingers were long and thin and very pink. He didn't appear to have a thumb.

Ash shied away. He didn't look very fierce or threatening, but she was still wary of him. "What you want?" she said.

His whole face and body shuddered. He looked at something over Ash's shoulder. "Take it," he said.

Between his four thin fingers he held some kind of metal object. Ash hesitated before reaching nervously forward and taking the thing from him. It was just a little piece of shiny metal. Ash looked at the strange boy. He didn't look as if he could do her much harm. He certainly didn't look big enough to have carried her from the camp.

He pointed with his face at the front of the cage.

Ash turned and looked. There didn't seem to be any way out. The little metal thing looked as if it was of no use at all. No good as a weapon or as a tool to break anything with.

"I stole it," he whispered, proudly puffing up.

"Oh," Ash said. She waited.

"The key," the boy said. "The key!"

She held the thing up. "This?"

He sighed, which came out like a little squeak. "Don't you know? Look—Shsh! He's sleeping up there. The others are foraging. No, hunting. The key opens the door. Don't you know anything?"

"'Course I do," Ash whispered, harshly. "I'd forgotten, is all. You make me nervous."

"Then why don't you open the door, idiot?"

Ash looked down uncertainly at the metal key. She did remember about locking and unlocking doors but wasn't certain exactly what to do.

The boy looked around, shuffling from foot to foot. He had on a pair of shorts, but his pink feet stuck straight out from the bottom of the leg-holes. "Look," he said, "look, put the key in here. In here!"

"Can't you?"

He held up one of those thin inadequate hands. "You have to do it," he said, "or you don't get out. And you'd better hurry up, or they'll be back. Come on. Key. Keyhole. Now turn it. The other way, idiot. Why are you such an idiot? Turn it. That's it. Now push."

Ash pushed and the front of the cage opened and she jumped down onto a road. A road! How long was it since she had actually seen one? There had been pictures of cars and roads and houses in their magazines. The thing she'd just jumped from was something like a car from one of those pictures, except that it was open at the back with the cage fixed onto it.

"Don't stand there!" the boy ran by her. "Come on, idiot! What's the matter with you?"

The forest pressed right up onto either edge of the road. They ran together into the trees, which were deep red and glowing in the morning sun.

"Red trees?" Ash said.

"All trees are red, idiot," the boy said. "Except the blue ones. Or the yellow." He scampered along so quickly on those little legs in those big yellow shorts that Ash had to almost run to keep up with him. "You don't know anything, do you," he said, as if to himself.

"Where we going?"

"Why were you there?" he asked. "Why did they bother capturing you? Why didn't they just eat you?"

"That's what I—eat me? You say eat me?"

"Of course, idiot."

"Who? Eat me? Who?"

He slowed, turning, stopping. "Where have you been?" he said. "They're Raptors. Who else?"

"Raptors?"

"Raptors. Raptors! You know, Blue Raptors!"

"Oh, Blue Raptors," Ash said, overwhelmed by all the new information coming at her. "Oh. And what're you?" she asked.

"What am I?" he said, swaying his yellow backside. "That's a good one. What am I? What are *you* supposed to be?" he said. "That's more to the point."

"Me? A girl."

"Agle? You're Agle? Never heard of 'em."

"I'm Ash."

"The Agle Ash. I'm Rat. Rodent."

"Rat Rodent? Oh. I know. I saw pictures before. Rodent."

"Yeah, Rodent. The best. Everyone knows. We can go anywhere, everywhere. No one can catch us. No one."

"Rat," Ash said again, trying to get used to such a name. "Rat Rodent."

"Shsh! Be quiet. Nothing can catch me, but you? If I'd known what a giant useless idiot you were, I wouldn't have bothered. How did you learn to speak Rodent?"

"Rodent? I don't."

"Oh yes you do. Not good, but not too bad either. Listen," he said, with his hairy round ears twitching. "Can you hear them? They're back. They've found out. Quick!"

At that, a roar went up. The red leaves trembled with the power and fury of it. Rat turned and ducked and zipped through the tiniest hole in the undergrowth. "Rat!" Ash cried. "I can't! Don't fit!"

"I can't help you," he called back, echoing from way down a hole. "Run! Don't ever tell them it was me that let you out. I wouldn't have bothered if I'd known what a giant useless idiot you were."

He was gone. Another roar rustled the leaves of the red trees. Raptors! That was what he had said. Ash didn't need to know what a Raptor was to be afraid of that roar. Run! That was also what Rat had said. That's what she did, away farther from the road and into the forest, just running without direction, with no purpose other than to get away from Blue Raptors forever. The ground was slipping under her as if she wasn't doing it, with her legs working on automatic, nothing but a blur beneath her.

Ash ran and ran until she burned herself out. The air felt better against her face than the rasp of that sack. When she began to feel that she had gotten far enough away, Ash slowed to a walk, trying to catch her breath. She had come a long way. The canopy above her as she crouched gasping against the trunk of a huge tree was brilliant red and turquoise blue. The trunks were bright green, with deep thick moss on them. Vines were growing upward, except where there was a break in the canopy and the forest floor erupted with growth. Birds shrieked at her from high up in the branches. Huge frilled lizards hissed and clumped slowly away.

For half her life, Ash had lived so close to the forest, constantly aware and wary of it. Others had died screaming in it. Derri had escaped but hadn't survived it. The forest was beautiful, charming, like one of Baz's colorful snakes. Ash's legs were scratched and stung. The birds screamed down at her. Vicious nettles stabbed her ankles. A lizard, an iguana stood beside her, eyeing her. It wasn't afraid. It despised her. The whole living organism did.

The more Ash looked around, the more she *felt* like some kind of disease here, where she didn't belong. There was no telling where this was. She was lost. There were thorns on the ground. Ash had to pick one of them out of the heel of one of her feet. She was bleeding, hungry, and thirsty. She sucked at the dripping moss. The moisture was sour, but at least it was cool. She looked around. The iguana never once looked away.

The forest spread out endlessly in every direction. Ash was all alone, but she felt surrounded. The whole thing, the powerful undergrowth, the animal eyes fixed her to this spot. She couldn't move without being stung or scratched. She was a surfer, an ASP camp dweller. She didn't belong here. She wanted to go home.

But she didn't know which way home was!

FIFTeen

The floor *was* very rough, with splintery scratches that hadn't been there yesterday. Not that Laura could remember, anyway.

Yesterday had been a strange and monumental day. As she made her way into the blast of the sunshine, looking to find another full daffodrill trumpet, Laura saw some of the effects of last night in particular. ASP dwellers were still asleep under bushes, with just the crinkled soles of their bare feet showing. Some others were appearing from huts that were not their own, in direct violation of the Camp Commandments.

"With you," someone said to Laura, although she couldn't bear to look through the glare to see who was speaking to her.

"With you," she said. "Seen Ash?"

"No. Not since."

Since when, Laura never found out. She doused her head again in fresh daffodrill water, which was always slightly yellow and sweetened. The water usually helped her, making her feel better. Not this morning. She still had that feeling of a great weight pressing her harder into the ground, as if she weighed twice as much as usual. She had to look down at herself to be sure she was still as slim and as slight as ever. She was, but the feeling was not assuaged.

Alex passed by, looking for Nicholas.

"Seen Ash?" Laura said.

"Oh," he said, not having noticed her there, "with you. No. Seen Nick?"

"With you, too. No."

"Some night," Alex said, walking away.

Then Laura realized that she was in pain. Her shoulders went from merely aching to stabbing her in the back, on both sides, at the blades. She tried to stretch, but the stabbing felt worse if she moved. It was the old thing but harder, heavier, and sharper. Laura had always suffered with pains in her upper back where those things were . . .

She ran back into her hut and took off her top. Reaching behind as far as she could, her fingertips touched the hard skin over the shoulder blades, the very, very hard skin. She couldn't bear to touch them for very long.

"Seen Ash?" she said to Jess, dashing back outside pulling her top in place. She ran to where Jess was standing taking a drink. "Have you?"

"With you, too," said Jess.

"Yes, sorry. With you. Seen Ash?"

"No—Will!" Jess called. "Seen Ash?"

"No—Anyone seen Ash?"

"'Course not," came Jon's belligerent voice from the other side of the bushes.

"Sulking, isn't it. Seen Ash? Course not!"

"Where's she?" Laura said, running, suffering, in such pain that only her best friend could help her deal with. "Ash? Ash!"

Tori appeared. She shrugged. No Ash.

Laura ran. She started to cry, the pain was so bad. "Ash! Where's she?"

She ran to the water's edge, looking out across the lagoon to the crash of the reef. As she stood peering out, she felt another pain, smaller, but stinging and sharp, in the sole of her foot.

Laura sat and looked at it, at a splinter of wood from the scratched floor of their hut sticking in her skin.

"Where is she?" Laura said, looking out to sea. "Where's she gone?" she said, to no one.

SIXTEEN

Rat hadn't known what Ash was. But what was *he*? A rat-boy? A rodent? He was so surprised that Ash spoke his language. *His* language? Yes, it was, by the sound of it, the way he used words, so many and so complicated they made Ash's head spin. What was she then?

The way Rat scuttled through the rough undergrowth, the way he knew what to do and where to go showed how he belonged here. What did Ash do? She huddled down at the base of the biggest tree she had ever seen, watched by a million bird and beast eyes, and cried.

All she did was cry her eyes out, feeling lost like this, hopeless and stupid, unable to decide what to do. Rat would know. He'd called her an idiot. She felt like one.

Things started falling down on Ash's head. Sticks and nuts of all kinds were dropping from the branches, missiles aimed purposely by the angry birds squawking up there. A growing flock was screaming at her, throwing things, doing bird droppings, anything to let Ash know how much she affronted them. She buried her head in her arms, but the barrage of debris from above rained harder and harder, and insects landed on and near her, scratching and nipping until she was forced to get up and move quickly away.

On almost every branch, iguanas blinked sidelong as she went by. They opened their red-pink mouths in disgust. They hissed so hard Ash could smell it.

She kept on moving through the trees. Ash was looking for any of the fruit and nuts with which she was familiar. There were none. There were vines, creepers, mosses and hard, plasticated leaves. Now the forest was almost entirely blue, except for the odd yellow bush dotted here and there. Bushes, blue and yellow, shook with rage as she passed. Hostile eyes peered out. Across the forest floor, countless soldier ants marched in line with military precision. Chameleons changed color, from blue to yellow to out-raged red. Under the scream of birds, the hiss of reptiles. Beneath that sound, the hum and buzz of insects. All Ash's senses were heightened, until she could hear everything, all at once. She could smell and taste it as everything around her consumed everything else. This place was all eating and being eaten. If she stayed still long enough, Ash was sure she would be consumed, eaten up, taken to bits by the organism that the forest was. Dismantled and chewed up, swallowed and digested and forgotten about in no time at all.

If Ash ran, the forest seemed to pursue her. It overtook her. It overwhelmed her. The ASP dwellers had been right to be afraid of this place. Their home was by the sea, where there was at least some sky. Here the canopy cast everything in permanent gloom. Any break in the leaves and the undergrowth went wild. It all craved the sun.

Too many times Ash stumbled, falling over hidden logs, scratch-ing her arms and face. There didn't seem to be a single inch of her skin that wasn't scratched or stung or bitten. At this rate, she wouldn't need to stand still to be consumed. Move far enough and she'd be worn to nothing.

"Rat!" she cried aloud, once, twice. "Rat! Rat! Show me out! Rat! Please!"

She ran without stopping, still crying, frantic to be out of the trees and into the sunshine, running and stumbling until she fell with a soft plop and had to drag herself out of the sucking mud. She found herself on the banks of a fast moving stream. Clear water bubbled through the trees. It was such a relief to hear, this sound that was not like the forest but was water freely running. All her life the sound of water had soothed her ears against the outcry of the land. Now it sounded like her savior, like an old friend reminding Ash of home and of her family.

She plunged into the stream. Almost as much water was coming out of her eyes as was flooding around her ankles. She dipped her face and drank deeply; fresh water, clear and cold. Good, running water. Ash rinsed all the sack dust and dead leaves from her arms and legs and hair. Now she could walk in the water, following it downstream. Perhaps it would take her out of here? Perhaps water would take her home.

It was so good to paddle on the smooth stony bottom of the stream. The current was too fast to let any of the insects rest on top.

At one point the stream dropped down about ten feet very quickly, falling over green rocks. The overhanging trees were turning green too, looking far more familiar. Reptiles and birds still lined the banks, but the flowing water wouldn't allow them to halt Ash's progress. Here and there, the sun broke through as the canopy separated to allow the passage of the stream. To be in sunlight and in water again made Ash even more homesick.

Up ahead, through the tunnel of the trees, she could make out what looked like a great clearing shining in the sun. She would have run toward it if the rocks hadn't been too green and slippery. But the forest did finally give way to what was much more than a simple space in the trees. The stream had led Ash to the very edge of the forest through to where a great grassy plain stretched out into the far, far distance. The sun here shone on everything at once.

It was like standing on the beach, gazing out to sea. The oceanic grassland quivered in the heat haze, with gentle local breezes creating waves that swept and crashed into the rocklike bushes that were dotted like small islands. Between the bushes, all sorts of animals grazed on the grasses. Herds of large and small horned creatures wandered on four legs, heads down, heads proudly up, from side to side of her view. They were peaceful, eating grass, looking up every now and again, keeping an eye out, every one of them covered in hair, fur, which was brilliantly white. The whole green plain was populated by white grass-grazers, each with one, two, three, four, or five horns.

Crawling out of the forest and crouching out of sight in the rich warm grass, Ash gazed at the spectacle, the welcome and safety of it, the beauty of the beasts grazing, some coming really quite close. She sat downwind of them, so they didn't see or smell her there.

Ash felt she recognized them, from the loose pages of some of her old books back at the camp. These were like cows, or deer, or antelope, except that everything here was albino, with bright white fur and pale eyes. Some came so close it was possible to see the translucent pinkness of their eyes. They reminded Ash a bit of Rat. He was albino too. Except that Rat was funny, with his pointy face and thin hands and long shorts and big feet. These animals were nothing like that. They moved with grace and poise, slowly grazing across this kind, clean grassland.

Ash smiled. Exactly as she did—smiling, breathing, and relaxing a little for the first time since she had been taken from the camp—a frantic blur of blue and green crashed on huge hard legs, flying, running, flying, throwing itself, launching with a hideous scream onto the neck of one beautiful clean white antelope. The poor creature had been feeding with its head down when this other thing, a nightmare of reptile scale and feather and sinuous muscle screamed through the air and fixed itself onto the antelope's long neck. The antelope tried to run, but its white was spoiled by a terrible spurt of red as the eagle beak of the other creature dragged out a vein. The blood went everywhere as all the other grazing beasts took fright and ran, leaving this one behind as another of the thrashing tearing torturers flung itself at the raw wound and the antelope went down, crashing onto its side with the twin terrors tearing into its open neck.

THE
BLUE
KINGDOM

PART TWO

SEVENTEEN

The antelope tried to kick out as another appeared, a third of the scale-and-feather monsters, throwing itself at the dying prey. As she stood up in panic, Ash could see into the victim's frightened pink eye. Ash fell back into the forest. The green-and-blue beasts were too frantic and fired-up to notice her, but Ash knew she would become prey too if she didn't get away right now.

She turned.

It was there!

It was there, hugely, horribly in front of her, muscle and sinew and green scale and blue feather. No pink in this stern face, as two blank, black eyes stared down at her. A great beak, like a giant sea-eagle's hook, broke that face into pieces. Ash turned into it, into the danger of this thing. Still behind her, she could hear the thrash and flesh tear of the fresh kill dying in the long grass. In front of her, a fourth deadly hunter, its eyes boring, driving, burning into hers.

Ash ran! It didn't seem to move, but the terror of its clicking grinding breath was instantly behind her. Close behind her! Forgetting tiredness, Ash's legs were pumping like life rings under her. Heart pounding, she ran like she had never run!

The thing pursued her, panting on the back of her neck as if about to bite her as the others had gashed the antelope to death. She could feel the thing at her, upon her. She could hear it. She could smell the raw meat exhalations of its breath, like something dead rotting in the heat. It was all predator, accustomed to killing without compunction.

As she ran, through panic and sheer terror, Ash got a flashback glimpse of the seagle with the ASP dwellers after it with spears. Now this thing was pursuing *her*, hunting her in the same way, right after her, its feet and legs and arms and terrible beak much better adapted for pursuit than she was for flight.

It was about to launch forward, to take her down, to tear her at the neck. She had run back into the forest, ducking and weaving to avoid running into the trunks of trees and branches. As she swerved suddenly to one side, Ash heard and felt the beast dive past her on its brute hefty legs. It crashed into a bush. She was away in another direction. It came after her. Its breathing had hardened. Ash could hear its awful beak clicking, like the serrated seagle's. In a moment, it was almost upon her. She swerved again. Again it trundled on in the one direction, too heavy to turn as quickly as she did.

She turned and turned. He—it turned some time after her. It could never catch her like this. But it was faster than she was, stronger, much fiercer. Ash was tiring. Her legs had started to feel as if they had weights attached to them from all of the running and walking she had been doing. She'd had nothing to eat. She was weak.

Turning again, Ash felt the weakness in her legs beginning to tell. The Raptor was upon her, its handlike claw catching her hair for a moment, for an awful, terrible moment! It almost had her. She could never fight it off. She was going to die. It was going to kill her.

She swerved. Again she swerved. She ran madly into another after another direction. Her lungs were about to burst, her heart to fly out. She turned again. Again, again.

As she turned in panic, too tired to go on much farther, she stopped. Suddenly. Something had halted her.

Around Ash's ankles, the snakelike constriction had whipped and tied her to a halt, very nearly tripping her over. She only just managed not to fall, stumping still, left swaying, held hard so suddenly by the ankles with the Raptor right behind her and on and on toward—

She felt like screaming, begging for her life, but nothing would come out. There was a great and monstrous sound in her ears that was the gush of blood and fear as Ash began to collapse, crouching down in sheer terror with her arms as very poor protection over her head.

But nothing happened. That moment, the screaming wailing second before the end, ticked on through, into another second, then another. Ash's eyes were screwed shut; her whole face and being was. She had closed herself down, expecting the worst. Gradually, she opened up again, lowering her shoulders from around her ears, looking out at the dappled dark and light forest, listening for the roar of her attacker.

None came. She looked down: wrapped around her ankles, some kind of thin green ropes. Ash tried to move. The strings wound tighter, with more whipping from the ground to tie her harder and tighter. They were the branches or brambles of some kind of vine, some kind of creeper from the treacherous forest floor. It had her tied down by her feet, and every time she tried to move, other brambles were excited to twang and fling and wrap her around. Ash steadied herself, determined to keep still.

Keep still! But what had happened to the Raptor at her back? Why was she still alive?

Risking a glance behind, as afraid as the antelope with the Raptor flying for its neck, Ash was relieved to see him, her pursuer, brought down and roped and tied like she was. But unlike Ash, he had fallen, being that much faster and heavier. In all the frantic excitement, she had not heard him fall. But fall he had, completely into the brambles that had snapped and constricted tightening against his struggles. He was so big, so mighty, but there were just too many vines here, too many thin strings roped over his limbs, across his reptile thighs and around his strangely familiar arms.

eighteen

Jon, flailing his arms: "She's somewhere. Sulking, is all. I'm right."

"Help, look!"—from Laura. She was sweating, running through the sunshine. "She's nowhere! I tell you!"

Jess came out and ran with Laura. "Will," she called. "It's Ash."

"Listen them!" Jon said to Rich.

Rich nodded. He and Jon were kicking sand into the sea, trying not to notice Will coming out of his hut with a purposeful look on his face. They were trying not to have anything to do with the growing commotion, with Alex and Nicholas shouting out Ash's name, with the echo of that same name bouncing back from the slope of the far green hill as if two more twins were out there looking for her, calling, "Ash, Ash!" "Ash, Ash!"

"When you last see her?" Will tried to ask Laura as she flitted by with a look of pain on her face. Will took two strides to catch up and take hold of her. "Slow it."

"It's Ash!" she said, looking up at him, wild with worry, or more than that. Laura looked as if the pain of worry was real, that she was carrying it on or in her shoulders.

"When you last see her?"

"Last? Last night. We all did. She went off."

"After that?" Will said. "No?"

"Something's happened," Laura said. "Something! Something!"

"Here," Jess said, trying to take hold of Laura now, just for a moment, to ease some of the pain from her. "Here. It's all right."

"Not!" stated Laura, because Jess just did not know, she did not understand how un-all-right it was. "Need to find her! Now!"

"Come on," said Will. "Everyone! Here!"

"No," kicked Jon, as Rich went to move. "She's a sulk. She's up there," he said, pointing toward the dunes.

"Not on her own," Laura said. None of them ever went up to the dunes on their own.

"Who cares?" Jon said. He looked at Rich, who, he knew, cared very much. "We don't," Jon said, for both of them.

Rich kicked some sand hard, out across the surface of the calm water of the lagoon.

"She lost," Jon went on. "She can't take it. Is all."

"Not all!" blasted Laura, as if those words hurt her some more. "Not all! Cret!"

"Cret yourself!"

"Crap! Ash'd make a proper search for you!"

"She wouldn't have to."

"We'll do it," said Will, stepping into the middle of all the ASP dwellers gathered now on the strand of the beach. "We'll search."

Jon just shrugged. Rich kicked at the sand, with his face down, looking at no one.

"Up there!" Will pointed. "Down there! Look in the huts. The bushes. The dunes."

As Will was indicating toward the different places to look, little bands of volunteer dwellers were setting off. "Jess," he said, "you go with Laura." He turned to Jon and Rich. "You in, you two?"

"Out," said Jon.

"Out?" Will said, with a look of disbelief.

"Out," Jon said again.

"Rich?" Will asked. "Rich, you?"

"Out," Jon said, once more.

Rich kicked the sand.

"Rich? With us?"

"Look!" said Jon, trying to square up. "He's out! I said!"

Rich tried to look at Will without Jon seeing. He didn't say anything.

In the end, Will shrugged and walked away, following Jess and Laura down the beach.

"Craps," Jon said, watching Will's shoulders moving.

"Yeah," said Rich, without enthusiasm.

"Bad loser, Ash. Is all," Jon said, kicking more sand. "Hate that! Bad losers!"

"Yeah," said Rich, who never really hated anything.

"Over here!" "Over here!" the twins' duplicate cry came from the far side of the camp where the dense forest crept up to the wire. The dwellers went running.

"Where you going?" Jon said, as Rich went to move toward the call.

"They found something," Rich said.

"Yeah. What did I say? Said they would."

"The wire!" the twins were calling out. "It's the wire!"

"It's the wire," Rich said, starting away, unable to stand still any longer.

"Stay!" Jon shouted after him. "Oi! Hey! You! I said!" But Rich had run off and Jon found himself kicking on his own, with something happening on the other side of the camp. "Crets!" he swore. "Craps!" as he sauntered over, taking his time, as if he was not concerned, as if he was not eaten up inside and aching to be listened to and taken seriously.

"Who cares?" he said, to himself. "Just who cares?"

nineTeen

From where she stood, risking a glance backward, Ash took her first chance to look properly at the Raptor. It had fallen onto all fours, so its massively powerful legs were wrapped in brambles, but she could still see the sheer size of its thighs. It was covered in reptile scales to the waist. But its body, the trunk of it, and its arms and hands, looked something like a man's, only bigger. Even Will's huge hands would have looked small next to those. And then, which looked most savage and fantastic of all, across its shoulders, covering its head and neck, a blaze of blue feathers that gave way on the face to a fringe of scales that in turn smoothed away into the skin of a man again. The bird eyes were solid black and blank over the hook, the cut of that terrific pointed beak. The Blue Raptor.

It was the blue, the poisonous-food blue of the plume of feathers that joined head and shoulders that struck the eye most vividly. Turquoise, clean and shining, the feathers seemed to show, even more than the threat of that beak, the deadly intensity of this beast.

Ash glanced back again and again, horrified, fascinated, and terrified all at the same time. This was what had been chasing her, what would tear her open, dragging out her blood vessels, as the other three had the pure white antelope. This one though, the fourth, the one on his own, looked bigger and even more powerful than the others she'd watched and witnessed on the plain.

Considering the ferocity of the attack on the antelope and the chase after her, Ash expected the constrained Raptor to be thrashing wildly, but it wasn't. It was perfectly still. Its face was down as if studying the vines wrapped around its thick wrists. The Raptor looked as if it was thinking.

Ash seemed to very nearly feel the Raptor's brutal thought processes. All through its attack on her, Ash had been able to feel the terror of its intention, its violent purpose. Then it had seemed like just a beast whose instinct was to kill and eat her: now that Ash could see how it could think so calmly and rationally when in danger, the horror of what it intended to do to her felt much, much worse.

The Blue Raptor crouched so quietly, considering its next move, Ash swallowed hard on her fear, took a few deep breaths, and considered hers. She was only up to her ankles in the low-lying brambles. They covered the ground like creepers, waiting to snap up and over and wrap the feet and hands, the paws and claws of their prey. Now, as she looked around, Ash could see remains, the scattered skeletons of big lizards and other things, all of which had died and decayed where they stood stuck in the brambles, their rotten flesh eaten. Ash thought fleetingly of the other ASP dwellers who had tried to escape the camp, kids screaming from the forest floor for help before the insects came, in their millions, as Ash could feel them now like needles and pins in her feet and ankles.

It eats! That was what Derri said. It all eats! Ash didn't have much time. The biggest Raptor was down and tied to the floor behind her, but the ants were soldiering up her legs and the termites were on their way marching with the millipedes.

She looked around. Above her head there was a branch that was just within her reach. If she stretched, ever so carefully without moving her feet or ankles, she was just tall enough to get her fingers over to get her grip and—

And then she saw it. The Raptor was watching her; those deep, round, blacker-than-black eyes both trained upon her, studying her as she stretched. Ash had to catch her breath. The Raptor's concentration was so piercing. To be studied, scrutinized like this by something that would kill her without compunction—this was more than unnerving, terrifying, eerie, the most strange sensation. His head had turned to face her, his eyes translating what he saw into how he thought and felt. That was the eeriest, the weirdest part.

Then the Raptor's beak moved, ticking a couple of times as if he was about to actually say something. Shivers ran up Ash's spine as she and this brute murderous monster breathed the same forest air, both bound by these carnivorous plants.

As the Raptor watched, Ash suddenly ripped herself straight upward onto the branch, tearing her feet and ankles from the clinging creeper. Her scratched and sore feet pulled free as the vines twisted and snapped and flailed about as if in anger at being denied. Ash dragged herself clear, pulling up onto the branch and into the safety of the tree, scrabbling the biting ants from between her toes.

The Raptor watched her all the way. His head moved with her to keep those eyes fixed on her. Ash sat in the tree for a moment or two, one leg on either side of that branch, trying to collect her thoughts, unable to resist the compulsion to look down on him, at the size and shape of him, his blue, blue feathers, his skin, and his scales. But he was looking back at her with those eyes, so piercing, so knowing, so deadly.

Ash couldn't bear to look at him. She knew he was watching her as she climbed down from the tree on the edge of where the brambles started. Ash was going to run back to the stream, follow it again, keep within its banks through the open plain and not stop until she got to the sea. She turned away.

From behind her, from where the Raptor crouched on all fours, a sound. Ash had heard that sound before, of course. It was that kind of purring, a soft clicking, that sort of ratchet sound she had heard from inside the sack. Now Ash knew that the Raptors had been talking to each other, that the sounds were part of a spoken language and not just the spontaneous purring of a wild animal.

Now she knew that this Blue Raptor was speaking to her. It was actually speaking to her! The sound stopped her. She glanced back. She couldn't help it. She had to take a last look, as he was speaking to her. This creature was capable of such a roar of aggression. This sound wasn't that. It was definitely saying something.

He was watching her intently. His beaked mouth opened slightly to emit that soft purring sound that turned into a series of clicks accompanied by nods and little flicking movements of the head.

"Dead down," she said, shaking her head. That did it! Shaking her head at the Raptor like that! He roared again, struggling to break free and get at her. He couldn't. The vines whipped across his broad back, tightening still further around his upper arms.

Ash watched his struggle with satisfaction. "Sick," she said. But as soon as Ash said it, she regretted it.

From immediately close behind, another, similar series of clicks, then another, another, a third. From behind her, the other three: one right behind, one a little to her left, one to her right. The brambles were in front.

Ash had nowhere to escape.

TШEПTY

Laura's nightmares were like this: "She's gone! Ash!"
In her bad dreams Laura would wake at this, relieved to find her friend still with her.

But, "Look," Will said. "The wire. Broke."

"She's nowhere!" said Jess.

"No," Laura said, with a line of salt sweat breaking out like panic over her upper lip, "not nowhere. She's somewhere."

"Not here though," Jon said.

Laura hadn't noticed him. She thought he'd stayed on the beach kicking sand into the sea. She turned on him. "You did this!" she said, into Jon's face. She was very small, but so was Jon.

"Oh yeah?" he said, facing her out. "What'd I do? Win? Yeah? Well I did, okay? Get used to it! I'm the winner!"

"No you're not! You'll never be a winner. You're nothing! Just a useless jealous stupid little —"

"Leave it," said Will, stepping in.

"No, don't leave it," Jon said. "See to it. I'm in charge now, so—"

"What?" said Will.

"Cret!" Laura said. "You, in charge? Where's Ash? Where is she?"

"I won," Jon said. "I won! The Fifth Commandment!"

"Doesn't mean anything," said Laura. "It's crap!"

"No crap," Jon said. "I'm the winner. It's what I say from here on. That's it. Is all!"

Will laughed out loud. So did Jess, but nervously. Others were smirking.

"Me!" Jon roared, stamping. "It's me!"

Rich looked at the ground.

Will laughed louder. "You?"

"Me!" Jon cried. "Me! Me!"

"Stop it!" shouted Laura. Her face was wet with pain and panic. "Stop it! Something's happened. It's Ash. So stop it! Where is she? It's Ash. Are you stupid? Are you all crets? *Are you?*"

"No," Jon said, turning away. "You are."

"You crap!" Laura said, as Jess tried to console her, putting an arm around her shoulders. But Jess found her arm shrugged away, with Laura letting out a cry as if Jess had hurt her.

"What's the matter with you all?" Laura shouted at them. "Look!" she pointed, with a rigid and trembling forefinger. "Look it! Marks in the sand. What is it?"

"Laura," Jess still tried to comfort her, "Laura. Come on."

"No. Look it! Marks! See? Come see the floor, in our hut. Marks. Like these. See?"

"I see," said Jess.

"I don't," Jon said, from a few paces away. "Nothing there."

"Show me the hut," Jess said, drawing Laura away from Jon before she could physically attack him. "Show me marks."

"Cret," Jon said, speaking toward Laura's back. She didn't turn. She couldn't. She was in too much pain.

"You, cret," Will said to Jon. "Shut it, can't you? Ever?"

"No. Why should I?"

Will tried to ignore him. The twins were lugging the wire-mending machine over. Tori and her friends were signing to each other over the marks in the sandy soil. All Tori's friends signed now, preferring it to speech.

"What they say?" said Jon to Will.

Will still tried to ignore him, inspecting the marks as Tori signed, miming something strange and dreadful.

"Mind," Alex said, shoving Jon in the back.

"Look it," said Nick as they came through the crowd with the machine and the reels of bright wire.

"Yeah," Jon said. "Fix it."

"Wait," said Will, still trying to read the marks in the soil. Tori tapped him and signed, clawing the air.

"Fix it," said Jon to the twins.

But Alex and Nicholas had set down the machine and the wire and were waiting for Will, watching Tori's claws.

"Fix it," Jon said again.

Jess came running from Laura's hut. "Something's been here!" she rushed up to Will. "Something's done something!"

Tori scratched at the air.

TWENTY-ONE

Ash was still looking at the Raptor in the brambles and he at her. He had stopped struggling again now. He was making clicking noises, moving his head, clacking his beak, speaking to the three others behind her.

They were there. Behind her. *Right behind.* The biggest Raptor, wrapped in brambles, was speaking to them, telling them to—

Ash fell to the floor before they could do anything. She scrambled backward, trying to wriggle between their huge legs before they could think to grab her. They didn't need to think about it, they just picked her off the ground and held her in the air as if she weighed nothing. Ash was too terrified to cry or cry out. She was rigid with terror.

The leader of the Raptor hunting party was raging and roaring from the bramble bed, shouting out his orders to the three with Ash stick-stiff in their hands. Their beaks were clicking in her face, about to tear her flesh, but they suddenly dumped her on the ground, picking her up and holding her there with her hands held behind her back in a grip so tight she could feel her arms beginning to swell. As one held her, the other two set about tearing systematically at the brambles. They were strong enough to wrench the nearest plant up by the roots as it squirmed and send it flying before it could catch a hold. In this way, they worked toward the trapped Raptor and set about releasing him.

But all the while they were working closer to him, he was watching Ash, as she, too afraid of him, tried not to return his stare. The others were going to release him, and then what? Ash felt her legs going too weak to bear her weight. She would have fallen down, but the Raptor at her back was holding her too tight.

Every now and then, without breaking his gaze, the largest Raptor sent out a few clicks and nodding grinds, which were his words to his helpers. The way he spoke to them, rather than they to him, confirmed that he was their leader and that they were doing as they were told.

When they eventually got to him and dragged his bindings away and he was able to stand, it was easy for Ash to see that he was in charge, because he was much bigger, with richer feathers and a self-important arrogance about him as he stalked toward her and his two rescuers fell back in respect.

He came to where she was being held, so close Ash glanced and saw her own reflection in his eyes, as if two of her were stuck petrified inside his head.

Ash had been trying to fix her stare as if into the middle distance to avoid seeing inside that crowing mouth into the horror of his meat-digestion system. The roar struck her face like the aftershock of a bomb, sweeping over her and into the chest of the Raptor holding her so tightly by the wrists.

When at last the noise ended, Ash could still feel it thumping inside her chest as the Raptor turned her face, inspecting her cheeks, one after the other. Ash clenched closed her eyes, afraid that the beast was looking for the best place for a first bite. But then she felt her face released and was thrust forward from behind.

She opened her eyes. The Raptor leader was walking away, gesturing with his arm. The one behind shoved her forward again and they set off, with one to the left, one right, and the leader in front. He led the way back through the trees to the plain. Ash tried not to look at the red and white carcass that lay ripped apart in the grass.

They turned shortly after that. They didn't have to go far, along the edge of the trees to where the caged car sat waiting on the road.

The head Raptor clattered out a command to his soldiers. One of them ran to fetch the old sack to fit back over Ash. They weren't going to kill and eat her! Not yet, at least. Ash's legs finally went, and she buckled.

The Raptors let her lie on the road. They gathered around her, clicking over her. Then she felt herself lifted and placed in the cage on the back of the car, with the sack thrown in after her. The door was locked with the key she had left in it earlier.

Ash slowly gathered herself. She could hardly believe she was still alive. But she was, and now she could sit up and breathe and look about as the car went along the road.

Cars, Ash had imagined, were supposed to go along on their own. She didn't know how, but that was what they had always thought, she and Laura. This one didn't. The three Raptors pulled it, with the leader in the cabin doing what Ash thought was the steering.

She still felt sick and wobbly, lying back to watch the sky as she was moved beneath it. Why keep her?

After a long while, Ash tried to stand without being seen to watch what they were doing. The car was heavy, but once it was underway, it just kept on rolling. They pulled it along the road, steering it around the worst ruts and holes, cutting through the trees and across the plains.

Ash sat back down and watched the landscape unfold as they rolled through it. The trees were always changing shape and color. In some places, they were massive, in others, tiny. The animals kept changing too. The birds were always different from place to place, so were the reptiles. Insects stayed the same, as far as Ash could tell, as they attacked her. There were masses of them, everywhere, and her dandeliar milk was either worn away or washed off in the stream.

There was no sea. Ash ached to see and hear and feel it near, but the land stretched out in every direction, scattered with the bodies or bones of dead animals. Here and there, the odd ancient building appeared, ripped apart like the skeleton reptiles in the brambles, or like the old library hut back at the camp, murdered, eaten, wind and weather worn and useless. The birds and reptiles had everything out here. The insects mopped up after them. Ash felt she could almost hear the termites working away.

Up front, the three Raptors pulled tirelessly as the road followed the contours of the hills. Their strength seemed limitless. They dragged the car up and along the side of a massive wooded hill as the road turned a corner that felt as if it was never going to end. They were veering left for such a long time that Ash thought they were going around in circles, when the hill seemed to give way and they had a view over the trees of another plain spread out below, going on and on as far as sight had ever seen. On this level plain though, no grass, no bush, no white grazing animals. Glass glinted in the sunlight and metal gleamed against the high-rise walls of the most incredible, unbelievable sight yet.

Ash caught her breath. She was stunned.

A city! A city, rising out of the plain!

There was a city, all laid out below her, like Laura's every lovely city dream come true! All Laura's dreams, true, Ash thought, for a moment, before she knocked her head on the bars of the cage as the vicious Raptors dragged the car over a huge ragged hole in the road.

TWENTY-TWO

"You can see it," Jess said, wide-eyed. "The floor's all torn. The floor's torn!"

"All right!" yelled Jon. "Enough! She's not here, right? So what? We are."

"Something took her," Jess said, staring at Will, as Tori froze, her mouth and fingers clenched, tooth and nail.

"Leave it to me," Jon shouted out. "Don't be 'fraid. I'll fix it. Me an' Rich. Right, Rich?"

Rich took a swift step backward.

"Oh yeah?" said Will. "What'll you do?"

"Whatever," Jon said. "Whatever it takes. We'll do it. You want we go out there?" he asked Jess, Tori, everyone. "Me an' Rich? Shall we? We'll go get her. Right, Rich?"

Stepping farther away, Rich fought with the urge to shake his head in alarm.

"No," Will said. "You won't."

"Who says?" said Jon. "You? You can't. I won. I won!"

"No one leaves," Will said.

Rich almost collapsed with relief.

Jon puffed up. "Hey! No! Hey! I won! You can't say!"

"Fix the wire," Will said.

"Yeah," said Jon to the twins. "Fix it. After we leave. Me an' Rich. Come on, Rich."

Rigid with fear again, Rich stood petrified to the spot. "Come on, Crap!"

"Stay there," Will said to Rich.

"What?" Jon said. "What you say? You can't say. Only me! Rich!"

"Stay there, Rich," Will said.

Jon looked as if he was going to try to punch Will, until Will stood tall, towering too far over him. "Rich," Jon said, without looking at his friend, but staring up into Will's staring-down face. "Come on."

Will held a hand out to Rich, as if to hold him in place. It wasn't necessary. Rich couldn't have moved, even had he wanted to.

"Rich," Jon said again, but more menacingly.

Nobody moved or said a thing.

Jon glanced around at his friend. "With me? Or what?"

But Rich was truly petrified.

"Right!" Jon bawled. "Right! That's it! Out of my way! Get! I'm away! Out of my way!"

He would have gone, leaving the camp through the hole in the wire had Alex and Nicholas not gripped him under the arms and run him backward with his little legs rotating beneath him and dumped him in the dirt.

"Stinking crets!" he was wailing. "Craps! All you!" He leapt up and ran to where Rich stood red-faced wondering what to do. But before he could do anything, Jon had punched his best and only friend in the face and Rich was running away and crying out and the girls called after him while Tori signed her shout and Will took hold of Jon and lifted him from his feet and threw him backward.

Laura, from where she was lying on her bed, heard the cries. She tried to get up, because if whatever had been there and taken Ash had come back, then she, for one, was glad and would gladly stand and face the threat—if only her arms didn't feel as if they had been disconnected.

If only she could move!

TWENTY-THREE

Laura's dreams were never like this! The outskirts of the city were like the roads, dilapidated and badly repaired. Nobody lived there. Or birds did. And reptiles. And billows of insects. City birds and reptiles were different again from those living in the forests. None of them looked the same, but the biggest difference was that these small birds and quick lizards were afraid. Every time they turned a corner from one derelict, ruined street to another, a thousand birds and as many lizards flew off or scuttled away in alarm. These creatures were naturally timid, always looking this way and that, ready to take flight at any instant. They never did that back home or in the forest. There, they were more inclined to peck or hiss, as if they were the rightful owners and ASP dwellers the interlopers. The birds of those damaged roofs didn't own the houses. The lizards on the walls did not belong there and knew it.

Crashed and smashed cars, some of them big, like the one Ash was on, spewed insects from the vacant spaces of their broken windows. There were gardens here, where the forest was reclaiming ground but in a mass, a blaze of fire flowers. Everywhere burned with red and orange and yellow blooms. Giant butterflies, about fifty times bigger than those in the gorse of the camp dunes, glided on patterned wings from flower to flower. Masses of green bees hummed—no, they were blue. Then some were striped—striped bees! Ash had thought that bees were green only, not yellow and black in bands.

It was wonderful, very lovely, and very sad. Ash had the feeling that in none of these houses the fresh water would run showers from their walls. The only perfume here was that which she could smell from the flowers. All the young, beautiful people, the magazine models were dead. Come nighttime, there would be no bright lights, no restaurants, no perfectly prepared food.

Ash had seen what the Raptors eat and the way they do it. As they moved through the ruined suburbs, all she could see or feel was decay or growth of forest flowers, fear of the threat of Raptor predation.

As they moved closer toward the high gleaming towers of the inner city, Ash wondered if she would ever see Laura or the camp, Jess or Will, Jon or Rich or any of the other dwellers ever again. She was being taken into this place for something. It made her shudder to try to imagine what.

Farther in, the gardens grew smaller and began to disappear. There were more wrecked, decaying vehicles between the buildings. Shattered glass frosted the pavements. The birds and reptiles were even smaller here, even more elusive. As they passed through, the city seemed to die around them.

Then Ash spotted another Raptor. It was a long way down the end of one of the side streets. She didn't catch much more than a glance at it, but it was enough to see the stalled curiosity on its face at the sight of them. She just had time to see it look away from what it was doing and raise its head in puzzlement.

Not long after that, another appeared from inside one of the buildings to stand and watch as they went by. Another. Then two more. They started to follow the vehicle, gazing up at her in her cage.

Ash hid her face from them. She was too afraid of the way they looked at her and the noises they made, click-talking to each other, raising their heads and roaring. They were shouting out, in their way, shouting at her.

There were more of them. The roads and pavements started to look blue with feathers, green with scales. Their beaks were moving, opening, clacking closed. They raised their arms in the air. Their clumping legs were terrible.

Suddenly, one leapt in a single bound from the crowd on the pavement onto the side of Ash's cage. She fell back. Its reptile feet held onto the platform of the vehicle while its man-hands clung to the bars of the cage. It roared at her, its feathers ruffled, almost on end. It was agitated and the crowd of following Raptors reacted in the same way. Ash could see, from where she cowered in a corner, the ruffle of agitation as it swept through the blue crowd. Another Raptor leapt in from standing on the road to perching on the very top of the cage. Its hard claws clanked hold of the bars over her head. She was looking up past its horrible lizard legs at its birdman face peering down at her. The excitement they were all affected by was turning into sheer aggression. These creatures, for all their apparent intelligence, lived this close to naked hostility all their lives. Ash could see it in their impassive eyes and hear it in the cluttered chatter by the roadside and easily in the roar from one side and now the top of her cage.

Then, before Ash could move away, one had leapt onto the corner where she cowered, catching hold of her hair. Ash's head was wrenched to one side as it tugged at her. She screamed.

The car came to a halt. As it did, the crowd took it as a signal to rush forward. Ash must have left handfuls of hair behind as she dragged herself away, screwing down into a ball in the center of the cage. The car was being rocked from side to side as more and more Blue Raptors leapt up, clanking hard to the sides, reaching through the bars. As Ash looked up, all she could see was arms and hands reaching for her through a mass of pressed blue feathers. The clatter of sound was appalling. All the light was being blocked out. Ash's own cries hurt her ears. She was sealed away with her screams in a cube of feathers as arms reached for her in the dark and quickly growing heat. Furious fingers scrabbled her hair and clutched at her back.

But then the light started to come back on. From the top, the feather blanket broke, peeling away in pieces, falling, dropping off. There was a roar above all the others, so powerful Ash could feel it vibrating. It was painful all over, just listening to this sound. The Raptors fell, flew from it. The cage cleared very, very quickly, leaving just Ash crunched into a ball in the center with the one last pair of clawed feet immediately above.

He stood there, the biggest, bluest of them all, not roaring now as she risked a look upward at him. He glared from his perch up top, peering down at the crowd all around them. His feathers were up with the aggression and excitement. His shoulders were massive, his arms powerful. As he moved, turning in a slow circle, his legs flexed as his toe claws clamped like metal on the horizontal metal bars.

TWENTY-FOUR

From there on, it was threateningly bright Blue all the way. He stayed where he was, the alpha Raptor, with his claws clanking above, holding back the braying crowd. One of the others steered the car through blue-green streets clicking with Raptor-speak.

They looked at Ash as if they couldn't figure her out. They seemed so surprised then, as if they were frightened, then angry that she should be here, in this city.

There were very few birds or lizards to be seen now and hardly any insects. This territory was pure Raptor, with no gardens to speak of, just the odd distorted green tree struggling out of the pavements here and there between the biggest, most fantastic buildings imaginable.

But what lived here now was lining the street in blue feathers under an avenue of trees on both sides that led to massive ornate iron gates. Ash tried to look at the leaves of the trees rather than the feathers under them, but Raptors jumped and climbed and their beaks clacked in her face from the branches. All the way up the avenue to the iron gates it continued, their hate, their unbridled aggression and Ash's fear.

The massive gates, through even more massive stone walls, were an entrance to some kind of open space beyond. As they approached the end of the avenue, it looked like an enclosed plain. The city crowded in right up to the walls as the forest had gathered against the perimeter wire fencing of the ASP camp. This place, it was now becoming clear, was where they were headed.

As the car came up to the massive gates, Raptors rushed on the other side to open up and allow them through. The first thing Ash noticed as she peeped at these Raptors, as they struggled with the heavy creaking gates, was that they were wearing something. Not clothes exactly, but a loose kind of wraparound, plain brown in color, fairly short. Their legs looked massive moving against the fabric. Being clothed didn't make them look any less vicious. When the camp dwellers wore the clothes or the wood or bone jewelry they'd made, they were decorating themselves, making personal statements with their special, individual adornments. The clothes on these guards seemed to be doing something similar for the Raptors wearing them, as they roared back with aggressive authority at the braying crowd outside. The guards stood together as the car passed, snapping at and holding back the crowd where he above had controlled them by gesture and expression of threat alone.

The great wall swept away in either direction, enclosing a huge park. Ash could hear water running. The grasses were all kept short and neat by hundreds of peacefully grazing animals, small, woolly, white, unmolested. The trees each had their own space, huge and full and mostly multicolored, starting with green at the bottom, changing to yellow then red then violet at the top. There were giant fruit trees and nuts like those the camp dwellers were used to eating, only about twelve times bigger. They passed a small sea, like a lagoon in a garden. A lake. Ash must have seen one before, long ago, but she'd forgotten. Dragonflies were flitting at the edges of the water. These were not like the insects the camp dwellers called dragonflies, but reptiles with wings like real flying dragons, about as long as Will's huge hand.

Ash wanted more than ever to escape, to get out and run among these peaceful parklands without the threat that was hanging over her. There was just too much to take in. She was hungry, starving in fact, but even that was altered and turned sour, like indigestion, when felt through terror.

She crouched, wound into a ball on the bottom of the cage as the car crunched up a stony road through the stripy trees and rounded a bend.

Then, all of a sudden in front of them with nothing between here and there but short grass and little lakes and gently grazing animals: a huge, huge house. Huge, huge! Not one of those big purposeful buildings they had passed in the city, but a place for living in. This house was beautiful. There were so many windows! Ash was astonished to see the glass intact in every one of them. On the corners of the roof, or roofs, as there were many walls and corners, carved out of stone, stood figures, statues, all looking outward. These didn't resemble Raptors: these stone representations were like ASP dwellers, but with wings. Most of them, as far as Ash could see from where she craned up at them, were female, about to take flight, looking out and down at them as they drew up close to the front of the house. If only they were for real, Ash thought.

"Swoop down," she whispered, looking up, trying to pin some hope on these immovable figures.

"Help me," she whispered as the car stopped. She was looking up to the figures against the sky, almost praying to them, when her view was blotted out. The Raptor on top of the cage stepped into

Ash's line of vision. He glared down on her. His face, before she looked away, seemed to say, "No help. No hope."

The Raptor rattled, calling his assistants, calling others from the house. Those that came out were all wearing the same things as before, like togas, but now colored, or patterned.

They rushed at Ash, much like the crowd outside the walls. Then they seemed to think better of it and stood back, silent, maybe scared.

But they couldn't be as scared as Ash, she knew. Ash hid her face again. She listened while the Raptor hurriedly unlocked the cage and rattled out some more orders. Ash peeped out from behind her hands. The other Raptors stood in their loose clothes looking uncertain. It appeared as if they didn't know what they were supposed to do.

Their leader rattled and roared at them. As Ash cowered, they bounded into the cage; three of them, four, taking hold of her, covering her with the filthy sack. They shoved her inside, lowering her to the floor so that they could tie her back in. They carried her, as before, but now could hear from the sound of their claws on wooden floors that they were inside the big house. She was being hurried through, bumping down and down, scrambling over stone now, being lowered onto another hard floor. Outside the bag she heard metal doors clanging closed, more keys turning, locking, confining Ash to room, to cell, to sack. Just like before.

TWENTY-FIVE

The ache in Laura's back eased slightly. She shifted on her bed looking for a more comfortable position. There wasn't one.

ASP dwellers were shouting outside. There were arguments going on, a crash that sounded like one of the huts falling down, a peal of laughter, a scream. Laura could hear the dwellers running from one place to another, clattering sounds, like wood, sticks, the clanging of bits of old metal. She would have clambered from her bed to see what was going on, if only she wasn't feeling quite so sick. Her head was swimming. Her mouth had been so dry all day. The water bucket by her bed had long since dried up. Or she had drunk it all. She couldn't remember. Half the time she was nearing delirium, believing Ash was back with her, only to wake to herself, to a hot empty hut and a face dripping with sweat. Everyone else seemed too busy to come and see how she was.

"With you!" she heard them cry.

The first few times, Laura had expected someone—if not Ash—to enter the hut with daffodrill water and fresh fruit and a kind word. But the cry was always echoed, "With you," from elsewhere and Laura was left alone to deal with her suffering. She had never felt this bad without her friend on hand to help her through it. Laura didn't know if she was going to make it on her own.

When "With you" came again, Laura ignored it until the door of her hut opened tentatively and Rich's soft voice entered before he did. "With you, Laura."

"With you," she said, desperate for company at least. "With you, Rich. Oh!"

"All right?" he said, from her bedside, with one side of his face swollen and bruised.

"Rich," Laura said, "your eye!"

"Yeah, well."

"Who did it?"

Rich shrugged.

Laura knew. "Rich," she said, "need water, bad."

"Right," he said, taking the plastic pail from her bedside. As he opened the door of the hut, which was on the opposite wall to the open window, the sounds of clattering, hammering, tearing and swearing came in.

When Rich came back in, "What's on?" Laura asked, after having taken a huge drink of yellow tinged daffodrill water. "So noisy."

Rich was looking at the floor. Laura thought, at first, that he was inspecting the splintered scrapes, the marks she had found in the wood of the floorboards. He wasn't.

"What's up?" Laura said, softly.

"Digging," Rich said. "Making holes. Spikes, traps, trip-wires, everything. Everyone's 'fraid. The camp's changing."

"Yes," said Laura, simply. "Yes, it is."

"Ash is gone," Rich said, looking at her.

Laura could see a tear about to fall. Rich was having trouble controlling the muscles in his face. His chin was wobbling.

"You've lost your best friend," Rich said.

"No," Laura said. "Don't believe it. Can't." She tried to sit up.

Rich reached out to help her. As soon as his hand touched hers, he went, falling into his bursting tears. "It's all gone," he said.

Laura was in agony as he held onto her. "Not gone," she said. "Don't believe it. Don't believe it," she said again and again as he held on and held on.

They stayed together like that until Rich could breathe properly again. The sounds outside were stopping as the day wore on into evening, when ASP dwellers foraged for food.

"She'll be back," Laura whispered. "Ash won't go."

"Jon will," Rich breathed, without looking at her. "I know. Jon will."

TWENTY-SIX

Unlike before, the tie at her feet soon gave and the sack fell open around Ash's ankles. She had been dumped on another floor. It was cold and hard. There were Raptors, she knew, waiting outside to see her. She didn't want to let them, so gritted her teeth and stayed where she was.

But not for long: big hard Raptor hands reached through the thick metal bars of her new cage and spun her around and tipped her out. Out she came, dirty and disheveled, onto the hard stone floor.

There were two of them. The one Ash had assumed to be the alpha male, wearing a gown now, stood with another just like him, or perhaps even larger, with an even more impressive set of head feathers. This huge Raptor wore a mane of magnificent blue from head to upper body that made him look as if he were flying. His arms hung slightly bent, as if tensed and ready for action. Every scale on his legs beneath the colorful gown he was wearing, looked separate, pristine, glistening under the electric light-bulb overhead.

Electric light! Ash glanced at it, the way it shone like a little sun overhead.

But they were watching her, talking about her. Click, click! Tack tack tack! Then a low, low rumble as the other Raptor bent down to examine her through the iron bars. He looked away as Ash collapsed against the ground to get farther from these terrors.

The two Raptors exchanged a rapid succession of head movements, a few hand gestures, ticks and tacks and beak clacks. The biggest of the two then stood, towering over her. He held his hand palm outward at her.

The other Raptor—Ash's attacker, her rescuer—stepped away. His beak moved so quickly, biting out a series of quick clicks. His great toe claws scraped over the stone floor.

Ash didn't know what to do. They were discussing her; that much was obvious. But their clicks were turning harder and faster, their low rumbles changing into growls. The way their bodies moved suggested Raptor agitation, the tapping of that bottomless well of aggression and violence. The fact that she was in a cage and they were outside did nothing to make her feel any safer. Their arms were pumping full of blood. Their eyes were darkening. Ash had thought from what she had witnessed, that their eyes were always pitch black, but no. Now, any hint of gray or light went from them. The blacker a Raptor's eyes, the darker their outlook. Anything could happen.

They circled one another, slowly shaking their heads.

Ash scrambled back until she was against the far wall that her new cage was fixed to. Just outside the cage, piled against the wall, were pieces of meat, bits of dead animals, some with the white fur still attached.

The Raptors went around and around in a circular dance of warning to each other. Limbs were pumped hard, feathers raised. The rumbling sounds they made were like controlled roars. It looked as though they were about to have a fight.

And the winner would get to do what to her, Ash wondered.

The first roar came. It was terrible. Ash thought her head was contained inside it, and her chest. It thudded through the air inside her lungs. Nothing could beat that.

Until the other roared. Until then, Ash thought she had heard the mightiest, most hideous sound a living thing could make. But this, this more-than roar, this sheer power in sound pressed her harder against the wall, hurting her ears, her nose and throat. The air was forced out of her. She was punched in the chest, in the gut, winded, wounded.

But still it didn't stop. It went on and on. To try to breathe through it was to gasp. Ash couldn't back far enough, hard enough into the protective wall behind her.

Outside the cage, the roar of the biggest male flattened the feathers of the other, taking him down, killing every bit of his threat. This new blue king Raptor shouted his domination into the face of the other.

There seemed to be no other side to this—the silence at the end belonged to that roar every bit as much as the sound had, saying everything the noise had not. It was the end of all argument, whatever it had been about. There was a clear winner and a definite loser.

Surprisingly though, the winner, the bigger brute, having established the silence as his own, then turned and left the room through the one door in the corner. The other Raptor, the one Ash was familiar with, stood alone. He wasn't looking at her now. He wasn't looking at anything.

The silence was terrible. It had changed, now that it was the loser's frustrated absence of sound.

The electric bulb that had seemed to glow like the sun gave only a cold light. Ash glanced at it again. The room was made out of stone sunk under the ground, with just a single wooden door and an air grille in one corner. Sound couldn't escape from here, or light. Or Ash. She was stuck as far in the corner as she could get, trying to squeeze out of the light and into the wall. No escape.

He looked at her, eventually. It took a long time. Ash kept glancing at him, glancing at him. He never moved.

Then he did, with his feathered head ticking in a kind of quick motion, fixing his eyes onto hers. This was even worse than before, now that he was black-eyed with rage, his few movements too fast to see, so that he seemed to go from one position to another without moving.

Ash tried to look away. But in a split horrendous moment he was there, in her line of sight. She tried again. Again he was there. He would not let her go. She screwed her eyes shut against him.

There was no stopping him. The crash against the iron bars shook the solid stone of the wall and the floor. He had leapt up on them, shaking them, about to bend them apart and get inside.

Ash opened her eyes again and he was there, even bigger than before with his feathers flying. He flexed at the bars like a devil, shrieking at her, tearing the air with beak and talon, with his outraged scream. He would have taken her apart, using just the terrible blank hatred of his eyes if Ash hadn't hidden her face away from him.

The bars were too heavy and strong to be bent, but he was at them, Ash could hear, thrashing through at her, his hands like claws, his claws like rending knives.

He screamed, he raged. The noise was awful, hideous. Of all the night and forest terrors she and the other ASP dwellers had lived in fear of, Ash had never, ever thought of anything like this, never imagined being up against anything so totally intent on harm. Against her!

He screamed. He thrashed at the bars. He clawed, he pushed and pulled and roared himself into a frenzy, a death frenzy, thoroughly committed to killing. That was all he was now, a killing thing that would never stop.

Ever.

TWENTY-SEVEN

"Where's he? Where's Jon?"

"The beach. Building a fire. On his own."

"Why don't you—"

"He won't. Is all."

Laura flinched as Rich touched her back.

"Hungry?" was all he said.

"You?" Laura said, deflecting the question. She hadn't eaten but wasn't sure she could. Ash used to mash nuts and fruit for her, actually chewing them up. How could Laura tell Rich that Ash fed her from mouth to mouth to get her over these times.

"Not hungry," Rich said. "You, though. You feel like—all bones. Sticking out. You feel like—"

"Just skinny," Laura said.

Rich was shaking his head. "No. Not just skinny. Like—there's—what's up?"

The pain of shrugging Rich away, the agony of moving her shoulders from him almost made Laura faint. The effort broke out a sweat all over her face. "Skinny, is all."

Rich stepped back. He was still shaking his head, slowly, trying to figure it out. "You're not—" he was saying, as a shout broke outside, then another, followed by a girl screaming.

"Jon!" Laura said, looking toward the door.

Again a shout came, an aggressive voice, which was not Jon's. Rich turned away. Jon's voice came in then, with the sounds of a fight, a wrench, the breaking of wood and another scream.

"It's Jon," Laura said.

Rich glanced at her.

"Go!" she exclaimed.

He faltered, for another moment, as if committing something to memory, before dashing to the door and flying out, disappearing into the noise of the next fight. The camp was now a series of squabbles.

Laura could hear what was going on as she lay listening to the dwellers laying traps and trying to arm themselves. They were more afraid than ever, but she, falling back on her bed, flinching and turning onto her stomach, was terrified.

As the sounds of the latest outburst died outside, Laura breathed into her hot damp pillow. "Come back. Ash. Please. Need you. Come back. Please. Need you. Ash. Need you. Ash!"

Again and again she said Ash's name, as if repeating it could possibly help stop what was happening to her. And it seemed to work. As silence fell with the dusk in the camp, so the pressure in Laura's tiny body eased, the thumping pain reducing to a background throb, and Laura's breathing evened out, lengthening as she dropped into a deep, profound sleep.

TWENTY-EIGHT

Never, ever stop!

And so it went. Screaming toward her, tearing at Ash until she could almost feel what he would do to her.

"Please don't!" she cried, with her hands over her ears. She couldn't look at him but couldn't help but see and hear what it was like, this level of rending, ripping hatred.

"No more!" Ash screamed.

He couldn't hear her. He wouldn't. She threw herself down flat on the cold floor, wishing to sink into it, rather to be swallowed by hard stone than have to bear this torment a moment longer. If only he would stop, she kept telling herself. It would be over, if only he would stop.

But of course it wasn't over. It never would be now. Even when he flew from the room with the door crashing closed behind him, Ash still heard him, still felt what it was to be the brunt and object of such sharp rage. That anger was madness and she was locked in by it, both physically and mentally. She was terrified.

All of the fear Ash had ever felt, all her time crying in the camp, being left alone, kids screaming in the night, boy Baz falling foul onto the dusty floor of his hut, none of it was a match for how she felt at that moment.

This was worse than being chased through the forest, thinking she was just more food for them. To be prey was one thing, to be so murderously despised was infinitely worse.

"Don't," she still cried, to herself, to her feelings of being brought down, reduced to near-nothingness, to less than an enjoyable meal for this appalling, vengeful beast. "Don't!" she cried out, as if to the thing itself, the creature's leftover hatred hanging in the air like a putrid smell. "I want out! I want to go home. Is all. Let me. Just—let me!" She was crying. She was never going to get out of here. "Why? Why me? What'd I do?"

"Agle," said a voice, suddenly.

Ash leapt. There was nobody there.

"Agle, you are such a giant useless idiot, do you know that?"

"Rat?" she cried. "Rat?"

"Shsh!" he hissed from between the bars of the grille over the air duct in the corner. "Agle, why are you such an idiot? Keep your voice down."

"Rat," she cried, with the tears streaming down her face. "Rat. You, here? Rat, I—how? How here? You."

"Shut up, Agle," he said, as the front of the grille pushed away and his thin hands and pointy snout appeared through the gap.

"Rat, I—"

"Hang on," he said, wriggling through the small space in the wall. "It's bigger on the other side," he said, smoothing the dust from the fine white hair on his head and shoulders.

"How? Rat—how you find me?"

"Find you? I never lost you. I was following all the way. Besides, I knew where you were going."

"How?"

"Because they hadn't killed you. They wanted you, so they wanted you here. Simple."

"Why?—Rat, it's just, oh," she tried to smile, as he scampered warily across to her. He had a way of keeping one ear directed always toward the door. He had on his long yellow shorts. Against the stonewalls and floor, contrasted with the horror of this place with its bits of dead animals in the cold light, Rat looked so funny. Ash wiped her face with her hands and tried to hang on to her smile.

He peered at her. "You've got such a stretchy face," he said, studying Ash's mouth.

"Stretchy?" she said. The smile slipped from her as a tear fell. She forced the smile back into position.

"Why do you do that?" Rat asked. "That funny mouth," he said, widening his mouth into the strangest, funniest parody of a smile.

Ash almost laughed, then almost cried. "You're here," she said. "You're here!"

"You are such a strange thing," Rat said, standing there in his floppy shorts with his big feet sticking out in almost opposite directions. "You're so weird looking," he said.

Ash coughed out a little wet laugh.

"What are you making that noise for?" he said.

"Noise?" she said. "No noise."

"This," Rat said, snorting.

"That?" Ash said. "A laugh."

"Laugh?"

"When something's funny. You laugh."

"I don't," he said. He looked about, with his attention caught for a moment by the bits of dead animal meat. "Anyway, I don't see anything funny."

"No," Ash said. "With you, there. But if there was?"

"What, something funny?"

Ash nodded. "What you do?"

"Bot-blag," he said.

"What? Bot-blag? What's bot-blag?"

He wiggled his little bottom inside those full flowing shorts. "Bot-blag," he said.

Now Ash did find something funny. She laughed. It made her feel dizzy and confused, but she couldn't help it. "You really are weird," he said, nodding his head.

"I suppose," she said, wagging her backside. Rat responded by trying to stretch his mouth again into a smile. He really was funny. Ash burst into tears again.

"No," he hissed, "be quiet." His ears were twitching. "No more noise. Listen—listen!"

"For what?" she whispered, swallowing hard.

He listened hard for a few moments more. He relaxed. "It's all right," he said. "False alarm. I thought he was coming back."

"Oh," she said, with her legs going weak and wobbly under her. "Rat, help me. Can you? Help me!—Can you?"

He glanced around. His pink eyes were so bulbous, but so beautiful as they caught the light. "If I could even get you out of the cage," he said, "you're too big to fit through the hole in the wall. We're in the middle of the Blue capital. I don't know how—"

"Blue capital? What's it?"

"The city. It's the capital of the Blue Kingdom. You're in, right in the middle under the king's council chambers."

"The king?"

"The king. The Blue Raptor king. You've met him."

"Him?" she said, indicating toward the door. "Him? That one? Him?"

"No," Rat said, glancing around. "No, not him. He's the king's brother. He only thinks he's a king. He isn't. He's the worst of Raptors. He's what they could be, if it wasn't for his big brother, the king."

"Big brother? That other?"

"Yes. He's the Blue Raptor king."

"But why they want me? What for? What they want?"

Rat blinked. His eyes bulged. "They don't. Talon thought you were—"

"Talon?"

"The king's brother. Talon, he calls himself. His name's Tallion in actual fact, but he always says it's Talon."

"You know all this. How?"

"I'm Rodent. We're the best. We're all over the place. Raptors, they think they own all this. How can they? They can't stop us. I know all about them. They don't know anything. The way they speak! They talk like children."

"You can talk like them?"

"'Course I can."

"They can talk like you?"

Rat wagged his bottom. "They don't even recognize Rodent as a language. They can't hear any clicks or clumps or grizzles in it. They just don't get it. See how stupid they are?"

"Are they?" Ash said, admiring Rat for daring to have such an opinion of so truly terrifying a beast. "Are they stupid?"

"Compared to Rodents they are. We're the best. I don't know about Agles yet, I haven't quite made up my mind. I think probably they're all pretty stupid. If they're anything like you they are."

"But why they want me?"

"Why? Because of the Yellow Raptors."

Ash looked. She blinked, shaking her head slightly. She didn't understand.

"Right," Rat said, "listen. The Blue Raptors and the Yellow always fight. They're all stupid. Talon, he wanted to use you against them."

"Use me?"

"Yeah. Use you. He thought you were, you know, not an angel."

"I don't—angel? Not an angel?"

"No wings. Not an angel. It's what Raptors believe. They think there are angels and demons, good and bad spirits. They believe in the power of the planets, the sun's and the moon's influence on events. They see good omens and bad omens influencing fate and determining their future."

Ash stood and listened and tried to understand. She blinked.

Rat sighed. "You really are an idiot, Agle, you know? The Raptors see good or bad in everything. Angels have wings. They're good. They look a bit like you, but they can fly. You can't fly. So you're bad—a demon."

"I am?"

"Talon thinks so. He says you killed a giant sky-brother. You're a demon. That's what Talon thought he'd caught—a demon."

TWENTY-NINE

"A demon? Me? How? I don't get it—don't remember the word."

"That means some kind of devil, a mischief, a bad omen. That's what they believe, Raptors. Outside, on the top of the house, stone angels. They look a bit like you do."

"They're angels? That means good, right?"

"Right. Angels, with wings. They're good omens. Only you don't have any wings. And Talon told Tomb—"

"Tomb?"

"His brother. Tomb. He's the king. He's like—well, he's not like Talon. Talon's crazy. He wants war with the Yellow Raptors. That's why he's always going out hunting in no-Raptor's-land, trying to start a fight. That's where he found you. They didn't know you were there."

"Did you?"

"I didn't. But my Elder did. We don't go that far away from the city, but the Elders knew about you."

"Elders?"

"You know, Elder. Old, that means," he said, bot-blagging, wagging his backside. "They prefer Elder."

"He knew us?"

"He knows about everything."

"You said Yellow Raptors? There are yellow ones?"

"Yes, yellow. Some were white, but they all died out. They were the weakest. They're always fighting each other, always have.

The White Raptors died because the Blues and Yellows killed them all. Raptors hate each other just for being the color they are, even though they're exactly the same apart from that. You can't get much more stupid, can you?"

"No," said Ash, although she couldn't help but feel relieved that there were fewer Raptors around.

"The Blues think they own this city, but they think the Yellows are trying to take it from them. They've had so many wars; it's ridiculous! Raptors! Idiots. Have you seen what they eat? Oh, you eat like that too, don't you."

"Like what?"

"Like they do."

"No."

"No? Talon told Tomb you killed a sky-brother. A bird, that is. He said you and others like you killed a giant sea sky-brother. Talon said you stuck sticks in it and then you ate it. Did you?"

"No—I—some. Not me. I didn't. I didn't eat."

"But you all killed it?"

Rat was waiting for an answer, but Ash couldn't admit it. She couldn't look at him.

"Are you a demon, then?" he said. He waited again. "Are you?"

"Rat, I—"

But he stopped her. His ears turned, as if automatically, on his head. "Shsh! Keep quiet!" he hissed as, on the instant, he was back inside the ventilation duct and the grill was wedged back on behind him. "Shsh!" his voice came out.

Outside, Raptor claws scratched across the stone floor. Ash froze: someone was coming back, to do whatever they had next in mind for her. She held her breath. But the scratch steps continued on past the door with a few clicks of ordinary Raptor conversation. Ash held her breath until they had gone and all was quiet again and Rat reappeared.

"Oh," she said, shaking. "Rat. I can't. This is—" she said, with the tears flowing again. "I'm no demon. I didn't do it. Help me, Rat. Why they bring me here? Why, if I'm so bad?"

"Talon wanted to use you against the Yellows. He wanted to scare them away by having the devil on his side. He was going to use you to beat his enemies."

"Use me? I wouldn't."

"You wouldn't have the choice. He was going to show you to them tomorrow—"

"Tomorrow?"

"When they come here."

"Here?"

"Agle, do you have to put your little questions in all the time when I'm trying to tell you something? What is it with you? You can hardly put more than two words together, but you keep throwing your little single sentences at me all the time! How am I supposed to talk to you?"

Ash didn't say anything. She had never heard anybody use so many words as Rat, not all at once, like he did. Ash decided to keep quiet.

"You are such an idiot. Let me tell you, will you? The Yellow Raptors, some important ones, are coming here tomorrow. Tomb wants to make peace. He's sick of war and fighting. He wants Raptors to change, to advance. He's an optimist." He looked hard at Ash. She blinked. She didn't understand. Rat sighed. "You're such a—right. Tomb sees good omens—good things in everything. He thinks angels are real. He thinks Raptors should try to keep them on their side. All Raptors."

"If he thinks angels are real," Ash said, trying to string together a whole load of words, "then what about demons? No?"

"Oh, he believes they're real too. But he doesn't think you're it. He thinks you're a freak, a lesser thing. He thinks you're vermin."

"Vermin? I don't—"

Rat sighed again. "Vermin. Garbage. A nuisance species."

"Species?" Ash said. She couldn't help it.

Rat turned in a circle with frustration. "You are such a—listen. Listen! Tomb thinks you're nothing."

"Oh."

"Well, don't worry about that," Rat said, "he thinks Rodents are too. It's a compliment, coming from a Raptor."

"Tomb and Talon?" Ash said. "Why they fight?"

"Fight? That wasn't a fight. That was just Tomb ordering around his little brother. He told him to stay away from the Yellow Kingdom, stay out of no-Raptor's-land. He said he wasn't going to risk the peace talks with vermin like you. He said Talon had to take you back to the forest and let you go."

"Oh," Ash breathed. "Oh." She almost fainted with relief.

Rat's big bulbous pink eyes bulged. "No," he said, "don't think—it's not as easy as that. Tomb called Talon a fool. His patience is running out with his headstrong little brother. But the way Talon sees it, you let Tomb humiliate him. And if there's one thing Talon can't stand . . . "

He trailed off. Ash let him. She felt faint. "Food," she said. "Can't eat that," pointing at the dead meat piled against the far wall.

Rat shuddered. "Raptors!" he said.

"And the toilet," Ash said, shaking her head. "Need to go, bad."

"Don't do that to them," Rat said. "Shaking your head. It means threat, aggression. Nodding is a friendly signal."

"What's food, when Raptors talk?"

He did a couple of clicks with his head to one side, then nodded once. "You have to get the head movement. You can't speak Raptor if you can't see who you're talking to. If you ever see a Yellow, don't nod. That's aggression to Yellows. Shaking your head's friendly. That's why they keep fighting. Every time one wants to try to be friends, the other thinks he's about to be attacked. Raptors!"

"The bathroom?"

"The bathroom?"

"The toilet. Raptors go, don't they?"

"Oh. That's this," he said, pointing to the ground, looking to one side then the other.

"Is all?"

"Is all? Yes, is all. They talk like children, like you do. It's all threat or friends with Raptors, pointing, clicking, feather-talk. Only Raptors can speak Raptor fully. I can understand it, but I don't have the head-gear to speak it properly. I can't do the clicks or the throat sounds. Neither can you. Your own language must be something like Rodent, isn't it?"

"Something like? No. Like this?" she said, shrugging, using her body and hands expressively, in the way that all the camp dwellers did. Rat was studying Ash's hand movements. "So like a Raptor!" he said. "Your kind—how many of you are there?"

"Thirty-one."

"Thirty-one? Is that all?"

"Is all. There was room, in the camp, for more. No more came. Thirty-one, is all. In there, just me and the others. Rat, I want to go home. I want to see Laura."

"Is he your Special?"

"My—oh, no. Laura's a friend. Best friend. She's a girl."

"You're all Agles. You mean she's Fe."

"Fe? Yes. Fe. She's my friend. And Jess and Will. They're together. They're Specials."

"I have a Special," Rat said, proudly.

"Really?"

"Yes. Really. How did you know?"

"Know what?"

"Really. She's my Special."

"Really?"

"Yes, Really."

"Oh. She's called Really? Really Rodent?"

"Yes," he said, shaking his head. "Really—Agle, you are such a—what are you, exactly?"

"I'm—just a—I'm just Agle, no?"

"Did you kill the sea sky-brother?" he said. "Did you?"

"Rat, I—"

"No, I need to know what you're like. Did you eat it? Is that what you are? Are you Raptor? Are you demon-Raptor?"

"Rat, I—"

"No," he said again, nodding. Nodding and shaking the head were all mixed up. Nod for yes, shake for no; that was the Rodent way. Nod for friendly, shake for aggression if you were a Raptor. A Blue one anyway, because for Yellow it was the other way around.

"Rat, I don't—I'm all—"

"Shsh!" he said.

Ash noticed then how his sensitive round ears were fixed in the direction of the door. "What's it?" she whispered.

"Shsh!" he said again.

They waited. Ash couldn't hear anything.

"Rat," she whispered. But he was creeping across to the hole in the wall. "Rat, what's it?"

"Get ready," he hissed, peering out at her from the darkness of the air vent. "Get ready for this," he said, as he pulled the grille back into position over the vent hole.

"Ready?" Ash whispered to herself, just before the urgent claw clicks rapped on the stone outside and keys clinked and then the door crashed open and he stood filling up the opening with his outraged pride.

"Oh no," she breathed, as he held out the bunch of keys, showing her, warning her. Frightening her. "Talon," she said, backing away.

THIRTY

Talon stalked her, stepping in, carefully closing the door behind him. He scratched forward, clanking, jangling. He sounded like bone and metal, scraping and grinding across the stones toward her. Even his arms and hands no longer looked or sounded like flesh; he was talon-horn entirely, hard and unforgiving.

"Rat," Ash said, pressing back against the wall. "No demon. I'm what you say—I'm Agle. Rat, hear me?"

There was no sound.

But there was! Talon's talons screeched across the rock floor as he careered out of his mind with anger into the door bars of the cage. His dark, dense eyes deepened. A low rumble came from deep within his chest.

Ash couldn't back far enough away. "Rat!" she cried, unable to take her horrified eyes from Talon's. "Rat! Don't go! Not now!"

Talon bristled. His clicking sounds were like bones breaking. He selected one of the keys from the bunch of five or six on the ring.

Ash felt sick to see him fit the key into the lock. "Rat!" she breathed. "Rat! He's got the key! Rat! Please! Help! Help me!"

Talon tried to turn the key. He dragged at it, growling and grumbling, looking up at her. The key didn't work. He held the bunch up for Ash to see, carefully selecting another.

"Rat! Rat! He's coming in! Help! Rat! Please! Help!"

The Raptor outrage grew as the second key failed to turn. Talon looked up and let out a roar. He turned a circle. His legs were pumping bigger and bigger. The veins in his arms were sticking out. He dragged out the second key, madly fitting another into the lock.

"I'm not demon! I'm not! I'm only a girl. I'm only Agle! Rat, I'm not—we're crets! We're idiots! Is all! Just Agles—we make mistakes. But we're good!"

Talon ranted over another key. There weren't many left he hadn't tried.

"Rat! Oh, no! Rat! He's going to get me! Rat! There's no one else! Don't leave me! Please. Please!"

She screamed that last word, as Talon had another of the few untried keys in his hand and Ash was convinced that this was going to be the one. "Rat! I'm Agle! Help me!"

Talon had the right key. Ash knew it was the one. He was coming to get her. She cried out.

But then, so did Talon. His cry was far more a roar, but he yelled out in pain where Rat had dashed in an instant from the wall vent and bitten Talon on the back of the leg. Rat must have nipped him really hard to make him bellow out like that, to make him jump into the air and drop the ring of keys onto the floor.

Talon was fast, but before he could get over the sudden shock of the pain in his leg, Rat had collected the keys and scuttled back into the hole, leaving the grid where it lay on the floor.

"Rat!" Ash shouted after him. "Go, Rat! With you!"

"I'll get help!" she heard him shout back up the ventilation shaft before Talon reached the hole, roaring, trying to dive into a space hardly big enough to allow his head. He smashed himself against the wall, feathers flying, out of his mind with fury.

"Get help!" Ash screamed back to Rat, although she knew he probably couldn't hear her by now. "Get help! Rat! Get help for me!"

Talon flew from one side of the room to the other. One moment he was crashing at the open vent shaft, another and he was at the bars of the cage, ferocious, crazed. His tantrum was terrible, even worse than before. He dashed back to the vent, reaching into it.

Rat, of course, was much farther away than Talon's reach by now. "Go, Rat!" Ash was still shouting out. "Get help! Go, go, go!"

Talon halted, suddenly. He had been scrabbling in the vent, finding it empty, as far as he could feel. He stood slowly, breathing in, turning to face her.

"Go, Rat," Ash said, more quietly, backing as far away as she could. "Get help," she said, as if to herself.

Talon came and stood at the bars looking at her as if he understood what she was saying.

"No keys," Ash said, quietly, as if to reassure herself. "No keys," she said again, but without completely forgetting how hungry and thirsty she was.

Talon was watching her intently. He made a sound, a single tick, before looking around at the vent.

"Go, Rat," Ash whispered. "Go."

Talon took a glance at her. Ash shook her head as violently as she could. All Talon's feathers undulated. He ticked. He turned.

"Go, Rat."

But Talon was gone, flying from the room to look for the Rodent.

"Make it, Rat," Ash whispered. "Get away. Help me."

Help me!

THIRTY-ONE

Laura started awake, as if someone had shouted into her ear. There was no sound, but Laura's head rang as if a cry for help were still reverberating through her inner ear.

It was night. The camp was quiet below the screech of owls and the cries of the night creatures. A single ASP dweller might have been speaking, somewhere fairly near, or it may be the chatter of a frightened monkey lizard or a non-stop bird. Inside Laura's head though, bells rang, alarms were going off, dizzying, flitting from one side to the other, as if the bed were moving under her.

She raised herself. There was no pain now, just that feeling of massive weight bearing down on her. Moving took an extreme effort and quickly sapped what little strength she had left. The bed tipped and was about to toss her to the floor, when Laura felt arms, not strong, but much more powerful than her own, catch her and hold her in position. "Who's it?" she said. "Who's here?"

"Me," said Rich's voice from the darkness. "You been moaning. Crying."

"Have I?"

"Stay there," he said, lowering Laura back onto her mattress. He went out.

The raging, burning thirst was back with her. "Need water," Laura said, as Rich came back in with a lighted green candle.

"Here," he said, hurrying to put the candle down, to prevent Laura from trying to get up again. "Here," he said, catching her, lifting her water pail from the floor.

She tried to drink, but her sore, dry throat wasn't responding properly, and she started to choke.

"Easy," Rich said. "Go slow. There. Better. Easy now."

Laura drank. As the water went into her, she could feel its effects almost immediately. Every cell in her body was dehydrated, crying out for moisture. Laura felt the water replenishing her, settling the chaos in her head, leveling the sickening tilt of the world.

Bringing her face from the pail for the fourth or fifth time, she noticed the difference, the huge and startling change in the hut. "The magazines!" she said.

"Drink," said Rich. "More."

"The magazines," she said, staring at her bedside table, the bare top of which she hadn't seen for years, ever since the night of the big storms when the library roof went. "Where're they? What's on? The mags!"

"I know," Rich said.

"You know?" She stared into his face. "What you know?"

"It's Jon," he said. "I tried."

"Jon?"

"He took them. I tried. He wouldn't stop."

"Took them? Where? *Where?*"

Rich glanced toward the window. "The beach," he said.

"The beach? Why?"

Rich didn't answer.

"The fire!" Laura answered for him. She struggled on her mattress. "Help!" she said. "Help me! Get me up."

"Are you—"

"Rich! Do it! Do it now!"

THIRTY-TWO

What Rat had done had been so brave. It made Ash feel like crying just to think of it. The danger he had put himself in, just for her! Not many Agles would have done such a thing. Ash felt so lucky to have met him. He made her think that the ASP dwellers should be more like Rodents, more like Rat, the way he could use words, the understanding he had of all those different things—they didn't have anything like that, the Agles.

Ash waited and waited, dizzy with worry over what would happen next. If Talon caught Rat, he would certainly bring him back down to the prison cell to show her. Time went by so slowly. But nothing happened. She concentrated on the electric light. From her early childhood, she remembered being able to switch lights on and off. But now the bare bulb looked too stark, too cold, all hard glare or dead shadow.

She concentrated on looking and listening so hard she started to feel unwell. Ash had to sit down. Suddenly she felt out of breath, hot and clammy, as if about to be sick. She needed food and water. She needed to get out and go to the bathroom. If somebody didn't come soon . . .

But as soon as Ash started to think that, she could hear somebody—something—coming. Claws clipped outside, more than one Raptor click-talking between themselves with some urgency.

The door opened and he came back in. Talon. Ash stood up, afraid, but at the same time relieved that there was no sign of Rat.

Then, immediately behind Talon, Tomb entered the room, along with another three female Raptors. Talon didn't look at her. He was doing all the talking. He showed Tomb and the others Rat's tooth marks on the back of his leg, then indicated toward the vent, with its covering grid still lying on the floor.

As Talon looked over at Ash, his eyes darkened.

Tomb glanced in Ash's direction, then looked at the air vent. He spoke to Talon. Talon nodded quietly, without much threat, before glancing back at Ash. His eyes told her the truth of how he was feeling. There was no friendliness or respect in them. He tried to hide them from his brother. He went to the hole in the corner and kicked at it. The empty sound that echoed back reassured Ash that Rat was safe somewhere else entirely.

Talon, Ash could easily see, was trying not to throw another temper fit in front of his big brother. He wasn't very good at controlling himself. His head was almost jammed into the vent hole again.

But Tomb didn't notice. He was looking at Ash. Talon was handsome, in a brutal kind of way, but Tomb had a stronger, more controlled beauty. He looked older, as Ash nervously glanced back at him, although she couldn't really say why. His eyes were quite different from his brother's: more expressive, a little grayer, less opaque. The female Raptors around him were with him, not with Talon.

One of them spoke to King Tomb. He glanced at her, but didn't really break his concentration on Ash's face and hair. He said something back.

Talon came stomping over with much more to say on the matter. They all let him talk, with none of them taking too much notice.

The way Talon was agitating himself made Ash think of when she was much younger, when the camp was filled with little kids left on their own, throwing tantrums of frustration and fear.

It looked as if Tomb was used to not listening to him. He was too busy looking at Ash because she had decided to nod at him, giving the Blue Raptor the friendly signal that Rat had told her about. She was astonished to see puzzlement in his eyes, and curiosity. Talon's eyes were always opaque and threatening, but the king's expressive gaze let Ash think that he was not about to bite her.

Ash tried going a tiny bit closer, nodding all the time. She noticed Talon, from one corner of her eye, trying to resist the urge to spring forward and try to grab her. The only reason he didn't, she presumed, was the massive, imposing presence of Tomb, the king, watching her and wondering. Ash had an idea that she could try to make him understand a bit more about what she was and how much she needed protection.

Not that she really *knew* what she was, not now; but what Ash did know was that she was so desperately in need of the Raptor king's approval. Rat had told her that Tomb had ordered Talon to let her go. Somehow, she didn't know how, but she needed to use Tomb to stop his brother from murdering her.

For a moment, she almost smiled at Tomb. But Ash had remembered from Rat that this was not the thing to do to beings whose mouths did not naturally stretch in the way hers did to show pleasure or amusement. Showing her teeth to Tomb may well be taken as a signal of aggression. So Ash kept nodding and nodding until he couldn't help but recognize that she understood what she was doing. She nodded until he nodded back. Ash felt a wave of relief.

But Talon could no longer control his temper. He drove forward, as if Tomb's nod was a signal to attack. It wasn't. Tomb shouted at him, ordering him back. Tomb had seen, as Ash backed away, how afraid she was of Talon. He ordered his little brother to back off. Ash watched as Talon clumped away, seething all alone on the other side of the room.

The king turned his attention back to Ash. She swallowed hard on her fear and stepped forward again immediately, determined to press her advantage with the king over Talon. She was nodding and nodding. Tomb again nodded back at her. The three female Raptors looked at each other with curiosity in their eyes. Ash breathed. It was always the eyes; they were so very expressive, Ash had come to learn. If at any time their eyes said nothing, if they were opaque and blank, then it meant trouble. Talon's eyes were nearly always like that.

But the king's were clear, or cloudy, but in the kind of way that doesn't look like rain. Tomb's clouds were readable, like the daytime weather. He nodded again. So did the three females surrounding him.

Ash nervously pointed to the floor and looked from one side to the other; the Raptor sign for going to the bathroom. She hoped she had it right. She did it exactly as she remembered Rat doing it. But the king just looked at her. She nodded, then did the sign again.

One of the lady Raptors said something. She was the smallest of the three. As she spoke, Talon went to come forward. Ash backed away, but Tomb stopped him, sternly, before sending one of the other females from the room. Then they all seemed to be waiting, with Tomb speaking briefly every now and then but with everybody else silenced.

The female Raptor came back in with another set of keys. She came to the cage and opened the door. Ash's heart was thumping. There was still a strong possibility that they were going to kill and eat her. She couldn't move.

Tomb was watching her. Then he stepped into the cage. Ash tensed still further. The female Raptors started to chatter and chatter excitedly while Talon tensed and rippled over the other side.

Ash truly thought she was going to faint, with the giant Tomb, the king, towering over her. It was obvious that he was infinitely stronger and more powerful than she. He nodded, looking down at her.

Fighting against herself, forcing her muscles to move, Ash looked up at him. She nodded. As she did, he held out a hand to her. Ash flinched as the chatter of the Raptor females increased in volume and excitement. But the king's hand was extended toward her. It was huge, but it was the same as Ash's hand. She didn't know what to do.

He took her arm and led her carefully out of the cage. The females stepped back as Tomb led her from the room.

As he led Ash past Talon, Tomb eyed him threateningly, fixing him back into position, away from her.

Away from tearing her to bits.

THIRTY-THREE

His fire was blazing as Laura, assisted by Rich, made her way slowly onto the beach. From a long way off, they could see Jon tossing printed pages into the flames.

"Don't!" Laura tried to call out. She was too breathless to shout loud enough.

"Jon!" Rich shouted for her. "Leave it!"

They saw Jon's fire-lit face glance at them, once, before going back to what he was doing. Beside him, the diminished pile of magazines.

"With you," Rich called, trying to put a more friendly tone into his voice.

"Don't!" Laura said, now that they were close enough for her weakened voice to carry.

Jon took not the slightest notice. It might have been that he wasn't even aware of the existence of anyone else on the beach.

"Jon," Rich said. "You can't."

"Why not?" Jon said, still tearing and tossing the loose pages onto the fire.

Rich felt Laura try to shove him away. She was going to go for Jon, to physically prevent him from doing any more damage.

"Yeah?" said Jon, with a smirk, as he saw Laura staggering with that purposeful expression on her face.

"Get gone!" Laura said, slanting sideways. The disruption in her ears was tilting the beach so that the black sea sloped down and uphill away to her left and right.

"Oh, yeah?" Jon smirked.

Laura staggered and fell. Jon laughed.

"Leave it!" Rich said to him.

Jon's attention switched immediately. "You?" he said. "Want it? Or what?"

Laura scrambled across the sand and laid her body across the pile, trying to protect the magazines she had shared for so long with Ash.

"Why you doing it?" Rich said.

"'Cause it's garbage," he said. He turned and took another magazine, tugging it away from under Laura. She was just not heavy or strong enough to prevent him.

"Garbage! Is all!"

"No!" Laura cried out.

"Don't," Rich pleaded. "Jon."

"*Jon!*" Jon wheedled, squirming at Rich. "She's gone. Ash, out of it. Me, now. My time!"

"No," Will's voice came out of the shadow from nearer the huts.

But Jon turned and tugged another magazine from under Laura and turned again and tore it and threw it on the fire.

Will's face appeared out of the gloom. Behind his, Jess's, saddened and concerned.

"No, Will," Rich said. "Leave it."

"Yeah," Jon sneered. "Leave it, Will."

Will looked from Rich to Jon and back again.

Jon, still sneering, turned to tug another magazine. Laura tried to scratch him away. He started to laugh but stopped when he saw that someone else had grabbed him by the wrist. Jon laughed in his face when he saw that it was Rich's hand holding his. "Off, Cret."

"No," Rich said.

Others—Tori, the twins, all the disparate ASP faces—were gathering in the gloom to watch.

"Don't," Rich said, his face, his voice and demeanor pleading with Jon to stop.

"Off, you," Jon said, with the smirking smile sliding from his face. "Off. Now!"

"No," said Rich, tugging Jon's hand away from Laura and the magazines. "Enough. Jon, enough."

"Never enough," said Jon, suddenly trying to shake Rich from his wrist. "Off! Cret!"

"No!" Rich shouted at him without letting go.

Jon stopped. "Warning you," he said, steadily, with all threat. "Off. Is all."

"Rich," Laura said.

But Rich didn't flinch, not this time. He held on to Jon, trying to stop him, trying to protect him. "Don't, Jon."

"You telling *me?* Jon said. "You telling *me?* Are you?" Jon glared into his eyes. "You—you nothing—you crap—telling me the winner—the champion of all the—"

"It doesn't mean anything," Rich said. His face was very pale, but he wasn't trembling.

"The fifth?—*Honor the Best Rider*—that's me. I'm the winner."

"I wrote it," said Rich, without so much as a blink.

"You—what?"

"I wrote it," Rich said again. "The fifth commandment. I scratched it on the signs, that day."

"What day?"

"When boy Baz went. When Ash took him out and showed us all what to do. It was her—it was Ash, that's all. Her."

Jon was shuddering with pent-up rage. "You—You—"

"Don't do it," Rich said again, holding his voice steady.

"You," said Jon again. "I don't have to do what you say."

"Neither do we," another voice came in. Will had stepped forward.

Jon broke his stare at Rich to look up in disgust as Will looked down on him.

"I wrote it," Rich said, drawing Jon's attention hard back onto his face. "I did it. No one has to do what I say. It was Ash, all long. No competition."

Rich and Jon were still staring into each other. Staring until Jon swung out suddenly, trying to hit Rich in the face again. Will started forward, but Rich had already turned Jon around, forcing him down flat on his back in the sand.

Rich fell on Jon, sitting on his chest with his arms pinned under his knees. Jon was struggling, spitting up into Rich's face. Rich couldn't stop him. He had to leap off of him, drag him into the dark water and hold his friend under. There they thrashed, splashing and flailing while the other ASP dwellers watched, until Jon gagged and gasped and had to give in. Rich dunked him one more time to be sure, before dragging him out and throwing him down onto the sand.

"Now!" Rich said, standing over him. "Enough!"

Jon was coughing, trying to get his breath back.

"Laura," Rich said. "You okay?"

She had positioned herself between the fire and the pile of her magazines.

"Will," Rich said, with some authority, "bring the mags back, yeah?"

"Yeah," said Will.

"No," Laura said, watching Jon. They all looked at her. "No," she said again, picking up as many magazines as she could hold at one time. "It's over," she said, turning, tossing them into the flames. The fire crackled enthusiastically.

Jess stepped forward as if to stop her. Will prevented Jess, taking her by the arm.

"It's gone," Laura said, struggling with another load, then another.

By the time the magazines were gone, Jon had stopped coughing. He sat up and watched Laura looking into the fire. He watched Rich taking Laura away, helping her back to her hut. Jon sat alone while the ASP-dweller faces faded into the night and his wet beach clothes began to steam from the enthusiastic heat of the fire.

"Crets," he said, to himself. But his voice failed as a splutter of a cry broke from him and he hugged his knees, falling sideways on the sand.

Laura let Rich lead her back to her hut. She was thirsty again but was surprised to find herself hungry now too.

"Crets," Jon said again, watching them go. "Craps. All. All!"

He had never felt so entirely, absolutely alone. Ever.

THIRTY-FOUR

King Tomb took Ash from the barred cell, from the stone room, away from Talon and up the first flight of stairs that Ash had seen since life before the ASP camp. Other Raptors stood aside to allow them to pass. Ash tried not to look at any of them. She wanted to examine everything but was still too afraid. She was in a house full of Raptors!

The one by her side, the king, halted and turned. Ash flinched. She was ready to fall onto the floor again, to curl up into a ball. From behind her, she could still discern the growling frustration and anger of Talon.

But so could the king. He turned and spoke, touching Ash on the shoulder before leaving her there. Ash had her eyes fixed mostly to the floor, but she glanced and saw the king taking his brother away, with Talon swaying and looking behind at Ash. The three females approached and stood around her. They were speaking sporadically, one, two, three. Ash cowered in the middle, wondering what to do. In the end, the smallest of the three showed Ash that she wanted her to follow, leading her along the wide corridor as male Raptors in patterned wraps like togas stood to one side or the other.

The three took Ash to a small room and opened the door but didn't go in. They all stood waiting outside, with Ash growing more and more nervous, until she suddenly realized that she was supposed to enter alone, that this little room was where they were going to keep her now. She had to go in, to stand alone in there, expecting the door to slam behind her.

It didn't. It closed gently. Another electric light shone, but this time more kindly. The light was softer. The source was shielded and the light reflected. Ash stood in the middle of the tiny room collecting her thoughts.

She was still alive, for a start. A good start, but locked in a little room in a house full of Raptors—what could she do next? There was no window through which to escape. Just strange things, white lumps fixed to the floor and to the wall.

Ash took a closer look at the thing on the wall with the two metal—then she remembered! Faucets! A sink! A toilet!

She tugged at the faucet, then pushed it. When she tried turning it, water came out. Clear cold water. She couldn't believe it! She drank and drank. It was like life coming back into her. She tried the other tap and the water from it started to get warm. Then hot! Hot and cold running water and a toilet! For a few moments Ash forgot what was on the other side of the door.

Not for long though. As she was taking another long drink, a knock came. Ash waited, thinking that it might have just been another Raptor bashing by outside. The knock was repeated, again, again. But there was, by the gentleness of the sound, no anger in it.

Ash finally found the courage to go to the door and crack it open to peep through. It was Tomb. The king was waiting outside for her.

He stood back away from the door with his three ladies-in-waiting. There was no sign of Talon. Tomb nodded at Ash. She started to feel confident enough to allow herself to look at him. He offered her his hand again. She had to take it. It was warm and strong without being too hard. He was nothing like his younger

brother, walking calmly, escorting Ash to another room and opening the door for her, inviting her to go in. There was a huge room
on the other side of the doorway. Ash could see a bed, a real bed,
like one out of the magazines. She entered. The king and the
females followed.

The room was huge. The bed was giant. Half the ASP camp
could have slept in it. But as Ash looked around, trying to take
it all in, her eye was drawn to the tray of things by the bed, dead
things, cut into pieces, raw meat, as if it had been prepared for
Ash to eat.

Ash baulked at the sight of it. The king looked at his lady-escorts.
They didn't understand. Ash started to feel more afraid again as
the Raptors bristled, thinking that perhaps she had insulted them.
From her experiences in the city streets, it seemed to Ash that all
Raptors were constantly on the verge of aggression and violence.
The way they were reacting to her now didn't make her feel com-
fortable at all.

She thought about trying to make the sounds that Rat had told
her meant food in Raptor, only she'd forgotten them. Ash looked
around. The bedroom was beautiful, the bed made up and ready
for sleeping in. But there was no real food.

Then she noticed the thick curtains hanging on either side of
the windows. They were patterned, showing flowers and fruit, none
that Ash recognized specifically, but still they looked good enough
to eat.

The three female Raptors trembled as Ash moved to the windows. The king calmed them. Ash felt him watching her with curiosity, as she went to the curtains and pointed at the fruit and indicated toward her open mouth. The Raptors watched her without

moving. She indicated again and again, starting to feel slightly more confident.

Ash continued her dumb-show until the littlest of the three females made a soft sound, speaking to the king. She, this little Raptor, not very much taller than Ash herself, went to Tomb and spoke to him again before she approached Ash, very warily, and nervously reached out with her hand.

Still too afraid to move, Ash waited to see what this little Raptor was about to do to her. All that happened was that the Raptor took Ash's hand in her own and led her back out of the beautiful room and back down the huge staircase with the king and the other two following on behind.

The littlest Raptor took them down the magnificent staircase they had come up to go to the bathroom and out of the huge main door of the house. The robed Raptors on guard out there immediately swung their heads into assault mode. The king calmed them, following into the gardens.

It was night now, so good to be back outside. The warm evening air felt wonderful against Ash's skin. The little Raptor ran to the nearest fruit tree, picking a huge ripe plumlike thing Ash recognized. She brought it back to Ash. As she held it out to her, Ash's eyes met those of the Raptor. This soft female exchanged a look of kindness and sympathy that almost knocked Ash over.

Biting into the fruit, Ash's taste buds went wild as the sweet juices flooded her mouth. Tears of joy and gratitude came. She closed her eyes tightly and tried not to sob. Before she knew what she was doing, Ash had scoffed down the whole thing. In a moment, just the big pit was left in her hand.

Tomb was watching her closely as the other Raptors went from tree to tree picking massive fruits and succulent nuts. He signaled to the three females which fruits and nuts looked the biggest and the best, and they all went back into the house with arms full, more than Ash could eat in a week.

They tossed the food onto the bed upstairs. They bounced! The bed was like that, soft but kind of firm and bouncy at the same time. It was like—like everything Laura and Ash had ever fantasized as they dreamed in the dry and dirty camp. The whole room was made of this dream stuff, with mirrors and tables and clean windows with curtains and all kinds of things she couldn't figure out but really wanted to.

The king's eyes appeared to be full of amusement and approval. Ash was still afraid and the three females still very nervous, but Tomb stepped up and took Ash's hand and looked into her face. Ash had to look straight back at him. She thought she was going to crumble for a moment. She had to fight against the urge to tear her face away. In her confusion, she smiled.

The king studied her face, so closely. He didn't seem to mind the smile, reaching up to touch her smiling lips, so gently. Then he touched her hair, holding it out to look more closely at it. Ash only wished it could have been much cleaner. But he nodded and so did she, putting away her smile.

He let go of Ash and stepped away. He indicated left and right, showing that this room, all of it, was for her. Before he left, he turned and spoke to the three females.

Then he was gone and Ash was alone with them. They didn't seem to know what to do, neither did Ash. She waited until they found the confidence to come close to her again, now that the king wasn't with them. Ash nodded and nodded. She was nervous but not afraid any longer. Not so very afraid, anyway.

Led by the smallest, they approached and waited until Ash held out her hands to them. They touched her fingers with theirs, which were just like hers but bigger and cleaner and softer. Their finger-nails were perfect. Ash's were dirty and split.

They took her through another door into an adjoining room. There were more faucets and things on the walls, and a big glass cabinet Ash mis-guessed for a moment might have been for locking her up again. But no. This was—fantasy of fantasies—a shower! This was where the warm water sprayed out all over, like Ash and Laura—Laura! If only Ash could have shared this with her!

The female Raptors, so gentle, so very nearly afraid, helped her undress and left her to clean herself under the spray of warm water. They gave her some plastic bottles of shower gel and shampoo in sealed bottles that had never been opened. The scent was still fully intact.

Ash couldn't think of how she was going to describe the luxury of washing her hair properly for the first time in years, shower-ing under warm water with the smell of the gel and the shampoo, washing out the grit and dust and everything the forest birds had dumped into her hair. None of the dwellers had experienced any-thing like it in the whole history of the ASP camp. To feel so clean! She thought she was never going to get over it.

There were towels and a robe ready for her when she came out. The three graceful females were waiting for her, wanting to do nothing but help where they could or else simply watch what Ash was doing. They were all three simply fascinated by her. It made

Ash feel more than a little self-conscious and still scared, but they weren't doing anything other than watching her.

All three gathered around as Ash sat at what she recognized as a dressing table and looked into the mirrors. There were combs and brushes laid out on the tabletop. These were not things designed for Raptors, but beings with hair, long hair, like hers. They had hairbrushes at the camp, but not like these. Theirs were old and worn and dirty, these were old but clean, big and ornate, beautifully designed. Ash picked out one of the best-looking brushes and started to tug out some of the tangles from her hair.

The Raptors were mesmerized. All three gathered at her back, but very close now, watching the brush starting to glide through her hair.

Ash found that she didn't mind them being so close to her. She stopped and looked at them in the mirror. They started to nod. One of them, the smallest, that neat little figure not a great deal taller than Ash, nervously reached out to touch her hair. She stopped halfway, wanting the courage to carry on. Ash felt suddenly confident enough to turn on the stool and face her. Taking her hand, Ash put the hairbrush into it. She nodded.

The littlest Raptor glanced at the other two. They were already nodding at her. She approached Ash's hair carefully. She started to brush.

A Blue Raptor was brushing her hair!

THIRTY-FIVE

Jon slept. He dreamed he was alone and afraid. He woke. He was alone and afraid.

The fire had died down a lot. "Not 'fraid," he said, shifting closer to the diminished heat and light. His clothes were still damp. The magazines were all gone, forever.

All that time Jon had been practicing his surfing, trying to be, dreaming of being the best. He was always going to be somebody! Now he was nobody. Nothing he did, no matter how good he was, was ever good enough. What was it? Why was everything and everybody so against him?

He hated the camp now. He hated everybody in it. For a moment, for two moments, he toyed with the idea of taking a burning branch to the huts. They deserved it. Why shouldn't he, after what they'd all done to him?

"Sick," he said.

If he could get out of the camp, if only there was anywhere else to go—

There was a sound. Jon turned toward it. "Who's there?" No answer. "Rich? That you? You better go," he said. "Cret!"

He listened. There was definitely somebody hiding in the shadows just outside the fire's low light.

"Who's it?" Jon said. He heard a scrabbling sound. Jon stood. "Who's it? Who?"

"Agle?" a voice said.

Jon didn't recognize the voice. "Agle?" he said.

THIRTY-SIX

Ash slept. She couldn't rest to begin with, because her mind was too full. Several times she woke with the image of the three Raptors taking turns to brush her hair, them allowing Ash to touch their head feathers. The ASP camp dwellers were on her mind too, especially Laura. Ash was worried how she, and Jess and Will and everyone else, were managing with Jon left supposedly in charge.

Before she went off to sleep, Ash had been trying to picture the disbelief on their faces when she told them about everything she had been through. It was so much, she'd be boasting about it around the beach fire for years to come.

When she got back—and the kindness of the king had allowed her to believe she would get back, somehow—the very thought of going home! Ash was able to curl up in that big bed and dream of seeing and being back with all her friends.

Ash did wake, many times, with a head full of frightful feathered images, with feelings of danger and dread, but the comfortable reality of the bed she was in wrapped her securely, and she was able to relax again. Going in and out of sleep was a luxury, with the curtains drawn to prolong the night and this feeling inside her that everything was somehow going to be all right.

When she woke for the fourth or fifth or sixth time, Ash leapt to see three Raptor faces hanging over her. Two out of the three disappeared as soon as she opened her eyes. Number three, the little one, Little Number Three, stayed exactly where she was, peering down at her.

It was getting quite late in the day, Ash saw, as they drew back the heavy curtains to let in the full daylight. Until then she'd been looking back at Little Three in the half-light leaking in through the chinks around the window's edge. Forgetting again that she probably shouldn't, Ash smiled as the afternoon sunlight lit the room.

Little Three might have taken fright at the baring of teeth, but she and the others had grown more accustomed to Ash now. Instead of running away, she took her finger and drew a smile on her Raptor beak to say that if she could, she'd be smiling back. Ash nodded and nodded. Little Three showed her drawn-on smile to One and Two, in order of size, which seemed to matter a great deal in Raptor society. They too drew on their beaks, and they all smiled and nodded until Ash's neck was aching again.

She ate some more fruit for breakfast and rinsed her teeth in cool clean water and showered again in warm. Two showers in two days! Ash already knew that, given the opportunity, this was what she'd be doing every day. There was nothing like feeling this fresh and clean. Standing in the rain was the nearest she had to compare with it. It didn't compare.

One, Two and Three had a special tunic already prepared for her when Ash came out of the shower. It was like theirs, smaller of course, but just as colorful. The fabric was heavy, like something the thick curtains were made of. Ash couldn't help but think that all the wonderful things the royal Raptors had were here to begin with. Somehow she felt that this whole place, the wooden floors, now scratched by claw marks, the fabric coverings all picked and pulled, were designed and created exactly for her. She fitted in here. The Raptors, even Little Three, looked as if they'd be more at home running across the open plains.

But Ash wasn't going too far into that way of thinking, trying to ignore her recollections of Talon's friends felling the lovely young antelope. Everywhere things ate other things.

She couldn't imagine Raptor Little Three killing anything. She was as shy and tentative as an antelope herself. She was gentle. All she wanted to do was touch Ash's hair, play with it, brush it through and through. They spent a long time together as Little Three groomed Ash, looking in the dressing table mirror at one another. She ran her fingers through Ash's hair. Ash watched as she looked at her own reflection and touched the bright blue feathers on her head.

Ash stood up and faced her. They were very nearly face-to-face, each studying the other, marveling at the differences between them. Ash held up her arm. Little Three held up hers. They marveled at the similarity.

As Little Three looked at her, Ash knew that Rat had never experienced Raptor friendliness like this. From the outside, Raptor society looked fierce and unrelenting. That was all Rat would have seen.

Ash saw more. Much more. The three females were excited as they helped her dress, as they encouraged her to accompany them out of the bedroom and along the grand upstairs passageway to the top of the even grander main staircase. Ash felt as excited as they were. "Where are we going?"

The three clacked excitedly, hurrying her along toward the upper hall. But as they made their way, the mood suddenly changed, falling precipitously as Talon stepped like a specter from one of the other rooms. He turned to face them, with his eyes darkening, his low-growling head moving steadily from side to side.

They halted, pulling up at the sight of him. He had on a very ornate coat, as if dressed up for some special occasion. He looked as civilized as Ash had ever seen him, but his face, his mood as soon as he saw her, showed the truth the fancy coat couldn't hide: the other side to this Raptor could never be dressed up as anything but pure predator. All his hatred, his disgust at being dressed and presented was being directed at Ash.

Her three chaperones gathered closer as Talon stalked toward them. This they had expected at some point, Ash could feel. They had probably had instructions to ensure her safety.

Talon bruised on by, crashing between them, growl-shouting his way through, stamping too hard on the floorboards with such an inflated sense of self-importance, blistering down the great staircase in a ceremonial huff.

As soon as he'd gone, they continued where they left off, One, Two, Three, and Ash, excitedly gathering in the upper hall with another couple of chattering females. Raptors were not like ASP dwellers; the girls never let the boys get away with much. Here they were left in the wings, watching backstage as the male Raptors gathered in the great reception hall downstairs, all dressed for some extraordinary event Ash could tell, from the way so many grand Raptors were presenting themselves downstairs and so many females were gathering up here, creating such an atmosphere of excited anticipation.

Ash surprised herself by suddenly realizing where she was, completely surrounded by Raptors and feeling only excitement and curiosity. All the while she sensed Little Three by her side, concerned and caring for her. Ash shivered with excitement.

From where she was allowed to stand, positioned out of sight, peeping over the heavy banister, Ash was able to watch Talon as he lurched from one place to another, snapping and snarling out his orders. All around him Raptors deferred humbly, inflating Talon's sense of self-importance.

But as soon as King Tomb appeared, the reverence switched from the younger to the elder brother, leaving Talon alone, seething in another wet sulk. He had so much jealousy and resentment in him, the only approach for Tomb and the other Raptors was to ignore him.

Even Ash could see that Tomb commanded respect, while Talon craved it. Tomb was respected naturally, holding his authority with ease and generosity and grace. All the tension was released when the king appeared and the prince was put back in his place.

Ash's three female keepers were careful to hide her, letting her see while ensuring she could not be seen. Ash was wondering why, of course, and what could be happening that was so exciting and important.

They were peeking over from upstairs as the great doors of the house were opened wide to admit the visitors.

Of course! Ash had forgotten. Rat had told her. The talks, today, here, with the Blue Raptors' sworn enemy. The peace talks that

Talon had hoped to disrupt by bringing her here. Another type of Raptor was coming here to speak with King Tomb.

Ash looked over as the doors opened. King Tomb's Blues threw open the doors, wide, and there they were.

For a moment Ash couldn't breathe.

They were magnificent. Yellow. *Yellow Raptors!*

THIRT५-SEVEN

So yellow! With maybe deeper green leg scales and slightly darker skin. But the yellow of the feathers Ash would never have anticipated. How any color could be that bright—not just that, so vivid and sincere! True yellow. The Yellow Raptor!

All around her, an astonished, frightened but respectful hush as the female Blues looked down upon the six, no seven, eight, nine, now ten brilliantly beautiful visitors. Ash felt that most of these Blues were seeing Yellows for the first time, just as she was. They were all as astounded and entranced by what they saw.

The Blue ranks downstairs drew back to allow the ten mighty Yellows to enter the house. From where she crouched out of sight, Ash could see and feel the tension, as the Blues tried desperately not to nod but shake their heads. This, for Blues, normally meant aggression, but they did it as a sign of friendliness toward their old enemy.

At the same time, Ash could see the Yellows struggling not to shake their heads at Blues, so they came in nodding and the whole thing was confusion for a moment or two. The talks looked as if they were about to break down from the very start. Talon, along with the other Blues, was shaking his head; but with him, Ash noted, from the look on his face, this meant only the one thing, the Blue definition, the fight stance.

Tomb had to put a stop to all head-movement on both sides by stepping forward into the amassed yellow to welcome them into his territory, his kingdom and his home.

From the Yellow ranks, the biggest Raptor stepped up to meet the Blue king. The two stood, as if preparing for a terrible confrontation, both straining not to nod or shake, shake or nod. It wasn't difficult to see how relations had broken down so easily in the past.

The standoff looked as if it would continue until something snapped on one side or the other. Tomb broke the deadlock eventually, by doing something that surprised Ash greatly. He held his hand out to the Yellow commander, in the way the ASP dwellers did, as Jon had, offering to shake hands on the beach after the surfing competition. The huge Yellow looked at Tomb's hand for a few moments before taking it. The two shook hands exactly in the same way and for the same reasons as the ASP dwellers.

All around them and all around Ash on the balcony of the upstairs hall, nods broke out, some shakes of the heads downstairs, more confusion, but overall relief and approval.

Except from one individual. Talon's talons flexed and gripped, his leg muscles tensing, growing, his head lowering. He was seething with rage at the sight of his elder brother taking the hand of a hated Yellow. Several of the other Blues had gathered closer to him, noticing his rising temperature, effectively closing him in and away from the Yellow ranks.

King Tomb and the stately Yellow continued to shake hands. They wanted to make a show of their intentions to end the animosity.

This was a great and special moment. Ash felt the importance of it, as did all around her. The great halls, lower and upper, settled into silence.

But something was going on. Something else was happening.

Downstairs, a sudden flare of yellow feather, of nodding yellow heads all turned to one side to look at—what was it? What could it have been to so perturb the Yellow Raptors this suddenly?

The female Raptors all around Ash leaned farther over the banister to see. Downstairs, blue heads turned and shook. Something moved along the side of the great hall. Against one wall were fixed some kind of crossed ornamental battle spears. Not the sort of thing a Raptor would use.

But an ASP dweller might.

That was when she saw him. All eyes were on him as he ran for the weapon.

Ash stood up.

He ran to the spears and pulled one from the wall. "Where's she?" he screamed.

Jon!

"Where's she?"

Oh, Jon!

THIRTY-EIGHT

He screamed at them!

"Oh, Jon," Ash breathed, "you cret. You—cret!"

"Where's she?"—screaming out like that, with teeth showing, head going in every direction, threatening, insulting everyone. The spear he had dragged from the wall was being thrust at Raptors, Blue and Yellow, as he cried out. "Show me! Savages! Where's she?"

The Yellows were filling up with fear and resultant aggression as they were in the most vulnerable position. They had come here to try to talk peace with King Tomb, only to find themselves under attack by a wingless no-angel, a devil-faced demon boy. They backed away into a protective huddle, nodding as Yellows, ready to defend by attack.

If only Jon hadn't gone for them! If only, Ash felt, she'd have spoken up sooner, then it wouldn't have seemed as if the thrust of the spear coincided with what must have sounded like a war cry from upstairs as she shrieked, "Jon! No!"

The Yellows in battle formation, full furious ten of them, fought back. The Blues had set devils against them; they were going to have to fight for their lives. The whole center of the great hall erupted in volatile yellow, with a thunderous roar as the females all around Ash Raptor-screamed, fleeing, flying away as she ran to make the steps downward.

Jon thrust wildly at the Yellows and the Blues. Yellows fought Blues, as Blues followed suit and fell into their own formations to fight back hard and fast. In an instant, a full-scale battle raged, roaring and thrashing, with one blue figure forging ahead into the block of yellow—the Blue prince, with his elder the king still trying in vain to calm everyone down.

The flock of females around Ash were scattering, all except Little Three, who clung ever closer.

Jon was down there, flailing with the spear, his back against the wall.

"You cret!" Ash screamed over the balcony at him. He couldn't hear her. As she went to run for the stairs, Little Three was there by her side, trying to prevent her. She showed Ash her eyes, reflecting the fear of the Blue and Yellow battle raging just below.

Ash revealed her own eyes, hoping that some of the feeling of respect she had inside showed through. But she had to try to get to him, to one of her own kind because he was in so much danger.

Little Three touched her hair. Ash took her hand and squeezed it. She held on.

Then she let Ash go and she was dashing down the huge staircase toward Jon, but the Yellows saw her as swooping upon them, another no-angel, a wingless devil flying on the side of the Blues. The Yellow roars bellowed out, louder and more ferocious as they backed out of the doors, fighting beak and claw on the stone steps outside.

"Cret!" Ash shrieked at Jon. "What you doing?"

"Come to get you!"

"You cret!" she dashed up to him. "You don't know! You just don't know!"

"He said," Jon said, pointing.

And there was Rat's pink snout about to disappear down the smaller staircase that led to the basements. "Come on!" Rat cried. "Quickly! Come now!"

"You crets! You idiots!" she shouted, using the word Rat was so fond of calling her.

The Raptor battle ripped and raged just outside, with horrendous roars and claw splits and all the sounds and sights of Blue and Yellow violence, but inside the hall now, pumped massively from the fight, Talon, staring at them.

"Now!" screamed Rat, from halfway down to the first under floor. "Now! Now!"

Prince Talon bore down upon them. He moved his mighty limbs with slow deliberation, magnifying the threat, but as if to give them the chance to run.

They ran! Ash almost went chest-first into Jon's spear. "Go!" she screamed. "Go! Go! Go! Do it!" Her throat was very nearly shouted out. "Get out!"

Down the stairs they went, following Rat, with Talon's knife-claws cutting against the steps immediately behind them.

"Throw the spear!" Ash shouted at Jon.

"I'll never get him!" he shouted back.

"Not *at* him, cret! Throw it away!"

"No! No! Go!"

Ahead of them, just, Rat's yellow shorts swaying onto the room where Ash had been held captive in the cage. "Not in there!" she tried to say. But there was nowhere else to go at the end of the stone corridor. Behind them, just, Talon roared down the backs of their necks. Behind him, another Raptor-cry: they were after them,

Prince Talon and his followers, the wild Blue youths, the cold-blooded killers from the open plains.

Jon dashed into the room after Rat. Ash followed Jon, smashing the door closed behind her. The room was as empty as the open cage.

"Come on!" cried Rat from inside the open air-vent in the wall. "Quickly! Quickly!"

Jon went to follow him. This was obviously the way they had arrived.

"Can't!" Ash cried. "Can't get through!"

Jon was smaller than she. He halted, turning. "Have to," he said. "The only way. No other."

"Can't fit!"

"Try!"

"I can't fit!"

"We have to go now!" Rat was calling. "We have to leave right now!" His voice sounded farther and farther away.

Jon and Ash were looking at each other as the door crashed open. Jon turned, with the spear at the ready.

"One chance, Jon," Ash said, stepping back against the bars of the cage. Talon stepped through the open door. He took it all in, in an instant: the open vent, Ash, Jon with the spear, their one single chance.

"Don't miss," she said.

"Don't worry," he said, bracing himself.

Talon's eyes darkened still further. He bristled with anticipation.

THIRTY-nine

Talon charged.

Jon held firm, standing his ground with the sharp stick pointed toward his attacker. Jon closed his eyes. Ash saw him do it. The idiot! He closed his eyes, somehow expecting a fighter like Talon to just lumber in and impale himself.

He soon found the thing ripped from his grip; and if he had kept his idiot eyes open Jon might have stood at least half a chance of doing something about it. When he did open his eyes, what he was confronted with was the massive prince of Blue Raptors heavily armed with beak and talon and now a sharp metal spear.

They were finished! Their one chance gone, squandered. Talon would never allow them to walk away from this. Ash could see it in his eyes, the bloodlust, the urge to kill. He had strength and weapons; they had nothing.

But through the doorway, behind the prince, stepped the king. Jon was watching, his face gaunt and white with fear. He obviously could never tell one Raptor from the next. But Ash did. She nodded wildly at the king as he stopped behind his brother.

King Tomb looked at her for a moment before speaking, very rapidly and urgently to his younger brother. Talon towered over them. His hard hands gripped the steel shaft of the spear. His eyes were full of dark blood, swimming, swirling.

Tomb spoke to him again. Ash knew he was trying to talk Talon down, the king trying hard to reassert sovereignty and to salvage what little he could from the mess that this day had become. He tried to reason with Talon. Tomb's click-words were soft and measured, reasonable.

But Talon's eyes would not be reasoned with. He didn't seem to hear his brother. He didn't even seem to be aware of the spear he was grasping. His head was swaying with menace as he took a step farther toward Jon and Ash.

Tomb growled at him threateningly, trying to halt him. The king did not want to see them killed by his brother. He gave Ash hope.

But Talon would not stop.

He would not stop, so Tomb leapt forward and grabbed him by the arm, and Talon turned and—

And Talon turned.

And Ash couldn't—she didn't—

He ran at him!

Talon ran at his brother and—

And it was intentional, running at him, or rather through him like that in a blind rage thrusting the spear into—right into King Tomb's stomach and, so terrible to watch, right out the other side, such was the force and ferocity with which he impaled him.

Talon impaled Tomb and Ash was screaming and so was Jon and so was Talon but Tomb, the king, royally, regally great, fell back slowly against the wall so that the spear was pushed part of the way back out of him again.

He didn't cry out. He fell slowly back with that thing through him and stopped their cries with his intelligent, thoughtful last look into his brother's face. That was all King Tomb did as he died. He looked at Talon and felt sorry. Ash could see he felt sorry for what had happened, and he felt sorry for Talon too.

Talon stood over his dying brother, with his pumped arms bent and twitching. He stood transfixed as his brother's blood came out onto the floor so quickly that Tomb just faded away. The life leaked out of him, and he was gone.

THE
RULE
OF
CLAW

PART THREE

FORTY

Ash and Jon stood rooted to the spot. Ash found her hand over her mouth. "Jon," she whispered from behind it. "Jon. The door. Go soft."

Talon didn't seem to notice them at all. He stood twitching over his brother, as if shocked and astonished at how it had happened.

They slid silently from the room. "Upstairs!" Ash breathed hoarsely. "Run! Follow me."

From behind them, the most hideous roar of rage and disgust and lament. The door of the cell room crashed from its hinges.

"Quickly!" Ash shouted as they ran up the stairs, through the empty hall, and onto the stone steps just outside.

They dashed out, almost stumbling over him: face up, with blank open eyes, the commander of the Yellow Raptors, dead. All over the park, everywhere they looked, Blues and Yellows ripped one another in terrible combat.

"Keep by," Ash whispered to Jon. They ran in the shadows into the parklands behind, moving from bush to bush, looking for a way out as Talon's dreadful cries broke through windows and doors all over the beautiful big house.

"All that," Jon was saying, far too loudly, "what's it?"

They had taken refuge in a bush, crouching together in the dark. "Jon! Shsh! Keep quiet. Follow me."

"Follow you?"

"Keep it down! What's it with you, cret?"

"Follow you?" he said, still too loudly. "I'm leader, not you."

Ash felt like getting hold of him and stopping his stupid mouth with a smack. From inside the house, roars splintered wood and smashed out glass. The walls were shaking. "You're such crap," Ash hissed, before running off, whether he was with her or not.

But Jon did follow, dashing with Ash from one bush to the next. The farther they got from the house the more they left the noise of Raptor rage behind. They crossed the park that surrounded the house, skirting a large pond in which the mirrored full moon shone. Here and there, the round woolly creatures grazed, moving away from their shifting moon-shadows.

Far enough away, they ran toward the almost complete darkness at the base of the periphery wall. Beyond the wall, the blank stalks of the darkened city buildings.

"Where you going?" Jon whispered as they huddled under the trees that grew in the park just this side of the wall.

"Out there," Ash said. "Somewhere. Don't know. Can't stay here, is all. Got to get out."

"Down to me," Jon said. "I'll get us out."

"Yeah?" Ash said, still fighting the urge to smack Jon one in the mouth. "How?"

"Got you out, didn't I?"

"You—what?"

"Got you out," Jon said, puffing up. "Told Rat I would. I did. I'd fight 'em, I would."

"Crap!" Ash said. "Such crap!"

"No crap. Got you out."

"Jon," Ash said. "I'm gonna—"

"Yeah? What? What you gonna?"

"Look!" Ash had to say, with her hands itching to take Jon by the scruff of the neck. There was so much she wanted to ask him, about Laura, about what was happening back at the camp, but "It's all crap," was all she said, "right?"

"No crap."

"It's crap! But we got to get away. You don't get it. Talon's gonna—"

"Talon?"

"Him, back there. With the spear. Prince Talon. He'll take your idiot head off."

"Yeah?"

"Yeah. So shut it. Come on. Over the wall."

"Then what?"

"Then what? I don't know. Out of here, is all. Find a place to hide. How'd you get here?"

"Tunnels."

"Tunnels?" Ash said, excitedly looking about. "Where? Where're tunnels?"

"All over. Rat knows. He runs them."

"Small tunnels?"

"Pretty small."

"Like the air vent?"

"Yeah, bit. Bigger, some. One place, really big. Smaller, others."

"Where? Where're they?"

"I don't know! Where's he? Where's Rat? He knows. I don't. Where you going?"

"Where you think? Up, over. Try and get us out. Now."

Ash clambered up the gnarled trunk of an old, colorful tree right next to the wall. The branches farther up overhung the city streets outside. Jon watched from the ground as Ash hauled herself onto one branch that was in reach of the next and the next until she sat high enough to see into the moonlit street.

Jon started calling up to her, "What's there? Anything?"

Ash had to wave him down to silence him. "Cret," she hissed from between her teeth. She indicated to him to follow her up.

"You think you're leader," he was complaining, as he climbed the tree trunk after her. "You're not. I won. It's me. Not you. Me!"

As soon as he was close enough, Ash grabbed him by the torn and tearing surfer's top, dragging him up to her level. She clapped a hand against his mouth and forced him to look down into the street below. At Raptors.

Raptors, everywhere!

FORT⅄-ONE

Jon was silent at last. So was Ash. They stood on one of the biggest branches hiding behind the trunk of the tree, looking down into the streets between the buildings. There seemed to be some kind of riot going on. Excited Raptors were running, snapping, snarling.

"They know," Ash said. "They found out."

"What? What they know?"

"Their king's dead."

"King?" Jon said.

Ash didn't bother explaining. Jon was looking down into the street, sneering and snarling, noticing nothing of what was really going on. Ash knew he wouldn't spot the differences between the males and females, the old and the young, except when it was obvious, as it was with that Raptor family. The young ones were only the size of a Raptor-child: about as big as Jon, the really small one.

At one point Ash noticed a couple of older Raptors with two tiny ones trying to make their way peaceably through the thronging crowd. The little Raptors seemed to be quite afraid.

At first Ash had thought that it was purely King Tomb's death bringing them out in this way. She mistook their noisy aggression for a form of Raptor mourning. She was wrong. The more Ash watched them, the more she became convinced of the truth. These Raptors were celebrating!

The king's reign had come to an end. A new era was just about to begin. The news must have flooded through the streets, bringing out this wild tide of revelers so soon after the old king's last breath.

"How'd they know?" Ash whispered.

"Savages," Jon said.

"No. Not."

"Look at them," Jon said. "What else?" he said, showing too much of himself from behind the tree. "Filthy animals."

"Keep back!"

"Not scared."

"No?"

"No. Not scared, some pack of animals."

"That what they are?"

"What else?"

"What are we?" Ash asked. She gazed down as the Raptors ran in streams along the street below, their feathers blowing like blue eddies against the flow of the main current. "What are we?" Ash asked herself, quietly, as she watched. In the world before the ASP camp, the question would probably never have been asked; but now they were Agles, in what kind of world did they belong? "We shouldn't be here at all," Ash said.

The Blues below roared louder, as if in approval of what she had just said.

"With you there," Jon said. "Look at them! Just look at them!"

Ash was looking at the unbroken Blue city streets. Along the shifting stream of blue feather, another color flashed by at the far end of the street. The Blues saw it. The excitement and agitation levels rose instantly. The two older Raptors bustled their children to safety as the ticking growl of the streets flared into roar and ruffles of animated blue.

"What's on?" Jon asked.

Ash had seen what Jon hadn't. She pointed toward the end of the street. From where they sat they could see him quite clearly. He was big and wild, tormented, afraid, and therefore extremely dangerous. He was injured. He was Yellow, but his yellow had been reddened horribly from many substantial wounds. He roared like a scream, death-defying and challenging to the Blue males out on parade below. The Yellow tried to run. He staggered sideways.

The wild young males raged, furious but delighted at the opportunity they were being given. Their worst enemy loped yellow and red on their very streets, roaring at them, rearing up at them. The blue of outraged feathers flocked horribly, scraping over the surface of the hard street as they scrambled after the lone Yellow. The street sounded like a single roar, one word of simple explanation for those that had not yet spotted the enemy: Yellow!

Yellow!

He backed against a wall, preparing himself for a final stand against the other color. Ash wished, as he must have, that the Yellows had never come here today, like this. Any other time would have been fine, but not now. Not now!

"All wrong," Ash said, as the amassed fury of Blue billowed at the end of the street and another Yellow was lost. This was what could happen, what would happen as soon as the influence of kind King Tomb disappeared and Talon was unleashed. And this was just the beginning!

"Yellow one, that," Jon said.

"It was," Ash said, quietly. "Not now."

"Good," he said.

Ash clenched her teeth. How could she begin to explain all she knew, about the damage Jon had done. "Come on," she said. "Quick. Jump!"

Jon clumped down onto the pavement beside her. "Ow!" he bellowed. "Ow! Ow! I've hurt me—"

"Jon! Shut up! Come on! Run!"

"But I hurt me—"

Ash didn't bother waiting to find out what Jon had hurt. Whatever it was, they had to get away, and now. They had to run for it, as far from the royal palace as they could, where the news might not have reached yet.

They ran through the streets in the shadows of the big buildings, with broken glass scattered everywhere, making it much harder for them in bare feet. Raptors were fine on these sharp shards, but Ash and Jon had to dodge and leap from one clear space to the next.

"Ow!" Jon kept crying out whenever he got it wrong. "Ow! Ow!"

"This way!" Ash called, looking into a shadow-darkened side street.

"No," he shouted, "this way." He could see the moonlight between the buildings when the road ran in that direction. "Need to see. Glass!"

"No," she called. "We'll be seen. Jon. Come back. Jon!" But he was already taking that path, into the milky moonlight. "Jon!" she shouted, running after him, turning the corner and bustling into him where he had halted suddenly.

There was no need to ask him why he had stopped.

The street was full of Blues!

FORTY-TWO

"Don't move!"

Jon glanced toward her.

"I said don't move! Keep still!"

There must have been twenty or more of them, young Blues. Very young. This was some kind of backstreet young Raptor gang, hanging out, doing nothing in particular. They were a little bit too young yet to be included in the furor of the main thoroughfare. Jon and Ash had blundered in on them as they kicked around on this patch of waste ground.

"They don't get it," she whispered.

The blue heads were all turned toward them, although their Raptor bodies still looked as if they had been caught in the act. They were very, very young. Not fully grown. Kids. Raptor kids out without supervision, looking for new experiences. One or two heads started to move in a worrying sideways sway.

"Young ones," Ash said. "Babies."

"Babies?" Jon said. Most of them, male and female, were substantially bigger than he was. "No babies." Then he roared at them, baring his teeth, raising his arms, his hands up, fingers splayed like claws.

An instant flurry of feathers. The Raptors scattered, frightened, every one of them running for a few paces, stopping and turning back.

"Jon!" Ash cried, as he laughed. "Don't!"

But he would not listen. "Rar!" he blared out at them, taking a step forward, scratching at the air with his little fingernails. Jon had no talons, he should have realized. His roar wasn't very impressive, and he had no feathers to ruffle and rise to make him appear any bigger.

The frightened Raptors shook. They clicked. They did not run. Jon looked small and ridiculous posturing there in front of them. They had no doubt heard of the wingless angel-demons as they had heard of the demonized Yellow Raptors. The Yellows had been vanquished, killed, in the king's home, or here in the city. These street-wise adolescent Raptors knew a thing or two.

"Jon," Ash hissed. "Turn now. Run!"

"I'll not," he said. He tried another roar. All it did was to inspire a wave of feather ruffle, a louder clack of snapping beaks and low ticking growls.

The Raptors in front and to the sides were growing in courage and stature. They were like a bunch of kids similar to ASP dwellers: stronger together, braver, fiercer, more hysterical, more likely to do something stupid.

"Jon! Now!"

But Jon had a look on his face. The dwellers had seen it so often before: Jon, trying too hard to assert himself. But the face was even sterner now that he seemed to have so much more to prove. "Not running," he snarled.

"Run!" Ash said, grabbing hold of his top, hauling him backward as several young males made the first dash forward at them. "Now!"—as she dragged him away.

They had a few moments before the Raptors arranged and encouraged each other into a single-minded entity, a street gang tooled with talon, pumped up and prepared for anything. In that short time, Ash had turned to Jon and made him run with her around the corner, around the next corner, the next, turning right and left. "Keep going!" she screamed.

"Not running!" he shouted, although they both were.

They were running from the sound of the other streets, the ones they had just left, from where the Raptor pack ranted, regretting their initial fear, committed now to making up for it.

"This way!" Ash called out, running out of one side street and into a main thoroughfare. Some distance away she could see more blue feathers. "Here!"—as she took them loping over broken glass into the fully open front of one of the buildings. All of the huge house fronts on this street were like this one, wide open, full of giant shards smashed from massive panes of thick glass.

Ash and Jon ran into this open space. It was huge. There was a staircase in the center, another to the side. As they moved out of the moonlight, it was difficult to see anything. The staircases stood out, with a couple of free-standing shelves or counters picked out in the leaking, bare white moonlight.

"There," Ash said. "Behind this."

"Not hiding," Jon said, although Ash didn't have to drag him there, to the old counter where they crouched and listened as the talon gang crunched by outside. "Not hiding," he whispered.

Ash's heart was thudding. "Keep it!"

They waited until the claw crunch marched away. They waited, listening to the silence pressing in. The young Raptors had gone.

Jon sat down. Ash stood and looked around. "Look," she said. "This place. Look it."

"Sick of it," he said.

"Look. I know. This place. A shop, this was. Department store. We've pictures, Laura and me. They had everything. All you had to do was—"

"Listen to me," Jon hissed. "Why don't anyone listen? What is it? Crets! What is it? Why they think they can—"

"Listen," Ash whispered.

"No, you listen. What'm I, nothing? You win surfing, it's all you. I win, and it's—"

"Jon! Shut it!"

"No. No more! Sick of it! I'm—"

But she reached down and put her hand back over his mouth, listening as the outside silence broke like glass underfoot, under claw, crunching more and more as the Raptors gathered outside. This was a department store, and they had come shopping.

FORTY-THREE

The Raptor gang was never going to give up that easily. The gang members knew Ash and Jon were hiding somewhere and had figured out that they would have run in here. No Raptor spoke as they gathered just outside the store. The broken glass grinding told Ash how many hard feet had collected out there.

She bent down to whisper right into Jon's ear. "Follow. No noise." She was hoping there would be a way out at the back of the building. If there was, she was pretty sure it would be broken open like every other entrance way or window in this damaged city.

"No noise," Ash whispered again, as forcefully as she could. She still had her hand over Jon's mouth. He was so upset and erratic Ash couldn't trust him. But she had to let go of him and start to make her way to the back of the store, hoping that he would choose to follow.

He did. They worked their way back, keeping to the absolute darkness in the corners, while the claws at the front stepped in, catching the splintered boards of the floor, scraping heavily, a small army of tearing talon horn.

Farther back, they could see a door open to the moonlit street at the rear of the building. Jon touched Ash on the shoulder and showed her something he could see near the door. No need to show her, Ash had seen it for herself. Something, somebody, not a Raptor, stood waiting, its ASP-dweller type figure picked out by a silver line of leaking light. The figure looked male, young, upright, and strong. He looked very like the magazine models they had seen and studied, Laura and Ash, in the fantasy of their magazines.

They stopped. The claws clamped against the splintered floor behind them. In front, the door sentry never moved. He must have heard the claw crunch as well as Ash and Jon did, but it had no effect. He didn't even seem to need to breathe.

Ash moved forward toward him. Between the magazine model and the wild young Raptors, she knew which she would choose.

Behind them, they could hear the Raptors fanning out, coming for them. Ash and Jon moved with hardly a sound as the claws behind caught and held onto the wooden ground as if about to be thrown off. A Raptor's feet just did that gripping thing automatically, Ash had observed. It meant she and Jon could hear where each and every one of them was, whereas they couldn't hear a single sound from—

"Ow!" wailed Jon. "Ow! Ow! Ow!" He was leaping up and down on one leg.

"No!" Ash screamed, although she didn't think he heard her. Nobody could have heard anything above the howl of young Raptor, a united growling roar that shuddered through the boards under their flying feet.

Ash had Jon by the scruff. "What is it? Cret! You crap!" But she still didn't think he heard her. They were tearing toward the back entrance with the Raptor rabble ganged up behind them, with feathers flying for the chase.

They dashed to the door where the sentry stood impervious to the cries and roars. He never moved a muscle, even as they mashed by him. Ash had thought he looked like one of the young models from a magazine, and that was exactly what he was. He wasn't real. Up close it was easy to see his face was made up, idealized, too plastic perfect.

Jon smacked him one on the way by, sending him rocking on his plastic feet, or whatever he had down there to stand on.

As they dashed out into the back street, Ash heard the Raptors stall. Their plastic man staggered at them, halting the Raptors for a moment. Then the model came to pieces under a snarl of rip and wrench. "That's you, next!" Ash shouted just behind her at Jon. She shouldn't have said it.

"Oh yeah?" he said. "Let's see. Let's see, eh?"

Ash had to stop and turn and drag him away again. "What is it?" she asked, exasperated. "What you *want*?"

But Jon shrugged her away. "Don't want. Come on," he said, running again. "Down here. Follow!"

Ash let him lead, because he seemed to need to so much. He was a bit better like this. It was easier to be sure where he was and what he was doing if she just let him go ahead. He was running with a limp now, so Ash guessed he really had hurt himself back in the shop.

He was bleeding. His foot was cut quite badly. Whereas before he was jumping up and down—Ow! Ow! Ow!—now, when he had a real injury to complain about, he didn't. He just kept running.

"Jon," she called. "Need to find somewhere. Hide! Jon!" Ash

speeded up, drawing level with him. He could never have outran her, even without a damaged foot. "They're too fast. Need to hide."

"I don't," he said. He was breathing too heavily.

"Jon. Do it."

"No!"

"Look," she said, dragging at him, stopping him. "Look! I don't wanna die! We have to hide." They had stopped beside a heavy car, one of the bigger ones for carrying cages and things around on the back. "Here," Ash said, dragging him to the ground. "Under here." They struggled under the old car, where it stank of wet seats and bad breath.

"I'm not—" Jon started to say.

"Keep quiet!" Ash said, holding him by his top, wrenching the fabric into the ball of her fist so that she held tightly onto him.

They watched from the street's surface level as the Raptor feet scraped by. Their talons looked and sounded like hooked knives scratching over the skin of the road.

"Your foot," Ash said, after some while of waiting in silence. "It's bad."

"Yeah," said Jon, lifting his head to look, cracking his forehead on the underside of the car.

"Tires flat," she said.

He didn't say anything. Ash wasn't sure he knew what a tire was.

"We'll wait," she said. "They'll go."

"I hope they don't," he said.

"Maybe they won't. We'll wait."

They waited. They breathed.

"Stinks," Ash had to say. "Car's gone rotten—"

"No," Jon said. "Rat-runs."

"Rat-runs?"

And Jon pointed behind her. Ash turned. There, from a slotted hole in the side of the street, a dim light showed.

FORTY-FOUR

"Rat-runs?"

"Yeah," Jon said. "Told you. The tunnels. They're all over. There're Rodents underneath, all over the city."

Ash looked into the metal slot in the edge of the pavement. "But there's light. How come?"

"Fire-butterflies," Jon said. "They're everywhere too, under there."

"But it means—Rat! Under there. He can help us."

"Okay," Jon said. He raised his face slightly. "Help!" he shouted. "Rat! Help!"

Ash took a tighter hold of his top, dragging him toward her. Their faces were almost touching. "You do that again," she said, deliberately, staring into his eyes, "I'm gonna—"

"Yeah?" he said, with an almost tired expression. "Oh, yeah? What you gonna?"

They were eye to eye in the slight fire-butterfly light coming from the drain. There was nothing Ash could do. If Jon was determined to behave in this way, she couldn't stop him. She sighed. "Sick, you are," she said. "Something's wrong."

"Nothing wrong with me."

"No?"

"No. Not me."

"What's happened, Jon? Talk to me. Tell me."

"Nothing to tell."

"Look, we have to wait. So talk. Tell me. How's Laura?"

She felt Jon shrug. "Okay, I suppose."

"No, tell me. How's Laura?"

"She burned the magazines."

Ash stalled. She had to wait a while, to take that in. "Burned?"

"Yeah."

"Why?"

"Don't know. She's sick."

"She's sick?"

"They all are. The lot of them."

"I don't get it," Ash said. "Didn't anybody offer to come with you?"

"Rat came to me," Jon said. "The leader. That's why he came to me."

Ash lay listening to Jon, trying to make sense of it. "So nobody saw Rat—nobody know where you are?"

"Hate them all," he was saying. "Hate them! Make me sick!"

Ash waited for a few moments. Jon was breathing so hard she thought he was actually going to *be* sick. "But Laura? She all right?"

"I don't know! What do I know? She's *your* friend. Not mine."

They lay silent for quite a while. "Why'd you come, Jon? Why you? You were in charge. Why just you?"

"What are *they*? Big lump like Will! What use is he, down rat-runs? Rich? Messed his pants. The rest of 'em. Alex, Nicholas! Don't make me laugh. They all make me want to—"

"Wait!" Ash said.

"For what? I'm not—"

"Jon," Ash hissed, as a solitary stalker, a pair of large looming Raptor legs clumped up the street toward the vehicle under which they were hiding.

He walked slowly, steadily, deliberately. The size of the feet, the raw rip-knives of the talons, showed his maleness, his steady nerve, his adult Raptor purpose. This was no street gangster, no young blade out finding out about his powers in the mean darkness of the city backstreets.

Ash and Jon watched in silence as he walked by. Just after he passed the vehicle, he halted and turned. One of his toe blades ticked against the surface of the road as he, it seemed to Ash, stood thinking. From where she lay on her back with her head to one side watching the huge hard feet, the tapping toe, Ash felt as if she could feel his thoughts. The air rippled with danger and the real potential for harm.

"Got to go," she said to Jon, urgently, as they watched the Raptor stalk out of sight. "Get help. Risk it, Jon. Call out. Are they there, Rodents? Are they?"

"They're all over," he said. "Everywhere. Under the city. Raptors don't know. They don't see it. Raptors!" he said, sounding a bit like Rat. He squirmed to get closer to the glowing hole. His face was softly and angelically illuminated by the weak, fire-butterfly light.

"Hey!" he called, with his mouth practically down the drain. "Hey, Rodent! Hear me? With me? Rodent?"

They waited a moment or two. Ash kept watch up the road for any signs of claws.

"Hey! Answer me. I'm Jon. With me?"

"Are you Agle?" a voice came back.

FORTY-FIVE

"I am!" Ash cried excitedly. "I'm Agle!"

"We are!" Jon shouted down the hole. He turned to Ash. "We are. It's what they call us. We're Agles."

A pink nose twitched at the other side of the hole for a moment before a pair of pink eyes appeared. "I heard about you," he said. "But I didn't believe it."

"You know Rat?" Ash called over Jon's shoulder.

The eyes redirected and focused on her. "Rat?" the little voice said. "Yeah, I know Rat."

"Coward ran off," Jon started to say.

"Jon, shut up! Can you tell Rat where we are?" she asked the eyes glowing in the hole.

"Didn't you know," the eyes seemed to speak back, "that about half of us are called that? Do you have any idea how many Rats there are down here?"

"Rat Rodent," Ash cried. "You know him? Rat Rodent?"

"Oh, bot-blag!" he Rodent-laughed. "Rat Rodent, that's a good one! Did you hear that?" he said to someone else behind him.

"Bot-blag!" came another Rodent voice, but female. "Rat Rodent!"

"Got pink eyes," Jon said to the pink eyes peering out from under the pavement.

"He's got a Special called Really," Ash said, quickly, before the Rodents could start their bot-blagging again.

"Rat and Really," the eyes said, with a look of recognition in them. "Rat and Really, yeah, I know them."

"Tell him. Get him. Tell Rat we need help," Ash said.

"Can't *they* help us?" Jon asked.

"We can't get away," Ash said. "Raptors. We need help. Can you help?"

"What can we do?" came the other voice, the female, the one they couldn't see. The other's eyes blinked at them.

"The rat-runs," Jon said. "How can we get in?"

"Through this hole," said the eyes.

"We're too big," Ash said.

"We don't want the Raptors after Rodents," she heard the other voice say.

The eyes disappeared.

"Don't go!" Ash called out. She had this feeling that something was set to go dreadfully, disastrously wrong. "Come back! Come back!"

The eyes reappeared. They didn't say anything.

"Help us, please," Ash said, with that bad feeling ticking at the back of her mind. But the voices had ceased. The pink head on the other side looked away, as if a quiet voice of warning was tapping at his shoulder. "Raptors won't find out about you. I promise. They won't."

But the promise was empty. That ticking at the back of her mind reminded Ash that she was in no position to promise the Rodents anything but trouble. Rat had bitten Prince Talon on the leg once already. And now the prince was king. "Look," she said, "I get it. Please, tell Rat. Tell him we're here. Say we need him. Could you? Please?"

The eyes were widening, reddening, as if growing in alarm.

"Don't be 'fraid," Ash said, because of what was happening in those eyes. Her head was ticking. She was dreading being left alone again with Jon in this mood, trapped with him under a big car in the middle of the capital city of the Blue Kingdom. "Don't go!" she cried, as he was fading away into the fire-butterfly distance that Jon and Ash would never reach from here.

"Tell Rat!" she shouted out. "Tell him where we are! Tell him we need help! Rat! Hear me? It's the Agle! Need you, Rat! Need you now!"

Ash's heart was accelerating again. Her temperature was rising, her head ticking. The smell down here reminded her of sick. "Rat!" she called.

Jon was watching her.

Then Ash realized that Jon was not watching her. He was looking past her, out at the open backroad behind. The ticking in her head no longer felt as if it was situated there.

Jon was staring.

Ash turned into the ticking. It wasn't in her head at all. Not at all! It was behind her, right behind. She turned into it.

The blade of a single Raptor talon tapped on the road going tick, tick, tick, tick, very, very patiently. The foot was the one they had seen from there a little earlier. It was huge. Ash had certainly seen it before.

It ticked away, as if keeping time. As time ticked by, the Raptor was joined by another. Then another. Another. Another. Another.

Until every direction Ash or Jon looked into was filled, overfilled, crowded with claws. The big old car was surrounded.

"Well done," Jon said.

Ash didn't look at him. She kept her eyes fixed on the biggest claw, the nastiest talon. She knew who it was even before he bent down to take a look at them.

Raptors cannot smile. But in his eyes Ash saw the equivalent of a cruel grin, a self-satisfied smirk. He looked under the car at them, ticking. Without understanding his language, Ash knew what he was saying.

"Now I have you," he was saying.

Talon.

Prince Talon.

The new king.

"You are mine," his look said. "You are mine to destroy and devour."

And his face showed how determined he was to do just that.

FORTY-SIX

"Oh no," Ash breathed as she stared back into those dense eyes again, those eyes that spoke to her, ensuring that Talon and she, at this moment at least, totally understood one another.

All around Talon the street gang were dropping to their knees as if in worship, peering under the vehicle at them. The young blades, the big baby Raptors were back in force, only now they had their prince, their king with them. Now they would not back down or run or even hesitate as they had with the shop dummy. Talon's energy, his fierceness was inspiring the worshippers on their knees. The Blue Kingdom was about to be subjected to unbridled savagery with the new king surrounded by his most loyal subjects.

Jon kicked out. One of the young Raptors caught him by the heel for a moment, before Jon kicked himself free. "Filthy animals! Piles of crap! Gonna kick your flat faces off!"

"Stop!" Ash cried. Talon was still staring at her. "Jon! It's him! Prince Talon!"

"Filthy animal, too! They all are!" He kicked out again. This time any number of Raptor man-arms came clawing, reaching under to try to grab and drag him out. "No!" Ash shouted.

Talon was the biggest of them by far. But the big car was all broken and low down against the road. Jon and Ash were squeezed under it. There was no room for the bulk of a Raptor body. The reaching arms stretched and grabbed at the air in front of them. Jon kept kicking back at their hands.

"Don't!" Ash shouted. "They'll catch you! They'll drag you out!"

He kicked and kicked.

"Help us!" Ash cried out, with Talon's hands scrabbling in front of her face. "Somebody. Help us!"

But there was nobody. Who could help them now, surrounded by Raptors led by the king of savagery? Nothing in this kingdom could stop the attack of these Blues. Their dense, dark eyes peered over serrated beaks at Ash and at Jon, as their hands reached out all around, grabbing and grabbing without yet catching. They couldn't quite reach, but they would find a way.

"No!" Ash called, as soon as she saw the way occur to Talon, as soon as she saw the idea pass over his clouded features.

Talon called out. The moment he did, the arms left off, withdrawing, leaving Jon and Ash huddled together in the center.

"What's happening?" Jon said.

"Oh no," Ash said, as Talon sat, as he crouched low, hooking one long reptile leg under the low-slung vehicle. "Jon!" she said. "Get ready!"

Talon's huge hooked claws struck an arc toward Ash. She had to pull hard away to prevent the knife-edge of his sharp toe-blades from slicing her from face to foot.

"No!" she cried.

All around them the young Raptors were positioning themselves to reach farther under, much farther under with much stronger, sharper talon-nails, each naturally well gifted to tear and to sever. Positioned correctly, a single Raptor leg could reach in with those fine toes and nothing could stand against it.

"Help!" Ash cried out, to no one. There was no one.

The prince's peering face knew it. "You are mine, now," his expression said. "Now and forever."

"Oh no," Ash breathed, reading Talon's features. "Not this. Not this!"

"Filthy animals!" Jon shouted by her side. A leg flicked by and caught him and cut him. Jon's arm swept away bleeding. He screamed out in pain. "Let's fight! Let's fight!"

But there was no getting out of there. They were hemmed in completely by thrashing toe-blades, Talon's talons, his own and those of his young subjects.

"Thanks, Jon," Ash said. He couldn't hear her. Not above the Raptor roar, the crackle and scythe of scales and knives. "For coming to get me."

"Laura," Ash sighed, with black talons flashing before her eyes, "I wanted to see you again. Once more. I would have loved that."

The prince—King Talon—was staring into her face.

"I'd have so loved that," she said.

FORTY-SEVEN

A flash of yellow!

Just a single glimpse, but enough to tell Ash it was not the color or texture of a Yellow Raptor, but the fabric of a pair of shorts.

Talon was staring at her in cruel satisfaction when his head suddenly wrenched away and he roared to the sky with that voice of pain and terror that penetrated the cavity of the chest. Ash felt his cry, his call of agonized anger, as did everyone else, Jon and the other Raptors.

The roar of pain and anger did not stop as Rat ran so quickly on all fours across the road and flattened himself to almost nothing and slotted his whole body into the pavement opening on the other side. In an instant, he had bitten Talon again, harder than before by the sound of it, and he was gone.

Talon leapt into the air. He intended, in his fury, to land on his attacker and rip him to shreds in an instant. But all he found was the empty road on which to vent his anger. All the other young Raptors jumped up to watch their regal leader thrashing, all scales and feather and flashing beak.

Jon and Ash were watching as the gang watched Talon, with none of them having seen anything of what had happened with Rat. "Ran out on us, eh?" Ash shouted at Jon as they watched Rat reappear from another pavement slot farther up the road. "Look at him go!" she cried as his floppy yellow shorts slipped with him, almost running around him as he showed himself to Talon.

The battle cry of all the Raptors was terrible. Rat's ears were plastered closed, collapsed against the sides of his head. He could do that. Agles couldn't. They had to listen.

They had to watch as Rat plunged into the next drain hole, but the back of his shorts got caught on the metal surround and his pink Rodent feet were left rummaging in the air. His yellow-covered bottom was left out and exposed to the Raptor rage as they, led by Talon, closed in on him.

"Come on!" Ash shrieked; but Jon was ahead of her, scrambling out from under the car, running around the other side to join her.

"Hey!" they shouted, jumping up and down, flailing their arms. "Hey! Hey! Hey!"

Talon stalled. That was all it took. He turned, the others followed. Talon watched as Ash and Jon started to run the other way.

Ash glanced behind and saw him wavering between chasing them and dragging Rat back by the pants. All this took long enough to give them a bit of a head start and for Rat to untangle his shorts. By the time Talon got around to giving the order for some to come with him after Ash, the rest to go for Rat, he—Rat—had shot back into the safety under the pavement and Jon and Ash were tearing across the junction of two roads and disappearing into the moonless gloom of a very dark alley.

They ran up there because it was so dark and because they could still see moonlight at the opposite end. As it wasn't a blind alley, they would be able to make their passage through impenetrable shadow all the way, unseen until they slipped out at the other end and ran off in search of another, better hiding place. That was Ash's plan.

Jon seemed to understand. He didn't question her. Ash couldn't trust him but had to hope that Jon would fall in with her. They both turned the corner and simultaneously slowed to a stealthy walk, creeping along the corner of the darkest side, feeling their way along the long brick wall.

Scattered Raptors ran straight by behind them, as if they could still see them up ahead. They stopped to ensure that not a single Raptor had thought to turn into this darkness. But they ran by in a swarm of scale, a flock of feather, until all was quiet again and Jon and Ash continued to creep toward the other end.

The alley was narrow and long. One of those big cars wouldn't have fitted. It felt safe but was too close to where they had been hiding. The Raptors were bound to figure it out and come back. They had to get to the other end and make another run.

As she crept, Ash reached back to ensure that Jon was still close behind her. She touched his arm. It was wet and sticky. Jon was bleeding. That cut on his arm from a claw must have been quite bad.

Ash stopped. "Jon," she said, "you okay?"

He stood in the pitch dark beside her. It was so black she couldn't see anything of him but heard his breathing and felt his heat shimmering there. At first Ash thought he felt like anger. Then she thought he was feeling something else. He was bleeding so much, from arm and foot, he must have been in pain. But he touched her gently, holding Ash by the upper arms. He might have been staring in the direction of her face; it was too dark to see. But then he turned her to face the other way, as if encouraging her to get going.

Jon wasn't doing that. He was showing Ash, directing her eyes toward that end of the alley.

A young gang Raptor had appeared in the moonlight. He wasn't alone. As soon as another joined him, a third appeared, a fourth, a fifth, the whole gang. That end of the alley was blocked, choked with Raptors.

Ash and Jon were about halfway along. One end was now closed to them. They turned.

Talon.

On his own. At the other end.

Massive. Absolute Raptor. Clicking and swaying with threat.

FORTY-EIGHT

They stopped. One way, the street terror gang. The other, their terrible new king. In the alley, one way or the other is all the choice there was. One way or the other, they had no way out.

"What now?" said Jon, with that deadpan kind of sarcasm to his voice, the sound that comes from extreme fear.

Ash looked both ways. The Raptors never moved, one way or the other. It made her angry and disgusted with herself that they should have captured them again so easily. "Not Talon," Ash said, with all anger and bitterness in her voice. "Not him. Oh, anything but him."

"We'll fight!" said Jon. "Go down fighting."

"No. They'll rip us!"

"Don't care."

"Jon," Ash said, through tears of sorrow and regret, "you're brave. You are. And stupid. But I'm just—I'm 'fraid. I'm scared, Jon."

"Come on," he said, taking her by the hand. Ash clasped him hard as they went for the end of the alley together, side by side, with nothing left to lose. "Doesn't matter now," he said "None of it."

"Jon, I'm not—I can't!"

"Filthy animals!" Jon cried, starting forward.

"Agles!" a voice cried back, from behind them, as if Talon had suddenly found a voice like theirs, only milder.

"Rat!"

"Aaagh!" Jon battle cried.

"Agles!"

"Rat! Jon, wait!"

He wouldn't. Ash had to rush for him in his fight frenzy, to stop him and turn him back to where Rat's friendly frightened face peered out of an opening gently lit up by fire-butterfly light.

"Look!" Ash screamed.

"Here!" Rat was calling, waving like crazy. "Here! Over here! Quickly! Now! Now!"

"Now!" he was crying out so feverishly, as Ash and Jon had to run back the way they had come, in the direction of Talon, and go for this unexpected exit before any of the Raptors realized what was happening.

Too late! The Raptor roar went up and they were coming for them as Ash and Jon were going for the gap in the ground.

Rat was waving crazily.

They were far enough from the Raptor gang, but going toward Talon, with him coming for them at the same time—they were never going to make it! He was driving at them, growing in size and ferocity as he neared.

"Jon!" Ash screamed.

Rat was crying out, but his voice wouldn't carry over the noise that now filled the alley. They were nearly there—so very nearly there!

Just before Ash could get to Rat and the exit, Talon was too hugely over her, leaping forward and about to come down on top. Ash wasn't going to make it! He had her, Talon, the killer king.

As he sprang into the air, about to fall upon her, Ash folded down under his flashing claws. He was going to pull her apart from back to front.

Ash was shoved away into the direction of Rat and the warmly glowing exit.

Rat and some other set of Rodent fingers clasped her clothing and pulled Ash away as she looked to the side to see—

If she could have—

She should have—

She couldn't do anything!

"Jon!" Ash screamed, louder than her voice was ever supposed to go. "Jon! Jon!"

As Rat and the second Rodent pulled her into the opening, Ash had to see Talon, King Talon, land heavily, mightily onto Jon's back, falling fully open clawed and terrible, ripping and tearing at what he thought was her.

Talon thought he had her.

He had Jon!

Ash called Jon's name again as the Rodents pulled her away, as the other Raptors arrived, as the metal door clanged closed on the thrashing, tearing, and terrifying scene outside. All Ash heard was Raptors, their horrible predator cries as Jon—

Jon!

She would never forget.

As that metal door closed.

Jon.

Ash would never, ever forget.

THE
BRINK
OF
EXTINCTION

PART FOUR

FORTY-nine

They were pulling Ash away, two of them. She was screaming. Crying. She tried to go back. "Let me go! Let me go! Jon!"

They would not let her go. Neither would that memory, not now, not ever. Those sounds. The metal door clanging closed, shutting off the scene outside where Jon—

He had pushed her out of Talon's way and taken her place. Talon came down on him with all his force, with all the hatred he held for her.

"Jon!" Ash was still screaming, being led down and around and down again into the dark labyrinth under the city of Raptors. The whole place was aglow with the soft safe light of the flitting fire-butterflies, but Ash hardly noticed anything.

"He came for me," she kept saying. "He came for me!"

"We know," Rat kept trying to reassure her.

"But that was Jon," she said, time and again. "It was Jon. It was."

"We know," Rat said. "We know."

Ash was in shock. Her head was in a whirl and she felt unwell. Every so often she would kind of come around, although they were walking or clambering through tunnels or chambers, turning corners, climbing up and down ladders. It didn't seem to be of any importance any more where they were or where they were going, who Ash was with, or what they were planning to do with her. Every time she woke to herself it was with another more powerful bout of sobs, spiraling down into grief and a sense of self-loathing that she had somehow allowed this to happen. The fire-butterflies flitted before her eyes. Ash felt dizzily sick and confused, unable to breathe properly, unable to stop grinding her teeth and clenching and unclenching her fists.

"Sit her down," a voice was saying. It sounded like a girl, like Agle Fe, someone like Laura, or Jess. But there was no one like that here, not even Ash. Her voice didn't sound like that any more. Hers was broken, a voice thick with mixed emotion and regret.

"I left him," she was saying, as her legs were going from under her. "I left him!"

"There was nothing you could have done," the voice said.

The lights were spinning around her. They were butterflies, but not fluttering now, flying around and around in sickening circles. The dark and light confused and disoriented her. "What's on?" she said.

"Lie down," the voice said.

Ash went onto her side. It didn't make any difference, she still felt as if she was about to fall over. "Feel sick," she said, closing her eyes.

"I'll get help," one of the voices said. "You stay with her. I won't be long."

Eyes closed or open, the effect was the same; the dark and the light sent her spinning. Ash was holding onto the ground as if she was just about to fall off the edge of the world.

FIFTY

She fell. A long, long way.

Then bang! Ash hit the bottom. With a massive violent start, she was struck awake as if a giant Raptor had landed on her back. Wham! And her eyes were wide and Ash was up and ready to run for her life.

"What's on?"

"It's all right," a gentle voice was saying. "Agle, you're here. You're safe now. They can't get you."

Ash found herself sitting on some kind of bed against a wall, more like an ASP dwellers' camp than the luxury she'd slept so well in back at the palace. The little room she was in was lit by masses of glowing yellow glass jars. The air was quite cool, but it was stuffy and a bit stale. There was a sweet flavor in Ash's mouth. Her ears were buzzing.

"Where am I?" she said, breathing more steadily.

"You're safe with us," she said, the little pink and yellow figure by her side.

"Who are you?"

"I'm Really. I've been looking after you."

"Really? I mean—have you? And you—you're Rat's special. I know. He told me."

Really Rodent made a tiny swaying movement that Ash recognized as a bot-blag of pleasure, like a Rodent smile. "He told me about you too," she said.

She came toward Ash. Really looked a lot like Rat, with similar ears and sloping shoulders, pink eyes, an expressive pointy nose. But Really was all-girl Rodent, and not just because she was wearing a golden yellow dress. Her face and manner, a way of moving showed, even though she had small legs and big feet like Rat, that she was considered to be beautiful. Her every motion was different, more considered and more expressive than what Ash had thought Rodents to be like.

Really had a little cup clasped between her two thumbless hands. "Here," she said, blinking with soft kindness, "drink some of this."

"What's it?" Ash said, nervously. "Can't have it."

Really's body swayed gently in a Rodent smile. "It's sap water. Sweet, from the trees. It's nice. Try some. It'll give you your strength back."

Ash took the cup and sipped some of the thickish fluid. It was very sweet. The taste was that which she had discovered in her mouth when she'd awoken. Really must have been moistening her lips with it as she slept. "With you," Ash said, before drinking the rest down. It did make her feel a little better, almost immediately.

As Really took the cup from her, a fire-butterfly flapped in through the open doorway. This was the first time Ash had had the chance to take a good look at one. It was huge. Its wings were cream colored and very dusty and glistening in the light of its big bright body. The butterfly flapped and glided about the room. Ash had never seen a butterfly so big and slow, even compared to those she had thought so huge on the outskirts of the city. The body was so bright, it did seem as if it might burst into flames at any moment.

"Look it," she said.

That a creature like this should be stuck underground, hidden away, seemed such a sad waste. "It's so—you know—I can't—" Ash said, wiping away the tears streaming down her face. "So a waste," she said.

"It always seems like a waste, when somebody dies," Really Rodent said, thinking that she had been talking about Jon.

Ash's tears showed her that perhaps she was; that all waste of life and beauty was the same thing. "Came to help me," she said. "Get me out."

"And that's what he did," Really said. She came over to Ash, placing the cup on the bed and reaching out to hold her. Ash had never been hugged by a Rodent. It was, well, she needed to be held so much, that Really Rodent felt like all the world's kindness and strength in one tiny pink, slightly furry body.

She held Ash away after a long while, holding her with padded, four-fingered hands, looking into her face. The pink of her eyes was glossy and astonishing in the fire-butterfly light. "Look in the glass jars," she said.

Most of the light in this room was in fact coming not from the single butterfly, but from a glowing fat blob on the base of each jar. "What's it?" Ash said.

"It's the butterfly pupae, the chrysalis."

Ash shook her head. She didn't understand.

"Let me tell you," Really said, sitting on the bed beside Ash, "about the life of the fire-butterfly. The butterflies down here are all doing one thing—they're looking for a mate. That's why the males fly around lit up so much. Have you seen a female? You won't have. You have to look pretty hard to find one. That's what the males are doing. But when they are found, the females then make their way out into the open air to lay their eggs on the leaves of trees. The eggs hatch and the caterpillars come out and eat and eat leaves until they're big and fat. Then they make their way underground, in caves or back down here with us where they go into this hardened state." As she said this, Really took one of the jars to show Ash the chrysalis.

"So lovely," Ash said. The tears on her face were lit by the brightness of the light emanating from it. "So, so lovely."

"This is the chrysalis of the male. The females don't glow. They don't need to. When the chrysalis has built a butterfly inside, out it comes, hanging from the ceiling while its wings inflate before it flies off to find a mate."

"Don't get it," Ash asked, wiping her eyes. "Why tell me?"

"The point is," Really said, "that when the eggs have been produced, the adult fire-butterflies die. That's all they do, as fully grown butterflies—they fly about in the dark looking for each other, then they die. Only the dark they fly in isn't dark any more. They change it. They make it light. Is it a waste?"

"I—I don't," Ash said. "What you're saying. I was saying—about—Jon."

"Were you? So was I. What he did for you is like what the butterflies do for their eggs, for the caterpillars, for the fire-butterflies to come. Don't waste it, what he did for you. It was a gift."

Ash was crying.

Really held her again. Her little hand was gently patting Ash's back. "That's all right, that's all right. Cry for him. Don't waste his light, that's all. I'm sure there are others that need you as much as you needed him."

"Yes," she said, "yes. Some."

"All your children," Really said.

"I don't—none of us. We don't. Not yet. We're young."

"How old are you?"

"Not sure. Sixteen? Bit less?"

"Sixteen?" she said. "And no children?"

"No. No. You? How old?"

"Fifteen," she said.

"Fifteen. Rat?"

"The same."

"You have children?"

She nodded proudly. "We have ten," she said.

FIFTY-ONE

"Ten children?" Ten kids by fifteen years old—it wasn't possible, was it? "Ten? All yours?"

Really blinked at Ash. When a Rodent closed those big pink eyes, the also-pink lids came down like rounded shutters and back up again, so that it was possible to see the mechanics behind the action. A single blink from a Rodent was a very expressive and significant act of communication.

"No," Ash went on quickly, "no, it—fifteen? How old are they?"

"Thirty-eight days," she said.

"All of them?"

"Yes, of course. I love them at this age. But they grow up so very quickly, don't they?"

"Suppose so," Ash had to say.

"Yes, they do. It only seems like yesterday," she said, "that they were blind and snugly, without any hair."

"Blind?"

"Before they open their eyes," Really went on. "They're so helpless. So lovely. I didn't want them to change for ages and ages, but they do. Before you know it, they're all over the place, getting into everything."

"Ten of them?"

"Yes. But it's worth it. I love them. I do love them. Are you going to? Soon?"

"Oh," Ash said, taken aback. "Oh, no. Not me. Jess, maybe. Jess and Will. Maybe. Not ten though, I don't think."

"We wanted more," Really said.

Despite the way she was feeling about all that she had so recently been through, Ash had to smile. "More?" she said, stifling a con-fused laugh, like a hiccough.

Really was staring at her through those pretty pink orbs. "He told me you had a stretchy face and made those kinds of noises."

"It's my—it's Agle. Doing a bot-blag," she said.

"We don't say "do" a bot-blag. We just say bot-blag. Your way's so funny though," she said, swaying, bot-blagging. "Are all the Agles like you?"

"Suppose so," Ash smiled, stretching her face. She thought about Laura, about Jon and Jess and Will. "Not all," she said. "They're dif-ferent."

"Like Rodents," Really said.

"Yes. Like Rodents and like Raptors," Ash said. She stopped. "Raptors? No, they're all the same. Raptors will kill and eat you. That's all Raptors do."

"No," Ash said, as gently as she could. "Not true."

The way Really was looking at her showed that she was remem-bering what had happened to Jon. Ash had to remember it too, because the feeling of it would never leave her, but Ash had to relive Jon's last moments as the iron door clanged closed on him forever.

"How long'd I sleep?" she asked.

"More than a whole day," Really said.

"More than?"

"Yes. I've been watching you."

"All that time? The babies? Where're they?" She looked down. "Really?" Ash said, using the Rodent's name for the first time. Really looked up as if surprised. "Where's Rat? With them?"

"He's out. He has to go out, every day."

"Who's with them?"

"My Elder. He's good with them. He helps me all the time, when Rat's out. And now Rat's—" She stopped. Again she looked down, reluctant to go on.

"Really? What's on?"

"Nothing. He'll be all right. I know he'll be all right. He's Rat. Nothing can happen to Rat."

"Happen? Where's he?"

"He's in—he's been sent out. We shouldn't have done what we did. We've brought attention to ourselves. We were never supposed to do that."

"Attention? From Raptors?"

"They never paid us any attention. We lived down here, going out up there, going about our business. They left us alone. They never knew how many of us there were. We're more all the time. We're not supposed to do anything to draw the attention of the Raptors to ourselves. If the Raptors find out about us, they'll start to fear us—"

"Fear?"

"It's what happens. Raptors think they're the highest species. They think everything else is either food or vermin. If they feel at all threatened, they'll destroy. It's what Raptors do. I don't need to tell you that."

"So where's Rat?" Ash asked, trying not to picture again the iron door closing on life. "Where's he?"

"The rat-runs were buzzing with talk and rumors about the Agles and the Raptors. When Rat told me what he'd done, biting Prince Talon, I—I was so worried. Then when King Tomb was killed. I told Rat, I had to tell him to stay away. We couldn't afford to be involved."

"Then, why'd you come?"

"We couldn't just let you—not both of you. Rat was so sorry about leaving you before. He couldn't do it, my Rat. He's just—he's good."

"Yes. And you. Saved my life."

"But we couldn't stop the rumors. Rat has now been ordered to go out and find information on what's going on up there. Our Lady sent word that she wanted to know—"

"Our Lady?"

"Our Lady. She's our Elder Elder. She's so, so very old and wise. She's our first mother, our Origin of Species. We're all related to her."

"All?"

Really nodded.

Ash nodded too, but without understanding. Really was like Rat with words—too many at a time! They seemed to have so much to say. "What's she like?" Ash said. "Our Lady?"

"Oh, we've never seen her. Hardly anybody gets to see Our Lady. She is our unseen queen. Some say she's a million years old. Some say she'll live forever. She's our keeper, our safety. We'd be lost without her. When she sent word to Rat—you can imagine. We were so afraid. But Our Lady needs to understand what's going on. She's—well, let's just say she's not pleased. We think it's our fault. But we couldn't—we didn't know what else to do. It's Rat—he's so headstrong. I worry about him. You can't just bite Talon and hope to get away with it."

"Twice," Ash said, confused by words but wishing she hadn't said that one.

Really's pained expression showed such suffering and concern. "I need him to be safe. That's all I want. Why can't we just be safe?"

"Safe?" Ash had to say. "Never felt safe."

Really looked at her with all of the Rodent concern. "Haven't you? Even when you were little? Didn't your parents ever make you feel it? Isn't that what parents are for?"

"Is it?" Ash said, trying not to have to remember, not now, not the way she was feeling. "I've forgotten," she said, unsteadily. "Or I don't want to have to—I don't remember feeling safe. Is all."

"Oh, Ash," Really said, reaching for her.

"No," Ash said, "it's all right. I just need to breathe. I'm fine. We all are. We're Agles. We were little kids, left on our own. Now we're Agles. Agles—not kids any more."

FIFTY-TWO

"Oh. Kids. Kids," Really said. "I like the flavor of the word. It's nice in your mouth."

Ash had to laugh.

"But you're right," Really said, "they shouldn't be left on their own, kids."

"Yours are," Ash said. "Too long."

"They'll be amazed to see you," Really said.

"Amazed? For me?"

"Oh, yes. You don't know how amazing you are."

"Really," Ash said, "I don't know how—thanks. Thank you. You and Rat."

"You don't need to thank us," she said. "Are you feeling strong enough now? Everyone's anxious to meet you."

She told Really she felt fine. She didn't, but doubted that she would be feeling fine for a long, long time to come. Ash felt confused, more than anything at the moment, dazed by the mass of emotions coming at her from every direction. She had to say she felt fine, because she lacked the words to explain it all to Really.

They left that small and cozy room and went out through a rough passageway lit by more glowing glass jars and huge gliding butterflies. Only a little way ahead they turned a corner and there, spread out in front and to their left and right, a great hall seething with life.

Rodents, hundreds, thousands of them. Every last patch of ground was covered. So crammed were they, the whole floor of the hollow underground cave seemed to be moving.

Until Ash appeared. As she turned the corner, upon the instant, the seethe froze into stillness and silence. Every pink-eyed, pointy face poked in her direction, doubly hundreds, doubly thousands of bulbous eyes blinking in the amazement that Really had spoken about. The stopping into stillness was so sudden and so total Ash halted too. She stood there, looking out, forward, left and right as every bright white and pink face pointed at her.

As if frozen, the whole scene stayed, with no movement other than the closing and opening of pink eyelids, the twitching of ears and Ash's head sweeping from one side to the other. Other than that, nothing, no movement—until Really made the announcement.

"The Agle!" she said, loud enough for the acoustic and the echo of the hall to relay the words into the twitch of the countless hairs in the ears of the waiting Rodents. At once the whole place erupted. There was a surge forward by the smaller ones, which had to be controlled by the larger. A cacophony of excited chatter broke out everywhere.

So many of the small ones got to her all at once, Ash was almost knocked over. Really had to help support her while trying to bring back a little order.

"It's huge," they were twittering, these little Rodents running around her legs.

"Look at it. It's got hair on top."

"What color's its hair?"

"It's supposed to speak," they were saying. "Why doesn't it speak? What can it say?"

Ash held up her hand. As she did, the atmosphere altered, going from excited curiosity to nervousness, with most of the little Rodents instantly backing away.

"Raptor!" they were saying. "Raptor! Raptor!"

"It's your hand," Really whispered. "They don't understand how you can look like you do. It's all right," she called, holding up her own four-fingered version.

"Oh," Ash said, bringing her arm down suddenly. "Oh—oh!"

"It's all right!" Really called out. "She's the Agle—she's good."

That was it. They all surged forward again, trying to hear her speak, throwing out questions, touching Ash's hands and arms, reaching up to touch her hair.

"Give us room!" Really was saying. "Please, give us some room."

"Hello," Ash said, smiling. "Hello. Hello."

The little Rodents started to stretch their faces as Rat had, grimacing while bot-blagging to each other in a mass sway of colored shorts and dresses.

"This way," Really said, drawing her to one side. "Up here," she said, leading Ash along the wall toward another exit from the huge cavern hall.

Ash looked out over a sea of pink-and-white heads. She waved to them all. So many tiny hands waved back, with so much mini bot-blagging going on she laughed out loud.

"Now you've done it," Really said, urging them along.

"Did you hear that noise the Agle made?" Ash heard them say.

"Why do Agles do that? Aren't they weird, Agles?"

After the initial crush of the smaller, more excitable young ones, the Elders were able to reassert their control, bringing order back into the hall, dividing the seething mass of Rodents into what Ash could tell were family units. The Elder Rodents were much less impressed by what they saw of her. As Really and Ash passed through, there were quite a few suspicious glances thrown in her direction, one or two looks of downright hostility.

The Rodents now stood back in their family groups, each with one, two, three or four taller Elders, any number of slightly smaller Rodents, and any multiplication of tiny Rats and Reallys running around their feet. The Elders were always the largest, as if Rodents were becoming ever smaller as they went along.

"The big ones," Ash whispered to Really, "not so happy?"

They were keeping to the outside of the hall, along the edge of the rough-hewn wall. "They're just worried," she whispered back. "Nothing like this has ever happened before."

"Agles eat meat!" one Rodent called out.

"Just keep going," Really said. "Don't stop."

But Ash had faltered.

The air of excitement in the hall had changed as soon as that statement came out, that Agles eat meat. As far as Rodents were concerned, meat eating was pure Raptor. Now the hall, everyone in it was concentrating on Ash's hands and arms. The little Rats and Reallys were clinging closer to their Elders.

"The Agle eats meat!"

"The Agle eats meat!"

Ash stopped.

"No," said Really, "let's go."

"No," Ash said, turning to the hall full of waiting faces. "Have to say. I've never!" she exclaimed, looking out at them all. "No meat. Me, no. Other Agles, only once."

"Agles eat meat!"

"Agles eat meat!"

"Only once," Ash said. "A bird, we killed. A seagle. We put it—"

She was going to try to go on and explain how it had happened, out of ignorance and fear, and that she was going to ensure that it never happened again now that she knew better; but Ash never had the words and anyway the Rodents had stopped listening.

"You killed!" Really said. She was as appalled as everyone else in that hall. The look on the Elders' faces told Ash that this was totally unacceptable to them.

"Only a bird!" she tried to defend herself, stupidly. "Vicious! A bird!"

"Quickly," said Really, bundling her away. "Through here. Quickly. You shouldn't have said that. To kill means to be a Raptor. That's what you are then. That's what Agles are—Raptors!"

FIFTY-THREE

"They ate meat," Ash was trying to say, "I didn't. That wasn't me. I'm not like that."

"You are," Really said, as they turned and turned again down the labyrinthine threads of the tiny corridors. "In a way you are. In a way you're like the Raptors."

"No. Not. I'm—like you."

"Yes. But when you kill things, you're doing exactly what Raptors do."

"Things kill. In the forest—"

"In the forest those things don't know any different. But you—you speak Rodent. You can understand what we say. Even then, you can consider yourselves so special, you can be arrogant enough to kill because others are not Agle. Next thing, you turn them into food. Before you know it, you think you can kill all other species if you feel like it just because you feel like it, because they get in your way or because you're afraid of them or don't like the sight or sound or smell of them."

They had stopped by this time, just Really and Ash in the middle of one of those long rough corridors. Really's pink face had grown a little pinker, she was so passionate about what she was saying.

What could Ash say? Everything Really said about the Agles, about Ash, was true. They had never thought about it in this way, or at all, back at the camp. "We just," Ash said, "we didn't—know. Stupid, Agles. But not like Talon. He's our enemy."

"And ours."

"But Really—you and me. Not enemies," she was saying, as Really bustled them through, as they turned yet another corner and came upon another room. "Really? Not enemies. Friends."

But more bunches, or little herds, of very young Rodents were clambering along, running riot through the long passageways. Suddenly Ash was surrounded and on her own with them. Really had disappeared into the other room. Ash managed to prevent herself from smiling. Instead, she did a slow bot-blag, or she bot-blagged slowly, as Rodents would say.

As soon as Ash did that the chatter broke out in an excited wave of sound. Everyone was speaking at once. Ash thought how cute it looked, surrounded by all those tiny faces, all those round, round eyes in the fire-butterfly light. Ash saw herself, her larger-than-Rodent-life reflection in those nearest to her. For that moment she saw in their pink eyes what they saw: a strange creature, a weird mixture of other things, or species, as Really called them: a curiosity.

To silence them, Ash put up her hand. It worked, of course. The Raptor in her reached out at them again. Those closest, in whose eyes she had observed her own strangeness, fell back in panic.

"No," Ash said, swaying gently, "don't be 'fraid." She still held up her hand. "These like Raptor?" But then she used that hand to pick up her hair. "Look. No Raptor. No scales, no feathers. Fur. Hair, like yours."

In fact, the Rodents didn't have hair like hers, like an Agle's hair, theirs being short and white and sparse; but they certainly did have hair.

"We're similar," she said. "Like all things—species—with fur. We're the same—family." Ash looked around. Really was standing at the doorway watching her. "We're the same family," she said, to her.

The chatter of excitement broke out again all around as the Rodents scampered up to touch her, to hold Ash's hand, each with a tinge of fear still, which must have been very thrilling for them.

Then Ash felt her hand taken by a bigger Rodent. Really held her hand. "Let me show you my family," she said. She blinked. That slow, significant closing and opening of the eyes said so much. Ash smiled. Really bot-blagged.

Really led her through the absolute throng, holding onto her hand all the while. As Rodents did not have thumbs, it wasn't possible to grip in the way Agles, or Raptors, did. Rodents like Really held another's hand by clasping it to the side of their body. Holding hands was always a very friendly thing to do. Laura and Ash did it quite a lot. Jess and Will did it all the time. But like this, Agle and Rodent, Rodent and Agle—this was something special. Really held her like this as they entered this other room together.

None of the other Rodents followed them in, just as none had come into the room where Ash had lain asleep for over a day. With so many crowded down here in the caves and corridors, she imagined there had to be clear rules on privacy that no one was allowed to violate.

Inside, a fairly large old male Rodent rose to greet them. His hair, his fur was quite long. His face was shorter than Really's and Rat's. He wore an ancient gray gown.

"Elder Father," Really said, "here is the Agle, on this momentous occasion, come to speak to you."

He came close to her and took Ash's hand between his. He was very warm and dry, with soft skin, which was whiter, not so pink as Really's. "So," he said, looking at her through darker than usual, but deeper and flatter eyes, "you are awake at last. How are you feeling now, on this momentous occasion?"

It had been so funny, strangely funny, seeing the underground home of the Rodents, meeting so many so suddenly, Ash had forgotten about feeling anything. Only when the Elder Rodent asked her that, did Ash realize how much better she was feeling. "I'm—not so bad," she said, truthfully, ignoring the stuff about the "moment of occasion" that she didn't understand. "With you."

"That is good," he said, swaying and bowing at the same time in what Ash took to be an old-style formal bot-blag. He turned and opened his arms. "Ah, Mother is home."

This he said because of all the cries that had started up, the tiny voices calling from behind. The old Rodent moved to one side to allow Ash to see properly the tousled bundle of tiny little limbs and the sweetest faces with the largest of bright pink eyes.

"Look," Really was saying, as she went to them, as the little ones climbed upon her, as she lowered herself to be among them, "look who's come to see you."

"Mom!" they cried, looking up at Ash.

"Dad!"

Ash had to laugh. The tiny young Rodents did indeed look at her with amazement. "Thirty-eight days old and they're already saying Mom and Dad!" Really's Elder, the big old Rodent said.

"I know!" Really said, with immense pride.

"They grow so quickly nowadays," the Elder said. "It's not like it was in my day. Nothing is."

"Look at them!" Ash smiled, as they crawled all over their mom.

Really waved her over. Ash sat with Really on the floor and the baby Rodents clambered on her lap, staring into her eyes and at her hair.

"They're like," she said, "they're up. Good. Lovely. Their names?"

"Well," Really said, "this one's called—where is he? This is Little Rat."

"Ah," Ash said.

"He is the eldest. And this is the oldest girl, Really Really."

Ash had to laugh again. "Really Really?—Really?"

"And this is Ready. This is Rip, that's Rap, and there's Romp. This one's called Rich."

"Rich?" Ash said. "We've a Rich."

"Do you? Well, that's funny, because we have a Rodent called Ash."

"Ash?" she said.

The Elder bent down and picked up one of the smallest female babies. "This is Ash," he said, handing her to Ash.

She took the baby in her hands. They were staring into each other. Ash could see herself in her eyes. "Ash," she said. "Me."

FIFTY-FOUR

"Oh," Ash said, searching for words. "She's—but—she's
called Ash—she's called Ash!"

"We changed her name," Really said, "when Rat told
me what you were called. It's such a beautiful name for
a Rodent."

Ash didn't know what to say. She could hardly speak. As
she held the baby Ash, as the tiny Rodent nestled into her,
Ash could so easily have cried. Seeing this, holding the young
Rodent, brought all her emotions raging again, all the feelings
she had been through with Jon were highlighted and exaggerated
by the vulnerability of little Ash. A tear crept from one corner of
her eye and made its way into the corner of her mouth. Little Ash
watched it go, fixing her wide bright eyes on it, following its passage down Ash's face.

"She's—perfect," Ash said, happy to have found the right word.
"They all are."

"Ten little loves," the Elder Rodent said.

Ash looked at them all. "So," she said, "let me. There's Little
Rat—Really Really—Ready, Rip, Rap, Romp, Rich, and Ash.
Yeah?"

"We wanted more," Really said.

"Ten's a good number," the Elder said.

"But," Ash said, "it's eight, no?"

"Eight?" Really said, looking at her with a puzzled expression.

"Yes," she said.

"What's eight?"

"Eight," Ash said. "You know. One, two, three, four, five, six, seven—"

"Ten," said the Elder.

"Ten?"

He held up his long lank hands, counting on his fingers. "One, two, three, four, five, six, seven, ten," he counted.

Of course! With four-fingered hands, Rodents counted in eights. Ash thought about it. "You must not be fifteen," she said. "Thirteen, is all."

"No," she said. "Fifteen."

"You count in Raptor," the Elder said.

"Do I?" Ash said, dismayed to be seen as like Raptor in yet another way.

"Where's Rat?" Really said, to spare Ash further embarrassment, now that she seemed to have decided to forgive her, to forgive the Agles for what they had done in the past.

"He isn't back yet," the Elder said, with reluctance.

"What," Really said, "he went back out?"

"No," he said, "he hasn't come back at all. Yet."

From Really's face, it was apparent that Rat should have returned a long time ago. She didn't say anything but attended to her children. Little Ash had fallen asleep in Ash's arms.

"Where'd Rat go?" Ash asked the Elder.

"Who knows where Rat goes," he said.

"To get information on the Raptors," Really looked up, with all that worry still in her face. "Where can he get information on what Talon's planning to do? Where would he have to go for that? I think we know, don't we."

They knew. They said nothing. Really was very busy fussing over her children. The babies were so cute, scuttling around on all fours, peering into everything, saying things like, "Me," "My," and "Mom," each wearing a little white loincloth diaper tied with strings.

"When they start to walk?" Ash asked Really, to try to end the silence the babies couldn't break.

"I don't know," she said, without looking at her. She was making herself very busy, concentrating too hard on nothing most of the time.

"It won't be long," the kind old Elder said, placing his hand on Really's sloping shoulder. "Nothing's going to stop these bright little buttons."

"I don't know," Really said again.

"Don't worry," said the Elder.

But Really had a look on her face, a worry that would not be denied. "Something's happened," she said, jumping up. The babies were all reaching up for her. The Elder took the tiny sleeping Rodent from Ash's arms. "I've got to go and find him."

"Nothing's happened to Rat," the Elder said, stepping close to Really with the baby Ash in his arms. "Your children need you here."

"Rat needs me! I know he does. I've got to go and find him."

"Think of these little ones," the Elder said. He held Ash out to her.

Poor Really. "He's been gone too long," she said. "He'd never stay out this long, ever. Something's happened to him. He needs me. Don't make me feel—he's everything. I can't do it without him. I've got to go."

"No," the Elder said, "you will not. Others can go. Let them find out for you."

"I'm going," Really insisted. "I have to."

"With you," Ash said, suddenly.

"With you?" said Really.

Ash nodded. "With you. Yes."

"Oh," Really said. "I see. But he'll be in the city. You can't go back there. Not with Talon and all his subjects after you."

"You'll never fit through the rat-runs," the Elder said.

"I fit here," Ash said, indicating the room, the corridors outside. "You brought me down from the city."

"There are only a few big runs," Really said. "Most of them are much, much smaller. We could take you back the way you came, but you wouldn't get very far. They'd pick you up in no time. No, I must go. Forgive me," she said to the children. She turned.

"With you," Ash said again. "As far as I can."

Really wasn't listening. She went out without looking back at what was left of her family without Rat.

Ash called out for her, running after her. "Really!"

She moved so quickly, as only a Rodent can. Ash had to run to keep close to her. They went back up the corridors the way they had come, bursting out into the great cave where all was commotion and noise.

This time the chaos did not stop. The Rodents looked at Ash but without faltering, talking as wildly as they were, urgently, seriously.

"Here she is!" someone said.

Really halted. Ash came to her side.

"She's here!" an Elder called.

From the crowd, a single Rodent was helped forward. "Are you Rat's Really?" he said, looking at her, glancing at Ash, looking again at Really. "You must be," he said. "And you must be the Agle Ash."

"Who are you?" asked Really.

"I'm Righteous. I've just come back—from the city."

"The city? Did you see him? Did you see Rat?"

"Yes, I saw him. Or rather I heard him. We spoke, through the runs."

"Where is he?"

"Really, get ready—the Raptors have him."

"Oh no," Really gasped. "Have they—is he—"

"He's all right, at the moment. They have him and they're keeping him alive."

"Why?"

"Why?" Righteous said, looking at Ash. "Because of her," he said.

FIFTY-FIVE

"Because of her?" Really said. "Why because of her?"

"They want me," Ash said simply, coldly.

The Rodent Righteous nodded. "That's it. They know just where you are." He looked at Really. "They want the Agle. They won't let Rat go without her."

"It's Talon," Ash said, spitting out his name like poison.

"But how," Really said, "how do they—they must know so much about us! How did they tell you this?"

"They were holding Rat. I was in the runs. He called out. He told me."

"But this means—" Really said.

"The Raptors know," Ash said. "They know you're helping me."

There were so many Rodents gathered around listening, as they spoke, as Ash said this, the information was relayed in a wave of whispered chatter that swept away across the expanse of the crowded hall; everything they said was effectively heard by every-one there.

"But Raptors don't behave like this," Really said. "They don't. We come and go under their feet—their claws. How do they know so much about us all of a sudden? We've always been so careful not to let them."

The Rodents all looked at Ash. It was no secret that she had spent some time in the royal household. Ash spoke Rodent. It would seem that she had somehow managed to show the Raptors how Rodents communicated.

"We needed them to take no notice of us," Really said to Ash.

"We'll outnumber them," Righteous said, "many times over, eventually. One day we'll overrun them."

"They know too much about us," Really said. "This changes everything." She stood as tall as Rodents of her age and size could. "This changes everything!" she announced. "You runners," she called, "you messengers, make sure Our Lady knows about this. Where is he?" She turned back to Righteous. "Where's Rat being held? In the city?"

"No," he said, "outside. He told me exactly where he was being taken. It's where the river runs out of the forest onto the grazing plains, on the edge of no-Raptors-land."

"Then that's where I'm going," Really said.

"No!" Ash said.

"They'll kill you both," said Righteous. "You and Rat."

"They might," Really said. "They just might. But I might kill them first."

They stopped. Everything was still. Even the energetic young Rodents had halted. This was not in their nature, this talk of killing. In her brief experience of them, in her short time underground with the Rodents, even Ash was able to see how set against any form of aggression they were.

"Might get a gun," Really said. "I might shoot them—all of them!" Some of the Elders were ushering the very young ones away.

"A gun?" Ash said.

"You can't fire a gun," Righteous said.

Really's face drained. She looked angry, but hopeless. "I don't care," she said.

"I couldn't care less."

"I could," Ash said.

They all looked at her.

"Fire a gun," she said.

FIFTY-SIX

"Ash," Really said. She had never before used Ash's name like this. "Ash," she said again.

"A gun," Ash said. "Talon wants me, he can. With a gun. Guns fire. I remember. *Bang-bang, you're dead!* Get me a gun."

They stood still, all of them, hundreds, thousands of them. A lone Agle among the Rodents.

"We hoped Talon would still think he'd got you the other night, when he—you know," Really said, sadly. "We hoped he'd forget about Agles and Rodents if he thought he'd killed you."

"I'm still alive. He won't stop." Ash stopped. She didn't need to put it into words. "You have guns?" she asked.

"No," Really said.

"But we know where there are some," Righteous said.

"Lots," said Really.

They were looking at each other. All around them, the Rodent faces pointed. For a moment Ash pictured the pretty pattern from above, all of those pink points, with a single Agle in the center.

"Guns are bad," Really said. "That's what we believe."

Ash nodded. "Him or me."

"Why would you do this?" Really said. "I mean, you don't have to."

"I do," Ash said. "Talon. It's never going to end. For Jon! And Rat. You. All of you," she said.

Really was starting to cry. Ash couldn't see, because Really was holding her, but Ash could feel it. A wave of soft whispers flowed away from them, carried by the crowd.

"Show me," Ash said, drawing Really away, looking at her face. Rodents never laughed, but they could cry. When they did, it was just like . . .

"Agle tears," Ash said, wiping Really's face with her fingers. "Like Agles. We're not so different. Same family."

"Yes," Really said. "We're not so different."

Ash turned. Really held her hand to her side. She was going to show her where to get a gun, but for the moment, there was no need. A swathe, a separation in the sea of pink faces, had split the whole cavernous hall in two equal halves with the clear-cut path across the center leading to a little exit hole way across the other side. Ash went to walk through, but Really stopped her. "I'm not sure I can let you do this," she said. "Not this."

"Come," Ash said. "Rat's waiting."

"He wouldn't want you to do this."

"He'd do it. I will. Here," Ash said, "this way."

She knew, because the only way to go was straight across the heavily populated hall of the Cave of the Rodents, through its heart with many, many soft hands reaching up to touch her on the back and the upper arms. Ash moved along the path they made for her, feeling gigantic as she looked across the parted sea of pink heads, with their soft four-fingered hands patting her on the way past.

One young Rodent stepped into their path. "Come back again, Agle," he said, as he was tugged out of their way by his Elders.

"Come back again, Agle," another called.

When the chant broke out—"Come back, Agle! Come back, Agle!"—when she stopped on the other side of the cave and turned, with the faces all pointing at her, with the voices all chanting for her, Ash was so overwhelmed that she couldn't think for a few moments how to express what she was feeling.

There didn't seem to be anything Ash could do to express how she felt. Bot-blagging wouldn't have felt right, so what she did was press her thumbs into her palms and wave two four-fingered hands at them all. They saw it. They understood. Their hands went up. They cheered.

Ash had never felt so proud in all her life.

FIFTY-seven

"Show me guns," Ash said, as she and Really made their way from the cave through the other corridor. "Show me the way. Is all."

"No, Ash. I have to go with you because—"

"Really," Ash said, stopping. She had to think carefully about what she was going to say. "You have family. Ten kids, all waiting."

"No, Ash, please don't. I have to go with you, for some of the way at least. At least until I know you are safely—" she faltered. "Until I'm sure you know the right way to go. I have to be sure you're going to get to Rat. Because when you're gone, when you leave me, all I'll be able to do is wait. Do you know what that's going to be like? Do you? How can I know what's happening, whether you're—if Rat's—how will I know anything?"

The walls they had been rushing between were closing in on them, widening out, closing in again. Everything about these runs looked as if it had been bitten out of the soft rock of the walls and floors and ceilings.

"Rat'll be back," Ash said, trying to sound more sure than she felt. "Whatever. He'll be there. His kids walk, he'll be there. You be sure."

Really wasn't sure at all, but she pretended too, and pressed Ash's palm to her side and Ash squeezed her hand in response.

"No Rodents?" Ash asked, looking left and right. The corridors were deserted, silent. Every now and then she could hear the beating wings of a passing fire-butterfly.

"This is a special way," Really said, "a runner's run. This is a communications tunnel, which cannot be used ordinarily, unless it is such a momentous occasion. The Rodents in the hall, all of us understood the importance of this—of you. This was a mark of their respect. I've never been down here before."

"Then, how—"

"How do I know where it goes? Oh, we all know where all the runs go. It's one of the first things we learn as children—as kids," she added, hugging Ash's hand to her.

"Really," Ash said, as they hurried on through, "how long since you were a kid? I mean, when are you grown-up?"

"Oh, you know, ten."

Which meant eight, by the Agle way of counting, the same age as Ash was when she and the others were first left all alone and crying at the camp. She was just a little kid at eight, but Really and the Rodents were pretty well fully grown by then.

Ash was about to try to tell Really about this, when they came upon the oldest and biggest Elder Rodent Ash had seen in all these burrows. He stood blocking their way, almost filling out the entire communications run with his large-limbed body. He wasn't very much smaller than Ash was, as she halted behind Really, almost bumping into her.

The huge Elder said not a word to either of them. He looked at Really, at Ash, then turned and walked ahead of them. His limbs looked stiff, his motions lacking range as if through wear and tear from great age. Like all the Elders, this one's face was shorter, but his hair looked longer and thicker, except on the top of his head, where the bald skin shone in the fire-butterfly light. He seemed to creak slowly along, so that they had to shuffle impatiently behind him.

"Who's he?" Ash whispered.

"He is one of the Elder Elders. He is one of the servants to the servants of the council, the inner chamber of Senior Elders that surround and advise Our Lady."

"Oh. Looks very old."

"They all are," she whispered. "They are great Rodents. They have lived a long, long time. Not as long as Our Lady, of course, but they are ancient and very wise in the world."

"Oh," Ash said, wondering what she would have to be like to be considered by Really to be that wise. "Agles know nothing about the world," she said, wishing that it were not so.

"But you are learning," Really said, "very quickly." As soon as she said that, Ash could see by her expression as she peeped at Really's face from the corner of her eye, that she was thinking that all Ash's learning could end soon, that she was possibly about to be taught the hardest, most final lesson in the world.

"No sad," Ash whispered, putting all her faith and hope in the power a weapon would allow her to have over Talon. One shot, from what she remembered of guns, one bang, and the whole situation could be changed.

They came to another hall, another rock cavern gnawed from the rough sandstone. But this one was smaller than the great Cave of the Rodents, with ancient ornaments and beautiful old carpets that looked as if they had never been laid on a floor adorning the sloping walls. There were pictures of landscapes in which all the trees were green only. There were metal objects that looked like weapons or traps or tools for digging at the ground. The whole ornamental appearance of this place reminded Ash of the huge entrance hall in the Raptor royal palace.

The Elder Elder stepped to one side, apparently to allow them to pass; but they soon saw that the six other exits were now blocked. The imposing figures of similarly stately looking large Rodents were wearing gowns, with long hair in varying degrees of baldness. The first Elder Elder had stepped into the tunnel through which they had arrived. All the seven exits were now effectively blocked, leaving Ash and Really nowhere to go.

"What's on?" Ash whispered to Really.

She had her head down, concentrating on looking hard at the floor. "It's nothing to worry about," she whispered back, without looking up. "I think they want to be sure of us. It's all right. Just wait."

They both concentrated on the bitten floor, looking down in silence, listening for any movement. For a long time nothing happened. Then footsteps clattered down one of the tunnels. Ash looked up. She couldn't help it.

Ash's mouth fell open. Standing in front of them, another Elder Elder. But this one's hair looked so long around his ears and face, it was like proper head hair and a beard. He was gazing at Ash. His eyes stopped her. They were not pink! He had violet eyes. And he was wearing shoes. A Rodent, in shoes! His strange eyes glinted.

"On this momentous occasion," he said, "I must ask you to come with me."

Really looked up now. She seemed as surprised at what she saw as Ash.

"You can wait here," the violet-eyed Elder Elder said to Really. "We won't keep you long. Please, Agle," he said, bowing slightly toward Ash, "you must come."

"Where?"

"With me. We must not keep Our Lady waiting. She wishes to meet with you."

"Our Lady?"

"Our Lady wishes very much to meet you."

FIFTY-EIGHT

Really waved to her pensively as Ash glanced back at her. She was even more astonished than Ash; neither she nor anybody she knew had ever had the opportunity to meet Our Lady.

"With you," Ash said, turning away from Really and back to the old Rodent she was following up and up the sloping narrow run. "With you," she said, again. "Sorry. I don't—Our Lady's—her name?"

He glanced around at her. His breath was quite labored. He looked very old. The incline in this uphill corridor was beginning to tell on him. "She is to be called Your Ladyship," he said with great pompous pride, turning away again immediately to concentrate on stepping ever upward.

Behind him, Ash smiled to herself.

But in another chamber some little way ahead, he gave in and handed her over to another Elder, this one even elder to him. They shared the same violet eyes. They both wore shoes. "The Agle," the Elder said to his Elder.

The latter bowed and gently bot-blagged before turning and tottering off into another climbing corridor and into yet another chamber and another even more aged violet-eyed Elder, who bowed stiffly and stumped around a corner into what Ash instantly understood was the final opening in their ever upward journey. Here a group, a council of ancient female Rodents, sat in conference at the longest table Ash could ever have imagined.

As they entered, the chatter of conference stopped, and maybe twenty female Rodent faces greeted Ash with slow, friendly blinks. They all stood.

"The Agle!" the ancient male Elder announced before disappearing back into the tunnel from which they had emerged.

Ash found herself in a huge chamber, beautifully decorated with printed silk curtains hanging on the walls, with molded glass containers for the glowing fire-butterfly pupae. The air here was lighter, with a scent to it like the open plains.

From the head of the table, the oldest lady Rodent tottered forward to present herself. This, Ash supposed, was Our Lady. She didn't know what to do.

"You must forgive our stares," the stately Elder Rodent said, "but we have never seen an Agle before. This is truly a momentous occasion."

"With you," Ash said.

Like all the Rodents, this one couldn't help but express surprise when she first heard Ash speak.

Then Ash remembered what she was supposed to call her. "With you, Your—Your Ladyship," she said.

Bot-blagging, she turned to look at the council of female Rodents. Every one of them was bot-blagging as enthusiastically as she was. "We are," she said, still swaying, indicating to the whole gathered council, "Our Lady's inner circle. Her Ladyship requests your presence as soon as you arrive with us. We are humble servants. Please follow me. It's just through here."

She showed Ash where to go through the flowing curtains at one end of the chamber. As there were curtains all around, it wasn't obvious that there was another room beyond, but there was.

Ash stepped into the other room alone. The curtains fell back behind her. The room was not very large, completely curtained and carpeted so that no stone showed anywhere. Light, daylight came in from immediately above.

There were just two chairs, one was vacant, on the other, a shrouded figure sat hunched under rich robes with a heavy shawl covering her head. Although she couldn't see her, Ash knew who this must be. From beneath the shawl, two ultra-violet eyes pierced the shadows, peering out at her.

"With you—Your Ladyship," she said, feeling big and cumbersome in this curtained room of outside air and light.

Nothing happened for a very long time. Those eyes did not waver or blink. Ash began to shift uncomfortably.

"Agle?" a voice said, suddenly. "Where did you get that name from? You are called Ash, but you are an Agle? What are Agles? Do you know?"

"They're—we are, like me. The name, Agle, a mistake. But a good name."

"Is it?" she said. There seemed to be humor to be heard in that voice, as if she was smiling under her shawl. Rodents never sounded like this, because they could not smile. "A good name, indeed! Please, Ash the Agle, please sit with me for a little while. I won't keep you long. I know of your mission. Please, sit. Let me look at you."

The light leaking in from some kind of open panels above allowed Her Ladyship to see Ash clearly. The same downward light made darkness of the shadow beneath her deep shawl. Those eyes only shone to show Ash she was actually there.

They sat for a long while, at least it felt so to Ash, before Our Lady said: "You are doing a great and wonderful, but a very dangerous thing. We had come to believe that it was not in your nature for your kind to make such a—such a gesture, on behalf of another species. You are not like the—the Agles I've always remembered."

"Always?" Ash gasped in surprise. "You—always remembered, us?"

"Yes," she said, "I always knew about you." She paused, another long, long while. "Tell me," she said, eventually, "tell me about 'us.' What do you think you are? In looks, color of skin, shape of face and eyes, all different sizes, what makes an Agle an Agle?"

Ash had been trying to think about this for some time. "Don't know," she had to say. "Not Rodents. Never Raptors—"

"Well, not entirely."

"I—I can't say. We're—not. Not Rodents, not Raptors. No feathers, no wings, can't fly. So—"

"Are you sure?" she said.

Ash could discern the sound of that smile back in her voice. Ash couldn't think of anything else to say.

Our Lady looked, long and hard, before she said: "Do you remember your father?"

"Oh. My father? Yes, I—yes. I do."

"So do I," she said.

FIFTY-nine

"My father?" The shock of hearing these words was ringing in Ash's ears. "You knew him?"

"No," she said, with patience and kindness. "I said I remember him. I knew of your father without ever having met him. He was very well known. Quite famous, in fact."

"Famous? Him? How, famous?"

"Well, perhaps I should have said infamous."

"I don't—infamous. No."

"It means well-known for reasons that are not necessarily good."

"Oh," Ash said, trying to keep the disappointment from her voice, recollecting only the kindness in his face and the sorrow of his last words to her.

"No, no," she said, "don't misunderstand me—your father was a good man. He did what he believed was of benefit to everyone. He wasn't the only one. There were lots of them, all over the world. It was, you might say, a joint effort."

"Not with you," Ash had to say, "Don't get it. He did—what?"

"Oh. They destroyed the world."

SIXTY

"But," Ash stammered, aghast, "but it—the world? Destroyed? The world's still here."

The face veil was moving as Her Ladyship slowly shook her head. "I can see you don't understand," she said. "The world I'm talking about, the old world that was destroyed by the work of Professor Helix and—"

"Professor Helix?"

"Some said it was total madness. Some said it was arrogance. Sometimes, high intelligence becomes intellectual arrogance."

"I don't—"

"I didn't expect you to. It doesn't matter. Let me tell you what happened. The world, the place your father helped dismantle, was very different to what you see around you anywhere now."

She stopped speaking. It felt as if she was remembering, or trying to remember that other, lost world.

"The world," Ash said. "The city world. The magazines."

"Yes," she said. "Agle ancestors, people like you, built the city above us now. Cities all around the world. They were a great civilization with the ability to do so much good and so much harm."

"Harm?"

"Yes, harm. Your father—some tried to say that he just made mistakes, he and so many others, that he was just a part of the error, part of the process. How many of you are there, by the way? How many Agles are there?"

"Thirty-one," Ash said. But then had to correct herself, because of—because of Jon. "Thirty," she said, quickly, trying not to think too much about it, "in tens."

"Ah, yes. Tens. Thirty? Do you know how many Agle ancestors there were, once?"

"Loads," Ash said. "A big city."

"Thousands of millions," Our Lady said. "Counting in tens. Thousands of millions of your ancestors. And they all had to eat every day and had to live somewhere and be kept warm and travel about and try to have a good life."

"All the world!" Ash said. "It's huge!"

"Not huge enough," she said. "Lots of Agle ancestors had too much, lots not enough. Lots were fat, lots were starving."

"Oh," Ash said.

"I know what you're thinking," Our Lady said, although Ash was just trying to keep up. "You're thinking, why didn't the ones with too much give to the ones with not enough? It's a good question. The answer is not as simple as you might think. The world is very, very old. I won't ask you how old you think it is—it is thousands of millions of years old. It took all that time to get it as it was. Everything was in balance, with different species living in different ways in different places. But then along came your ancestors."

"Where from?" Ash ventured.

"Ah, another good question. The world is powered by the sun. The sun is a star."

"The sun? Stars are tiny."

"Yes, but that means they're a long way away. The sun's a star on our doorstep. Everything that lives here is made from the sun's energy. We are the stuff of stars. That's what we're made from, all of us. Agles, Rodents, Raptors, birds, reptiles, fish, flowers, trees, and insects. Everything that lives."

"Oh," Ash said. It was all she could think of to say. Everything that lives. "Oh."

"Yes, oh. What you see around you is the struggle for survival. Why do species struggle to survive, do you suppose? I mean, why is it so important that you and your kind carry on living?"

"I—because—I don't." Ash couldn't possibly begin to answer such a question.

Our Lady understood this. "It's built into you," she said, with kindness. "You have fear, you have love and joy. Which do you try for? You run from fear, or you fight it. You continuously move toward love and joy. It's what you're for, at heart."

"Love and joy," Ash said.

"Yes. Well all species are like that, in their own way. But species isn't a fixed thing. An Agle isn't just an Agle."

"It's not?"

"No. Everything changes. Over time, nothing stays the same. Things adapt, they evolve. The world came into being, and the condition eventually became right for life to begin. It was very, very simple life. But the world changed, as it always had. And so did the various life-forms. They adapted, through evolution. Over massive expanses of time, the world changed and changed the life-forms dependent upon it. They, in turn, changed the world. Oxygen, the air we breathe, came about through living things, organisms. By adapting to change, gradually, life-forms altered, they evolved. Until one day, one day, the Agle ancestor came. But it was different. It was intelligent, more intelligent than anything that had ever lived here. Its ability to adapt to different environments or adapt environments to suit it, was unprecedented."

"I don't—"

"The Agle ancestor could live anywhere. It changed the world, very, very quickly. It changed the world to suit itself so very quickly, so totally, it started to tilt the delicate balance of the world. The world never used to be like this. There were other species here, once. But so many were destroyed."

"By them?"

"Yes. Because they were so many and they ran cars and built cities and made all kinds of things they didn't need, and they burnt the air all over the world and poison was everywhere."

"Poison!"

"Yes, indeed. The world started to change. The weather was made to be different."

"How?"

"By burning the air. By destroying trees and all kinds of other ways. The world never used to be as hot as it is now. The sun started to break straight through to the ground. At the same time, Agle ancestors like your father thought it would be a good idea to find a way to make food easier to grow everywhere, to help stop pestilence and disease and do this without poison to the land."

"But that's good—no?"

"It sounds like a good idea, but how can you do this? Professor Helix found a way. I'll give you an example of what he did. If you're growing a plant, some kind of stuff to eat, and the insects keep eating it before you do, instead of poisoning the insects, as was the way, you can interfere with the plant and make it different."

"Different?"

"There's a way of affecting the way things are. In everything that grows, in every plant and animal, there's a pattern that's laid down from the beginning. It's called genetics."

Our Lady paused. Ash was trying to understand everything. She felt Our Lady waiting for her to catch up. "I have a pattern?" Ash said, at length.

"Every living thing has its own individual genome map—no, I know you don't understand. But this pattern determines how things grow into what they are. If you take that plant and introduce the essence of a spider, the insects will think it is the spider so they'll be afraid and not go near it."

"A plant with spiders in it?"

"No. A plant that smells of spider."

"But how?"

"It can be done. But should it be done?"

Ash tried her best to think about it.

"The world had become as it was over thousands of millions of years."

"I can't think—thousands of millions. It's too much."

"Yes, it's unthinkable, isn't it? But your father used his intelligence to start to interfere with genetic processes. He and others after him made crops and medicines that altered the spiral heart at everything. They thought it wouldn't matter. They tried to test these things.

"For a long time it was fine. But a few years is a long time to us. That's nothing compared to millions and millions of years of evolution. The fiercer sun was shining through, making everything more volatile, less stable I mean. This caused a bird or some other creature to be born with something strange about it, so that when it ate the altered seeds that dropped from the plant, its droppings fertilized other plants growing wild, giving them altered spiral imprints, altering their genes, and things started to change.

"As soon as this happened once, there was no stopping it. The sun and the altered double helix imprints in plants and animals started to change more and more quickly. It was everywhere, all at once. Babies, new Agles, started being born with strange shapes and terrible things wrong with them.

"At the same time, the Adults started to get ill because they were becoming allergic to all the altered grains and fruits and nuts and meat. For a long time, they thought it was a new disease that was killing everyone. But it wasn't. Agle ancestors didn't belong here any more. Nothing from that old world did. Everything was either changing or dying. Changing and changing, ever more quickly. If you look at an old tree, if you can find one, the leaves at the bottom are a different shape and color to those at the top. The tree changes as it grows. The world used to be a stable place. Evolution, the process of change that brings new species from the old, used to take millions of years. Now it takes no time at all!"

SIXTY-one

Ash was left gasping at the end of what Our Lady was saying. She kept seeing in flashes of broken memory the care-worn worry written into her father's face. He had had such kind eyes—the eyes of a good man beaten and broken by the consequences of what he had done. She dropped forward in her chair with her face in her hands.

"Everything is changing," Our Lady went on, when Ash reappeared, "all the time. But once these changes started, they spiraled like the very creation patterns themselves, new species springing out of the old, surviving by change or else dying out very, very quickly."

"My father did this?"

"He did this. Professor Helix."

"And I'm his daughter—you know that?"

"I know you are Ash, the Agle. Your father had a daughter called Ash, and she was somehow unaffected by change. For a while, she seemed to be the only one. She was the Agle I suppose, even then."

"She?"

"You. You were—"

"Special," Ash said, interrupting Our Lady without thinking about it. "Something special inside me," Ash said, filling up with the words her father had spoken to her before he went away. "My—double helix? My genome map—I—he said one day I'd understand."

"It's right that you do," Our Lady said. "Your father must have thought that if you are here, there may be others. But he himself was not resistant to the allergy attacks. And with everything else changing and dying—"

"My mother!"

"And millions and millions of others. In all that, your father set up a place in which you and any others like you may be kept safe."

"The camp."

"He collected the New Agles from all over the world and put them in some secret place."

"By the sea."

"Yes, on the most remote part of our island where the wind blows in from the sea. He had a reef built to keep the waves from battering you. But the wind kept that side of the island green. It didn't change so much. Your father quickly collected any Agle children he could find to try to save his species. That's what we all do. Evolution writes the will to do that into our life-spirals, into our genes. It's why we are."

"Why? We have a why?"

"We do. We all do."

Ash sat in silence for a long while with her head spinning, watching Our Lady as she seemed to collect more and more thoughts, her recollections of the past. "My father," she asked, at length, "where did he go?"

"Professor Helix? Nobody knows. He was travelling as far as he could, looking for survivors. But everything was breaking down. People were fighting for their lives. Most couldn't understand what was happening to them. They were looking for reasons, coming up with all sorts of wild imaginings. This was punishment, many said, for their sins against nature. Against Genome, I remember them starting to say. Genome became a deity—a spirit, some kind of god, the essence of nature against whose laws people, not Agles, had violated. In a way, they were right. But they distorted Genome into a terrible spirit, a god of awful retribution. They sacrificed the lives of other species to him, to this new deity. They made up all kinds of rites and rituals.

"Nothing worked, of course. The laws of nature, physics, and evolution are mechanisms. No species is any more special or valued or chosen by evolution. The strongest, the best adapted mostly survive. People stopped understanding the truth of the world. They always saw their place in it as special, too special. Like Raptors do. Raptors believe in many signs and omens, in the power of fate written into the pattern of the planets and the stars. But they believe themselves to be the center of all things, as if everything was there for them and because of them. Raptors have never recognized their place in the world. We hope, one day, to teach them. But at the moment, like your father, they haven't the humility to learn."

Ash blinked, her head awash with words and their meanings. Or what she guessed to be their meanings. "Did you—do you—hate him?" she asked. "My father?"

Our Lady paused. "No," she said, carefully, "I'm indebted to him. That is why I'm telling you all this. Without your father and what he did, Rodents, as we are now, wouldn't exist."

"Oh."

"But then, neither would Raptors."

"Oh."

"That is how the world now is. Everything is in a state of flux, constantly changing. Every so often the world is unbalanced by one thing or another. It's how new species are born from the old. The earth sometimes stays as she is for thousands, maybe millions of years, but nothing lasts forever. The world has to go into these periods of sudden and massive change. It has happened many times before, but this was different, being caused by a few members of a particularly dominant species. Usually it's the earth herself. She shrugs her shoulders and a big freeze or a big thaw comes, or she's hit by a small planet or her crust comes apart. All different things. These periods of change last only a few hundred years—"

"A long time!"

"Not long. Not for the world. A few hundred years, maybe a thousand, and things will stabilize again. Evolution will still change us afterward, but in only small ways. And when the earth settles again, it would seem to me that Rodents should be an important part of that stable future."

"Yes," Ash agreed.

"You've seen us," she said. "I'm proud of what we are. I don't believe that any other species—that is to say that love like ours shouldn't be wasted or lost. If it is, the world will be a much, much poorer place."

Ash's head was down. "Agles," she said. "We—we're like," she said, looking up suddenly, "you."

"Yes," Our Lady said, leaning forward. Her face was much closer to Ash now. "I believe in you," she said, coming so close Ash could just begin to discern her face properly for the first time.

She reached out and took Ash by the hand. Her hand gripped Ash's. It gripped her hand! The only way one hand can grip another like that is if . . .

"Yes," she said, as Ash stared down at her hand. She stood in front of Ash and helped her stand. "Yes, I have a thumb."

Ash looked into her face, straight into her face, because with the two of them standing, they were eye to eye. Our Lady stood at Ash's height gripping her hand, Ash's Raptor hand with her own five fingers.

"And yes," she said, "I still count in tens." Then, with the hand that wasn't holding anything, she reached and withdrew the head veil to fully reveal her face.

It was a Rodent face, in many ways, but not entirely. Those vivid ultra-violet eyes burned above a long and sloping nose that was still yet half Agle. Her ears were hardly Rodent at all. Her hair was white, but obviously more from age than from albinism.

Ash stared at her. She stared at her.

Our Lady smiled. "It's years since I've done that," she said, touching the corners of her mouth.

"But you—you're a—"

"When I was born," she said, smiling again, "I was considered wrong, as if something had gone awry inside me. I was ugly, a freak. I was one of the first people to be affected."

"So you're—your mother and father—"

"Agle ancestors? Yes, although we didn't call ourselves that, obviously. I am Rodent. I was the first. I am the mother, the great-great-grandmother of every Rodent you see here. This is my family."

Ash's mouth was hanging open.

"Hard to believe? I gave birth to twenty-four children in all. Eighteen are still alive today. They have all had at least thirty kids each. I am no older than your parents would have been."

"But the Elders, they're—they look older than you."

"Yes, they do. Rodents always have many babies, but they age more quickly than you and I."

"Grown up at eight?"

"And that's likely to shift as the generations go on. You must have noticed the difference in size?"

"Yes, the young ones, always smaller."

"We are evolving. We are becoming a fully developed species. We owe our very existence to your father. And, after today, we will owe you an everlasting debt of gratitude. Rodents will never kill, unless we absolutely have to. You have killed, unnecessarily. Your species has always taken the lives of others, and not only for food. For fun, sometimes, in the old world. But now, on this momentous occasion, you must do it, necessarily. That is the difference. We Rodents will never forget you, ever. You will be always with us from now on, as long as our species survives. You will be in our hearts and in our myths and in our minds. You will never die from us."

SIXTY-TWO

They were rushing, dashing through the ever-diminishing rat-runs, with Really glancing at Ash again and again. In all their breathlessness and urgency, Really couldn't resist asking: "What did she say? What was she like? Is she a million years old?"

Ash wished she could have had time to sit and think about it all, everything Our Lady had told her. But there was no time, and the runs were closing in steadily over her head, these little burrows becoming so small Ash was going to have to get out and make her way across the dangerous surface. With so much to think and to worry about, her head felt as if it was about to explode.

"Is she a million years old?" Really asked again.

Ash nodded. "Yes," she said. "Old." She said that because she was, kind of, if Ash thought about the millions of years evolution would have taken in that old world, in the age of the Agle ancestors, to change one species into another. "So old," she said, "she knows evolution. She can see why. Ow!" Ash exclaimed, knocking her head again on the rough sandstone ceiling. "Ow!"

"Are you hurt?" Really said with concern. They had stopped, both stooping in the claustrophobic space they shared. "We have to leave the runs," she said.

"Yes," Ash said, as Really stretched to kiss her head where she had knocked it. She kissed her head like the mother she was.

As she did it, a memory, a feeling, the feeling of a memory came to Ash, sweeping upward as if from her toes. Her own mother, Ash's mom, had kissed her like this, once upon a time, when she was very, very young. She was gone now, and all the changes in the world pressed in on Ash harder than the mass of the sandstone and soil heaped above them now.

"Are you afraid?" Really whispered, as they hugged.

The strange thing was, Ash was surprised to discover that she wasn't. Just about every other emotion, but not fear. No hatred either, she then realized, even for the Raptors that wanted their revenge upon her. Even there, in that cruel and violent society, there were kind and hopeful characteristics, Rodent-like compassion shown to her by Little Three and some of the other female Raptors.

"Not 'fraid," she assured Really.

"I am," Really said. "I wish I was as brave as you."

"No," Ash said. "Not brave. Stupid."

"Oh no," Really began to say.

But Ash stopped her. "We didn't—think," she said. Ash was forever having to search for the words to explain herself to Really and the other Rodents. "We didn't talk. We didn't find out."

"Find out what?"

"Anything. We just—I wish we—when I get back," she said, determined to find her way home, somehow. "Come on," Ash said. "The gun. Is all."

So Really took her along a side-run that led to an opening. Before they reached the end of the run, Ash could smell the forest air suffused with another freshness, like running water.

They came up by a little stream. The forest animals peered at them in affronted alarm. An open-mouthed iguana hissed, so Ash hissed back. He swung his tail as if to lash out with it but was too far away. Ash tried to laugh, although she didn't feel like it. Really attempted to bot-blag halfheartedly.

"The water," Ash said. This was the stream she had followed before, the lifeline that took her through the forest to the plain. That was the place, according to Righteous, in which the Raptors were holding Rat. "Goes out," Ash said. "This is it. Down there."

"Yes," said Really, "it is. But first of all, we follow it the other way. Just a little way. Let me show you."

They began to wade upstream. "Be careful," Really said. "If you see anything swimming, anything at all, shout and we get out."

Ash was looking into the water, but it was so crisp and cool and clear, as it was before, she felt only safe in its shallows.

A little way upstream, and the forest had been taken down and fruit and nuts grown there instead. Just a little farther on, there was a broken fence. It was made of wire. In one place hung a sign, red lettering on a white background.

"Look!" Ash said, fascinated. "Look!"

"Yes," Really said as she led Ash out of the stream and through the broken fence. "This way," she said, taking them through the bushes to the clearing.

Ash stopped dead. The clearing was full of wooden huts, just like her own, all laid out in formation, spaced apart from each other, exactly as they were at home.

"Admission Strictly Prohibited!" Ash said.

SIXTY-THREE

The huts were dirty and in disrepair, just like their
own. There were old beds, rotten mattresses full of
insects. "An ASP camp," Ash said, walking through
with her eyes and mouth wide open.

"You know this place?" Really said.

Ash nodded, although she didn't. She felt she knew it,
because the only real difference, apart from the absence
of the sea, was that no one had lived here for a long time,
except the birds and the hissing beasts, the insects and the
encroaching vines.

"You know this place?" Really said again.

"It's like where I live," Ash said.

Really looked about. "You live in houses?"

Ash nodded. "Same. Exactly."

"They must have moved some to make your place," Really suggested. "This is an old military installation."

"Oh," Ash said, without understanding.

"The army," Really said. "Out there, beyond those trees, is what
used to be a firing range. This is where they kept the guns," she
said, leading Ash into one of the huts.

Inside, the hut was full of guns. They were in piles, all kinds of
weapons, heaped up, fixed to the walls, thrown about all over
the floor.

"All these!" Ash said.

"No," Really said, "there are more. The next two houses are just as well stocked as this one."

"Why?"

"Why did they need so many guns? Who knows! There must have been so many things to fire at."

Ash and the other dwellers had always known about guns. They remembered televisions, computer games, films; guns were there in all of them. But she hadn't imagined that so many were ready, that so many Agles had been prepared to actually take hold of these things and fire them.

"Choose one," Really said. "You need to be sure you can hold it properly."

Ash picked a big, black, oily, nasty-looking piece from the top of the pile nearest to her. She had to pick it up with both hands it was so heavy. "Like this," she said, holding it to her shoulder, as she remembered from something she must have seen long ago on a TV screen.

"Rodents can't hold them," Really said. "And we're forbidden from using arms against anything. If we must resist, we must use only our teeth to—"

BANG!—BANG! BANG! BANG! BANG!

Five explosions split their eardrums and smashed a great hole in the side of the hut. The birds were screaming as Ash dropped the automatic weapon that had gone off with the merest touch and smashed her in the shoulder as if it had come alive and was kicking at her. She and Really ran out of the hut and were halfway to the broken periphery wire before Really shouted for them to stop and they did and both stood looking at each other and breathing very hard. Ash started to laugh and Really bot-blagged.

"No," Really said, still amused, "no, quickly, let's go back and find a smaller one. There are some one-handed things in the next house."

But the birds around them were not letting up. Really stood to her full height and looked to the tops of the trees. She wasn't bot-blagging now. "It's the noise," she said.

"They're 'fraid," Ash said.

Really nodded. "No, not just that. Come on. Quickly. Quickly!"

They ran into another hut and Ash picked up a handgun, still a hefty lump of a thing, but at least she could run with it. That was essential, as Really was moving them along at such a rate, looking this way and that, leading them in a hurry out of the army ASP camp and into the forest, making their way back to the stream.

"Really," Ash said, "your kids. They need—"

"Shsh!" she said, with her ears twitching. She whispered, looking very afraid: "Quickly! Quickly! Hide here. Be careful of the snap-brambles."

Ash knew all about the snap-brambles that wrapped the arms and legs, the paws and claws and held tight, waiting for death and then decay to come. Really dodged around them and waved Ash into a yellow bush. Several disgruntled birds rattled and peered at them from their roosts. They peeked out.

"What is it?" Ash whispered.

Really pointed to the other side of a little clearing. They waited. From between the bushes over there, a yellow-clad figure appeared. No, a Yellow figure, a Raptor, moving tentatively, signaling to two others to follow. Together the three crossed the clearing and disappeared into the bushes, passing within touching distance of Ash and Really.

Ash gripped the gun, ready to fire it to at least frighten the Yellows away. They waited. "They've gone," Really whispered, eventually, extricating herself from the catches of the twigs. The roosting birds cackled at them as they moved.

"Yellows," Ash said. "Why? This the Blue Kingdom, no?"

"They must be trying to gather information," she said. "There's been so much Raptor movement. Things are going to happen."

"They are," Ash said, clutching the gun. "Things are."

SIXTY-FOUR

Ash couldn't look at the expression in Really's face when she left her standing there. Neither could bring themselves to say good-bye. Really looked away from her as Ash glanced back, her eyes darting here and there as if watching out for danger. But Ash knew she found it difficult to look into her face.

The water, as before, felt wonderful about her feet and ankles. The stream was smaller here, as they were quite a bit farther inland than where Ash had started to follow its currents once before. The dappled sun glistened on the water's surface. A little farther ahead, the canopy closed in. From there on, she'd be able to see nothing but leaves and branches for a while. Ash looked back again. Really was not there. The place in which she had left Really standing just a few moments before, although it was vacant, seemed to say something about her, as if Really wasn't entirely gone from it, or from Ash yet.

Then, as she passed through the multicolored tube of the forest funnel, Ash noticed a flitting movement between the leaves. The excited birds were again cawing and crying out at her, but also at the something else moving by her side.

Every now and then she caught a glimpse of the color of Really's dress, and once her face as she appeared on the bank of the stream looking back.

Ash was about to call for her, to tell her again to leave, to go home, but her pointy face had disappeared from the side and there was no sign of her. But then the birds just over there let Ash know that she was still with her. She was about to call out to her when a flash of yellow ahead reminded Ash of the Yellows they had seen skulking through the bushes earlier on. Ash walked with the gun held out in front. This time it was nothing more than a brilliant parrot with huge legs, like a lizard, or a small Raptor. It was about to break a nut with its huge beak before deciding to throw it at Ash instead. She snatched it out of the water, broke it with her teeth and ate it, waving the gun at the staring bird, crunching the nut happily, for Really's sake, as Ash knew she was still watching her from somewhere.

The stream met with a little tributary, another small brook, and the water began to fill up the banks until Ash thought she recognized where she was from where she'd been before. There was a clearing up ahead, a blaze of unbroken sunshine as the canopy gave way to the sky. Yes, she did recognize this place, the same sunshine on that dead tree, the shape of the gap against the sky. Now Ash knew there wasn't very far to travel, she looked again for Really, to try to signal to her that they were near, that she should go. She stayed hidden.

Time and the stream's current both similarly pressed her onward, toward Rat, toward . . . everything! To Ash, there was nothing now, except what was ahead, what lay in wait for her around the little river's bend. The canopy enclosing her again, shutting out the sun over her head, funneled Ash through into her future, toward that pinpoint of light at the end. Which could *be* the end, possibly . . .

No, she would not let in thoughts like that! She took a drink from the stream and steadied herself, looking about for Really. There was still no sign. The stream ran on and she followed it, holding hard onto the gun. The bird-caw and lizard-hiss and the musical notes of the water all combined in her ears, in her head, preventing Ash from thinking straight. Her thoughts were buckled, curved and misshapen images of all that she had been through since she had lost the last surfing competition. Jon was there, stalking up the beach, holding out his hand for her to shake. Then the handshake was between King Tomb and the leader of the Yellows. Little Three was with her for a moment. Really never left her side.

The edge of the forest showed through as that light at the end of Ash's green tunnel. The stream met the plain up there. Ash stepped out of the stream early, taking to the woods for a while to try to come unexpected upon whoever she would meet, so that she could at least see them and ensure that Rat was there, alive. Skirting a snap-bramble animal graveyard, the place in which Ash had seen Talon properly for the first time as they were both tied to the ground by the plants, Ash crept from bush to bush as she had seen the Yellow Raptors do. Rat and Really and all the Rodents had surface runs through the undergrowth, but she'd have had to be much more evolved to use them. She had to creep up to the edge of the forest so slowly, but continuously on the move in case the affronted birds gathered against her with all their fighting and racket.

Out beyond the last bushes at the edge of the forest, the oceanic waves of the plain undulated in the heat of the sun. Ash peeked out across the open grasslands at the point where she had last seen the fallen antelope lying broken. There was nothing there now, not even a bone picked clean. No other animals grazed here, as if they had all run from the Raptor kill that day never to return. Now the hot breezes ran freely, interrupted only by the intermittent yellow bushes, until they met with the heat haze of the horizon. There, she now saw, several shimmering white forms watched what was happening from a safe distance, a small herd of antelope stood peering over in nervous curiosity, ready at any moment to run away. They were watching something quite close by, a little to Ash's left, that she could not quite see from where she crouched.

Leaning farther forward from the camouflaged safety of the forest edge, Ash looked left at what the white antelopes could see and felt, as they did, that she should prepare herself for flight. She gripped the gun. The antelope herd was afraid of the brilliant blue of feather against the green of leaves, as Ash feared that same blue against the grass. From where she watched, Ash could count four, no five, no, six blue feathered heads, twelve monster lizard limbs stalking through the grass.

And there! Between two Blues, a sack, tied and tossed and carried as she had been the day they took her from her home at the camp. There, just there, as they put the sack on the ground, a movement from within.

Rat! Ash knew it was him. It was! He was alive!

She was going to—what was she going to do to save him?

She was going to—Ash would have done something, if she'd had a little more time to think, but just then, everything went black.

SIXTY-FIVE

Everything went black, exactly as before, on that night back at camp. Then she felt afraid, unknowing of what was happening to her, who her abductors were and why they wanted her. Now she felt afraid in a different way because she knew, only too well, who was behind this and what he wanted.

The dirty, dusty sack was back over her head and Ash was bundled off her feet and trussed and tied, bagged up before those familiar hard Raptor hands tipped and tilted her, carrying her from woods to wide open free grass plains. Inside, in the grit-hard dark, Ash felt the force of the midday sun on the outside of the sack.

This time she did not struggle, as she knew it to be futile. And she had the gun. Nothing could stop the Raptors taking her where they wanted, before tipping Ash out at the taloned feet and at the mercy of the new king.

But King Talon had no mercy, especially not where Ash was concerned. Back at the camp, she had made enemies, of course; she had been head girl, champion surfer, and event leader. There were always those that did not like her, or the way she got things done, or the equality she gave to girls and boys alike. Enemies, but not like this one. Not like Talon. He was never going to rest now, as long as she still lived. In the confines of the dusty sack, Ash could see him, she could picture him at home in that huge house as it fell quickly into disrepair under his reign, the cold King Talon pacing the floor, destroying carpet after carpet with his stress-related talons as he gripped and hardly ever relaxed, gripped and hardly ever relaxed. His obsession would be keeping him awake at night. He had killed his brother, the real king, and Ash was the only one who knew, now that Jon was gone.

Ash would show no mercy either. She carried the gun as they carried her. She was more than ready to use it, to put an end to Talon and rescue Rat.

She felt herself being lowered to the ground, just before the bag Ash was in opened, and she was tipped out onto the grass next to the other sack, right next to it. As soon as she saw light, Ash rolled over and over, jumped up and found herself face to face with a Raptor.

No time to think, she pointed the gun at the Raptor's head and pulled the trigger. Click, it went. Ash ducked. She jumped up again and aimed once more and fired.

It didn't fire. Another click, nothing more.

"Agle," Rat said, matter-of-factly, "are you quite finished?"

Looking about, three Raptor faces peered back at her. One set of Rodent features appeared among them. "Rat!" Ash cried, leaping toward him. "Rat!"

She wanted nothing more than to take hold of and squeeze him to make sure he was real, but they were surrounded by Raptors.

They were standing next to them and near them and farther away, Blue Raptors, watching them without moving.

Rat clicked a couple of times and wagged his head, pointing at Ash. It took a moment or two for Ash to realize that he was talking to the Raptors.

It took another moment before she realized, before she recognized who it was standing speaking to Rat. Ash had been expecting merciless Talon, when here stood Little Three!

"Lucky that thing didn't work," Rat said. He took the gun from her and tossed it into the long grass.

Ash nodded and nodded, she was so relieved. Little Three reached out her Raptor-Agle hand and brushed some of the bag debris from Ash's hair.

"Rat!" another voice screamed. "Rat!"

The Raptors were perturbed for a moment as Really came rushing from the woods. Rat calmed them, clicking and gesticulating and pointing at his heart. The Raptors, Ash now saw, were all female, all, as far as she could tell, from the house of old King Tomb.

Little Three took her hand as Really dashed blindly through the Raptors and threw herself at Rat, nearly knocking him over. "Oh, Rat. My Rat."

"It's all right," he said, holding onto her. "It's all right. I'm fine."

Ash looked at Little Three. She was staring back. Before she could stop herself, Ash smiled at her. Her smile was reflected in those massive Raptor eyes. Little Three touched Ash's mouth.

"Oh, Rat, I've been so worried! How can this—" Really was saying, stopping, looking about suddenly alarmed, as if she had only just noticed that they were completely surrounded by Raptors. "But how—why are you—how it is—"

"Little Three," Ash said to Really, before Rat could start speaking. "A friend." Saying that, she held up Little Three's hand in her own. Ash could see Really looking closely at their clasped hands, noting again the undeniable similarity.

"Look," Ash said. "I know this Raptor. No harm."

"She's right," Rat said. "I never knew that Raptors could be so—"

"But now they know you can understand them," Really said in hushed wonder, almost as if she was afraid that the Raptors could now understand her. "This should not be!"

"And you shouldn't be here!" Rat said. "But you are. And so am I. And so are they."

"What do they want?" Really said.

"They want to talk to the Agle," Rat said. "That's all they want."

"And I want to talk to them," Ash said.

Really was looking from one to the other to the other of the Raptors surrounding them. She was still afraid. She looked at Rat, with all her doubt and misgiving showing in her face.

"Let them speak," Rat said. "Let's hear what they have to say."

"But how—" Really went to ask. She had a thousand questions she desperately needed answers to.

Rat stopped her by hugging her again. "How are they all?" he said, asking after his children.

"They want their father," Really said.

Rat looked up and said something in click-speak to Little Three, who nodded, saying something to the others with her. "They had to do it this way," he turned and said to Ash, "in case they were being watched. They are very afraid."

"Talon?" Ash said.

"There's so much for them to be afraid of," Rat said.

"And for us all," said Really, still nervously looking up at the hooked beaks or down at the claws clinging to the ground.

"They want to speak," Rat said, turning to them. He clicked and nodded.

Little Three nodded back before beginning to speak. She talked for a long while. Rat was her interpreter. He had to keep interrupting her, as he didn't fully understand everything she said. Little Three kept on, patiently explaining. This is what she said:

"Talon is king of the Blue Raptors. His authority is absolute. In the space of a couple of days, he has undone all of King Tomb's advancements. King Talon is a warrior-hunter. He decrees we forget Tomb's misguided compassion, his philosophy of weakness and fear, his un-Raptor-like reforms that led to the treacherous prospect of peace talks with our sworn enemies. To be a true Blue Raptor, Talon says, is to revel in our strength and our might. We have, he says, only one hope of survival, surrounded as we are by hostile colors and verminous species, and that is to fight."

When Little Three said this, she looked away, as if she couldn't bear to see Ash with these words in her mouth. Ash didn't understand what she was saying as she said it, as Rat hadn't yet interpreted it, but she understood how it made Little Three and the other female Raptors feel.

"King Talon," Little Three continued, after Rat had finished putting Rodent words to everything she had said so far, "is a warrior-king, a hunter-Raptor. He believes in the Rule of Claw. He has declared war on the realm of the Yellows as retribution, he says, for the death of his dear brother."

She paused again to allow Rat to interpret and to allow the significance of what she had said to sink in. Ash and Little Three exchanged a long look.

"King Talon, ruler of all True Blues, has determined that he will lead our species into greatness. It is written in the stars, the king decrees. It is our destiny."

Again she paused. Rat spoke. Ash understood. *They* understood, Little Three and Rat and Ash. Really did too, as she moved in closer to Rat. Little Three looked at her friends, the other female Raptors with her. They nodded. A shiver ran up Ash's spine.

"King Talon," she said, slowly, as Ash was beginning to understand at least the click notation of those two words, "is determined to fight the good fight. The sun and moon are on our side, he says. We will vanquish our enemies and rid our fatherland of pestilence. The Blue army will destroy the Yellow; that is to annihilate the Yellow race from the face of the earth. That is our destiny, King Talon has decreed."

Rat's face told it all before he did.

"Once the blight of the Yellow scourge has been eradicated, then the superior species, the mightiest, the purest Blues will rid the earth and the underearth of all its filthy vermin."

Little Three stalled there, looking at Really for a few moments, sadly nodding her head.

"King Talon decrees that the new Blue conquerors will cleanse the earth by ridding it of the vermin that is the Rodent population as it creeps, as it crawls through the city's filthy underbelly."

Now she looked straight at Really as Rat interpreted this. "I'm sorry," she said, still slowly nodding in sadness. "I'm so sorry."

Then she looked at Ash. "The Blue armies are amassing at this very moment. Almost everyone has volunteered. No one dares protest. Already there have been Rule of Claw executions for traitors."

Someone unfamiliar with Raptors would not find it very easy to see through to their emotions; but Ash had spent enough time with Little Three to tell what she was going through, to discern it in her eyes, the slope of her wretched shoulders, the sorrow in her slowly nodding head.

"Almost every Blue Raptor of fighting age is preparing for battle. We are a nation of thousands, tens of thousands, all prepared to make the ultimate sacrifice. Nothing can stand in our way. All the Blue omens are good. Our armies are gathering on the border at this moment, in preparation for the invasion of the Yellow Kingdom."

Now she concentrated on Ash alone.

"But before that invasion can take place, King Talon will take no-Raptor's-land and destroy everything and everyone in it. This is, in fact," she said, looking into her, "his immediate priority. He will destroy everything, and everyone. The Agle, he says, is a violation of Raptor purity. It is a vile abomination, he says, and must be the first among all vermin to be eradicated from the face of the earth forever. There is only one solution, in the king's mind. Every Agle killer will be honored, immortalized. The Agle's head must be severed and shown, if Blue safety is to be assured. This is of the king's foremost priority. The attack will be swift and absolute. No mercy will be shown."

She shuddered. Rat looked at the ground. Really reached out to touch Ash. The other Raptors looked away.

"But," Little Three said, still staring at Ash, "the priority of priorities for the Blue forces, is the obtainment of the head of the king's first and foremost foe, the Chief Agle, the one called Ash.

"Talon will have the head of the head Agle, first, foremost, entirely, finally. There is no other solution. The king will never now rest until Ash the Agle and all her kind are dead!"

SIXTY-SIX

"The camp!" Ash said, to herself as much as anybody else.

"He'll destroy you all," said Really.

Little Three looked. She couldn't understand their language, but she knew what they were saying.

"You will have to get them away," Rat said.

Little Three touched Ash's hand. She made a sign Ash had never seen a Raptor use before. She laid her hand flat against her chest then extended it to Ash.

Rat went to tell her what this meant.

"No," she said, before he could, "I get it." Ash laid her hand against her heart and offered it to Little Three. "Tell her, Rat," she said. "Tell her I feel the danger she's in. Tell her I don't blame her."

He told her. She nodded.

"Please tell her, Rat, that—that she's my friend."

She nodded. Blue Raptors did not hug, as a rule, but they broke that rule this time. The other Raptors didn't quite know what to make of it. Little Three understood. She held Ash with such strength almost all of the air was forced from her lungs.

"Ash," Rat said, quietly, "Ash, you cannot—Agle, listen to me. The army of Blue is ready to advance. You can't delay any further. We have to go."

"We? No. Your family!"

"Really," he said, "please tell this Agle."

"You must go," she said, right away, "you and Rat. He will show you the way."

"No," Ash said. "I'll follow the stream. The sea's down there."

"That is the best way," Rat said. "But you won't make it on your own."

"I will. I'll just—"

"You'll just never notice when the life leeches creep up on you, or what if you fall in frog moss or get lichen bites, or what if you're spotted by infantry ants or Trojan seahorses—"

"Trojan seahorses?"

"Horses as big as boot-beetles," Really said, "with funny faces but full of lethal bacteria. You'll be dead in hours."

"You'll never make it on your own," Rat said.

Little Three spoke. "She says she'd like to go with you, only she can't, so somebody has to."

"How did she know what we were saying?" Ash said.

Rat and Little Three looked at each other. "Oh," Rat said, bot-blagging softly, "she understands a whole lot more than I'd have ever believed." He nodded at her in great respect. "Now we must—" he was saying as a great rumble of sound rolled over the horizon. They all looked to where the far plain met the sky.

"That wasn't thunder," Really said.

Some of the Raptors were shaking their heads in alarm at the sound. Again it rolled in toward them like a giant wave. Again they all recognized it: a warrior roar, the battle cry of the Blues as they assembled in their ranks, preparing to leave for the coast, a mighty army primed for the massacre of a few innocent young Agles.

Little Three looked at Ash, tilting her head, purring and clicking softly.

Ash nodded. "Yes," she said. "We have to go. Rat, promise you won't get involved."

"I'm already involved. All Rodents are."

"No. Not yet. Find ways to defend yourself. Get those guns. Before the Raptors."

"They don't work," Rat said.

"One did," said Ash.

"One? They're just as likely to explode in your face. You were lucky. Now it's time to go. Really, I—"

"I love you," she said to him.

This was the first time Ash had ever heard those words spoken in this way: that they were from one Rodent to another seemed so natural, so characteristic.

"I love you," he said, as unself-conscious as Really had been when she'd said it. "I do. Now, we must go. There's no time. The Agles will be lost forever if we don't leave now."

Another low rumble of collective Raptor roar thundered across the horizon, as if to prove what Rat was saying.

"Really," Ash started to say.

"I know," she said. "I know, don't worry."

Little Three nodded gently.

"Come on," Rat said, quietly. "We'll follow the stream to the sea."

"I'll kiss the kids for you," Really said.

"Yes," he said, as they paddled away from the edge of the forest and out across the open plain. The horizon looked a long, long way away.

Ash looked back. Really stood among the Raptors, one tiny Rodent against the full-feathered bodies of the Blues. She looked so tiny.

Rat never looked back.

Ash did, again and again, backward and forward until the far dots of white turned into grazing plains animals and the firm wide bodies of the Raptors shrank to blue dots and Really disappeared altogether.

"She's gone home," Ash said to Rat.

He still didn't look around. That was where he wanted to go, home. He didn't say anything until the forest looked like nothing more than a fine line accentuating the horizon behind them. Not until then did he look at Ash. "She said she'd kiss the kids for me," he said.

Ash smiled. "Yes."

He frowned. "What does kids mean?" he said.

SIXTY-SEVEN

They were just like the little horses from the pages of a rotten book, except that these had no legs and were swimming after them. "Out!" Rat screamed. From the scales on the sides of the fresh-water Trojan Seahorses sprang spiny prongs like nasty poison spears shoved through from inside.

"Run!" Rat bellowed, as a million infantry ants assembled a spikelike attack of their own, each spitting a line of foul smelling acid that shriveled the grass on contact.

"Not that way—frog-moss!" Rat warned, as Ash narrowly avoided the spawnlike mass that belched around the bones of long-dead grazing animals.

All the way it was like this, one hard peril following the other as they paddled and scrambled or fled across the plain. Out there, away from the verdant cool of the canopy, the heat dried the ground to dust around the base of each individual stem of toughened grass. What looked from a distance like a sea of peacefully waving perfect pasture turned out to be another harsh environment of eat or be eaten, rough and hard and hoary, scratching at the feet and around the ankles. This far from the forest there were no bushes, no shade. They had left the grazing beasts behind some way back. The sun was relentless. This was insect environment, steel-hard creatures crunching one another with fearsome jaws under the overhead dead glare of the sun.

"Go faster," Rat kept saying. "Go faster." He seemed as worried as Ash was about getting back to the camp before Talon and his troops. "Run!" he cried.

"Can't run all the way!"

But Rat indicated behind them. The stream was flowing black. "The infantry!" Rat cried, meaning the spitting ants that were sailing downstream after them, each battalion on a craft of braided grasses, so many that the water just looked covered in ants.

"Splash them over!" Ash shouted. There were frog-moss bogs lining the banks, preventing them from moving across dry land. They were running with the current but it was still very hard going.

"Too many!" Rat shouted back as they ran. "You'll get half, the other half will get you."

"Nice little paddle," Ash tried to joke.

"Stop wasting your breath! Run!"

They had to outrun the current of the stream. Looking back, the water had turned into what looked like a big black snake sidewinding through the arid grassland. In the distance, hills shimmered in the haze, covered with trees, promising the luxury of shade.

"Not far to go," Rat said.

Ash was busy dreaming of the cool leaves, some respite from the endless sunshine. "Long way yet!" she said. They were still running, with the black sidewinder snaking toward them.

"No," he said. "Just around this bend."

They followed the curve of the banks to find a beautiful sight that had been hidden from them. The first she saw of it, Ash thought she was looking at a miracle of mini-rainbows interlaced spectacularly between the rocky widening banks of the stream. "A waterfall!" she said. "A real waterfall!"

They scrambled down the rocks to watch the water tumbling and splashing before the barrage of the ants started. "It's an ant-fall now," Rat said, as the water turned black with tumbling insects tipped from their grass crafts. They laughed, Rat and Ash, bot-blagging as the infantry tried to regain their former military precision on the mossy rocks. But they were drenched and ridiculously sodden, crawling over each other in a soggy mess.

As they watched the ants, the plains horizon rumbled as if through thunder, a low, threatening sound that went on and on like a neverending storm.

"We have to go," Rat said, scanning the sky as if searching for storm clouds. There were none.

"We have to," Ash agreed, turning to walk away.

Before she could take more than a dozen more steps toward the coast, Rat stopped her. "There's something you need to see," he said, too seriously for Ash's comfort.

"What?"

"I couldn't tell you before."

"What? What's it?"

"Your leg," he said.

She looked down at her legs.

"At the back," he said. "Don't panic."

Don't panic? "Oh—what's it?" she panicked. "Oh no! Derri!" she said, remembering the thing that had attached itself to Derri's back when he came out of the forest.

Fixed to the back of her lower leg, covering most of her right calf, another great brown jelly monster had suckered onto Ash's skin as if she belonged to it now and it was never, ever going to let her go.

"It murders!" she cried. "Derri died! Derri died!"

"It's all right," Rat tried to reassure her.

"No! Not! Get it off! Get it off!"

"Don't pull it! Don't pull it! You'll break off the proboscis and it'll be stuck inside you."

"No. Off! Derri died!"

"No, I mean it! If you pull it off it'll leave its tube inside and it'll go bad and you'll die."

"Oh, help! Help me! Rat! Do something!"

"Calm down. Just calm down. Come on, sit here. You'll be all right."

"How? Can you get it out, Rat? Can you?"

"Yes."

"Oh—please. Please. Do it!"

"I will. But to do that, to make it release its hold on you and not break off its tube, I have to kill it. I have to make it die, suddenly, or you die."

Ash shuddered, unable to look at the monstrous jelly-monster clamped against her lower leg. "Sick," she said, still shuddering. "Dead down! Evolution? It makes these?"

"That," Rat said, "is Raptor thinking. Like that, you'll start to believe the world was made for you and everything else has been put there for your sake."

"Didn't mean that."

"Maybe not. But as soon as you start seeing other living things in that way, you'll start thinking that you're superior to everything else, like Raptors do."

"Not all," Ash said.

"No, not quite all. But Talon does. He thinks he can kill everything he doesn't like because he doesn't like them. He thinks he's been put here to do such things. But nothing's been put here for those kinds of reasons."

"Then why? We all have whys. What are they?"

"We were put here to be here, because that's what here's for. That's all. Everything that lives has come from the same origin. No exceptions."

"But, this?" Ash said, pointing with disgust at the life-leech. Even as they were speaking it was getting bigger and changing color, growing deeper and darker as it filled up with Ash's blood.

"It has a right to live," Rat said.

"Not on me," Ash said.

"It's not for me to say. But I'll have to say, this time, because this leech will bleed you white, given enough time. It'll drink every drop of your blood or it will be pulled off and leave too much of itself inside you. Either way, you die."

"Unless you kill it."

"That's why I have to do it," Rat said. "Turn over. Lie on your stomach. This is one of the worst things I've ever had to do," he said, with his face approaching the elephant life-leech. "Forgive me," he said, as if speaking to the jelly creature.

Ash had turned away, but the force of terribly morbid fascination made her turn back and watch. Rodent-quick, Rat lunged forward with fearful precision and his razor teeth bit straight through the middle of the jelly with a huge spurt of rich red blood. The leech immediately deflated into nothing much more than empty skin.

Rat's pink and white face dripped red. "Hold still," he said, pinching the skin of the leech and winding it gently around his four fingers. Then, very, very carefully, he started to pull.

"Oh," Ash cried, as she could feel—she could actually feel something moving inside her, a feeling that she was being pulled from inside out.

Rat stepped away. He had to step back a good six feet before the last of the needle-thin black tube of the leech's proboscis finally came out entirely. It left with a bloody flick that spattered up Rat's body and Ash's leg was left with a red mark and a tiny puncture that bled and bled and bled.

The proboscis dripped as Rat held it up. It had curled into a bloody spiral. He looked covered in blood. Ash's leg was pumping red. They looked at each other. As they looked, a great thunderous roar bellowed over the horizon. They both turned toward it.

"Clouds," Ash said, nodding at what looked like a storm coming their way.

"Yes," Rat said, from a dripping mouth. "Dust clouds. Claws, talons, just over there. Thousands of them. Thousands and thousands."

SIXTY-EIGHT

Never had Ash seen the sea like this! Her first glimpse of it after the dangerous plain, having crossed the line of wooded hills, and she thought her heart was going to break.

The sea! Never had Ash realized just how much she loved it, how much she would have missed it, yearning to see touch and smell it. The sea was in her blood, as Rat had spat it out, complaining of its extreme saltiness. Ash's blood, she felt, and the sea, were very similar. One was mixed with the other.

That was how it felt to run from the trees out across the line of sand and plunge in. How she would have reveled in its small cool waves, in this feeling of being almost home, were the storm clouds not gathering behind them. But her homecoming was coinciding with immeasurable danger to her friends, her family, her kind. There was nothing else Ash could do but run along the soft sand of the beach, desperate to get there first. If she failed, if Talon got his way, the Agle would become an extinct species this very afternoon.

"How far?" she shouted to Rat as they ran.

"I don't know how far along the coast we are," he called back. "Not too far. We'll get there."

Yes, they would get there, but to find what? At this moment, the frightful Blue forces were forging their thunderous passage across the plains, oblivious to the dangers that had beset Rat and Ash. Infantry ants and frog-mosses were weak and powerless against such might of fury, especially in such numbers. The whole plain looked like it was on fire behind them and they were only just escaping being burnt alive.

Ahead of them were sand dunes. Seagles swooped. "Looks like—" Ash was saying, when she saw that it wasn't the wild end of the ASP beach as she had hoped but the beginning of another beach she didn't recognize.

The trees behind them seemed as if they were on fire on the far side. "Too slow! Too slow!"

"Run!" Rat screamed. "Just run!"

A seagle must have mistaken Rat for prey just then, because Ash had never seen one quite so determined on the attack, except after fish or lizards. She had to help him scare it off.

More dunes appeared. As they ran along the beach in front of them, Ash held her breath. They ran around the curve of the beach past the dunes and—

And there it was!

The wire!

Her home.

"Don't stop!" Rat screamed, clambering at once up the wire fence next to one of the "Admission Strictly Prohibited" signs, jumping straight over the top.

Ever since she was a little child, when that boy and girl had gone out into the screaming woods, Ash had never considered doing such a thing. Climbing the wire! It was against everything the fence and the signs were set up to achieve. But just to go over it!

It showed just what a trick the camp had always been—"Admission Strictly Prohibited"—with its empty promise of safety. There was no such thing. This feeble wire was as if nothing had ever, ever been there to protect them.

From the top of the fence Ash could see over the dunes to the sad gathering of little wooden huts, now surrounded by some kind of spiky fringe, between the beach and the forest. As Ash looked over from the top of the wire fence, Rat disappeared into the ground. He came back up, with bits of foliage falling from his sloping shoulders.

"Watch out for the hole!" he shouted back.

Ash followed him over the fence, going down into what she now saw to be a pit dug around the outside of the whole camp enclosure, covered in branches and leaves. Farther in, the fringe turned out to be spears, wooden weapons prepared by the dwellers.

Rat and Ash dashed between the wooden shafts and into the camp. It seemed deserted. Ash knew better. "Laura!" she called, rushing for their hut.

Will appeared suddenly, with Jess just behind him. They looked shocked, then amazed and excited. "Ash!" they shouted together as loud as they could, bringing an echo of that name bouncing back from the far trees.

"Ash!" Jess screamed again, running toward her.

Then there were camp dwellers, Agles running from all angles from where they had been hiding out of the heat.

Jess had Ash around the head in an overexcited bear hug, so that she couldn't speak or see what was going on.

"What's on?" Ash heard Will saying to Rat. "Who're you?"

"No," Ash said, pulling free of Jess's grasp; she and Rat were surrounded by Agles, more than she had dared to hope to see again. "No, listen, there's no time. This is Rat. Friend."

Rich was there, looking with strangely curious aggression at Rat. "Where's Jon?" he was saying.

"Where's he?" Will said.

Rat was looking very uncomfortable.

"Rich," Ash said, drawing his, and Will's, attention, "Jon didn't make it."

Nobody said anything. Rich was blinking. Will looked as if he was about to do something but couldn't quite make up his mind what it should be.

"Didn't make it?" Rich said.

"He saved my life, Rich," Ash said.

"Didn't make it?" he said again. "What you mean?"

"And what's this s'posed to be?" said Will, bearing down on Rat.

"I can't—Rich, Will, we don't have time."

"Make time," said Will.

"What happened, Ash?" Jess said, glancing at Rat.

"We don't have time, Jess," Ash said. "Jon was a hero. He's dead. But we don't have time. We have to go."

"You are in great danger," Rat tried to say.

The Agles looked at him with hostility, afraid of him, as if he had been responsible for what had happened to Jon.

"Go home, Rat," Ash said. "Please, now. And thank you."

"You all have to leave," he said, "now."

"What's on?" Will said.

"He's dead?" Rich was chanting. "He's dead? He's dead?"

"Listen!" Ash cried. "We have to leave, all! Now! Listen! A storm is coming, You can't imagine. None of us will survive! We're all going to die! Understand?"

"I understand," a voice said, a voice Ash recognized and loved. Laura was suddenly standing there, appearing from nowhere, even thinner and paler and more fragile than she remembered. "Was always going to end," she said, "life here."

"It's that time," Ash said. "Jon's dead. We'll all be dead, soon. We're to leave, now, right now! Right very now!"

SIXTY-nine

"Go!" Ash ordered Rat. "Go now! You've done enough!"

"Stay!" Rich ordered.

Will nodded in agreement, studying Rat with hostility.

"We can't just go," Jess was saying.

Lots of the others were saying similar things. They couldn't leave, walking away from their lives, from everything they had, everything they knew without so much as a glance back over their shoulders.

"Our place, this," Jess said.

"The Raptors are on their way," Rat kept trying to explain. "They killed Jon."

"We'll fight," Will said, as if about to attack Rat.

"We'll kill *them*," said Rich, with tears on his face. "We'll fight! We'll kill them," he said, arming himself with a wooden spear.

"They'll pull you apart," Rat said, hopping from one foot to the other. "They'll rip you open."

"I'll rip *you* open," Will said.

And all this while, all Ash really wanted was to be with Laura, to ensure that she was real and whole and not broken. But she appeared to be unexpectedly healthy and quite strong. She had grown less thin, with slightly more robust skin. Under the full glare of the sun, she still appeared translucent, flimsy enough to cast no solid shadow on the near-white sand, but no longer faint or near to sickness.

Ash wanted to touch Laura, to speak to her, but all she could do was beg Rat to leave, to implore everyone else to follow her, to get away, while there was still time.

"No time!" Ash screamed. "No time left. We have to go. All! Now!"

"Where to?" Will wanted to know, putting his question as if asking Rat for the answer.

"The city?" Ash just heard Laura quietly say.

"Don't know where," Ash said. "Somewhere else! Anywhere! Just not here! Rat, see you again, some day. Depend on it. Give my love to—"

"Where's he going?" Will was saying, too aggressively for Ash's, or Rat's liking. "Rich, where's the rat going? Stop him. Don't let him get away."

Rich was still holding onto the spear he had dragged from the sand. He looked uncertainly at Rat as he scuttled away into the undergrowth, before turning his attention back to Ash.

"What happened to Jon?" Will said. "Rich. Don't you want to know?"

"Don't, Will," Jess was saying.

One or two of the others made moves as if to try to stop Rat leaving. "Let him go," Ash cried, although they would never have caught him now. "Leave him. He's our friend. Jon was killed by Raptors, by King Talon."

"Then I'll kill him," Rich said, clutching his wooden spear.

"No!" Ash shouted over them all, above the general talk and shouts. "Listen to me! We are Agles! The Raptors won't rest till we are dead. There are thousands of them. They are powerful. More than us. I see what you've done to the camp. It's nothing to them. Believe me. We have to leave! We must run, before it's too late."

"Agles?" Will said.

He was joined by the twins, Alex and Nicholas. "Agles? What's Agle?"

"It's what we are. You don't know what the world's like. In the world, we're Agles. Believe me—"

"Yeah? Why should we?"

"Jon's been killed. Why should we believe her?"

"Because I know what it's like out there. You don't know, and I can't tell you. There isn't time to get your stuff! There's no time left!"

"Laura," Ash said, turning to her friend, speaking softly, "I'm sorry."

Laura was about to start crying. "I've missed you so much," she said. "I thought you were never coming back."

"I'm sorry," Ash said again. "I left it too late."

"Let 'em come!" roared Rich, sounding just like his dead best friend now, just like Jon.

"I'm fighting for him—for you, Jon. Who's with me? Who's with me?"

Some were gathering spears. Some were standing waiting, looking confused, afraid, looking to Ash for guidance. Laura was there for her.

"I'm sorry," Ash said. "I tried. I left it too late."

"Not too late," Laura tried to say, as the boys around them picked little wooden weapons out of the sand. "Not too late, Ash."

She looked so lovely. A tear fell from Ash's eye. Ash's back was to the sea, Laura's to the trees, so that Ash looked at her as if she was framed by the green of the forest outside the wire. From where Laura stood, Ash must have appeared surrounded by the blue of the ocean.

From where Ash was standing, the green surrounding her best friend was changing into the sea, turning, altering, changing color, going more and more, more and more and more and more—

More blue. More and more.

The forest poured blue.

Blue!

"Not too late, Ash."

"I'm sorry, Laura. I'm so, so sorry."

SEVENTY

From every side, Blue, running out of the forest. Just outside the wire Talon's forces gathered, crowding in on them, crushing down upon their little encampment, pressing against the wire. Blue surrounded them completely, Raptor or sea.

Now the Agle boys gripped their spears as if hanging on to life. The Blue front kept concentrating, growing, growling, rumbling, and ruffling outside the wire; which, it was obvious, was never going to keep any of them out.

"Too late," Ash said. "I'm so sorry."

From where she stood looking past Laura as she looked back in horror, Ash couldn't miss *his* horrible face. "This time," his expression was saying to her. "This time!"

Talon looked straight at her. His great Blue head rose above the ranks around him, and he let out his mightiest roar. The cry was picked up and magnified, amplified by the hundreds to his left and right and the thousands crushing in behind him. Talon's army roared at them, stamping and flailing, fully furious, wildly aggressive.

"The sea!" Ash screamed, as Talon took the low wire and severed it with one swipe of his harder-than-steel claw.

"The sea!" she roared, but Ash's voice was lost in Raptor battle cry as all along the camp periphery Blues leapt up and cut through in an instant so that the flimsy walls appeared to collapse inward with Blue and they were screaming forward, falling one over the other in a crazed attempt to get to the Agles, leaping over the dug ditches and casting aside the sharpened spears.

Ash ran. "Follow me!" she screamed, grabbing up a surfboard. The Raptors were feathered! They had claws! They didn't look like creatures that would be able to swim very well.

"Laura! Will! Jess! To the sea!"

To the sea! As the great wall of Raptors ripped across the sand at them, the main body of the Agles sprinted to the shoreline with their surfboards and started to take to the safety of the water's surface. But the Raptors in full rage were loud and swift across the sand to lift one of them, a boy called Parry, throwing him into the air. He fell at the unmistakable feet of King Talon. Parry tried to scramble away. Talon tore him terribly until he crawled more slowly, more slowly, then stopped. And shuddered. And stopped.

"Don't stop!" Ash screamed. "Go! Go! Go!"

Some were able to start to get away. But Raptors splashed and caught some more, and the water was instantly red there and some were gone, just gone. But no Raptors were. They were still streaming across the sands.

"No!" Will shouted. "I'm not! I'm not!" He was wild-eyed with fear, unable to go on a surfboard on the sea because he could not swim and was afraid of water. "No! I can't!" He still gripped his wooden spear firmly, very firmly. "Can't do it!"

Jess was halfway into the water. "Will!" she screamed, almost out of her mind with fear and passion.

"Do it!" Ash wailed at him.

"I can't, either," she found Laura's incongruously cool voice speaking in her ear. "I can't do that, Ash. You'll have to leave me."

"Not leaving you!" Jess was calling to Will, jumping from her board, splashing madly back to the beach. "Not going without you."

"Come with me!" Ash screamed at Laura.

There was no time. Raptor hands were on Jess, dragging her to one side. Talons were ready to tear.

But Will was there. His spear thrust so hard and fast through the Blue Raptor's neck that the thing was dead and Jess was screaming in the water and Will was trying to drag her and Blues were everywhere, and all the other Agles were confused and some trying to come back in were bumping into those coming out and they were being torn and ripped and they were going down and everyone was screaming and there was red in the sea and—horrible! Too horrible!

Ash saw one of the twins, Nicholas, dragged from his board and she saw his brother, the only brothers the camp had ever known, watch him being torn by the Rule of Claw and Ash heard Nick's brother Alex scream his name and it was nearly the worst thing she had ever heard. The worst was the tearing, the Raptor rip as Agles went down one by one.

But Will was fighting with his spear and so was Rich, so Laura and Ash ran to them, dragging Alex with them and Jess was there and some of the others, all of them tugging flagpole spears from the sand and forming a spiky circle surrounded by Blue. Utterly surrounded by Blue.

They were all that was left. Nearly a quarter of the others, so many, so many, gone, in a minute, or less. Lives lost, so quickly, so horribly, so permanently.

"Help us!" Ash cried. "Help us!"

All around, the Blues were closing in. The Agles battled them back with spears, but they kept coming, still tumbling by the hundred, hundreds, and hundreds of them flying with venomous spite from the forest, tearing the little camp to pieces, smashing the huts and dragging down the bushes, tearing and grinding the Agle belongings and the remains of their friends into the sand.

Everywhere was Blue. All force, all horrendous! The Agle's few and brittle spears were bristling, but Raptor talons more metallic. They were far better armed, naturally. Agles were weak. They screamed.

Talon, Lord Talon, the king, came to the fore, in the forefront of his troops, the one among thousands, hundreds of thousands. He screamed toward the tangle of Agles. He smashed a spear into splinters as if it were nothing. It was nothing! And the Agles would be too, soon. Too soon. All of them.

Through the reptilian legs in front of them, a small pink figure scrambled, wearing floppy yellow shorts. Rat had returned, was bravely, blindly flying in to try to help them, to bite Talon on the back of the leg for the third time.

Not this time! Talon took him and tossed him high into the air. His little body went flying.

"Rat!" Ash screamed. "Oh, Rat! Oh, Rat!"

What had she done? She had saved no one. No one! Now Rat—Oh, Rat—as she saw his floppy body flung still farther by more and more Blue Raptors crowded around.

Talon roared. His might was felt in the air even over and above the multitude. He roared to the sky. His was a cry of victory, a giving of thanks to the powers of the planets and the stars that Talon believed were on his side. Talon was the ruler of the Blue Raptors, given to reign by the very force of destiny itself.

The king's tyrant head wagged in victorious threat. All around, the Blues were falling to order, subordinated to their supreme monarch as he eyed Ash with a low tremulous growl ticking over in his throat. His massive head was wagging, slowly, slowly.

All around Raptor heads wagged in time with their leader. They were being ordered to take their cue from him. He wanted to savor this moment. He had waited long enough for it, his eyes told Ash, as they bore into her. "You are mine," he wagged, his head growing faster, faster.

Their heads moved in terrible time. Horribly, horribly! The low roar in their thousands of throats began to elevate and amplify. It was everywhere, that sound, all over and inside every Agle. It was going to tear them to pieces—Will and Jess, Alex, Rich, all of them. Ash and Laura. They were going to rip into Laura, Ash's sister. Ash should have protected her. She should have. She didn't!

Ash looked up to the sky. "Help us," she whispered. But the sun was as impervious as ever, and the sky was blue and beautiful. Like Raptor feathers. So beautiful, so deadly.

Blue.

Beautiful.

Deadly.

seventy-one

Ash didn't cry. She looked to the sky.

The Agles' few and splintered spears were being broken down. Only a few of them were left.

Talon's face was practically in Ash's. He roared as Agles screamed, easily drowning them out. They were so close to the end of everything with no way out.

All around, the blue of Blue. Agles could do nothing. Their camp had been destroyed, so many friends murdered.

Nothing could stop Talon now. After all Ash had been through! And the worst thing was that Laura was with her here, although she had slipped her hand from Ash's. But she was there. They were trapped inside an ocean storm of Blue, their little Agle space at the epicenter, the eye of the storm, in the very dreadful heart where, for a moment, all seemed peaceful.

Then the screams to the sky, the battle cries of victory and vanity all faded away. Even Talon's face took on a change as every Blue Raptor's attention was turned to something by Ash's side.

She looked around. Laura was there. Just Laura. She looked almost as frail as ever, translucent in the sun as she stripped away the loose white gown she always wore. Laura's skin was too thin for the sun. She never swam. She always remained covered up. Now she had stripped down to the underclothes Ash knew she wore but had never seen her in.

Laura, the weak one, the one among them Ash felt most duty bound to protect, had become the reason why the Raptors halted, why Talon stopped and looked and altered his expression. Laura, their weakest, their smallest, their most frail member Agle, stood on tiptoes on the sand with her arms outstretched and she flexed her back.

That seemed to be all she did. It was all she needed to do. The effect was instantaneous. The Raptors, every one of them with a view of her, including King Talon, emitted a sound Ash had never heard from a Blue before. It was a kind of reverse roar, a sound made by sucking in air suddenly, massively. It was the sound of Raptor fear.

Laura had done this, by simply undressing to her undershirt and shorts and flexing her back. She was—Ash had never, ever seen her! Nobody had, not like this!

As Laura stood tall, as she spread her arms and flexed her back, she showed what she had kept hidden for so long. Laura flexed and showed that she had—Laura had wings!

Wings of skin, lined with bone like a huge white bat, but with a great wide wingspan. The bones were like wires, the skin truly see-through, with a spectacular network of beautiful veins. The wings flapped out then flexed like another pair of arms, but much, much wider.

She looked at Ash as she stared with her mouth wide open. The growling gasps of the Raptors sounded all around, rumbling away into the distance as the word spread, as Laura spread her wings and, still watching Ash, started to move them. Laura opened her magnificent, paper-thin wings and she moved them up and down as though she knew instinctively what to do, as if she hadn't spent most of her life hiding herself away.

Talon stepped back. His face had changed completely. His eyes had paled to gray and the iron pump had disappeared with the blood from his arms. He cowered, he actually cowered, as Laura shook her frail white wings and started to flap them.

The air moved around us as she went. The force of the air was remarkable, moving under her as Laura lifted from the sand, as her wings gathered speed and she rose up and up, above the heads of Agles and Raptors alike.

The Agles were open-mouthed with astonishment, while the Raptor faces moved away as if struck, as if awestruck by terror and fearful wonder. With white wings spread, Laura rose into the blue of the sky. She looked like an angel. No, she *was* an Angel. Higher and higher, way above the Raptor blue with the Agle eye in the center, suspended beautifully on the air, as delicate and as frighteningly lovely as an apparition.

She was peering down at Ash. The Raptors were in raptures, nervous, awestruck, afraid. Ash called up to her: "You are an angel!"

As she said it, Laura swooped. She folded her wings and fell out of the sky toward Talon, dropping down on him as a seagle does to its prey, falling almost into his upturned, astonished face before opening her magnificent wide wings again and swooping low across the frightened faces of the Blue troops.

Talon, in the wind-wake of Laura's falling flight, let out a scream, not a roar, a desperate cry of fear as the angel of the skies flew in his face. His brother, Tomb, the real king, had been right: Angels did exist. The grandest of Raptor omens was true. She was here. And Talon had insulted her!

The cry of terror was echoed all over the ruined camp as the Raptors turned away in horror at what they had done. They were terrified of this wonderful white being, the spirit of pure perfection turned against them, about to do them eternal harm. They ran, scattering, falling, trampling. So many were injured or killed by wildly flailing claws as Talon turned and fled.

Laura swooped over them again and again, coming in low, swooping away as they ran, as they covered their eyes and heads with their arms, as they ran and fell and limped or crawled out of the broken confines of the camp and into the forest.

In just a few minutes, they were gone, all of them, every one, leaving just those trampled blue bodies here and there. Talon had turned and fled in terror.

Laura had done this, using everything she had been given, using all her gifts. Evolution had been generous to her and to the few of the Agle survivors.

They were still alive!

They fell on their knees in the sand. Will and Jess fell upon one another.

Laura landed as expertly as a bird, as an everlasting angel. She stood in front of Ash with her wings outstretched. They looked hard at each other for a moment or two, before Laura burst into tears.

RANDOM
DRIFT

PART FIVE

SEVENTY-TWO

Laura cried. They all did, all except Alex. His brother, Nicholas was gone, but Alex just brooded silently, white faced and alone as the rest of the camp held on to each other and counted the survivors rather than those lost.

Ash and Laura were still clasping one another when Will's voice rang out: "Look! It's him. Back again!"

Several of the ASP Agles cried out in panic before they saw what it was that Will had seen. It wasn't Talon returning in vengeance for his humiliation, but a small figure limping along in yellow shorts with a pointy pink nose and sloping shoulders.

Ash didn't know whether to laugh or cry. She cried out: "Rat!" Laura let her go and run to him. "Rat! You're alive!"

"So are you," he said, wincing in pain as Ash hugged him so hard. "Bruised, quite a bit," he said.

"Did you see what happened?"

"I saw it all," he said, "from the top of that bush where I landed. Agles with wings," he said. "I never knew."

"Nor me," Ash said. "Nor me. Laura's an angel."

"No," Rat said, right away. "She's an Agle with wings. Evolution, not magic. Try to understand—there are no angels. Don't start believing such things, or you'll end up like Talon. And even he won't believe it for very long."

seventy-three

Seven were gone, they concluded, adding up their new number, subtracting from the old. They named each one, although some could not be found, so many were the Raptors at them. But the Agles convinced themselves the sea had taken them, as it always did and would.

Ash helped Laura to fold her wings and put her clothes back on. "Why didn't you tell me?" Ash asked.

Laura shook her head. "Didn't get it. It was just wrong. Something wrong. Like boy Baz. Turning into something else."

"That's evolution," said Ash. "Rat knows it. Listen to him."

"Listen to Rat?" said Will, physically supporting Jess, as she had just been sick. "Why him?"

"He knows," Ash said.

"What?" Will said. "What's he know?"

"Let's find out," Rich said. "Listen, then decide. Right?"

Tori was there. She had lost two close friends. She made a sign to say that she was with Rich. Laura nodded too, looking at Rich with huge respect.

Will went quiet. The dynamic of the camp had changed considerably in Ash's absence. She watched Laura and Rich share a glance, an exchange. Laura's look, Ash could see, was telling Rich that he was doing what she thought was right.

"Right?" said Rich to Will again.

Will nodded.

"First, though," Rich said. "First, the boards."

"After," Laura whispered to Ash, knowing that Ash wanted much more time with her, just to be with her, and to find out exactly what had been going on.

"Ash," Rich said. "You?"

Ash nodded.

"Who else?" Rich said to the others, asking the friends of the deceased.

Ash looked at Rat as he stood to one side watching. He didn't understand what was going on. The Agles had wrapped their murdered friends in sheets, those that could be found, and had laid them out on boards on the sand at the water's edge.

"With you," Ash said, touching the dead boards. "With you. With you. With you."

Rat looked down at the ground.

"With you, Nicholas," Ash said, touching his bare board. "With you, Nicholas," she said, looking toward his brother Alex, who hadn't spoken since the Raptor attack.

"Alex?" Ash said, inviting him into the water to take his brother's board out, to float it away into the forever outside, where Nicholas now was.

But Alex's face was hard with anger, not mourning. Ash watched as Alex glanced at Rat, as if he believed that his grief was being intruded upon by this alien Rodent species.

Alex glanced at Will, who was also undecided about Rat.

"Alex!" Ash said.

He stood ready to spring, his face boiling, his every muscle fiber straining to go.

"Don't," Ash tried to say, noting the look of apprehension in Rat's face at all the tension and hostility he could feel.

The other Agles were waiting to perform the mourning ritual. They needed to cry, but there was so very much to be done.

Laura said, "Rich," quite softly.

Rich stepped up to Alex. "He came back," he said, indicating toward Rat. "Only friends do that."

Alex looked confused. His head was about to explode, his hands were twitching. There was nowhere now to direct his aggression, his loathing and fear but inward. He looked up to the sky with gritted teeth, his neck straining to break away from something only he could see. He threw himself backward on the sand, landing on the back of his head. It looked as if he was going to break his neck, but he started thrashing, hitting himself and pulling his hair. Laura made a move toward him.

Rich stopped her. Alex was flailing at his feet, not crying or crying out, but emitting a series of horrible snarling sounds, like a wounded beast in a trap. Rich stood over him as Alex's rage compounded, growing into an ecstasy of grief that could only climax in the breaking of an arm or a leg.

"Enough!" Rich cried.

Will started forward, but Rich halted him too. He bent down and took hold of Alex, unwinding him like a piece of ASP camp fence wire.

Ash hadn't realized that Rich was quite so strong. His character, until now, had always projected softness. Losing Jon after all Jon had put him through had toughened him. He held Alex down, gripping Alex's head, speaking into his face. "Enough," he said again, but much more gently. "Alex. Stop. Say good-bye properly. We've all lost."

Alex didn't say anything. He allowed Rich to calm him, to pick him up and help him to the water's edge, putting him on his surfboard. Rich then gave Alex his brother's board to take out, to let go, to see his life off.

"With you, Nicholas," Rich said, touching the empty board.

Tori signed toward the now silent Alex. Still he said nothing. He set off, paddling out to sea, towing his brother's bare board, with the other Agle surfers following, towing the boards of their friends, taking their friends out toward the barrier of the angry reef.

SEVENTY-FOUR

"Your fortifications are woefully inadequate," Rat said to the faces around the fire.

All of the survivors were out on the beach. Jess, still sick, had fallen asleep on Will's lap. Apart from her, the rest sat listening to what Rat was saying. After he had spoken, they sat blinking, every one waiting. Someone had to say something, eventually.

"It means," Ash said it, "no good. The camp. What you did."

"Yeah?" said Will to Ash. "How you know?"

But Rat intervened. "It does mean that," he said. "What you did to fortify—to make the camp more safe—it wasn't anywhere near enough. The Raptors didn't even notice it."

"So," Will said, "we walk away?"

"No," said Rat. "You can't do that."

"Who says?" said Will.

Rich leaned farther into the firelight. "Listen first," he said, before reclining like a background figure of authority.

"Go on, Rat," Ash was able to say.

"You'll never get through," Rat continued. "You're hemmed in, Blue Raptors on one side, Yellow Raptors on the other."

"Yellow ones?" Jess said, suddenly awake, sounding weak, weighed down by sickness and by the volume of Raptor numbers surrounding the ASP camp.

"I've seen them," Ash said.

"So did Jon," said Rat.

The tension seemed to ripple through the ASP Agles as Rat mentioned Jon's name. Rich disappeared farther into the shadows on the other side of Laura, as if to conserve his strength.

"The Blues are of course your worst enemy," Rat said. "But the Yellows think you are with the Blues. They hate you too. You'll never make it through their territories, unless you all grow wings."

Ash held Laura's hand. She had encouraged Laura to fly again that evening, trying to get her to glory in what evolution had made of her, and also to look for Raptors from the air.

"Talon won't just leave this," Rat said. "We all had a kind of victory today, but Talon won't stand for it."

"How you know?"

"He knows," Ash said. "So do I."

"Talon won't rest, not like this. He showed his fear today. He'll have to make amends."

"How's he make them?" Ash had to ask.

"I mean," said Rat, "he'll have to come back. Stronger. Fiercer. Less afraid. He won't stop next time. It doesn't matter what you do to your camp, you can't stop the Raptors. Talon wants every single one of you now, believe me. Especially you," he said, not to Ash, but to Laura.

For quite a while, nobody found anything to say.

"How can we get away?" Ash said, as Laura squeezed her hand with surprising strength.

"The sea," Rat said, "is your only escape route. I've seen what you can do on the waves and it's extraordinary."

"That means good," Ash guessed.

"Yeah?" said Will. "Not for some."

"Some don't surf," Ash said to Rat. "And the tiger sharks. Out there. You can't see 'em."

"I don't mean on your little boats," Rat said.

"Boards!" said so many of the surfers.

"Boards," Rat said. "I mean you're going to have to build a sea craft, a real boat to carry you far away."

"How far?" said Laura.

"I can't say," said Rat. "This place used to be part of a great country, a continent. There wasn't so much sea in the world then. The sea came up and swallowed so much land that islands were left, big and small. This is a big island. There are others, lots of them. Life's different on every one. Evolution is a localized process that develops individual species in specific ways, especially in isolated environments that have—"

"What's he on about?" gasped Will.

"Words and words," Jess said, breathing heavily, as if Rat's voice was nauseating her again.

"*What it mean?*" Will said, still gasping.

"It means," Alex appeared from nowhere, speaking for the first time since his brother's death, "we run. It means we run away."

"You build a boat—" Rat started to say.

"How?" Will said. "How, a boat?"

"You use your floats—your boards to—"

"We run!" said Alex.

"To where?" Jess said, wearily.

"To some other place."

"Islands?"

"What's there?"

"I can't say what's there," Rat said. "All I'm saying is it won't be Raptors."

"How you know?" asked Will.

"Because the random genetic mutations that modify a species, effectively creating another, are local to the—"

"Yeah—what's it *mean*?" Will half shouted, exasperated, with Jess falling limply from his shoulder.

Ash saw Alex advancing with all his pent-up anger-in-grief, with Will just about to stand and Rat looking left and right for the nearest, quickest exit route.

"You run!" yelled Alex. There was a vein pulsing in his neck, a thick angry rope of tension showing the pressure in his head.

Will was on his feet, Rich was jumping up, along with most of the other dwellers, as if Rat suddenly represented the threat to the camp, or at least an enemy that could be vanquished.

"No!" Ash shouted, with Laura struggling by her side with wings bound against her new instinct to flutter away from danger.

"Some rat!" Will yelled. "Why're we listening?"

"No run!" raged Alex.

"Stop!" Ash shouted at them, her voice falling to near nothing in the cacophony starting up all around her. "Stop!" she yelled again. "Listen! Listen!"

Tori stood and opened her mouth, as if to scream out. She had no voice, which was just about as effective as Ash at the moment.

Both Ash and Laura were about to step close to Rat, when Rich imposed his thick-set body in the way. He didn't try to say anything, but one by one the excited ASP Agles centered upon him, silencing, if not calming. Rich looked around at every face. As his glare fell on them, they fell back, self-conscious and ashamed. Will looked at Jess. Only Alex faced Rich out, but he too fell silent.

When every one of them had been so stilled, Rich looked over at Rat. "We're sorry," he said. "We're confused. We're stupid and 'fraid."

Rat just nodded. He was afraid too.

Rich looked slowly around the ring of faces again. "Ash," he said. "Ash, you know. You tell us."

"What can I say?" she said.

"Just tell us," Rich said, without looking at her. He was going from one ASP face to another again, fixing them, holding them all in place.

"You saw Raptors," Ash said, uncertainly. "Rat's right. Talon won't let them stop there. He believes in the Rule of Claw," Ash said, surprising herself. "The stars are on his side, that's what he believes. There are other Raptors—not like him. But he's their king. He doesn't know what he's doing. He's taking his struggle for survival, taking all the—the emotions that evolution has given him and growing them—making them—destroying—Rat? What is it?"

"He's distorting them," he said.

"That's it," said Ash. "Till they're out of control, wanting to destroy everything he sees as a threat or insult to him. He's a—he's unstoppable. Rat knows. Rat's a Rodent. They know. We have to listen. We have to!"

The whole camp stood without a word. Ash had, it seemed, used everyone's supply of words for a week. She had sounded like a Rodent.

"I think I'm going to be sick," Jess said, out of the blue-black sea darkness.

"I think she's changing," Laura whispered to Ash.

SEVENTY-FIVE

Rat was on his way home.

"What makes us change?" Ash asked.

"Evolution."

"No, I mean, what, exactly? What thing is there? What gets in us?"

"Your DNA. Your life spirals, your genes. All your life's written in them. Laura's changes were probably programmed into her when she was born. Laura was always going to grow wings."

"But boy Baz—snakes?"

"I don't know. DNA changes happen through exposure to the environment too, now. Mutations happen all the time. Nothing's stable. You don't know where you're going or what you're going to become. Rodents are changing, so are Raptors."

"So are Agles," Ash said. "I think Laura thinks Jess has started something."

"Maybe," said Rat. "Or maybe she's just unwell. It's difficult to say."

"It's difficult to say what we are," Ash said. "I never knew what the world was like. Nothing's how I imagined."

"How did you imagine?"

Ash had to think about it now. "I'm not sure. I just didn't, you know, question. We had a place, is all. Nothing more to think about, except where we came from. We didn't think where we were going. We wasted so much time."

"Wasted?"

"We didn't do anything. We were 'fraid. We didn't know and we let not knowing be it for us. Our library, our books, we let it fall away. Rodents wouldn't have," she said.

"No," Rat agreed, "but we always had our Elders to teach us. We always had them to help us in not being afraid. They loved us," he said.

Ash loved the way the Rodents talked of love. When Rat had gone, disappearing into the undergrowth with promises to return as soon as he had seen to everything at home, Ash started to think about home. She was looking around at the camp as the Agles dragged down some of the barely-standing huts, with Will throwing himself into the work when he wasn't taking care of Jess, and Laura sailing high over the canopy on the lookout for the next Raptor attack. What had been home was being dismantled and effectively destroyed. But it had to be done. They had to get away. They had to leave their home behind. Ash told them what to do. Nobody questioned her now.

Rich seemed to have some ideas on how to build a boat, or at least a raft big enough to float away on. Direction didn't matter; away was all that counted. If they lashed together enough surfboards and wood from the huts, tying it all into one piece with old rope and fence wire, they'd keep high enough in the water to float straight over the tigers out there beyond the bay. This floating platform would be all they would be taking with them of the ASP camp, other than its cargo of Agles.

"Admission Strictly Prohibited," the signs at the edges of the ASP craft would read, now that Rat had told them what it meant, as instruction to the sharks and to any other evolutionary sea monster waiting for meat morsels farther out there in the deep. Nobody really believed that the signs would hold off any hungry marauder, but Ash thought they might help to make the Agles feel slightly more at home for as long as it took to find another land.

Home. That was what they were going in search of. The attempt was desperate, especially as the new craft they were erecting at the water's edge looked no safer than the old library hut, which had collapsed with just the faintest of tugs. The twins had been sleeping in there. But there were no longer twins, or brothers or sisters in the camp. There was no library. One tug, they all fell down.

Rich had them wiring surfboards together, across which they were going to tie planks of wood from the huts. The plan was good, but Ash knew it really needed nails and—and nails and—other ways of attaching one thing to another. Nobody had much of a clue how it could be done, other than nails and wire and rope. And they had no nails.

They worked for days. Ash would have been more worried about Rat if she wasn't so very busy.

Laura flew. She spent most of every day soaring over the camp and its surrounding forest. They felt that as long as she was keeping watch up there, they were all much safer. Every time the forest birds around the camp erupted in panic, as they did and always periodically had, the Agles looked up and listened, waiting for a cry from Laura, their guardian angel overhead. The night was as it had always been, the time to be most afraid.

Many arguments broke out, but the work went ahead. Reels and reels of fence wire were wound around the wooden frame and old floorboards tied onto it. Everyone worked madly, dragging wood, tying it off, breaking it to size, where it would be broken, fitting it clumsily into the platform where it wouldn't break, as they had no means by which to cut it. The only cutter they had was for wire, useless for wood. But the construction started to come together and more or less stayed in one piece, however many splinters it shed onto the sea and into the Agle's skins.

Jess still kept getting sick and had to sit out of the sun, but Laura was in the sunny air as if born to it. Alex worked like a demon Agle, or else he went off into the dunes on his own and refused to be drawn back. Laura kept an eye on him from on high.

When Rat appeared beside Ash on the water's edge, he looked strangely at the mass of the splintery platform.

"Rat! How's Really? How're the kids?"

"Oh. They're—oh, they're just—is that it?" he had to say, nodding at the ASP raft. "Is that what's going to take you out over that reef? *Is that it?*"

"That's it," said Ash, trying to sound confident. "We're taking it out tomorrow. The lagoon, in the morning."

"See you in the morning then," he said.

Ash looked around for him, but he was already gone. She looked back at the raft as Tori tied down another plank, winding the wire so tightly that the end fell off the wood and plopped into the sea.

SEVENTY-SIX

"Say something," someone said.

"What?" said Ash. "What shall I say?"

"Shove it out!" yelled Will. He and Rich and Tori were standing on the platform of the raft. "Get it away!" Will was afraid of the water, so this was quite an act of bravery for him.

"What shall I say?" Ash said.

"On this momentous occasion," Rat whispered.

"On this momentous occasion!" announced Ash.

"On this momentous occasion!" repeated the other Agles. "With you!"

"No, wait," whispered Rat. "That's not all of it."

"On this momentous occasion!" Will and Rich roared from the top of the craft. Tori was signing the words as best she could from the sounds. She was jumping up and down.

"On this momentous occasion!" cried Ash again, raising her hands to the sky where her best friend flapped and fluttered, as if perched stationary against the blue.

Laura waved. Everyone, including Rat, but excluding Alex, waved back.

"On this momentous occasion!" they chanted. "With you!"

On this momentous occasion, the Agles pushed their ASP craft out from the beach and into the soft sea in the lagoon. The platform was somewhere about the size of the floor space of one of the huts. It would have been made simply of the floor of the library had not the whole thing fallen to pieces when the hut fell down. So it ended up as a kind of lashed together floating hut floor, tied onto pillars of piled-up surfboards, with other lumps of wood crisscrossing the whole heavy structure, all roped and wired more or less together.

The gentle waves that undulated toward the shore were replicated in the surface of the raft, with Tori, Rich, and Will rising and falling as the old floorboards creaked and rasped against each other.

"On this momentous occasion!" came the cry from the shore. "With you!"

"With you!" Rich called back, doubtfully.

"It doesn't look—" Rat started to say to Ash.

"No," she said, "it doesn't."

It didn't. It looked not like an *It*, not like a single, solid craft, but a clumsy collection of loose, ill-fitting parts. The ropes were going limp and stretching as they soaked up the seawater. The wire on its own started to bite into the dead worm-eaten wood, breaking it away in lumps that floated off like many little rafts with momentous occasions of their own. The three passengers were looking down at their feet, shifting position as the floor began to separate, with different size boards moving in different directions at different rates.

Alex appeared on the shoreline. "Momentous occasion?" he said.

"Don't know what it means—bet it isn't this." He looked up. Laura was calling down at them.

"It's useless," Ash was saying, watching the raft disintegrate, as Tori and Rich and Will jumped into the shallow water. "With you!" she called to Will, wading in to offer him her hand. The water was only up to his waist, but Will looked about to panic.

Laura screamed down at them. "There! There! There! There!"

"No!" Will was shouting out to Ash. "Not me! It isn't that. It's that!" he pointed. "*That!*"

Laura had landed on the sand. The ASP raft, tilting crazily, was tipping Tori into the sea, but Laura turned away from it, screaming out, "Get spears! Get spears!"

"Raptors?" someone said.

"Raptors!" "Raptors!"

"No!" shrieked Laura. "Not. Something else. Get spears!" she ordered, taking off again. "Get in the water. Now!"

Ash looked over toward the other side of the camp. "Quickly!" she screamed. "Now!" as she went to arm herself with a sharpened stick.

All around her, Agles bristled with spears, all up to their thighs in the water with the raft spinning slowly, tipping and creaking and falling farther into the sea.

Rat was up to his waist. He was without a weapon. "I don't know what that is," he was saying, as a very different creature lumbered from between the huts toward them.

"No Raptor," said Ash.

Laura swooped low over the square heads of the thickset but sharp-looking, man-shaped beings as another after another appeared, walking stiffly and slowly on two shining legs, with two shining arms and a sort of folded-skin body and a wide, blank face. Each was carrying a metal device, some of which looked a bit like the gun Ash had accidentally set off at the old Army camp.

The Agles and Rat stood clumped together in the water. "What is it? Rat—what are they?"

Four, five six, seven, eight of them appeared, white, but dingy white, no feathers, no scales.

"What are they? *Rat?*"

"I don't know," he said.

More of the strange, plastic-looking, square-headed creatures appeared and lined up on the shore.

"What shall we do?"

Alex started to move toward them. His face was ashen and pale. He was shaking.

The alien creatures tensed as he moved, as if flexing their plastic muscles. One or two of them glanced with what looked like curiosity as Laura swooped again. They were not alarmed or frightened by her.

Ash caught Alex and pulled him back into line. "Keep it," she said.

"Wait," Rat said. "See what happens."

"What are they?"

"I don't know," he said, "but they don't look too aggressive, at the moment. Wait and see."

They stood in their line formation in the water with the raft sinking on one side behind them. Facing them, a long, gray-white line of blank, featureless faces.

Nothing happened. For a long, long time they waited with tense and aching muscles and bumping hearts. Nobody moved until one of the plastic man-monsters slowly raised an arm and pointed with a crinkled forefinger. It was pointing out something on the sea. Not the raft, noisily collapsing nearby, but something way, way farther out.

Ash took a glance behind.

Laura swooped.

Ash looked again. She could not believe what she was seeing.

Moving against the skyline, as if drawing up out of the far dunes down that side, sleek and powerful, massive, gray and green and blue—

Ash dropped her spear. All of the other Agles looked around. They each let down their guard. Nobody could believe it. It was huge! Colossal!

"Now *that's* a raft," said Will.

"It's a ship," Rat said. "A ship!"

seveNTY-seven

A real ship! Made out of unsinkable metal, by the look of it. Metal that floated better than wood; hard, painted metal in the water with guns, massive cannons, mounted on top.

Ash looked back at the beings lined up along the shore. The one who had pointed out the ship placed its weapon on the sand and reached to its neck as if to make a sign. But its big blunt finger fumbled with something there before it made a popping sound and pulled its head clean off.

Inside the head, another, smaller one: a man's head. The man, a whole adult male, was inside a plastic suit. The head poked out of the top. "Who's in charge here?" he said. "Which of you is in command?"

A man! On either side of him, others, presumably other men or women, all wearing similar suits. Adults! A ship!

Rescue!

"Who are you?" Ash finally found her voice.

The man's eyes homed in on her. "Are you in charge here?"

"No," said Ash.

"Yes," called Rich, "she is." He glanced at Will. "She's in command. Commander Ash."

"Commander Ash?" the man said. "I'm Captain Beagle, of the *Ark*. Quarantine the vermin and the winged one," he said to the others with him. He turned back to look at Ash. "You're all under arrest," he said.

SEVENTY-EIGHT

"It's just a formality," Ash said. She had been confined to one of the last surviving huts with Jess and
Will and Rich.

"What's it mean?" said Will.

Ash wasn't too sure. She was just repeating whatever
had been said to her. She would have liked to ask Rat, but
he'd been put in a metal box, Laura in another. Outside, big
metal huts were being erected along with towers made out of
tubes. Wire with hideously sharp blades fixed into it was being
unwound and looped around the ASP periphery. The Agles looked
out of the window as the still-suited Adults bustled from place to
place, stamping all over the old camp. Most of the wooden huts
had been taken down and used for the raft, with the Agle survivors confined to the few remaining.

"A formality," Ash said. "It means rescue. It means we're saved,
that's what it means."

She said so as convincingly as she could. Outside, metal
clanged. Military boots clumped. The many Adults outside
had hardly a word to say to each other, as if they worked with
spontaneous organization like ants. Rat had been referred to
as vermin. Raptors did exactly the same thing. Laura was the
winged one. They had both been put into quarantine.

"Quarantine?" Ash had quizzed the one man whose face she had so far seen.

The Agles went quietly, in the end. Alex had wanted to put up some kind of a fight, but here were Adults, real forces of authority and control, stern and purposeful, with a giant battleship backing them up. And the one face, the bearing and the threat of the protective suits and the arms the adults bore, had intimidated the Agles. Ash felt, as did they all but Alex and Rat, that they had done something wrong. Laura looked ashamed of herself. Now they had to start being good again. It was a strange feeling, somehow connected to long ago, when they had first found themselves abandoned here. They had lain down their arms quietly, with their oceangoing vessel sinking in the foreground against the absolute authority of the battleship dominating the whole sea horizon.

"It's just a formality," the man, Captain Beagle, had answered when Ash had asked him the meaning of the word quarantine.

"It's a formality," she told the other Agles as they glanced warily out of the window. "Rescue! It's what we've been waiting for."

"Is it?" said Will. "I stopped waiting for anything."

"With you," said Jess. "Long time ago."

Rich didn't say anything at all. He went over to the window. From where he stood, he could look out and to the side at the big metal boxes with holes in them, inside which Laura and Rat were being kept. "I think," he said, when at last he did speak, "quarantine's prison. I think."

"I think," Jess said, "I think—I think I'm going to be—I think I'm—"

"She's going to be sick again," Will said. "We need some water."

"I'll go," Ash said, stepping to the door. She opened it and went out.

She dropped back against the wall of the hut. The barrel of what was definitely an automatic rifle was almost touching the tip of her nose. Several more guns approached her face, almost into her eyes.

"Admission Strictly Prohibited!" said a woman's voice from within one of the nearest protective plastic suits. "You will return to your villa. You will return now, without raising your hands or making any sudden movements."

"We—need—water," Ash said, very, very carefully. "Someone's getting sick."

"Go now," the voice said, "and attempt no further escape. Food and water will be delivered to your quarters in due course."

"Where's water?" asked Will, as Ash stepped back into the hut, quickly closing the door behind her.

"They're bringing it," she said. "Jess, can you hold out a few minutes? They won't be long. Water and food. Soon."

The heat inside the hut was becoming unbearable. Jess was lying on the floor bathed in sweat. An age went by. Huge metal panels were being unloaded from a gray boat, a landing craft, carried quickly across the sand and erected into more metal houses. These were bigger than huts, with steel shutters over the windows. Everything was painted in different greens. All kinds of fantastic equipment disappeared into the new buildings.

"Where's water?" Will was saying again. "She needs it now."

"I'll go," said Rich.

"No," said Ash, too quickly, remembering the rifles aimed at her head that she'd thought it best not to mention. "No, best not."

"But she—" Rich was saying as a shout and a crash sounded from one of the other huts. "Alex!" Rich said, starting for the door.

"No!" said Ash, standing in his way.

They stood looking at each other as heavy-booted feet were heard stomping, storming into the nearby hut. Something fell. It sounded as if it must have been broken.

Ash turned and went out of the hut. Once again she faced an arsenal of black rifle barrels.

"Admission Strictly Prohibited!" the female voice said again. "You are violating—"

"I want to see—"

"You must return to your quarters! You are violating—"

"I demand to see Captain Beagle!"

"Turn around, now!" a male voice came at her from one of the other suits. The guns were being leveled in anticipation. Inside the suits, the arms and shoulders were tensed and prepared to fire. "Turn around! Now! Return to your quarters! You will be sent for in due course."

Ash pushed her back against the wall of the hut. She peered past the first gun barrel into the female eyes she could just make out on the other side of the smoked face-screen. "I will go," she said, "when you bring us water."

"This is your final warning!" the male voice declared. "You must turn around, now! Now!"

Out of the corner of her eye, Ash saw Alex being restrained, held on the ground while some metal clasps were being fitted to his wrists. "We have someone sick in there," Ash said, as steadily as she could, fixing her gaze onto that pair of brown female eyes. "Jess is unwell. She has to have water."

"This is—" the male voice started to bray.

The female suit pointed its face toward him. He stopped. The woman inside looked back at Ash. She blinked and gave a tiny, almost imperceptible nod. "Go in," she said, in a measured tone, "and I'll bring water and food right away."

"No," said Ash. "Now."

They were looking at each other. The woman's plastic face mask moved away again. There was another brief nod before one of the other suits walked away. Ash looked over to see Alex being carried away toward another of the quarantine cells. "For his own safety," the woman said.

Ash could clearly see into her eyes. "I want to see Captain Beagle," she said.

The eyes blinked again. "He'll send for you, in due course. Now," she said, as the other suit returned, "take these and wait in your quarters."

"Bottles of water," Jess said, back inside the hut. She was watching Ash take the plastic top off. Jess took a drink, almost choking. Her eyes widened. "It's cold," she said.

"It's way cold," Rich said, with his own bottle open.

"And get this," Will said, unwrapping some silver foil. "Food. Look it."

"No food," said Rich.

"Is food," Will said. "Taste. Jess. Love it."

"Oh," Jess said, taking a teeny bite. "I know. It's—it's chocolate! Oh! I remember. Chocolate!"

seventy-nine

"And who are your enemies, Commander Ash?"

The air in the huge metal hut, even in the full heat of the afternoon, was cool. Captain Beagle was wearing some kind of silver suit that looked like the foil the chocolate came wrapped in. The captain's hair was cut very short. His hands were impeccably clean and his fingernails were perfect. "Commander Ash?" he said, requesting a reply.

He sat behind a big metal desk piled with books, manuals, diaries. Ash had to stand in front of the desk looking at the captain, thinking how much he looked like one of the models from the old magazines, while another Adult stood by the door still in full protective clothing and carrying a submachine gun.

"Enemies?" Ash managed to say. She was overawed by the captain's one-piece suit and the electric hum of the false atmosphere in the hut.

"From your little reception committee," the captain said, "it looked as if you had some experience of fighting your enemies. Is that not so, Commander Ash?"

"Oh," said Ash. "I'm not—that's not me. I'm Ash, is all. Not commander."

"You are not in charge here?"

"No, not really. In a way. Kind of."

The captain took a few moments to regard Ash. She, feeling foolish under his too-steady gaze, began to shift.

"My name is Charles Beagle," he said, when Ash had suffered enough. "I need—we need your full name, for our records," he said, tapping the top of a pile of manuals.

"Ash," she said. "It's Ash."

"Just Ash?"

"No," she said. Her conversation with Our Lady of the Rodents came back to her. "I'm—my father—my name's Ash Helix."

The captain regarded her again. "Helix? Really?"

"No," she said, shaking her head, "not Really—oh, I see what—Really's a name. Yes, really. My name. Ash Helix." She said it again not because it needed repeating, but Ash liked the sound of it, the feel, as Really said, the taste of it in her mouth.

"Helix," the captain said again, and not because he liked the feel of it. In his mouth, the word looked as if it must have tasted pretty sour. "That's an unusual name," he said.

"Is it?"

"Yes. I've only ever come across it once before. By reputation."

"Professor Helix?" Ash ventured.

The captain did not respond. The air around him, chilled by some trick by one of the machines Ash could hear humming, froze his pale blue eyes.

"He was my father," Ash said.

"Who are your enemies?" asked the captain. The pinch of his mouth, the nervous tick in his cheek showed a hot temper brewing just below his icy surface.

"The Raptors," Ash said.

"Mutations!" the captain said.

Ash wondered for a moment if this was a question. She glanced again at the kind eyes in the protective suit by the door.

"Mutations!" the captain said again. "Mutations are your mortal enemies. Why have you not grasped this? Why is this not your overriding survival principle?"

"I don't," Ash said, glancing at the guard again, "get it. I don't—understand."

The captain stood. He was tall, upright, clean, and very fit looking. "You are Professor Helix's daughter, you say?"

"Yes. So I was told."

"Told? By whom?"

"By Our Lady. The Rodent leader."

"Rodent? Like that vermin?"

"You mean Rat."

"I mean *vermin*, young lady. I mean *mutation*! Professor Helix. He and his scientific community—they are responsible for the flood!"

"The flood?"

"The flood! The tide of abomination, the corruption distorting Genome's purity of perfection on the face of the earth."

"I don't—" Ash tried to say, because she was having such difficulty following what the captain was saying.

"The *Ark's* humanitarian forces are committed to seeking out survivors, untainted, Genome-like human beings and preserving His holy likeness until this dread tide recedes and we are restored to our former preeminence upon the face of the earth!"

"Captain," the woman at the door said.

"Listen to me," the captain said to Ash. "Listen carefully. When mutations whisper blasphemies in your ear, when the devil tempts you, you are in mortal danger."

"Devil? Our Lady, she just—"

"Mutations!" he shouted.

Ash heard a sound from behind her. The guard's gun had been placed on the floor, leaning again the back wall.

The captain glanced over in that direction, breathing, taking another, another deep breath. "These abominations, these creatures will tell you anything to undermine the truth. They will say anything to get you to believe in the lie of evolution!"

"Lie?"

"A lie! A perfidious distortion. It is very, very unlikely that you are Professor Helix's daughter. You were told that for a purpose."

"I don't get it—don't understand."

"Genome," the captain said, steadily, with his passionate face whitening, "made man in His image."

"But genome's just a name for—"

"How dare you! Genome is Lord. Genome is the all-creator, the most powerful, the omnipotent all-seeing enlightenment. And man was perfected in His image! You may not question Genome's laws. The physical abominations you see around you everywhere are a direct result of such questions, such loss of innocence. Your father—Professor Helix, he was tempted by the serpent with the knowledge of that which should remain unknowable."

"I don't—I—"

"Captain," the woman came forward.

He halted her. "Six thousand years ago," he said, in a very measured tone, "Genome created the earth and everything in it."

"But isn't the earth thousands of millions of years—"

"Such numbers," the captain continued, his deep voice resonating with the power of his conviction, "mean nothing. They are measures of impossible time and imponderable distance. Genome alone exists in such stretches of eternity. He has always existed and always will. Not so for human beings. We have been made by Genome to worship in His light. We are the center and pinnacle of his universe."

"Human beings?" Ash said.

He nodded. "You. And me. Do you understand me now?"

"I think so," said Ash, although she thought not.

"Then who are your enemies?" the captain said.

"Raptors," said Ash.

"Mutations!" shouted Captain Beagle. His firm face was flushed, his deep eyes cold. "Mutations! Mutations are your enemies! Any base creature remotely humanlike is a distortion of the truth. It is an imperfection, an abomination. It is unclean! It is the devil incarnate!"

"Captain," the woman's gentle voice said.

Ash glanced and saw that her suit helmet had been removed. She was looking intensely at him.

"These—Raptors," the captain said, drawing, with some effort, his eyes from the woman's face, "what nature of beast are they?"

Ash started to describe the Raptors in general and Talon in particular.

"Their arms and torsos," the captain interrupted, "are human in form?"

"Torsos?"

"Bodies," the woman explained.

"Yes," Ash said. "Human. Like us."

"Like us?" the captain said, doubtfully. "That is like us meaning you and your vermin and winged distortions?"

"No," Ash said, uncertainly, "Rodents only have four fingers. Raptors have hands like ours. Talon is their commander, their king.

He will lead his Blue army, bring them here to kill us. We need help. You have to help us get away." She stopped.

The captain regarded her for a long, long while. He looked at the woman. "Lieutenant Hope," he said.

"Ash," she said, "it's time to return to your quarters."

Before Ash could say anything, Lieutenant Hope had taken her gently by the arm. "The captain will consider your request carefully," she said.

"But," Ash said, looking into the woman's caring face, "we have to get away. We'll all be killed."

"The captain will let you know of his decision in due course."

"In due course?" Ash looked in her deeply dark face. She looked back at the captain's dispassionate pale blue gaze. "Genome made man in His image?" she said.

"What color is Genome?" she said. "And who made Him?"

"Get her out of my sight!" the captain bellowed.

EIGHTY

In another place, a figure sat in the shadows thinking. This time of growth, this time of security and learning, was always going to end. A long time ago, a young, strange-looking woman had decided to take her huge family underground. If she hadn't, they would all have died. As it was, they flourished, cousin with close cousin, transforming, transmogrifying, turning from family to new species: the Rodent.

Our Lady sat alone in her rooms, where the light filtered through colored glass from above. Rodents lived an almost totally subterranean life, when they were not foraging for food. But Our Lady was not so completely Rodent as her offspring had become. She could not quite give up daily contact with the surface, with the outside air.

But now the air fell in on her, exploding over her head as the glass ceiling splintered into a hundred thousand shards in a single instant and the whole thing rained down all around. The top of Our Lady's chambers had seemed to atomize and fall, bringing with it a larger, harder body than glass, a mass of living substance downward falling but in control, roaring with aggressive delight. As if on a fantastic ride of joy, the creature dropped from breaking glass roof to torn floor, falling on its feet from far above, sturdy on sharp claws.

Our Lady, appearing from between her bleeding arms, did not cower before the exaggerated blue pride and beaked threat that towered over her. She lowered her arms from her face and stood before the Raptor, waving away those Elder Rodents who had appeared between the silken sheets over her doorway. "Go," she said to them. "Go now. The family needs you."

The huge, magnificent Raptor turned slowly to face her, ticking on its diamond-hard feet.

"You must be Talon," Our Lady said, nodding up at the Raptor's blank black eyes. "I've been wondering when we would meet," she said, as the king Raptor roared to the open sky.

From outside in the Rodent council chambers, the frightened departing Elders heard the roar, the forward thrust of the deadly attack, the dreadful crunch of impact, the fall, the horror of the first foul rip.

But what they never heard was the stately old Rodent lady's cry, her beg for mercy: nobody ever heard such a thing, for such a sound was never made.

EIGHTY-ONE

"Can't wait," Will was saying. "On a ship. Jess, eh? You'll feel better. Away, on a ship."

"Yeah," Jess tried to smile. She was feeling much better but somehow couldn't seem to share Will's enthusiasm for going away from the camp, from the lagoon especially, forever. There was no choice, they had to go, but now the time was almost with them, the camp did seem like home. "It's just a shame," she said.

"What is," said Will, looking from the window toward the skyline out to sea, on which the ship, the *Ark*, sat so still it looked like a picture plonked there.

"So many Adults," Rich was whispering to Ash.

"The camp," Jess said to Will. "A shame. All pulled to bits. Gone. For good."

"Good," said Will.

"Why don't they talk to us?" Rich asked.

"They—I don't know," Ash whispered.

"I mean," said Rich, "who are they?"

"Captain Charles Beagle and Lieutenant Elizabeth Hope."

"Yeah? Who else?"

"They're the Genome Militia. That's what they're called. She told me. Elizabeth. They were a military unit cut off on an island. Captain Beagle's their commander in chief and he—"

"What you two whispering?" called Will from the window. "What's on?"

"Nothing," said Ash.

"I don't get it," Rich said, so they all could hear. "Why they keeping us, like this?"

"Just a formality," Ash said.

"What's it mean? Rescue? Doesn't feel like it."

"We're going on the ship," Will said to Ash, "right?"

"Yes," she said.

"When?"

"What about Laura?" Rich said. "Locked up."

"I saw her. She's fine."

She wasn't. She was being kept in a box with holes in it. The box was cool inside, but Laura was like a bat with a broken wing. Lieutenant Hope had allowed Ash to see Laura on the way back from the captain's quarters.

"See?" the lieutenant had said, allowing Ash a peek through a spy hole. "She's fine."

She wasn't. Her wings were wrapped around her like fine smooth sheets, and her head was tucked inside. Laura did look very bat-like, huddled into a corner, enfolded in delicate leathery skin as if cocooned from the world.

"It won't be long," the lieutenant said, closing the spy hole. "Charles always knows what to do for the best."

"What about Alex?" Ash said.

"I have to take you back now. Your friend needs to be prevented from doing harm to himself as much as anyone."

"He's already harmed," Ash said. "The Raptors killed his brother. His twin. They were together, always."

"We'll look after him," the lieutenant said, "don't you worry."

"And what about Rat?" Ash said.

"The vermin?"

"No. Rat. He's a friend."

Lieutenant Hope's brow furrowed. She had left off her protective helmet to talk to Ash as they slowly made their way back to the hut. "You have no friends like that," she said. "Believe me, Ash, you cannot afford to fall for their tricks. Their ways are blind alleys of punishment where lies and sins are paid for in full."

"You sound like your captain," Ash said.

"He's a great man. A *great* man! His is a long-term view. It's not always easy to see the eventual good when evil seems so friendly and true. It isn't, believe me."

"You don't know what Rat's like," Ash said.

"Oh, but I do. I know exactly what he's like. He'd have you believe there's no Genome, that the world in all its glory is a result of the millions of actions of pure chance. He'd try to convince you that human beings exist by the accident of evolution, that everything can be known and explained and that we never have to answer to any higher power. All species are equal in their blasphemy—"

"I don't understand . . . blasphemy."

"A lie, a falsehood, an insult to Genome. Ash, let me tell you, you are in danger for your very soul. Even should Charles choose to—should you remain here, you must be vigilant—be always on guard and accept Genome into your hearts and pray for your salvation. Genome will be merciful—"

"But Charles might not be?"

The lieutenant stopped for a moment. "Ash," she said, turning to look at her, "you are much more intelligent than you think."

"Am I, Lieutenant Hope?"

"Yes. But you can call me Elizabeth, if you like. You are a bright girl and your—the others here need you."

"The Agles," Ash said.

"Agles?"

"We are Agles," Ash said.

"No," Elizabeth Hope said, "you are *Homo sapiens*. Humans. You do not have wings, you do not fly, you do not burrow. You live as humans live, as Captain Beagle lives. Don't forget that. You have a duty to live as Genome decreed and never to compromise that, as it is a gift from on high."

"So if we go with you," Ash said, "if Captain Beagle lets us onto the ship, Agles with wings will not be with us."

"Charles will save human souls," Lieutenant Hope said, escorting Ash back to her hut.

"Laura's fine," Ash said to Jess and Will and Rich again. "She'll be just fine. I'll see to that."

"Look it," said Will, pointing to the sun beginning to disappear behind the great black silhouette of the battleship.

"Doesn't look real," Rich said.

"No," said Jess, standing at the window with the others. "Doesn't look like we'd all get on."

"No," agreed Ash. "Doesn't look like we'd all get on."

EIGHTY-TWO

Under cover of darkness, the way was even more hazardous. But she was Rodent, resourceful, fast, and talented. The moon was almost half full. When scudfish snapped, Really was grateful for the silver seam in the sky reflecting just enough light for Rodent eyes to pick out the dangers.

She followed the stream to the coast, negotiating the frog-moss and every other peril the open countryside could throw at her; none of which compared with the danger of being caught by the Raptors in the city. Really had been lucky. She didn't believe in luck, good or bad; that was what Raptors did, always looking for omens from one side or the other. Things just happened: good or bad or indifferent, luck depended upon your point of view. But from where Really viewed the moon at the moment, from the fact that it was there shedding just enough light for a Rodent to see but not enough to help a Raptor, the fact that she had made it all this way and was looking at the lights in the Agle camp with no life-leeches attached to her and hardly any bites or scrapes on her feet and legs, Really had to consider herself very lucky.

The camp was surrounded by razor wire and was attended by watchful guards with guns. No matter. Really was Rodent through and through. She soon burrowed past the periphery defenses, slinking through the shadows beyond the guards toward the big metal hut from where most of the light was leaking.

In no more than a few moments, Really was under the wire, through the camp, and beneath the cover of the darkness at the base of the metal wall below the lighted window. One single glance through the door and she was like any Rodent on the search for something to eat—spot an opportunity, take it! She shot into the big cool hut and hid in the shadow between a cabinet and the corner, waiting to find out exactly where she was and what was going on. This place didn't look much like Ash's description of the camp, so better to be cautious, she thought.

There was water running. It stopped. Someone was washing. Really heard the water running away before an Agle came from another room through a second doorway on the other side. But this Agle didn't look how Really had expected—this one was an Elder: not an Elder Elder but still quite senior to Ash. Strange, as Ash had told Really that all the Agles were about the same age. This one looked very different, with extremely pale skin and flickering blue eyes. His hair had been shorn very close to his head. He wasn't bald; this was deliberate.

Really watched closely as the Elder Agle came out into the center of the room wiping his face then his hands, looking at himself in a long mirror affixed to a big wooden cabinet. He wore a silver suit. He was looking very closely, very carefully at his reflection, his eyes meeting their mirror-image before scanning up and down the body. Then he reached to his throat and ripped apart the top half of his suit. Really could tell, from the way it readily split open, that this jacket was designed to come apart like that.

But the Agle did not take off the jacket. He stayed where he was, looking into his own face with the garment split apart. Then he turned and looked over his shoulder at the reflected image of his back. He pulled the jacket off with a sudden, violent jerk and stood with it hanging from one hand, studying the line of his backbone.

Really sucked in the air. For a moment, so loud was the noise she made, she thought she might have given herself away. But the Elder Agle was too engrossed in surveying the line of his back, from the top of his shoulders down to where his waist narrowed. Really had seen enough of Ash to understand that Agles did not usually develop plates, like huge leathery armored scales along the vertebrate line down the back.

"Forgive me," the Agle said.

As there was no one else in the room, Really thought, with a prickle of fear, that he had spotted her after all. She cringed farther back into the shadows.

"Oh, forgive me," he said.

Really peeked around the corner of the cabinet. The Elder Agle had fallen to his knees, perfectly unaware of Really's presence.

"I have sinned," he said, looking up toward an electric light shining down directly from above. "I have sinned and have been justly afflicted. I must hold my peace, for who can bring a clean thing out of an unclean? Not one! Oh that I were as in the months of old, as in the days when Genome watched over me; when His lamp shined upon my head and by His light I walked through the darkness."

Really ducked at the name of Genome. She shivered and watched and listened with nervousness and apprehension. All Rodents were taught, from a very early age, about genes, the beautiful DNA double helix and their nucleotide sequences. They learned that genome is a word made out of the words gene and chromosome, so it means how all the genes fit together to form chromosomes in living tissue.

Everything that lives has DNA and an individual genome sequence. This was the first time that Really had come across the belief in Genome as a spirit, the jealous, vengeful god of all creation. That was a frightful power, quite separate and apart from the simple stream of natural information in the four nucleic acids that constituted the DNA of organic matter.

"Although I have sinned, Lord Genome," the kneeling Agle seemed to implore the electric light above him, "I have endeavored to remain pure in heart and intent. I must remain committed to my holy mission—nothing must stand in my way if I am to ensure a future for Genome's Chosen—even should it mean no place for my own weak, corrupted flesh. The future must be dominated by Genome's perfection made flesh, when the flood of abomination is reversed and the world replenished. That I am afflicted by corruption is merely weakness on my part," he was saying, reaching over his shoulder to try to strike at his armor-plated back, "this I understand. I have sinned, but please, give me time and I will serve Your higher purpose, whatever the cost to me personally and to those—"

A knock sounded, firmly, but not too loudly on the outside door. "Captain Beagle?" said the voice of a Fe. "May I enter?"

Really drew her head back in as the Agle hurriedly dragged on his upper garment, rushing to hide his back and to stand and compose himself all in a single moment.

"Yes," Really heard him say. "Come in. Good evening, Elizabeth. How are they?"

"They're anxious, Charles. Ash especially. She needs to know what's likely to happen."

"Yes," he said.

Really took a tiny peek. The Male and Fe Agles both stood facing one another. She couldn't help but notice the stark contrast between the lightness of his skin and the darkness of hers.

"I appreciate their anxiety," he said, the Male to the Fe, "naturally. I only pray that they have been granted the wherewithal to appreciate mine."

"But their lives are in danger, Charles."

"So are ours," he said, sternly, "all of ours. You, above everyone, must appreciate the complexity of the matter."

"Yes, Charles. But I can't help—"

"But you *can* help, Elizabeth. There is so much you can do to help."

"How?"

"By ensuring that these young people are prepared for an adverse decision. They have been subjected to venomous influences, vermin. One among them has grown wings. Another is at this moment sickening with something. How can I possibly take the chance with such abnormalities?"

"But this means that you have already made up your mind, Charles. This means that they will be abandoned here to fend for themselves against overwhelming odds."

"Did you imagine that this does not distress me, lieutenant? Do you not think that my decision is a matter of conscience for the greater good?"

"Charles, I—I can't help feeling—did you see their pathetic attempt at building a raft? They're desperate to get away from here. Surely we could simply transport them to another island?"

"And risk the integrity of the *Ark*? The ship is our only safe environment, Elizabeth. You know as well as I do that—"

"But I can't help—"

"No, Elizabeth. No. Help me, if you will. Grant me one good reason why I should risk jeopardizing the safety of the *Ark* for these few young people. If you can give me such a reason, Elizabeth, then I could rejoice in my decision to take them somewhere else. Then perhaps I could sleep. Can you give me such a gift, Elizabeth? Can you?"

"No, Charles. I'm sorry. I can give you one thing only. You know what that is."

Really, still peeking around the corner of the cabinet, saw the Fe Elizabeth start toward the Male Charles. She wanted to hold him. Really could see that she had done it before and was desperate to do it again.

"Charles, come to me."

"No, Elizabeth," he said, holding her at arm's length. "We must sin no more."

"Is it such a sin to love? Is it, Charles?"

"It can be. Believe me, I know."

"What do you know, Charles? Tell me."

"I can't. There are things I just cannot tell you. But I will be informing the young people's leader, Ash, of my decision, first thing in the morning."

"That you intend to leave here without them?"

"That I intend to continue my mission. That I cannot compromise the purity of our objective."

"Poor little things," she said. "Poor, poor little things."

"We have to be strong, Elizabeth, in every way. You and I have been weak, in the past. Now we must be resolute. One day you'll realize that I was right. Goodnight, Elizabeth. Get some sleep. Tomorrow we prepare to ship out."

EIGHTY-THREE

Suddenly, standing in front of his desk, Ash knew exactly what she needed to do. All of the dreams and the dreads of the night before, having listened to everything Really had to tell her, drained away and she stood listening to Captain Beagle with her mind made up and her body tensed but ready and her breathing easy.

"Having taken everything into consideration," Ash listened to the captain saying, "especially your extended exposure to adverse environmental influences, the infiltration of certain alien species, and your own experiences of transmogrifying mutations—"

"You're going to leave us here," Ash cut him short. She didn't understand half of what he was saying, but she knew what he was going to say. Really had woken her last night and told her everything she had seen and heard in the Elder Agle's quarters. Really had made her way to the camp in the dark because she needed to find Rat. She needed him more than ever now that Talon had burst through into Our Lady's chambers and—and the inevitable had happened.

Ash expected to feel shocked, saddened, and dismayed when she heard about Our Lady. She felt all of these, but mostly, anger. When Really had told her what had happened, Ash had had to go outside and scream and kick and lash out until her anger subsided and left her with her shock and sad dismay.

Talon was as murderously obsessed as ever, and he was never going to stop. The Rodents were being kept underground by the Raptors, as Talon's troops were being positioned at every Rodent exit from the runs. Some foragers had been caught and killed. Even the Elder Elders were in disarray, bereaved and confused after the murder of Our Lady, unsure of what to do, how to handle this threat to the whole of the Rodent species. The young were crying of hunger and their mothers and fathers were in distress. More and more young Rodents were making reckless runs for food, with more and more getting caught.

If ever Really needed Rat, it was now. So she had made a reckless run of her own to find him, to bring the bad news to him. His family were desperate and in danger. She had to try to bring him home.

Ash had spent the rest of the night trying to understand the significance of what Really had seen in the captain's quarters. The *Ark* was going to ship out without them, leaving Agles and Rodents alike to their savage fate at the hands and beaks and talons of the Blue and Yellow Raptors.

"You're going to leave us here," Ash interrupted the captain, suddenly sure of what she was going to do. "You've seen our raft. We're useless, but we're trying to get away. And you're going to leave us here!"

"I have deliberated long and hard," he said. "I have tried to justify subjecting my people to such an influx of risk as you represent—"

"I don't understand your words," Ash said, "but I know what you're saying. You think our genes are—you think we're changing."

"Genes?" he said, sitting back in his chair. "You speak like a scientist. You sound like your father."

"My father? But you said you doubted that—"

"Science would destroy us, left unchecked. You can see—you have experienced the corruption everywhere. The world has been made unclean."

"Everywhere?" Ash said.

"Almost everywhere," the captain said. "The holy forces of the *Ark* represent an untainted ideal—"

"Everywhere?" Ash said again. "You said everywhere. Is there anywhere without genes—with no changes, Captain Beagle?"

"The *Ark* represents the only—"

"Is there anywhere—is there anything, not being changed. In some way or another, is there anything not changed?"

"Man has lived in a state of grace since the world began six thousand years ago—"

"Only man?"

"Humankind."

"What color?"

"All colors. We are all equal. The question is not one of race. It is a question of the human qualities of mind and—"

"So what of Laura's mind? She has wings."

"She is unclean."

"But it's about the . . . human qualities of mind?"

"Of mind and body."

"So what's a human's body like? How can you—"

"No wings!" the captain half shouted, standing up.

"No wings? What about scales, like some kind of a shell going all the way down the back."

The captain almost fell, stepping backward into his vacated chair.

"What about that, Captain Beagle? Should your *Ark* people have to live with something like that?"

"How did you—"

"Or don't they know?" Ash said. Her heart was thumping. The captain's face had whitened with shock and anger. Ash wondered if he had enough power over the *Ark*'s forces to have her taken out and shot.

It didn't matter; she had nothing to lose. Shot or taken apart by Raptor claws, either way, Ash had just this one chance of doing something about it.

"You can't leave us here like this," she said. "We can't fight the Raptors."

"I cannot take you with us. It's simply—"

"And I can't just let you leave."

"Are you trying to threaten me? How dare you even—"

"Captain Beagle, please. I've got to do something. We'll all die—all of us. You have to make this place safe."

The captain glanced to his left and right. "I don't think that's possible, not without an impractical level of fortification."

"No," Ash said, with determination. "Not here. I don't mean the camp. I mean this place. The whole of this island. This is an island, isn't it?"

The captain nodded. "A substantial one, but yes, it is."

"If we held the city," Ash said. "If we took the city and were given— if we could hold that."

"The city?"

"You and your troops could push Talon and the Raptors out of this kingdom, couldn't you?"

"Kingdom?"

"Yes. If you pushed them into the Yellow realm, they'd be at war. With the Rodents and your guidance, we could hold the city, if the Raptors are busy fighting each other, couldn't we?"

The captain regarded Ash for a long, long time. "Is this your idea?" he said.

Ash nodded.

"You think you could hold the city?"

"Our only chance," said Ash. "The city, is all."

"The city is all," the captain said. He stood staring at Ash. "And how did you find out?" he said, at length.

Ash thought about her answer before she spoke. "I'm my father's daughter," she said.

Captain Beagle inhaled sharply. He looked at her and looked at her for a long time before speaking again. "I remember," he said, when at last he did speak, "seeing pictures of him. The famous Professor Helix, giving a presentation at one or the other of the scientific and political institutes. You look a lot like him."

"That's his half of my DNA," Ash said, repeating something that Really had told her. "That's my genes," she said.

The side of Captain Beagle's mouth twitched as he clenched his teeth. "You are your father's daughter," he said, stiffly. "Return to your quarantine. You will be hearing from me in due course."

EIGHTY-FOUR

"After careful consideration," the captain announced to the crowded camp, "given the complexity of the situation," he said, without looking at Ash, "I have decided that there is only one solution that will serve the greatest good."

Ash held hands with Laura and Jess. "He's going to help us all," Ash whispered as Laura's pale wings twitched and juddered.

Rat had been let out of the quarantine box with Laura and was reunited with Really. Captain Beagle chose to ignore them. Alex was also freed and stood blinking in the light, glancing angrily at the Adults in their full protective suits to the left and right of him. The captain was obviously well aware of Alex.

The camp was still under armed guard. Most of the Adults were still hidden behind semitransparent smoked visors. All carried weapons, except Captain Beagle, who wore his protective suit without the helmet.

"You people," the captain said, standing on the back of a low vehicle, looking over the Agles, ignoring Ash and Laura and the two Rodents, "you have survived here, flourished, in your own way, against the massive odds stacked against you. But the threat to your very existence is greater than ever. The *Ark*'s forces have reconnoitered the entire area. These abominations—the Raptors, your enemies are all around you. But the Yellow mutations on one side appear interested only in defending their territories from the threat of the Blue. The Blue Raptor so-called king, I am given to understand, is your main adversary. The Blue Raptors have attacked your camp, killing any number among you, murdering your brothers," he said, looking directly at Alex, "and your sisters," he added.

Alex seemed to shudder with disgust, as if he was shivering in the oppressive heat of the late morning.

Will was standing protectively over Jess as she sat near Ash in the shade. Really and Rat tried to keep out of the way, hiding under Laura's flickering wings.

"But this is your natural environment," Captain Beagle announced, throwing out his arms. "Your enemies are formidable, the dangers great, but should you run from them?"

"No," said Alex.

"Should you retreat in the face of sheer animal savagery? Or should you fight for what is rightfully yours? Yes!" he yelled toward Alex. "You should fight the good fight. You have right on your side, for you are—you are the inheritors. This place has been bequeathed to you. No, not just this modest camp—this whole island environment is rightfully yours, all of it. The camp, of course, but the countryside, the city!"

"The city," Laura quivered.

"The city," Ash heard Rat say to Really.

"The city, the capital of your island country, is yours. It was built for you by people like you," he said, ostentatiously peering away from Laura and the Rodents. "You cannot allow all this to be taken from you, can you?" he said, staring from one face to another. "You cannot let that happen, can you?" he glared directly at Alex.

"No!" Alex said, almost shouting it out. "No!"

"No!" shouted Captain Beagle. "And the holy forces of the *Ark* cannot allow this to happen to you. We, together, yourselves and us, we shall take back your rightful territories from the aggressor. This enemy of yours, the Blue Raptor, is our enemy. Together we shall vanquish the beast and liberate the city for you and your allies. The *Ark* forces will leave you as a nation in the making, a great people with a secure future. These filthy beasts cannot keep you from your destiny or continue to threaten your security. Together we shall eliminate this threat, once and for all. We shall eliminate this abomination for good. For good! Are you with me?"

"With you!" shouted Alex.

Most of the other Agles were watching, wide-eyed with astonishment, glancing at Ash, staring at the captain as he seemed to expand and flow outward from his higher platform.

"If you are with me, you shall secure your future. If you are with me, you shall live. If you are with me, you shall wreak your revenge on the murderer of your brothers and your sisters!"

"With you!" Alex screamed. "With you! Come on!" he shouted at the other Agles. "With you!" he shouted again at the captain.

"*With me?*" the captain shouted out. "*With me?*"

"With you!" Will called back.

"With you!" "With you!" "With you!" The ASP Agles were calling out, whipped up and excited, suddenly powerful, suddenly unafraid.

"Commander Ash?" Captain Beagle stopped them by saying.

Elizabeth Hope looked from the captain to Ash. Her eyes could be seen flashing behind her smoked visor.

"Commander?" the captain said again. "With me? Do we do this together? It is the only way."

Laura quivered by Ash's side. "The city!" she hissed.

"Eliminate this threat?" Ash said. "What's it mean?"

"It's the only way," the captain said.

"The only way to save my children," Really whispered.

"Yes," Ash said, eventually. It was the only way. "I'm with you!"

A cheer went up. The Adults raised their arms in a victory sign. Each and every raised arm held a weapon, dark and glistening with oil, absolutely at the ready.

EIGHTY-FIVE

The busy landing craft were still bringing more Adults in full protective plastic armor, more military equipment, many more armaments. An army of *Ark* forces were gathering on the sands with just a sprinkling of Agles and two wary Rodents. Many guns had been pointed at Really and Rat, some at Laura, until the order came to stand easy. The bodies in the suits stood but didn't seem very easy about the order.

"Are you with me?" Captain Beagle called above the heads of the amassed troops, the newly armed Agles.

"With you!" cried Alex and Will and Rich, holding up their sharpened steel machetes, big brutal blades for cutting through thick vegetation.

Tori held hers in the air too, but Ash kept hers by her side. Laura wasn't allowed one. Neither were Really and Rat, but they would never have taken such a weapon.

"You have right and righteousness on your side, you crusaders for truth! Your full rewards will be in paradise at the right hand of Our Lord and his heavenly host. Nothing can stand in our way!"

Ash watched Really holding onto Rat as Captain Beagle delivered his words. She could see how uncomfortable they were with such words, whatever they meant. The Agles didn't understand them. But at that last sentence, they were stirred into raising blades again, crying out: "Nothing can stand in our way! With you! With you!"

Will turned around to ensure that Ash and Laura were taking care of Jess. As he looked back his face showed surprise to see the sheer number of *Ark* troops positioned behind them, all the way to the sea and out along the beach.

Ash, noticing Will's face, looked back too. They were an army, a solid well-equipped force forging forward as the ASP camp wires and the razor wire were brought down and the front flanks moved off into the forest. "Are you all right, Jess?" Ash said.

Jess was shaking. "Yes. I've never been—we're going out."

"A long way out," said Ash. "But it'll be fine. We'll be fine."

"Yes," said Jess. "We'll be fine."

"The city," Laura said.

"The city!" the captain called from the front, as if confirming Laura's reason to be excited. "We shall liberate the city!"

"A momentous occasion!" shouted Alex, flailing his machete blade very, very dangerously. As much as he hadn't understood those words when Rat had first said them and Ash had repeated them at the failed launch of the raft, he *felt* the momentousness of this occasion.

Captain Beagle, with Lieutenant Hope by his side, caught the phrase and expanded it in volume and significance. "A momentous occasion!" he repeated, inspiring his troops with the Rodents' words, distorting them out of all proportion.

Really and Rat kept close to Ash and Laura and Jess as the armed forces moved into the forest immediately hacking through the undergrowth using machete blades that glinted malevolently under the canopy in the dappled light. The Agle boys along with Tori were there with blades, attacking the low plant life, seeing off the hissing reptiles as if to try to wreak some small revenge for their long years of captivity.

Ash watched as the army marched forward. From the first step out of the camp they were on the attack. The shrieking birds were now afraid of this other type of Agle, this armed-to-the-teeth Adult letting off a gun aimed at a squawking parrot, slashing the tail from a distressed iguana. The forest was nothing to fear now with the front wave of protective suits cutting such a swath that every Agle walked without scratch or sting across the open forest floor.

Captain Beagle had not once to ask Ash the direction of the city. His people had old maps that they seemed able to work from. They asked nothing of no one. They stopped for nothing.

"This is great!" Will ran back to shout at Jess and Ash, before darting ahead again to be just behind the forward thrust of the *Ark*'s forces.

Up ahead, Ash spotted a huge bed of snap brambles. She moved forward, trying to catch Captain Beagle's attention. Elizabeth Hope noticed her and fell back.

"Those plants," Ash said. "They'll catch a hold of you. They won't let go."

"Leave it to me," the lieutenant said.

Ash watched but was astonished to see the lieutenant doing nothing about it. Then she saw the front troops slowing and falling back and a dozen or more others taking their place. This new front line looked armed with something other than a gun. Each carried a weapon with a barrel, but that was about it, other than the huge tank that every one of them carried on their backs.

"Look out," Ash said to Laura.

As soon as she said it, the first fiery tongue flew lashing into the brambles as they snapped and curled and burned away. The weapons breathed fire, threw flames, lighting up the forest with more than a dozen fearsome spitfires flashing. The gloom under the canopy was lost as the glare of flame affected everything. The air was burnt. The snap brambles writhed and sparked and were gone, leaving just blackened thumping stumps sticking out of the ground. The animal bones of the brambles' old victims crumbled white onto the scorched ground. The leaves shriveled on the trees, and the creatures went very quiet as the army marched on through.

"A momentous occasion," Ash heard them cry from up ahead. The call was echoed from the sides, from the back.

Guns went off, automatic weapons unleashing another after another stutter of tearing malevolence.

"They'll wreck everything," Rat said.

Ash looked at him.

"It was always going to be horrible," Really said, noticing the look of uncertainty and apprehension on Ash's face.

"It's the only way, isn't it?" Ash asked Really, trying not to feel regret that she had unleashed the destructive force of fire through the forest.

The army advanced at almost running pace. Flames were thrown out, guns fired, machetes wielded. Behind them, the sun shone through onto a new strip of cleared forest land, blackened and shriveled and broken down. The air there smelled like the sun, like heat, dead energy, stuff stored up for millions of years then ignited all at once.

Up ahead of the army, the squealing creatures ran, informed by some language of terror and dread that something terrible and dreadful was this way coming.

Will ran back again. "This is really great!" he shouted in everyone's face. "Why'd we wait? Why'd we wait so long for this?"

He didn't wait for an answer to his question. But Ash would have told him it would never have been like this. Until now, the forest ate Agles like Will and like Ash and like Derri.

"They'll wreck everything," Rat said again.

"They'll save my babies," Really said.

Rat looked back down the blackened ramp of a devastated hillside. He shook. "That's what believing in another, in a better world will do to this one," he said.

"They'll save my babies," Really said again, "that's all I care about at this moment."

"Is that what Agles are?" Rat said, surrounded by plastic suits, machine guns, forest-fire machines, flashing blades. "Is it?"

"No," said Ash. "Adults are like that. Agles can have wings," she said, holding onto Laura. "We are evolving. And that's good. Jess is changing."

"Am I?" said Jess.

"That's why you're sick," Ash said.

"Is it?" said Really.

"Only Adults wish to stay the same. Our Lady told me they made Genome into what they wanted to believe. They believe they can do anything."

"But they can," said Rat.

"They can save my babies," Really said. "Only they can do it."

EIGHTY-SIX

They were out of the forest, all the way along the road and into the outskirts of the city before they saw their first Blue. The Raptor saw them at the same time and disappeared down another side street.

"The city!" Laura had been saying. Ever since they rounded the long bend in the road and looked over the trees at the far glittering towers, Laura had wandered open-mouthed with astonishment. "It's so big, the city! It's so—so big!"

"Down there!" came the call, as the Raptor disappeared in a feathered flurry.

"We'll see more soon," said Ash. "They're all here, somewhere."

Ash had been expecting to find more in the countryside, watching the foraging exits to the rat-runs. But the runs were unattended and silent. "Where are the Rodents?" Ash asked Really and Rat, immediately wishing she hadn't.

They said nothing, looking into the empty runs. No Rodent had got this far, for some unknown reason.

But the reason became clear as soon as the army marched into the city suburbs. All the drain-hole covers had been ripped off, all the metal pavement entry doors removed and stuffed with huge blocks of granite. The Raptors had evidently moved on to the next level of persecution, ripping into the runs, destroying as much of them as they could, driving the Rodents farther underground.

Houses were set on fire as the army marched on, in case the enemy might be hiding inside. One of Genome's soldiers poked inside with the fire stick and the whole place burst into flames. Small burning birds fell fluttering from the broken roofs, turning as they dropped on charred wings, flipping and tumbling along the ground. Gunfire stuttered, smashing inward any windows still intact on the upper floors of other buildings.

"Fire at will!" called Captain Beagle. "Let the enemy know we're here!"

"Yes!" said Will, punching the air with one hand, slashing at it with the bladed other.

"Let the enemy know we're here!" repeated Rich. "Let the enemy know we're Jon's friends, and we are here."

"Fire at will," Alex was saying almost, but not quite, to himself. "Fire at will!"

"But not at me," Will said.

"Give me a gun," said Alex.

"It means fire when you like," Really explained to them.

"Just gi' me a gun," Alex said, louder this time, looking ahead. He glanced at the machete in his hand. "Gi' me a gun," he said again. As he said it, the bullets ripped open a wooden door on one of the big buildings just up ahead. Door down, the flame thrower poked into the open space and lit up the whole of the inside like an explosion.

"Fire!" Alex screamed, not at the fire but at the gunmen closest to the building as two Blues came roaring out from the hot interior, feathers ablaze, shrouded in flaming oil fuel, screaming in Raptor rage and terror and terrible pain. They flew like live flames into the street and tried to run.

"Fire!" Alex screamed again.

"Alex!" Ash cried as he ran toward them.

"Fire at will! Gi' me a gun! Gi' me a gun!"

"No!" Ash ran after him, with Rich close behind her. "No! Alex!"

"Don't stop that man!" the order rang out.

Ash looked up to see Captain Beagle making his way back from the very front of his line of troops. "He is a true volunteer!" he barked.

"He's hurt," said Ash.

"Not!" yapped Alex.

"Hurt? Where are you hurt, young man?"

"Not hurt!"

"Arm this young fighter."

"No," Ash tried again to insist. Although she couldn't see them, she could feel Really's and Rat's eyes on her. Ash wanted Agles to be like Rodents. She looked into Alex's raging red eyes and saw that they were almost as opaque as a Raptor's.

"Lieutenant Hope," the captain called. "See that this man is armed, immediately." He turned at once, making his way through to lead as ever from the front. He himself remained unarmed.

"Don't," Ash tried to say to Elizabeth.

But the lieutenant was in uniform, in plastic armor with full protective head and eye gear. Like this, she was impenetrable.

"Me too," Will leapt in, as Alex was being given his own heavy automatic weapon. "I want one."

"No," said Jess.

Ash and Jess watched relieved as the lieutenant turned away, ignoring Will and Rich, who would have had to ask for arms too, although he secretly never wanted to fire a gun.

"Why him?" Will wanted to know. "Hey! Why him?"

Everyone ignored him. Elizabeth Hope made her way back to be the protective armament at the right hand of her commanding officer and Alex followed her, glancing back at the other Agles with a look that said, "Not with you. Definitely not with you!"

"We shall reclaim this city!" the crowing captain threw out his arms. "In ancient times, holy feet walked here. These walls," he said, as another building burst into flames, "were constructed by human hands to glory Our Lord's likeness. This is the same," he said, pointing out one house, another, "and this, as Genome builds by His holy design. We build as He would, as we have been built by Him. This is His land and these are His dwellings."

"Oh my," said Rat, by Ash's side.

"And here," called Captain Beagle, turning, gathering his strength, "and here and now are the enemy gathered, the usurpers, the very blasphemy of mutation! Here, look!" he pointed, to the blue, Blue wall ahead, completely blocking the street. "And look," he pointed behind. "And so, to the left and the right of us. The Blue mutation has come to collect. Let us brace ourselves, you *Ark* angels, let us pray. Amen!" he bellowed. "So be it! Amen! We find ourselves surrounded. Amen! In the valley of the shadow of death, shall we fear? A momentous occasion!" he shouted out, before the Blue walls fell toward the central troops and before the first flames spouted their reddest spate.

EIGHTY-SEVEN

The Blue Raptors prepared to charge. They came from nowhere, then they came from everywhere.

At a crossroads between big city buildings, the army of the *Ark* were taken by surprise to find themselves effectively surrounded.

"There's no way out!" screamed Jess.

Ash held onto her. Laura's wings were flitting and fluttering. She was desperately resisting the urge to take to the safety of the air.

The amassed Blues were about to surge forward in one huge four-way moving, collapsing wall of roaring terrifying claw-crunch and beak-bite.

"C'mon!" Alex screamed out.

Captain Beagle looked back at the Agles, at Ash, staring straight into her eyes. His look showed her that this was what she had asked him for; that whatever happened from here on was not his fault. His gaze wavered for a moment, falling significantly on the Agle screaming by his side, before settling back, full of obvious meaning, onto Ash's doubtful face.

"C'mon! Murderers!" Alex was screaming at the top of his voice, as the captain looked long and hard and too calmly at Ash.

"Fire at will!" the captain ordered.

Alex's gun was one of the first to sound out, to clatter forward at the oncoming blue of the Blues. His and many other guns met the full force of the Raptors with an even greater force, a rain of flying, indiscriminate bullets cutting straight from the blue and thumping home again and again.

"Fire at will!" the captain cried, again and again, needlessly.

The Agles stood in the epicenter as the four square walls of the plastic-coated army threw fire, emptied cartridge after cartridge of shells into the collapsing over-surge of Blue Raptors.

It was all over in a few moments. The wall of Blue Raptors met an even greater wall of fire-fighting equipment. The fine and furiously courageous Blues fell heroically. Ash was looking out for Talon the whole time, but he was not to be spotted in the chaos and the roar of flame and blue flail.

Not one *Ark* soldier had been harmed, and the Raptors were in retreat, wounded, burnt half brown, scuttling and shuffling toward the sanctuary of the city center.

"Advance!" the captain ordered, following the retreating Raptors along the city streets. "Press the advantage! Victory is Genome's for the taking!"

One or two wild young Blues attempted a suicide attack as the *Ark* forces continued, other Raptors perished flying from the buildings the flame-throwers continued to ignite. The air stank of burnt, broken feathers.

"Did you see it?" screamed Will, again and again. "Did you? Did you see that?"

But Rich had gone very, very quiet and stepped alongside Laura with Tori forever silent by his side.

"They're saving my babies," Really said again.

Rat said nothing. The force of the Adult counterattack had been too hard and too brutal he seemed to be saying, by saying nothing.

"Did you see it?" Will was crowing, running backward and forward. "They're on the run! We got them! We got them!"

Alex was ahead in the very front of the advancing line, aiming a shot at everything that moved.

Ash noticed that the captain gave the order to keep replenishing Alex's ammunition. Lieutenant Hope kept constant her vigil by the captain's side, offering up her own metal containers of unused bullets to keep Alex in the first firing line.

"Press the advantage!" the captain yelled again. "Onward and into them, you *Ark* angels, you defenders of the way! Our war is a holy war! Theirs is nothing but an animal's savage snarl. The devil works his way through such wretched abominations. We shall prevail. The truth! The way! Onward, in the holy name of Genome!"

And the machine guns spat, underlining that name, and the flame-throwers sent destruction upon everything that was not obviously of that name. Only Genome and his like could or eventually would survive this.

Really was holding onto Rat. "It is the right thing to do," she was saying. "It is—it is the right thing."

"Onward, into the center of the heart," the captain called. "The king's crown, the head of the alpha male, no less! He must fall!"

Ash wasn't sure that Talon was still alive, after the battle at the crossroads. But the captain was right, he could be.

"The royal palace!" the captain ordered. "We will dethrone the pretender king, the bluest beast. This Blue menace must disappear from this country forever!"

"Forever?" said Really.

"Can't wait!" shrieked Will.

Alex's gun rattled as some tragic young Blues scattered for safety. They never made it. All the way to the royal palace, the streets were cleared, forcing the Raptors farther and farther inward.

Between the trees along the avenue through which Ash had been brought caged, the Raptors were forced back until all that remained had taken refuge in the palace grounds behind the iron gates and the huge stone walls. The *Ark's* troops were ordered to search the surrounding buildings, and any Blue individuals to be "dispatched," which Ash was told meant sent away. She understood what it really meant.

Just about all the surviving Blues had run in through the palace gates. The grounds were crowded with Blue refugees, families, Raptor kids wailing with their mothers, behind their angry roaring fathers.

"Spread out!" the captain called. "We must take this place entirely! Contain the enemy!"

Ash was looking on in horror. Captain Beagle's intentions were clear. As he had said, the elimination of the Blue menace: now Ash began to understand what so many things really meant.

"Rocket launchers at regular intervals all around the periphery!" the captain roared. "We shall storm this last bastion! We shall show no mercy! In Genome's name, we shall cleanse this forsaken country with His holy righteousness. Blessings on you all and may He grant us a great and eternal victory!"

Ash looked at Elizabeth Hope. "This isn't right," she said.

But the lieutenant's visor was down, fixed into battle-stations position.

"Spread out there!" the captain ordered, making his way up the line, organizing his troops for the ultimate attack.

"Elizabeth!" Ash said, taking the lieutenant by the arm. "Not this. Not murdering all of them."

"They're the murderers!" Alex screamed. "They are!" He made as if to fly through the open Palace gates with his automatic rifle hot in his hands.

"You'll stop!" Lieutenant Hope ordered. "Hold your fire!" she yelled at Alex. "Hold your fire!" at the troops nearest to the iron gates.

Ash could see through the lieutenant's face visor just enough to see Elizabeth glance toward the captain's back as he disappeared barking orders along the line of the troops as they curved with the wall. "Please," Ash said to her, moving closer. "Don't have to kill them all."

Alex was twitching with nervous rage.

"Elizabeth," Ash said, quietly. She saw the eyes behind the lowered visor fix on her for a moment or two.

"You!" she snapped at Alex. "Accompany the captain!"

Alex shuddered, his head turning this way and that, his itchy trigger fingers flexing.

"Now!" the lieutenant ordered. "I have armed you, I will disarm you if necessary."

Alex twitched toward her. Several of the *Ark*'s troops stepped up to him.

"Go now," the lieutenant said. "I need you to protect Captain Beagle. That is your mission. Set to! Now, I say!"

Ash and Elizabeth watched him go until he disappeared after the captain around the curve of the palace wall.

"Now," Lieutenant Hope said, turning back to Ash. "You have two minutes. Stand down," she said to the puzzled troops. "Stand down, I said! Two minutes," she said to Ash. "Is all."

EIGHTY-EIGHT

The garden was full of Blues, so many it was difficult to see the green of the grass or the leaves on the trees. The whole space looked blue.

"Laura," Ash said. "Laura, get them out, all those that will go. Let them go," she said, looking into Elizabeth's eyes.

"Please," she said. "Not all Raptors are—some are—please, let them out."

The lieutenant looked toward the captain's troops.

"Laura," Ash said again.

Elizabeth Hope nodded. "Get them to come this way," she said.

"Fly, Laura," Ash called up, as Laura flapped from the ground.

"We'll give them one minute," the lieutenant said. "Hold your fire!" she called to the officers left and right to prevent them from shooting Laura out of the air.

Ash watched as her best friend flew around the outside of the palace gardens, as she dropped toward the Blue Raptors as she had before on the beach, scattering them, driving them toward that particular space in the wall. The first few through expected to be fired upon by shot or flame, to be killed on the spot. But the lieutenant was able to hold the *Ark* angels' fire as the real angel, Laura, shepherded hundreds of frightened Blues back to the palace gates. They came out, tumbling, running, almost flying through the breach to take to the roads and escape the city to whatever other fate would befall them in the open countryside. Ash and the military had to stand back to allow the Blue flood through as it poured out and ran away.

In just over a minute, many of the Raptors had evaporated. Laura circled around and around, indicating downward at something Ash couldn't quite see from where she stood.

Ash moved toward the great iron gates. Laura swooped low. On the other side of the wall, he stood tall, mightily proud, with his feathers full and his dense eyes profoundly opaque. His chest was streaked with blood. He was wounded, probably in pain, but would never show it.

Talon stared back at Ash. Laura flew low, just above Talon's head. He glanced up at her, unafraid. Now Talon was afraid of nothing.

Behind Talon, a few dozen very, very young Raptors, about the same age—Ash recognized them as the street gang she and Jon had been chased by. These were now the wildest, most fearlessly ferocious males, all under the influence of their proud and maddened king.

He, the Blue leader, turned and walked away, disappearing with the rest of his band of young Blue blood into the trees around the house.

EIGHTY-NINE

Captain Beagle gave the order. Along the lines at regular
intervals the shoulder-held cannons blasted. The wall
was thick and strong but the cannon shells thumped
against it, exploded, and the wall went, throwing debris
and dust in the royal palace garden behind.

"See how they retreat!" the captain cried out joyously. "See
how they cower from Genome's image? Take heart, you true
crusaders, you carriers of the burden of truth and purity! On!
And on, into glorious battle, in His name, on! We shall pursue the
devil and overcome, and his house shall be the house of Our Lord,
for ever and ever. Amen!" the crazed captain cried, advancing into
the palace grounds.

The order to advance upon the house was sent via the officers all
the way around the wall. From every angle, as Laura alone could
see from where she flew, plastic *Ark* forces lurched into the palace
grounds. She alone could see the house from above, surrounded
as it was by a ring of blue feather, with the white of plastic armor
closing in and closing in.

The *Ark's* troops started to shout as the Raptors began to roar.
As Ash broke through the circle of trees and bushes that ringed
the house like another wall, sound met sound, shout into roar
and back again. She could see the circle of very young, pristine
blue feathers around the house as she ran toward it shouting,

hoping that their defenses would break down and they would scatter and escape.

They did not. They stood. Then they fell. Ash saw how they wanted to protect the house as their own, the symbol of the old king and the new, Tomb and Talon. Not many of those brave and foolish young Raptors could have realized that Tomb would never have brought them here; that only Talon, as he stood raging on the palace steps, would have asked this of them.

Ash saw it all. She knew the old king better than did the young dying Blues, and she recognized the catastrophic rage of the new king as he lashed and tore at the air between himself and his enemy.

The ring of blue was as nothing to the severe advance of the white: natural resources give way to plastic and lead and oil-fueled fires. Ash ran forward with the *Ark* soldiers, as Talon turned away from the end of the last of his fine followers and stalked back into the house. The door slammed behind him.

Almost as soon as it did, a rocket launcher sent a missile flying and the doors shattered into a hundred thousand splinters and just about every window in the entire house blew out and the palace was opened in an instant with its rich curtains flapping like torn tongues hanging out.

ninety

The *Ark* troops closed in, with Alex one of the first up the steps and into the broken open doorway. His gun was the first to fire inside.

Ash ran to get there. Inside, Raptors were running up the great staircase and across the upstairs hall. Alex and the *Ark's* firepower was directed toward them as they ran.

"No!" Ash cried. She could see at a glance that these were not young warrior Raptors, but gentle females of the old king's court. "They won't harm you!" she screamed, running across the down-stairs hall.

Alex's gun was poised to rattle out into the running Raptors, until Ash flew into his side and knocked him down. "Stop!" she shouted down at him. Elizabeth Hope appeared next to Alex. "Stop him!" Ash shouted, turning, running up the stairs and into the upper hall.

Blue Raptors ran from her in fear, with nowhere to go. But Ash knew exactly where she was headed. She ran along the corridor and into the bedroom in which she had slept that night. She knew she would be there. Ash knew they'd all be there.

Little Three stood with One and Two and many other female Raptors. They flinched and ruffled their feathers and click-cried as Ash ran in through the door. The noise they made was more in Raptor fear than roar of threat.

Ash stopped. The blue feathers before her shimmered and ruffled. Little Three stepped away from the rest of the frightened females, coming closer before stopping and standing face to face with Ash.

"I've come for you," Ash said. She remembered to nod.

Little Three didn't do anything.

Ash stretched out a hand. The other females fell back, with shocked and shaking heads. But Little Three nodded. Ash held out her hand. Little Three didn't take it. She nodded. She nodded. She nodded again as the door behind her closed and Ash turned.

Talon's chest was streaked with blood. He stepped forward. His massive presence filled up all of Ash's senses. He stood over her. His eyes were like black mirrors. In them Ash saw Little Three's reflection as she finally reached out to take Ash by the hand.

ninety-one

Little Three reached out for Ash but Talon dragged Ash away. He lifted her off her feet and held her in his fists. Talon had roared at Ash before, straight into her face, but it was never like this. Now he had lost everything, his brother, his brother's kingdom. Now Talon was in pain. He had nothing more to lose. All he could possibly gain was his revenge.

He opened his huge hard beak again, not to roar but to bite. He had his worst enemy, the little insolent Agle he had hated for so long. She was in his hands and about to be torn, to be taken to pieces in Talon's last act of crazed savagery.

Ash was too shocked and afraid to cry out. Lifted from her feet she felt the roar of the injured king Raptor, felt the heat of his breath as she was flung forward, backward and forward in his hands. This moment, she was surprised to feel herself thinking, was always coming. It had to happen. There was nothing for it but to accept her fate.

But she, like the Rodents, did not believe in fate. Things happened that felt inevitable, but they never actually were. Like Talon's first bite into Ash's cringing flesh: it never came. It almost felt as if it did, as Ash anticipated the pain of it, but everything stopped.

Ash dangled from Talon's hands at the ends of his outstretched muscular arms. He had her. There was nothing between them now but his arm's length of open air, nothing to prevent him from wreaking his revenge upon her body.

But he didn't do it. He halted.

Ash noticed another pair of hands that had taken hold of her—no, arms going around her. Little Three's arms held on, wrapped around Ash's waist.

Then other's hands, more arms were pulling her away from Talon's grasp. His head was swaying with massive threat, but so many females were around him, drawing Ash away, that he had to release her. He took a small step backward as the female Raptors took Ash with them as they huddled against the wall on the other side of the big bedroom.

Talon looked down on Ash where she knelt on the floor with blue female feathers and Raptor scales at her back. From immediately behind her, Ash heard Little Three saying something, speaking to Talon. He looked from Ash to Little Three and back again.

He roared and in the instant before the eye could detect that anything was moving, he had crossed the room and taken hold of Ash and flung her spinning across the carpet to the smashed open window.

Ash looked back to see him roaring with rage into the face of Little Three. As she looked, the bedroom door was smashed apart in a hail of bullets, and Captain Beagle and Alex stumbled through. Talon turned as Elizabeth Hope appeared in the doorway.

Talon leapt through the air at them. Ash saw him from the side, the fearfully magnificent sight of him in full flight with feathers flowing, with razor talons stretched and toes aching to tense and tear. He flew at Captain Beagle but Alex was there and his gunfire lit the room and Talon took the full force of it and he dropped onto his back and lay fighting with his own flailing body as if a great weight were pressing down onto his chest. Talon fought and fought with his terrible wounds, roaring and thrashing against the floor.

As he crashed and cried out, as the female Raptors backed farther away in shock and fear, Rat ran into the room followed by Really. Tori appeared just over Really's sloping shoulder.

"Finish him!" the captain bellowed, shouting at Alex. "Finish the job!"

But Talon was putting up such a fight, such a noble, hopeless struggle, that Alex could only stand in awe and watch.

"Finish them!" the captain screamed, pointing at the female Raptors crying along the opposite wall. "What are you waiting for?"

"No!" shouted Ash. "No! They're harmless!"

"Finish them!" roared the captain. "That's an order! Finish the job!"

Ash was about to cry out again when, tearing himself from the floor against all his terrible wounds, Talon rose up, lifting himself, as if being resurrected. He stood tall, taking a bubbling but huge breath and roared majestically for one last time before another burst from Alex's gun sent him down forever.

He crashed onto the floor, Ash's worst-ever enemy, the king of the Blues. This was the end of the Raptor society as Talon would have had it.

But the captain still screamed out at Alex. "Finish it, boy! I order you to finish it! Now!"

He was pointing madly, trembling and white, his blue eyes flashing with crazed hatred, pinning the frightened female Blues back to the far wall with his accusatory finger.

"No!" Ash cried out.

"They are your enemy!" the captain ranted. "They killed your brother!"

"No!" Ash screamed.

"They killed your brother!" Captain Beagle shouted into Alex's receptive ear.

"No!" Ash cried, driving forward.

"Yes!" the captain screamed. "Yes! Yes! Do it! See to it! Now!"

"No!" cried Ash, as she dived across the carcass of the dead king, flinging herself at Little Three, throwing herself to stop Alex as he reacted to the crazed screaming in his ear, doing as he was told, seeing to it, now.

"Now!" the captain shrieked as Alex reacted and Ash drove her body across to try to protect the Raptor who had protected her against her enemy.

"Now!"

"No!"

The gun went off. And Ash was pushed back against the feathered breast of the Raptor she was trying to help, as Little Three caught her and fell with her and an angel flew in the open window and covered them with its white, ethereal body.

Laura flew in and tried to stop it. She protected her friend with her pale and delicate angel wings to stop the burst of bullets from a machine gun. The wings could not stop the bullets, not just because they were too frail, but the bullets were there, and there, and there, there, there and there, too soon.

"No! No! No!" Laura screamed.

Then Tori opened her mouth.

"No!" Laura screamed again.

But no one could hear anything through the sound that Tori made. Voiceless Tori opened her mouth in rage and fear and passion, wider than any mouth was ever meant to open, and she cried out, emitting a scream like no other scream in the whole history of the world.

Tori screamed and everyone fell down with the pain of it. The troops arriving at the open door dropped their guns and fell to the floor as the scream went on and on.

"Ash!" the scream cried out.

"Ash!" it said, although no one could hear it through the pain and the anguish and the cry for shame at what had happened.

ninety-two

"No!" Laura cried again and again. "Oh no! Oh no! Please, Ash. Please."

Tori stood shocked. Her scream had been shocking, especially to her, but that wasn't what had stunned her.

Will and Jess had appeared after the noise stopped.

"What's on?" Will was saying, looking over at the wide spread wings of Laura. "What's it?"

"Oh no!" said Laura. "Not this. No, Ash. She'll be all right, won't she? She will be, won't she?"

Little Three sat holding Ash, hugging her, holding onto her, wanting never to let her go.

"What have you done?" Will went at Alex. "What have you *done?*"

"I—" Alex was trying to say. He looked down at the machine gun on the floor at his feet.

"What have you done?"

"I—I didn't mean—I didn't —"

"Come here," said the captain, stepping forward. "Let me see—"

"Stay away!" said Rich. No one had noticed Rich when he came in. Captain Beagle did now though, as Rich stood blocking his way. "Stay where you are! And you!" he pointed to the captain's troops as they took up their positions again.

Elizabeth Hope waved them down. She took the captain by the arm. "Let them be," she said gently.

"Oh no," Laura was crying. "Oh, Ash."

Rich went over to her. He bent down, peeling Laura away. He looked at Ash in Little Three's arms.

"She'll be all right, Rich," Laura said, "won't she? She'll be all right, won't she?"

"With us, Ash," Rich said, too quietly. "Please."

Little Three let Ash go. She had to.

"She'll be all right, Rich, won't she?"

Rich took Ash in his arms. There was no resistance, nothing. He lifted her.

"Won't she? Rich?"

He held her. Ash was limp in his arms.

"Oh no!" said Laura. "Oh no!"

Rich carried her over to the bed in which she had slept so well that night. He laid her down. Rich covered her over.

"Oh," Laura cried. "Please, no. Please!"

Elizabeth Hope turned to look at Captain Beagle. "My work here is done," he said, glancing with malevolence toward Tori. "Too many mutations," he said.

Tori opened her mouth as if to scream at him as he turned and left the room and took his troops away with him.

"I'm sorry," Elizabeth said, to the silent Agles, to the Rodents and to the Raptors. "I'm so sorry."

"What have I done?" cried Alex.

ninety-three

"I'm so sorry," Lieutenant Hope said.

"You just go," Will threatened her. "Go now."

Laura had collapsed by the bed. The Raptors, all but one, had left the room. Little Three stood by the bed next to where Jess held Laura on the floor. Alex was in the corner with his head in his arms. Rat took Alex's gun and threw it out of the window.

"I am sorry," Elizabeth still said, with tears in her eyes.

"Go now," Rich said, with Will by his side.

But Really Rodent came between them, looking up at Elizabeth. "You must go," she said. "They'll be waiting for you. *He'll* be waiting for you. But before you do, let me tell you something. Let me tell you this, then I'll give some advice. The world," she said, looking closely at Elizabeth's face, "is not as you think. Even before, before now, the world always changed—always! Nothing stays the same. There is no image of purity, no perfection, not without everything else. You Adults lost your way. You forgot how to be a part of the world. You thought the world was *for* you, instead of accepting that you are just a small aspect of it. But that's what you are, that small aspect. That's what we all are.

"Genome is not what you think. It's in all of us. There is no higher power than what we are. And everything that lives is related. It's all the one, ever-changing thing. Yes, ever and always changing. If you don't believe me, just take a closer look at those you love the most."

Elizabeth looked at Really with a question written into her expression.

"Yes," said Really, "look to those closest to you."

"Now go," Rich said.

Elizabeth took one last look at the dark-stained blanket on the bed. "I am sorry," she said.

"That's no help," said Really, turning away. "That is just no help at all."

BACK FROM THE BRINK

PART SIX

ninety-FOUR

They followed the scars of the cut through the forest. The undergrowth was already erupting, healing
the wild wound, but it was still a path through, leading
them back.

It would have been much easier for the Raptors to do the
carrying work. The Agles did it. They tripped and stumbled
over the low bushes and would have walked straight into the
snap brambles if not for the Rodents, but still they did the carrying. All of it, all the way.

"And Jess is changing too," Will was saying. Jess was following on behind, being helped occasionally by Tori or Rich. "Not
feeling so good. Not the same as she was. She's changing."

"Yes," Really Rodent said, "she is. But not in the way you think."

"What way is she?" Will asked.

"Don't you know?" Really asked, stopping to allow Jess to catch
up. "Don't you know what's happening to you?"

"My body's changing," Jess said. "I don't feel the same. I don't
look the same."

"Can't you see it?" Really asked all the other Agles. "Tori,
can't you smell it? Jess, you're not changing in that way. You're
going to have a baby!"

Everyone stopped between the scorched trees just over the brow of the hill that sloped into the valley at the end of which nestled the old ASP camp.

"A baby?" Jess said, as if she was about to be sick again.

"Yes," said Really.

"A baby!" shouted Will.

"Yes," said Really.

The birds shrieked down at them from the trees. "A baby!" Will shouted back.

"You certain?" Jess said.

"Of course," said Really. "It's obvious."

"Is it?" Jess said, looking down at herself.

Little Three came up to Jess and touched her on the stomach. She nodded. She clicked, softly, then nodded again.

"That confirms it," Rat said.

"A baby!" said Will, taking Jess in his arms. "A real baby!"

Everyone else walked on and waited, taking a rest, giving Jess and Will a chance to take it in.

"We're going to have a baby!" Will shouted to them as he and Jess caught up. "Ash!" he shouted, looking up. "Hear that? A baby!"

"Where will it live?" asked Jess, looking down from the hill on the remains of the camp.

The whole place was a ruin. Not a single hut was left standing now. The fences were all down. The beach was littered with debris, garbage from the huts and from the *Ark*. The great battleship was gone. The ASP raft still swayed in the lagoon, listing drunkenly to one side.

"You'll all live in the city," Really said. "With us. We'll have a new society. We can all live together."

"Yes, we can," Jess said, nodding at Little Three.

The Raptor nodded back at her.

"We can live in the city together," said Rat. "Most of the Raptors want to live outside. They'll be our protectors, they say. They want to try to make peace with the Yellows again."

"We'll live in the city!" Laura said.

"Ash'll live in the city," Will said.

They all looked at him.

"Of course she will," said Laura.

"No, our baby," Will said.

"We're calling it Ash," Jess said. "Boy or girl—"

"It'll be called Ash," Jess said.

"Our daughter's called Ash," Really said. "There'll be an Agle baby and a Rodent baby both called Ash."

"It is right," said Jess. "Agle and Rodent. That is right."

"The city!" said Laura.

"We'll all live there," Really said.

"And," Rich said, "we'll put up some signs. 'Admission Strictly Prohibited,' they'll say. So if the Adults come back, they'll read the signs and they'll know it means them."

"But won't we be the adults soon?" Will said, touching Jess's stomach.

"No," Rich said, "no, we'll never be that. We're Agles. We are Agles. Adults Strictly Prohibited—that's what ASP means now."

"ADULTS STRICTLY PROHIBITED!"

NINETY-FIVE

"On this momentous occasion," said Rat.

They all repeated it. The Agles and the Rodents recited the words while Tori signed and the Raptors clicked. Little Three clicked something of her own and touched her chest and bent and touched the wrapped figure at the water's edge.

The return journey had been made for this single purpose. The surfboards of the lost Agles, some broken in bits, floated in the shallow water at the edge of the lagoon.

"On this momentous occasion," Alex cried. He bent to touch his lost brother's surfboard. "Ash," he said, "with you, like never before. I'm so, so sorry."

"It's okay," Laura said to him, gently. "It's okay, Alex."

NINETY-SIX

"It's okay, Alex," Ash managed to say.

"See?" Laura said to Alex. "Now look what you've done. Lie back, Ash. You'll hurt yourself again."

"I'm all right," Ash said, wincing from the pain shooting through her side.

"Please, Ash," Alex said, going to her. "Don't hurt yourself."

"And don't you hurt *yourself*," Ash said. "We're okay, both of us. Come on, help me sit up. I want to see. I *have* to see."

"We," said Rich, looking away from Ash, searching for the right things to say, "we—are Agles."

"We are Agles," Will and Jess said, following Rich.

"It means," Rich said, "it means—I know what it means—I just don't know how to say it."

"We don't have the words," Laura said, to Really and Rat. "We never did that. We should've. We didn't."

Ash smiled weakly as Alex held her sitting upright on the makeshift bed the Agles had carried all the way from the city.

"Tell us what it means," Rich said, looking at Ash then at Really.

Really wiped her face. "See?" she said, holding up her hand. "Remember, Ash? Tears. The same, Agle, Rodent. It doesn't matter. Evolution was once supposed to be about the survival of the fittest. Ash changed that. The survival of the most loved, that's what it is now. Now we all understand her. Little Three and all the Raptors understand. She did this. None of us would have done it without her. This," she said, looking around at Ash, at Agles, Raptors and Rodents, "is a truly momentous occasion. With you, Ash," she said.

They all touched her, before they let her go. "With you, Ash," they all said. "With you."

"Now it's time," Ash said. "Time to take the boards."

Alex left Ash to be supported on her bed by Jess and Will. He went to join the rest to take his brother's board along with the surfboards of all the lost others.

"Alex," Ash called. "Alex." He heard her, turned. "Take mine," she said. "Take mine, with all the others. It's over," Ash said, breathing heavily against the pain of the three bullet wounds that had pierced and plunged through her side and her arm.

"You'll surf again," Laura started to say. "One day, you'll be—"

"Take my board, Alex," Ash said. "It's only evolution. Things change. This is over. We start again, in the city. All of us, Rodents, Raptors, Agles."

Alex faltered. It seemed too final, as if Ash had died there on the floor of that sumptuous room back at the royal palace.

Rich made his way to the water's edge and picked up Ash's surfboard and handed it to Alex. Ash watched Alex take it. It was final.

"Come on," said Laura. "It is time."

So the survivors, those who could surf, took the boards across the lagoon, over the white turbulence of the rubber reef and out into the wild, wide open sea. An angel flew over them.

The angel hovered over the waves, watching the surfers body-boarding over the foam of the reef. She looked down as a mass of white surfboards were released into the sea on the other side. "Everything changes," she said, "always," as she watched the Agles below her making their way back over the reef, only to kick themselves free of their surfboards forever and start swimming back unencumbered to where their future awaited them on the strand of clean shore on the green side of ASP island.

COMING IN FALL 2009

Revisit the world created by John Brindley in

The City of Screams

CHAPTER ONE

Flying above, taunting the young male Green Raptors, Air Agles were on the wing. White against the violet sky, they flitted like Angels, with their leader, Gabriel, laughing demonically as the roaring Raptors leaped up and fell back.

His kind, Air Agles, lived neither in the city like the heavy Ground Agles and the sloping-faced albino Rodents, nor in the countryside like the lizard-legged, bird-faced Raptors. For Air Agles—fliers—flying was like breathing. If they didn't do it, they'd die. They were made for it. Evolution had produced them. They were Nature's chosen ones, the winged beings, the Angels.

Laughing along with them was a single Ground Agle. Evolution had denied Phoenix her wings. She sailed supported by three fliers, soaring with them, laughing down at the snapping rage of the gang of wild Green Raptors below.

"Take me down!" Phoenix shouted to Gabriel and Jay-Jay, the Air Agles on her left and right. Gabriel's pale green eyes looked down at the ground.

"Take me lower!" Phoenix cried to him.

"Fly me!" Phoenix screamed at Gabriel. "Show me what it's really like! Fly me down! Show me, now!"

Gabriel looked at Jay-Jay. Together, holding Phoenix by the arms and the back of her plain dress, they looked behind at Jay's Special, Ember, the beautiful Air Agle at the Ground Agle's feet. Ember shook her head. She looked uncomfortable, worried. Phoenix watched Gabriel looking at Jay-Jay. She smiled as they grinned at each other.

"Fly me!" Phoenix was mouthing to Gabriel. If she had wings, she'd never falter, not for a single second. If she had wings she'd be the best, with Gabriel, the ultimate flying Agle.

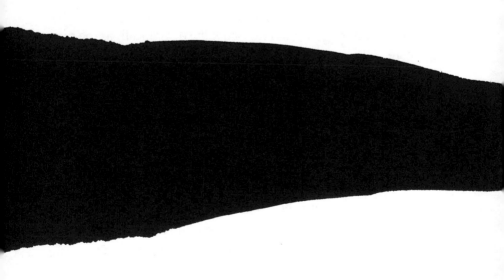

ABOUT THE AUTHOR

John Brindley's previous novels include *Changing Emma* and *Rhino Boy*. He lives in southeastern England and has two grown-up children. He enjoys music of all different types and plays squash and trains to stay fit. He likes to draw ideas and inspiration from all aspects of life, especially the people he meets.